D1085015

TIME WILL TELL

Also by Elizabeth Waite

COCKNEY FAMILY
COCKNEY WAIF
NIPPY
KINGSTON KATE
SECOND CHANCE
SKINNY LIZZY
THIRD TIME LUCKY
TROUBLE AND STRIFE

TIME WILL TELL

ELIZABETH WAITE

LITTLE, BROWN AND COMPANY

A *Little, Brown* Book

First published in Great Britain in 2000
by Little, Brown and Company

Copyright © Elizabeth Waite 2000

The moral right of the author has been asserted.

A CIP catalogue record for this book
is available from the British Library.

HARDBACK ISBN 0 316 85468 9

Typeset by Palimpsest Book Production, Polmont, Stirlingshire
Printed and bound in Great Britain by Biddles Ltd, *www.biddles.co.uk*

Little, Brown and Company (UK)
Brettenham House
Lancaster Place
London WC2E 7EN

BOOK ONE

LONDON, 1944

Chapter One

THE TALL TREES that lined the borders of Wimbledon Common were bursting with new life as the early spring sunshine streamed through their branches and a young girl with flame-coloured hair walked with her soldier boyfriend. Strolling over the thick grass, she slipped her hand into his. He smiled, whispered in her ear, and they both laughed. The lovers went to sit on a park bench looking out over a pond to eat their corned-beef sandwiches and sip bottled shandy. Later, as they kissed goodbye outside the Fox and Hounds, where she worked as a barmaid, passers-by sighed sadly for them. It was nearing the end of February 1944. Life was hard, and the war seemed unending. How much time had the youngsters had together? How long would it be before the young man would have to report back to his regiment?

Joan went through the double doors, across the saloon bar and into the comfortable sitting room that lay beyond. It was only a matter of minutes before she was confiding tearfully to her boss, Poppy Benson, that she was in love with Matt and terrified because he'd be on the move any day now. Eighteen-year-old Joan Harvey's life was anything but routine. And Mathew Pearson, the twenty year old born and bred in the East End of London had long realized his life would be far from normal as long as this war continued.

'I know it's your day off, but why don't you go and wash your face and come down to the bar for a drink?' Poppy suggested kindly. 'It's almost closing time, and you can give Bob a hand with clearing the tables if you like, take your mind off things.'

'All right,' Joan agreed quickly. 'I'll be down in a few minutes.'

Poppy and Bob Benson were really good to her. They had given her a cosy bedroom so that on the days she did work she lived-in rather than having to travel home in the blackout when the pub closed at half past ten. Although her home was only down in Haydons Road, Merton Park, a fifteen-minute bus ride, her parents would never have agreed to their eighteen-year-old daughter working if it had meant she'd be out late at night. True, the air raids had lessened somewhat, but in these terrible days you never knew what to expect.

She went slowly up the broad staircase of the beautiful old public house. Once inside her room, she took off her coat and hung it in the wardrobe, then stood before the black iron fireplace and leant forward towards the mirror that hung over the mantelshelf. She stared at her reflection: her hair was her crowning glory, and today her cheeks were pink from the sharp fresh air. Over a slim black skirt she was wearing an emerald green jumper, which emphasized her bright green eyes.

Oh, why can't we have more time together? She sighed.

Like everyone else she wished this rotten war would end but never more so than since she had met twenty-year-old Matt Pearson. She hadn't realized that you could love someone so much. He made her feel so special. To remember the way he had kissed her and run his hands over her breasts made her blush. Why had he singled her out? There had been dozens of pretty girls in the dance hall where they'd met. She giggled at that. No matter where she went her hair made her stand out from the crowd. She used to hate it when she was at school: Copper knob, Ginger, Red-roots were only a few of the names she'd been called. Now she didn't mind her mop so much. The colour had darkened a little, though it was still thick and uncontrollable. It had a life of its own, was what her mother said – speaking from experience because it was from she that Joan had inherited her colouring. Matt said he adored her hair, so that was all right.

They had been meeting for six months now. He had taken her to meet his family and she had liked them very much. Bit rough and ready, she had thought at first, until she found that all folk who lived in the East End of London spoke in the way they did. They were open and friendly – well, they were if they took to you – And they seemed to take to me, she told herself.

But now Matt was probably going away. No, that wasn't true. There was no 'probably' about it. He *would* be going away.

Just a week ago she had given in to him. No, *that* wasn't entirely true either. They had both wanted what had happened, had been carried away by their emotions. Matt had told her that he wanted them to be married before he was posted. 'I'll get a special licence,' he had insisted.

Joan wasn't sure that that was what she wanted. It had all been so quick.

But the minute she had first set eyes on Mathew Pearson she had gasped. He was every girl's idea of the tall dark handsome man they all wished would come into their lives. He stood six feet three inches tall, had short thick dark hair, big brown eyes, and broad shoulders. But it was the way he smiled at her that turned her legs to jelly. 'How can you talk about us getting married when you know full well you've got to go away soon?' she had asked.

'I've been dead lucky so far. I was almost sixteen when the war started and although me dad got me a good job in the timber yards I knew I'd be called up sooner or later. Me mates were just the same. We all knew we wouldn't escape. So, it's live for the day, ain't it? Has to be, or don't you agree?'

For a moment Joan had looked thoughtful. 'I was thirteen coming up fourteen, still at school, but I wanted to join the Wrens so badly. All my dad said was, "Over my dead body."'

'I should think so too.' Matt had been shocked to think that this gorgeous girl should want to be in the forces. Bad enough that the lads had to go without involving young girls.

Joan had been pampered from the Christmas Day on which she had been born in 1925. Her mother had been only eighteen herself at the time, and her grandmother the same age when she had given birth to her daughter, Joan's mother, so they all lived in a young, lively environment. Both women were petite and attractive, and looked younger than their age. With her mum and her nan, as she called her grandmother, still trim and smartly dressed, spending evenings working up west in clubs and often out dancing,

Joan had always been a daddy's girl. And if he failed to give her the attention she sought there was always Pops, her grandfather. He and Nan lived only four doors up the street.

Joan herself was a mixture: small-boned like her mother and grandmother, with their colouring of hair, she was also blessed with her father's kind, loving nature.

Having brushed her hair and tied it back with a wide velvet band, Joan gazed at her reflection in the mirror and said, 'I'll give Bob and Poppy a hand, then I'll catch the bus and go home for the night. Have a good talk with me dad. See what he has t' say about me getting married.'

With that, she went downstairs and into the main bar.

'Are you coming up to Rainbow Corner on Saturday night?' Peggy Watson asked casually, as she watched Joan, her best friend, bring two handfuls of empty glasses and set them down on one of the mats that protected the counter.

'I don't know. Depends on whether Poppy wants me to work or not.'

'Well,' Peggy answered slowly, 'if you can't make it then we could always go on Sunday afternoon. The girls where I work all say it's full of Yanks and Canadians for the afternoon tea-dances.'

'Good idea.' Joan laughed. Then, seeing her boss making a disapproving grimace, she added, 'The Yanks are smashing dancers. They're out to enjoy life when they get the chance. They're lonely, miles away from home, and glad to have a bit of fun now an' again. Can't see no harm in that.'

'Thought you were dead serious about Matt. Only minutes ago you were crying yer eyes out cos you feared he was going to be sent overseas,' Poppy said, polishing a pint glass so hard it was a wonder it didn't break in her hand.

Joan didn't answer, but Peggy did. 'You want her to live

the life of a nun just cos she's got a steady boyfriend, do yer? What I mean t' say is, you're only young once an' God alone knows what's gonna happen before this ruddy war comes to an end.'

Poppy looked across at her husband, who had just finished serving a group of businessmen. He shrugged his shoulders. He had a lot of time for young Joan Harvey. She was a good clean girl, worked hard and was always polite. His own thoughts were that she was far too young to get too tangled up with any man. She should be living her life to the full. This war had been hard on the young folk, made them grow up too fast. They were never going to retrieve the lost years of their youth. However, he had more sense than to voice his thoughts – he didn't want to upset his wife, who had a right old temper when she got going. So, very quietly, he said, 'Won't hurt for the lasses to have a bit of a dance, especially if it's an afternoon do. The Yanks must feel just as bad as our lads about being away from home, and the war can't go on for ever. There has t' be an end to it sooner or later and then things will all get back to normal.'

Poppy sniffed. 'It's not *after* the war I'm worried about. It's *now*. These Yanks have more money than our lads and they're not slow in flashing it about. It's turning the girls' heads an' – you mark my words – there'll be a lot of tears shed an' some heartaches when it's time for them to go home.'

Joan felt all this was getting out of hand. All she and Peggy were considering was whether they should go up west at the weekend or not. It wouldn't be the first time they'd been, and she admitted to herself that she'd always had a wonderful time. You could say that the Americans were a bit brassy, but on the other hand they were kind, too, attentive, great dancers, and they acted like gentlemen. At least, the ones she had met had. They didn't all look like Clark Gable – of course they didn't – but their uniforms were smashing, kind of elegant compared with the rough material of the British soldiers' battle-dress, and that made a big difference when they took you in their arms if the band played a slow waltz.

They didn't shout like the men in the East End pubs did either. Now Joan's thoughts made her grin as she remembered the first time Matt had taken her with his family to their local for a drink. Talk about noise! You couldn't hear yourself think. Their laughter was so loud it had covered the sound of the ack-ack guns down on the embankment. And when a man finished a game of darts on a quick double everyone in the bar went mad. And there had been a lot of crude remarks flying about. She knew she was being unfair to Matt's family but there was no getting away from it: a night out in the East End didn't compare with an afternoon tea-dance at the London Palais. She liked to dance with the Americans. There wasn't a girl in her right mind who would say different, but . . . she loved Matt. Quite honestly, though, she did wish he'd act a bit more gentle, like. There again, every girl they passed in the street envied her because, whatever else you might say about Matt Pearson, he was so good-looking.

'Well, let's leave it for now,' Joan said eventually. 'Maybe I'll have some news to tell you after I've been home this afternoon and talked to me dad.'

'What sort of news?' Peggy's curiosity got the better of her.

'I'm not going to say any more now cos I'm nowhere near sure myself. Wait till I've been home and got things sorted in my own mind.'

'All right,' Peggy answered, with a lop-sided smile. 'I'll pop in tomorrow in my lunchtime. 'Bye for now.'

'I'll walk t' the door with you,' Joan said, linking arms with her friend. 'I wasn't trying to be mysterious, I just want to have a chat with me dad before I decide anything.'

'That's all right.' Peggy smiled again good-naturedly. 'But think about Sunday. It'll be a bit of a laugh, an' if we hang around here Sundays can be a bit of a drag.'

'I will,' Joan called, as Peggy ran off. She thought, There's nothing feminine about those trousers and that duffel coat she wears all week, but it's hardly her fault she quickly chided herself, thinking it can't be any fun working in that factory. Weekends were a different story, though: when you saw Peggy dressed and made up no one would believe she was the same girl. God knew where she got the makeup from and the sheer stockings, let alone the clothing coupons, but Joan didn't ask any questions and that way they stayed good friends.

As soon as Joan put her key in the front door she felt that luck was on her side.

Her father opened the living-room door and stared up the hallway. At the sight of his daughter his face broke into a smile. 'I was just thinking about you, pet, and here you are in the flesh.' Big man that he was, he cleared the space between them in three strides, flung his arms around her and hugged her so tight her feet were lifted from the floor.

How lovely she is, Bill Harvey thought, kissing the top of her head. 'You smell of fresh flowers,' he told her, setting her down and leading the way.

'You in all on your own, Dad?' Joan asked, taking off her coat and laying it over the back of a chair.

'Yeah, I'm all you're gonna get this afternoon. Your mother

an' yer nan are doing a high tea in the Co-op hall. Some bigwig died and apparently it's a funeral on a grand scale so the mourners have to be fed.'

They looked at each other and burst out laughing. Joan recovered first. 'With a bit of luck, Dad, there'll be some boiled ham left over an' you and Pops will get it for yer tea. Beats me that with all the rationing there's always something going to provide for weddings and funerals.'

'Well,' her father said, 'that's the way of the world today. Some blokes have escaped being called up and are making a packet on the black-market. Supply and demand, that's how it is, an' probably how it always will be.'

'Ah, well. Have we got any tea?'

'Yes, yer mum got half a pound this morning. It's in the caddy an' the kettle's on out in the scullery. I was just about to make meself a cuppa when I heard you come in.'

'I'll do it, Dad, you set the cups out. And, Dad, I'm ever so pleased that you're on yer own cos I want to have a talk with you about me and Matt.'

Her father watched her disappear into the scullery and his heart sank. She was still his little girl and he didn't want to lose her. It had been six months and more since she had started going out with that Mathew Pearson, and he knew a lot more about that relationship than he had ever let on.

Bill Harvey worked in the smelting works at Colliers Wood, a reserved occupation. Because it was wartime the furnaces were never allowed to go out so a three-shift system was in place. Six until two was the morning shift, two until ten was the middle shift and ten at night until six a.m. was the night shift. If he was coming off work at ten or just going to sign on, it was a dead cert that he'd catch a glimpse of the pair of them. Time after time he'd had to curb his temper for there they'd be, strolling around in the blackout, with their arms entwined and practically eating each other. He didn't need to follow them: he knew full well they'd be heading for the park and the shelter of the trees.

Joan came back, carrying the teapot. With one look at her father's face she could guess what he'd been thinking. Her dad was well over six foot tall in his stockinged feet. His face was kind, open, with big blue eyes, a wide forehead and a friendly mouth. He had a thick shock of hair that, sad to say, was very grey. To Joan he always looked as if he had just had a good wash for his rosy cheeks usually glowed. Wholesome, that was how she would describe her dad.

They sat at each side of the table with a steaming cup of tea set beside them. Eventually Joan brought herself to say, 'Dad, Matt thinks the Army will be making a big push soon and his regiment will be sent to France. Kind of a second front is what the boys are calling it and, well . . . he wants us t' get married before he goes.' She brought out the last sentence in a rush.

Bill Harvey sighed inwardly. He wasn't a bit surprised. Girls as young as sixteen were rushing into marriage without a thought to the future. Half of them were doing it for the Army marriage allowance. Mind you, he'd been twenty-two when he'd married Daphne, but she had been only seventeen, barely turned eighteen when Joan was born, so he was hardly in a position to preach to his daughter. Nevertheless, he'd give his right arm to stop her from diving into marriage with this Matt Pearson. Although he looked like what every girl must dream of, there was something about him that stuck in Bill's gullet. Beneath that smooth surface he was a cocky bugger – he was as sure of that as he ever could be. He rested his elbows on the table and stared at his daughter. She had an odd, dreamy look on her face. All right, the lad made her happy. He'd give him that much.

'Do you love him?' he asked.

'Um,' she whispered, 'of course I do.'

'There's no of course about it,' he answered sternly. 'I think I'd better have a talk to him before we decide anything. In fact, it should be him to come to me, if not to ask permission – that would be too old-fashioned for you youngsters today – at least to put me in the picture as regards his plans for you.'

That statement frightened Joan a bit. 'Before you talk to Matt, hadn't we better tell Mum?' She paused. 'And we hadn't better leave Nan an' Pops in the dark else there'll be hell to pay.'

'Hold yer horses. At the moment there's nothing to tell anyone.' He leant across, took her hand and kissed her gently and lovingly.

'I'll talk to your mother and if anything is to be decided then the decisions will be made by both of us. I'll have a chat with her tonight, you leave it all to me. You know, Joanie, we both love you dearly, and all we want is for you to be happy.'

'I know, Dad, I know, but what if Matt does get sent away soon?'

Her father's lip trembled. He wanted to ask her some point-blank questions but he hadn't the heart for it. She was still his baby girl. How could he bring himself to ask if there was any particular reason that she and Matt should be marrying in such haste. Had he made her pregnant? He clenched his fists. I'll kill him if he has! He took two very deep breaths. But it takes two. She was all dreamy-eyed when she spoke his name, so it didn't seem as if he had forced her. Oh, for goodness sake! he chided himself. He probably hasn't got further than a few kisses. Anyway, he'd leave it for now until Daffy came home.

Daffy by name but not by nature. Oh, no! His wife had her head set squarely on her shoulders and if anyone could talk some sense into Joan then it would be her mother.

Changing the subject quickly, feeling a right coward, he said, 'I know where your mother's hidden some biscuits, chocolate ones. You sit still and I'll fetch them and we'll have ourselves a real treat.'

'You're the best dad in the whole world,' she called after him, which served to make him feel even more inadequate. He stood still for a moment and covered his eyes with his hands. Great changes were taking place in his daughter's life, changes he didn't like, but somehow he felt he had no power to stop them.

Chapter Two

IT WAS THE first Sunday in March, and the weather had certainly changed for the worse. There was cold rain and a bitter wind that went right through to the bone, as Peggy and Joan got off the bus at Piccadilly Circus. Scarves tied tightly over their hair, they tucked their heads low and ran. Once inside the dance hall, they each let out a satisfied sigh. This was a different world. There might be a war going on outside but here they could forget it for a time. They checked their coats into the cloakroom, spent fifteen minutes in the posh ladies' room titivating their hair and makeup, then came out and stood at the edge of the dance floor.

A few minutes later they looked at each other and grinned. This place was something else: gilt paint, red-velvet seating, and the lighting made for romance, soft and subdued. Blue cigarette smoke wreathed up to the high ceiling while a dazzling mirror-ball sent its reflections darting here and there. At the far end was a stage and a snazzily dressed band were playing all the latest tunes. They couldn't wait to get on the smashing sprung floor. There were loads of servicemen: Navy lads with their white dicky-fronts and well-scrubbed blue and white wide collars, and the Brylcreem boys from the RAF in their special blue uniforms. The poor old Tommies in their serviceable khaki battle-dress looked like the poor relations, and both girls felt a little sorry for them – more so today because the place was swarming with American soldiers, who were stealing the show: they danced with so much energy, jitterbugging in a way that you'd never see in a local dance-hall.

'Would you like to dance, ma'am?' Two lean young men stood before them.

'We'd love to,' Peggy answered for the pair of them, giving the two American soldiers a wide smile.

They allowed themselves to be led on to the floor as the band struck up a quickstep.

It was fantastic, the music was so fast. Within seconds Joan was beaming up into the tanned face of her young man, who was so far from home. 'My name's Hank,' he said loudly, as he led her expertly, following the beat. Suddenly the tempo changed and he asked, 'Can you jitterbug?' Not waiting for her to reply, he pushed her in the direction he wanted her to go and they were off. Joan glanced across the floor to where Peggy was sliding between the legs of her partner and laughed. This was wonderful! Ducking underneath Hank's outstretched arm, grinning as his feet seemed to move like lightning. His arms circled her waist and he had her high in the air one minute then down so low that her hair almost touched the floor the next. Turning this way and that without a break in his own steps. By the time the music stopped Joan fell against him and, for a brief moment, the lad held her close. 'I'll see you to your chair and then I'll fetch us both a drink,' he said.

He was as good as his word, as was his mate. They found a vacant table and asked the girls for permission to sit down with them. Both Joan and Peggy had asked for orange juice and neither of the lads had queried that. Joan's thoughts went immediately to what any of Mathew's relations would have said: 'I ain't going to the bar to ask fer no bloody orange juice. You 'ave a proper drink or go without.'

The juice was refreshing and by the time the band-leader announced the next dance, both girls were raring to go.

'Waltz, then, is it?' Hank asked Joan, while the other young man, who had introduced himself as Greg, stood and held out his arms to Peggy.

'So dreamy,' Peggy mouthed, as the two couples danced close.

The pattern continued: there were several more lively jitterbugs, and even a well-executed fox-trot, but neither gave a thought to changing their partners. Then, far too soon, it was announced that the next dance would be the last waltz and the band struck up 'Who's Taking You Home Tonight'. Joan felt a shiver run down her back as Hank let go of her hand and stroked her long hair. 'I've been wanting to do that all night,' he told her. 'I have a young sister, she's only ten, and she has ginger hair, though it's nowhere near as dark as yours.'

He sighed, and Joan suddenly felt sad. 'Mine used to be more red, and I expect your sister's hair will darken as she gets older.'

'Yeah, you're probably right.' Then, very quickly, he began to twirl her round and round as though to eradicate the memory from his mind.

The lights were brighter suddenly: the dance was over. 'Do you and your friend live within walking distance?' It was Greg, the taller of the two lads, who asked.

'No,' Peggy answered quickly. 'We get the tube, we'll be all right.'

'We can't allow that, not two young ladies out on their own in the blackout.' Greg glanced across at Hank, who nodded. 'We'll flag you down a cab.'

'You'll do no such thing,' Joan said indignantly. 'It would cost the earth. Besides, you'd never get a taxi driver to take a fare out of the West End – they haven't the petrol.'

Both girls had their coats on and were tying their scarves over their heads. Peggy produced a torch from her pocket and switched it on. 'See? We'll be fine. Me dad managed to get two new batteries yesterday.'

Hank whistled under his breath. 'Self-sufficient, eh? But, torch or no torch, we're seeing you to the underground station and safely on to your train.'

Greg linked his arm with Peggy's and smiled down at her. 'It's the least we can do. We've had the pleasure of your company all evening and it wouldn't be right to abandon you now.'

'Come on, then.' Hank had his arm across Joan's shoulders as they made for the exit sign.

Once outside they all stood stock still. There was total darkness, not a star in the black sky. It took a few seconds for their eyes to adjust, then Peggy switched on her torch and handed it to Greg, reminding him to keep it pointed downwards.

'Right,' he said to Hank, who still had his arm around Joan. 'Keep close to us – we don't want to have to send a search party out for you.'

They stumbled along, two in front and two behind, the torch held well down just showing where they could safely put a foot forward. In only a matter of minutes they had reached the tube station at Piccadilly Circus. Black metal shades covered each lightbulb set into the tiled walls of the station, with a small slit cut into the covering base allowing just enough light to show through to enable passengers to reach the moving staircase in safety.

'We'll come down on to the platform with you,' Hank stated assertively.

Peggy tripped as she set her foot on the fast-moving step but Greg's arm was immediately round her, holding her close to his chest, and Joan smiled to herself. Had the trip been deliberate? If it had, who could blame Peggy? There were so few occasions when they had the company of young men, these days, and this evening had been so nice. Suddenly she thought of Matt: maybe she should feel guilty. Then again, it wasn't the kind of evening he would have enjoyed. Come to think of it, he had taken her to many places – the pictures, the theatre, dog-racing, to watch him play darts in the pub, and he had promised her visits to the speedway once the war was over because he was motorbike mad – but he had never mentioned dancing. Perhaps he couldn't dance! She didn't like that thought and hastily brushed it away. All young people loved to dance.

The train was coming through the tunnel as they reached the platform. A little clumsily Hank took Joan in his arms and put his lips on hers. It was not a passionate kiss, just sweet and gentle.

The train came to a noisy halt and the doors slid open. ''Bye, Joan. Maybe we'll meet again. You take care.' Hank's voice was little more than a whisper.

Greg was calling out his thanks, saying what a wonderful evening they had had.

Joan and Peggy stood side by side as the doors closed and they both waved to the two American soldiers standing on the station. Then they moved slowly down the train. As they each found a seat Peggy declared loudly, 'Bloody war.'

It was a sentiment with which Joan, and everyone else in the carriage, come to that, was in full agreement.

Chapter Three

JOAN DIDN'T NEED telling that these next few days were going to be vastly different from any she had ever spent in her life before.

Matt had been given seven days' leave. He had suggested that she came home with him and spent the best part of the week with his family. That way he wouldn't be torn in two as to where he should be. Reluctantly Joan had asked Poppy and Bob if she could have the time off.

Poppy had laughed her head off. 'He's under pressure from his family, my love. You mark my words. And if you don't go, well . . .'

'Poor sod, I know the feeling,' Bob added. ''Tis only natural that his mother wants to have him around especially if the rumours are true that his regiment might be posted soon. I'd take a bet, though, he being the healthy bloke he is, he'd rather shack up somewhere with you.'

'Bob!' Poppy screamed at him. 'That's no way t' talk to Joan.'

Joan grinned. Two days ago, Matt had had a couple of hours off and turned up at the pub just as they were finishing the lunchtime session. They had spent the entire time in the wooded part of the common. 'Amorous' was the only word she could think of to describe Matt during the whole of that time. His passion had been such that she had ended up feeling grateful that it was daylight and that quite a few people were about.

Her own family's reaction to her going to stay with Matt's family hadn't been enthusiastic and it had taken a lot of persuasion on her part to get her mum and dad to agree. Matt's home was in Whitechapel, a district of east London in the borough of Stepney. The best way to get there was on a District line train, which, luckily enough, left from their local station at Wimbledon.

As always, these days, the train quickly became crowded. Many servicemen were returning from leave, their kit-bags slung into the string racks in every compartment. A young woman with three children boarded at Putney Bridge, and Matt jumped to his feet offering his seat. He bent low and whispered to Joan, who got up to allow the three children to squeeze into her seat.

There were so many people already squashed into the corridor that Matt had a job to find a space for them to stand. Not that he cared. His arm was already round Joan's waist to hold her steady, and when a sudden jolt threw her hard against his chest he laughed. 'We'll tell my lot we're gonna get married an' when I bring you back 'ome I'll tell your dad straight we don't intend to wait any longer,' he told her firmly, his big brown eyes showing how eager he was.

His grip on her was so tight that Joan was glad when at

last he bent down, picked up her small attaché case and said, 'Next station's ours.'

God! Joan was surprised, or perhaps a better word was shocked. She had been to visit Matt's family twice before but each time he had borrowed his brother's car and taken her door to door. Even when she had been taken to their local pub for a drink they had still driven there and she hadn't taken much notice of the area. Now, standing on the wide platform, she couldn't take in all that she was seeing. So many servicemen. So many different uniforms. Such crowds.

They emerged into a street that was busy, dusty and full of people. And the noise! It was deafening.

'Hold my arm,' Matt urged. 'We're gonna get on a tram. It's only a few stops.'

They surged forward, with half a dozen other would-be passengers, into the middle of the road to board the tram that clanged its way through lorries and cars. On each side of the road, in front of a good many shops, there was a never-ending open market. Joan lived in London herself but until now she had had no idea how vast the difference was between south London and the East End. As they made their way to the pavement she could see the beauty and the magnitude of Tower Bridge. It made her feel that she came from a different world.

'Everywhere is so busy,' she mumbled, as they walked down a side turning.

Matt was so happy to be back in his home surroundings that he didn't notice her discomfiture. 'Yeah, it's always like this, day an' night,' was all he said.

On her two short previous visits Joan had got out of the car and gone straight into the house. Now she was aware of her surroundings. A young woman came towards them pushing a shabby old pram full of babies, lots of children were in the road, and it sounded to Joan as if they were squabbling and fighting rather than playing games. A side road led off and, as they turned into it, Joan took note of a public house on one corner and a corner shop right opposite.

Matt's home was in the middle of a row of terraced houses. It was exactly the same as all the others, with a small fenced-in front garden and a path that led up to a dark-brown-painted front door. A bow window was on the ground floor and two flat windows above.

Matt opened the wooden gate. Amy Pearson, his mother, was hard at work scrubbing her top step. A sacking apron was tied around her skirt, a dark green jersey covered her bosom, and over her wiry grey hair was a flat cap, which she was wearing back to front to enable her to see what she was doing.

She looked up, smiling broadly, as Matt and Joan, doing their best to avoid the soapy water that was running down the path, gingerly stepped their way towards her. ''Allo, son. I wasn't expecting you till this afternoon. Give us an 'and t' get up,' she said.

Suddenly two young lads came tearing up the passage-way to the front door. 'It's our Matt. Wotcher, Matt, 'ow long yer 'ome for?' They fell upon him and pulled him into the house, both talking at once and leaving his mum and Joan to follow them.

'These are my sister's kids,' Matt told her, by way of intro-duction, once they were inside the cosy living room. 'This is Teddy,' he said, waving at the older one, whom Joan thought to be about ten, 'and this is Jack.'

Then, before he could tell her anything else, his mother cut in, 'It's that little 'un you 'ave t' watch out for. I know 'e looks like an angel but, believe me, love, 'e's a right little terror.'

'This is Joan,' Matt finally told them.

The younger boy certainly was a lovely child, hair so thick and blond it didn't look natural, and blue eyes that would tear the heart out of you. He looked up at Joan and gave her the sweetest smile before saying. 'You're his tart, ain'tcher?'

Matt's mother moved with speed that belied her bulk. She had removed the sacking apron from around her waist and now she flicked it so hard at the child that Joan winced. 'Yer little brat! One day that mouth of yours will get you into trouble. Go on, get upstairs, both of yer, an' don't come down till I say yer can.

'Sorry about that,' Amy said. 'Their mother works in a factory canteen and I suppose I've let them get away with murder. Still, they're back t' school tomorrow, thank God. I expect you're ready for a cup o' tea, ain't yer?' She was fat and smiling, with the same big brown eyes that had endeared her to Matt, and Joan felt that in spite of the way she spoke, she could really come to like this woman.

Soon they were drinking tea and eating home-made rock cakes in the homely kitchen. Then Joan couldn't believe her ears: Amy was telling Matt that his father and two of his brothers were going to be in the pub about now and were expecting him to join them. Matt got to his feet, bent over and kissed her. 'Shan't be too long,' he said.

'Can't I come with you?' she asked.

'Later on ternight I'll take yer for a drink, but right now me dad an' me brothers are waiting for me. Mum'll look after yer, won't yer, Mum? See yer later.' Then, as he reached the door, he called back over his shoulder, 'By the way, Mum, we're gonna get married. I'm gonna get a special licence. Now's yer chance to 'ave a good old natter, sort things out between yer.'

Joan wanted to say that they hadn't really settled anything. When he'd previously spoken about getting a special licence, she hadn't taken him seriously. Now he seemed so different. From the minute he'd walked into this house he'd become a different person. He'd even slipped into their way of talking, which she'd never noticed before. Well, not so much anyhow.

'He always does that when he comes home on leave.'

Amy's voice made her jump. 'Does what?'

'Goes for a drink with his dad. Lot of his mates'll be in the Blind Beggar about this time of day. If you've finished yer tea I'll show yer round. Won't take long, there ain't that much t' see.'

Joan was upset. He had brought her here, dumped her the minute they arrived and told his mother they were getting married when nothing had been agreed between them. Some cheek he had!

'I'd better show yer the lavvy first. It's out in the yard – expect you're dying t' spend a penny.' It was true, she was. But, my God, this was embarrassing. Here she was, sitting on a wooden seat of a toilet in a shed in an outside back-yard with Matt's mother standing outside the door.

The house was small, two rooms and a scullery down-stairs, and just two rooms above. The biggest bedroom was furnished quite nicely. In place of honour stood a wide double bed with brass rails top and bottom. There was a tall chest of drawers, which had brass handles, two wicker armchairs, painted green and gold, and a marble-topped washstand, which held an enormous china bowl and jug. Placed beside this on the floor Joan was amazed to see two big china chamberpots, each sporting the same floral pattern as the washing bowl.

'Jug's 'alf full of cold water if yer feel like a wash,' Amy offered, and before Joan had a chance to reply she added, 'You can sleep in 'ere with me. Ernie, me ole man, can kip downstairs in the middle room with Matt while you're 'ere.'

Joan hadn't given a thought until then as to where she would be sleeping, but now she was expected to share that big bed with his mother!

What with one thing and another being sprung on her Joan was getting more and more mad by the minute.

When Matt came back from the pub, bringing his mates as well as several members of his family, the house was so crowded she didn't have a chance to speak to him on his own. There were his two brothers with their wives, a sister, the mother of Teddy and Jack, and an unmarried sister. Joan got the feeling they were all there to inspect her. Everyone was talking so loudly, telling her how bad the air-raids had been and how glad they were that, for the time being, they seemed to have eased off. Crates of beer had been brought in and, as soon as it got dark, someone said that Mr Clarke had managed to get hold of a few boxes of fish and would be frying tonight. In a flash Amy had her purse out, and the youngsters were sent to fetch fish and chips for everyone. It was a noisy but happy evening. Joan heard songs that she'd never heard before. Then, still without having had Matt to herself, she was being guided up the narrow staircase. There didn't seem any point in protesing so she found herself lying beside Amy in a big feather bed that was far more comfortable than she had imagined.

'You'll meet me other daughter termorrow. She'll be round with 'er kids,' Amy said happily, already half asleep.

Joan sighed. She felt out of her depth. Whatever had she let herself in for? Just have to wait and see, won't I? she thought, as she turned on her side and snuggled down. I'll tell Matt in the morning I'm not staying, she decided, as she plumped up her pillow, hoping and praying for a good night's sleep.

But next morning Amy was standing beside the bed holding out a tin tray with a cup of tea and two slices of bread and butter, saying, 'Sorry there ain't any biscuits. Joe up at the corner shop had quite a few in this week but cos I ain't got no points left for this month he wouldn't let me 'ave any. He'll regret that – you see if 'e don't! There won't always be a war going on.'

Joan smiled at Amy's threat.

'I've brought you Ernie's dressing-gown. It's almost new, he never wears it, and I thought you'd be glad of it, if you want t' come downstairs to the lavvy. And yer can bring a kettle of hot water back up 'ere so's you can wash – be better than down in the scullery.'

'Thanks,' Joan said, appreciating the kind thought. 'I'll come down as soon as I've drunk my tea.'

As the day went on, Joan came to the conclusion that it was the busiest and noisiest she had spent in her whole life. As she soon discovered, Amy was determined to show her their part of London and, at the same time, give her neighbours and friends an eyeful of Matt's posh girlfriend, was how she put it.

Joan did her best to tell Matt that she would rather spend the day with him but he wasn't having that. 'We'll 'ave all the time in the world t' be together when we've tied the knot,' he said, following her up the stairs when she went to fetch her coat.

'No, we won't,' she protested. 'You said yourself your regiment won't be in England for much longer. And you had no right to tell your parents we're getting married before we've settled anything.'

Matt pulled her close and began kissing her face, then her ear and her neck. 'I'd like to spend the entire day on that big bed making love to you, but I can't see me mum standing for that, so suppose I'll just 'ave to be patient. Anyway me dad's coming down the town 'all with me while you're out with me mum. We're gonna get the licence and that means by this time next week we could really be Mr an' Mrs. Just think about it, Joanie, it'll be perfectly legal for us to stay in bed all day long if we want to.' Matt's eyes were half closed as he squeezed her breasts. 'God,' he murmured. 'I've got t' get yer to meself some time today or I'm gonna go mad.'

'Joan, are yer ready? If we don't get off pretty sharpish all the best fruit an' veg will be gone, not to mention the size of the queues there'll be at the offal shop.' Amy's voice, coming from the foot of the stairs, sounded like thunder.

'I'll have to go,' Joan said, and Matt grinned. 'You better 'ad, else she'll be up 'ere like a dose of salts and she'll whack me round the 'ead – not for what I've done but for what I've been thinking I'd like t' do. She's nobody's fool is me mum.'

So Amy and Joan set off for the market.

Much of the area they walked through was ugly and sordid, with slums, the like of which Joan had never imagined. And the bomb damage was beyond belief: whole streets had been razed to the ground. But it was strange: suddenly they would come to an area that was delightful, even beautiful.

The colour and life of the market had Joan laughing as she listened to the barrow-boys spouting off about their wares. Wimbledon had a market on Saturday mornings but it bore no comparison to this one. Offal and fish were not rationed and it stood to reason that more people stood in line outside these shops to have something decent for their dinner that day. 'Blast,' Amy muttered, as from the other side of the road she watched a man with a white apron and a straw boater on his head pull down one of the shop shutters by means of a long pole. Then, 'Come on,' she ordered, grabbing hold of Joan's arm, 'we might just be lucky.'

The fact that the fishmonger was shouting that he was closing because he'd sold out did nothing to deter Amy Pearson. She marched into the shop, set down her bag amongst the sawdust on the floor and folded her arms across her ample bosom. 'Bet yer got a nice little parcel left to take along to Miss High an' Mighty Morrison,' she said, so quietly that Joan wasn't sure that she'd heard right. 'Saved any for yer wife, 'ave yer?'

The fishmonger's face flared bright red and he took such a deep breath he looked ready to explode. Without a word, he placed the pole he was still holding against the wall and walked through to the back of the shop.

Amy winked at Joan as they waited.

'There y'are, Mrs Pearson. Four 'errings, best I can do,' the fishmonger told her, holding them out for her inspection.

'That's very kind of you,' Amy told him sweetly. 'But do me a favour, will yer, and tell me what I'd do with four little fish among my lot? You know 'ow big me 'usband is and me boys are even bigger . . . all employed on war work and Matt's 'ome on leave from 'Is Majesty's forces. They deserve a bit better than that, don't yer think?'

Joan looked at her in amazement. What was she implying? Her words, though spoken softly, sounded sinister.

The fishmonger sighed heavily. 'How many were you thinking of feeding today, Mrs Pearson?'

'Oh, only me own family but most of me lads would eat two of them little 'errings an' still say their bellies were empty, not to mention me old man.'

'All right, all right,' he said, turning so quickly that Joan felt he was now just anxious to be rid of them.

Joan couldn't help it, she wanted to laugh, the satisfied grin on Amy's face as they waited had to be seen to be believed. 'You're the bane of my life, you know that, don't yer, Mrs Pearson?' He pushed two newspaper-wrapped parcels into her shopping basket. 'There's eight 'errings and a couple of codlings. Give us three bob and let me tell you I'm a fool ter meself.'

'Course you are,' Amy agreed, and added softly, 'All sins carry a price.'

Over the next few days Joan became aware that London had many different sides to it. Not much housework seemed to get done, but no one could blame Amy for that. She seemed to spend most of her time providing enormous meals for everyone who cared to step over her doorstep. Joan grew accustomed to the family and laughed to herself when Teddy and Jack warned her to make herself scarce when their gran was in a roaring temper because Granddad had come home drunk.

The wedding was often discussed and everyone, young and old alike, seemed to want to put in their two-pennyworth.

Amy was all for going to the church and seeing if the vicar could do a rush job as Matt only had a few more days' leave. At this Joan was terrified. Get married without her mum and dad being there? And what about Nan and Pops? She'd never dare go home again!

For once Matt showed some consideration for her. 'Suddenly feeling all religious, are we?' he asked his mother. All he got for his pains was a swift smack round the head.

Then came her last day. Half of Whitechapel seemed to be crammed into Amy's terraced house. At least, that's how it seemed to Joan. Still, she had come to realize that they were genuine folk, kind, warm-hearted and generous. If they took to you you'd made a friend for life; cross any one of them and God help you. These East Enders certainly knew how to stick together. They had come to wish her and Matt the best of everything, and hoped to be at their wedding.

Joan smiled and kept her tongue between her teeth. If this wedding was to take place, she knew full well that it would be when and where *her* family arranged it. She was their only child, after all. But she wasn't brave enough to say as much. Instead she bade Matt's mother and father a fond farewell and thanked them for having her. 'Any time, my love,' Amy told her, squeezing her to her bosom. 'Just cos Matt ain't around don't mean you can't come and pay us a visit, so I'm telling you now, don't you dare become a stranger.'

Joan was touched. Maybe she would come up to the East

End to see Amy after Matt had been posted. That brought her up sharp. More than likely she'll be your mother-in-law by then, she thought, as she let go of Matt's arm and turned at the corner of the road to give a final wave.

Chapter Four

JOAN WAS SITTING in a corner of the kitchen, alone with her thoughts. I'll have to tell them, she thought. There's been so much talk already and still nothing has been decided. But this is a different kettle of fish, and there's no getting away from it.

Matt had brought her home three weeks ago and he had faced up to her father honestly and squarely. But Bill Harvey was his own man and no one swayed him easily: special licence or not, there was going to be no wedding until he and Daphne had settled in their own minds that it was what their daughter wanted. That had been his decision and no one could shake him. 'There is plenty of time,' he kept repeating.

Matt had returned to his regiment a sad young man.

Ten days had passed before Joan had seen him again, and then he had been down to take her out over the weekend. It was as they came out of the Odeon cinema at Shannon's Corner and went across to the Duke of Cambridge public house that she resolved to tell him.

It was warm and crowded in the pub, and the smell of beer and tobacco smoke was somehow welcoming even if it didn't make the telling any easier.

'There's an empty table over there,' Matt said, pointing a finger. 'You go and sit down and I'll get us a drink.'

It's as if he knows what's coming, Joan thought, as Matt set down a pint of beer for himself and a brandy for her. 'Not often a pub has spirits, these days, but the barman offered so I accepted. It's the uniform that does it, I expect.'

Joan took a sip and found it warming as it went down into her stomach. 'Matt . . .' she started, her forehead puckered with the effort of trying to find the right words to tell him '. . . about us getting married. I think I can get my dad to agree now if you still want to.'

He took a long drink from his pint, saying nothing.

'Matt . . .' she tried again . . . 'I'm pregnant. I've known for some time. I really am.'

He didn't smile, he didn't speak, he just set his glass down on to the table and drew her close to his side. 'That settles it. Now, I'll tell you what we're gonna do,' he said, sounding determined. 'First we'll finish our drink, then I'm taking you home and I'm coming into the house to talk to your father. I'm gonna tell him that some time tomorrow, depending on when I can get out of barracks, we're going down to your nearest register office, show them the licence I already have and get a date for us to be married.' Seeing the forlorn look on her face he added quickly, 'You know how much I love you, Joan, and I'm over the moon about the baby. And you're not to worry, I'll look after you.'

Surprise and pleasure at the way he had taken her news

had bucked her up no end. 'Well, that sounds lovely,' she said, smiling at him. 'But you may not be able to get the time off.'

Matt had told her to leave everything to him. He would see the padre, get him on their side, and he had no doubt that his commanding officer could wangle him a few days' compassionate leave.

The best-laid plans of mice and men do go astray.

When they had burst into the house, arms linked, faces glowing, it was to find no one at home. Matt had stayed with her as long as he could but finally had to leave. He didn't want to overstay his pass, especially as he was about to ask a favour.

It was very late that night when her mother and father came home, bringing her nan in with them.

'Where have you been?' Joan cried, but the sadness on all their faces made her lower her voice. 'Whatever's happened? Tell me!'

'It's Pops,' her father said, reaching for her hand. 'He had a heart-attack.'

Turning to face her nan, Joan said softly, 'Oh, Nan, he is going to be all right, isn't he?'

Her mother wrapped her arms around her and told her that Pops had died.

There were things that had to be done, or so they told her. That's why they had all gone out early this morning and she was on her own. Joan was frightened, overwhelmed by sadness. The more she thought about her predicament, the more she felt as if she were wading through a sea of mud. Matt would probably turn up here again soon, full of beans and acting larger than life. She would have to tell him to calm down and urge him to say nothing. She just couldn't let him talk to her father, not at a time like this.

Poor dear Pops. He'd loved her so much. And she him. She'd been so privileged to have had him while she was growing up. It had been like having two fathers – two loving fathers, who had not only loved her but spoilt her. Dear God, she was going to have to grow up now! Soon she was going to be a mother. 'Oh, Pops,' she murmured, as the tears trickled down her face.

When the doorbell rang, Joan got quickly to her feet. At least Matt had arrived before her parents had got back, which would give her time to tell him her sad news.

There he was, arms spread wide and laughing. 'Everything's sorted. You're never gonna believe our luck, darling.'

This burst from him before Joan had a chance to say a word. The sight and sound of his joviality annoyed her, and she greeted him curtly. It wasn't his fault that Pops had died – she knew that – but she just couldn't help herself. 'Hold on, Matt,' she said, pushing him away as he tried to take her in his arms. 'Come on inside. Something very sad has happened.'

Once in the kitchen he removed his cap and demanded that she tell him whatever it was without beating about the bush.

Joan did just that.

'I'm sorry, really I am, but we're still going to get married,' he said. It was a statement, a decision: there was no doubt about it.

Joan began to worry. 'We can't tell my mum and dad now, not with all the trouble they've got – and my poor nan, what would she say?'

It was at that moment that the door opened.

'Hello, Matt.' Daphne was the first to speak.

But, sensing that something was not quite right, Bill Harvey faced the young soldier squarely. 'You're not here this morning just on the off-chance, are you?' he asked quietly.

'No, I'm not,' Matt agreed. 'And I'm sorry the timing is all wrong but I do need t' talk to you about Joan and me getting married,' he said, stubbornly.

'I'll put the kettle on,' Daphne mumbled, and she went with her mother to the scullery.

Hester Burton had lived long enough to have learnt a few facts of life. As she watched her daughter go to the sink she murmured, 'Hear of a death and you hear of a birth.'

Daphne turned and stared at her mother. 'What are you on about, Mum?'

'Our Joanie's pregnant. That's what this young man is here about. Not that I'm surprised. I was going to say something to you days ago, but I thought I'd wait till she came back from visiting his folk. You only have to look at her to tell.'

'Mother, you can't be right! She's as thin as a rake.'

'I'm not talking about her showing. Just look in her eyes – you'll know then, right enough.'

'My God!' Daphne clutched at the sink for support. Talk about history repeating itself. She and her mother might have been eighteen when they had given birth but at least they had been married. There had been no hanky-panky before the wedding in those days. It's this damn war that's sending so many girls off the rails, she thought.

'I've laid the tray but I think you'd better put a bottle of the hard stuff out as well.' Hester was staying remarkably cool, considering. 'I'm not sure who's going to need it most, our Bill or that young lad.'

The atmosphere was tense when Hester put her head round the door and asked if it was all right to bring in the tea. Bill just nodded.

Joan was too tired, too stunned by her father's angry outburst to argue any further.

'By the look on the faces of you two you don't need any telling,' Bill said to his wife, and then, much more softly, he said to his mother-in-law, 'At least Matt wants t' do right by her. So, whatever we decide we'll keep it quiet. Well, quiet as possible. Let Pops's funeral be our first concern. I'm just grateful that we managed to get the death certificate and suchlike this morning. We'll have this cuppa and then I'll go back to the undertaker's with you, Hetty, and get a date set.'

Matt cleared his throat. 'Mr Harvey, would it be all right if I take Joan down to the register office this afternoon?'

'Register office?' Joan's mother was appalled.

Her husband gave her a look that silenced her. Then, sternly, he said, 'We can hardly have a church wedding and all the frills, now, can we?'

'I suppose not.'

She looked so forlorn that Joan got up, stood behind her and put her arms round her mother's shoulders. 'I'm sorry, Mum.'

Daphne Harvey wasn't an emotional person: she had always believed that what would be would be. Today, however, she was truly moved, and Joan, unable to stem her tears, had taken her arms from her mother's shoulders and was fumbling for a handkerchief.

'Come here, baby,' Daphne urged, wrapping her close in a tight hug. 'It's a very sad day for all of us but it will all work out for the best in the end, you'll see. Just think what Pops would have said. A baby! Another for him to spoil.'

'Yes,' Joan rubbed at her eyes with her sopping wet hanky, 'but he's not here, is he?'

'He'll be watching over you, wherever he is. You can be sure of that,' her grandmother said.

'I wish I was as sure as you are, Nan. I'm going to miss Pops so much.'

'We all are, pet,' her grandmother admitted sadly.

Daphne felt that things were getting out of hand, and although she was furious with Matt Pearson for having taken advantage of her daughter, she felt just a tinge of sympathy for him as he stood against the wall, ignored by everyone. She said, 'We've to make the best of a bad job and now we know that Joan is pregnant, her and Mathew should get married.' Then, looking across at her husband, she added, 'The sooner the better. It'll be all for the best, don't you agree?'

Her husband bit hard on his bottom lip, then muttered, 'I don't know, I just don't know.'

Daphne picked up the teapot and pushed past him to go into the scullery, leaving him staring at nothing, deep in thought. Then he shifted his gaze to rest on the young man attired in soldier's uniform, knowing that more than likely he would be sent miles away in the not too distant future. All for the best indeed! Yet what else could he do? He felt he had no option but to agree.

At two o'clock, Joan and Matt stood side by side in the register office, and she watched while he explained the circumstances and produced the licence he had applied for in a different area.

'You still have to give seventy-two hours' notice,' the elderly lady clerk informed him. 'We have a free slot at eleven o'clock on Friday morning.'

Matt thanked her warmly. In twenty minutes the whole thing had been set up and he felt a sight better for knowing that.

The next three days passed in a haze.

No one had much enthusiasm for the wedding preparations. Joan was to be a bride on Friday, but on the following Monday they were to bury her grandfather.

What about a honeymoon? Matt asked himself. I suppose that idea goes down the drain. He didn't feel able to ask Joan's father if they could slip away and not attend the funeral.

Then it was their wedding day. Joan looked lovely in a pale blue dress with a loose-fitting coat, both made of silk and embroidered along the cuffs and neckline. Clothing coupons had been begged from all the neighbours, and Sadie Bowman, who owned a dress salon at Wimbledon Broadway, had come to the house bringing three outfits for Joan to choose from. Poppy and Bob Benson had had to be told the news, and they had come up trumps. Indeed, the hat Joan was wearing belonged to Poppy. It had been retrimmed with artificial white daisies and loaned to the bride for the day.

Few were there to see them get wed. To Joan's disappointment her nan had said she wasn't up to it so on her side she had her mum and dad, her best friend Peggy and Poppy. Bob felt it wasn't possible for the two of them to leave the pub.

There were even fewer folk to be with Matt. He had managed to slip away and fill his family in on all that had happened. He still couldn't believe the way his mother had reacted to the news that he was getting married. Down in the south, in a register office, and no ding-dong afterwards? 'Least said soonest mended,' his mother was fond of saying, but that certainly hadn't applied on this occasion. She'd had plenty to say.

'Made her pregnant!' she screamed. If he'd murdered her she couldn't have sounded more scandalized. She practically threw him out of the house, and threatened never to speak to him again.

So, on that May morning the only person Matt had to stand up for him was one army mate. However, at the last minute, to his delight and relief, his eldest brother Stan had turned up.

It wasn't exactly the brightest of wedding days.

It wasn't until she and Matt were alone in her grandmother's house that evening that Joan fully realized that she was married. Matt had been as pleased as punch when Hester had offered her house to them for the weekend, saying she would be fine staying along the road with Bill and Daphne. 'It was very kind and thoughtful of yer nan,' Matt was saying, as he lifted a cloth off the cold refreshments she had set out for their supper. He only wished to God that Joan would cheer up a bit. He'd had it in his mind to take her to Southend or even down to Brighton for the few days he'd got left but they had the funeral looming over them. Still, they had a whole house to themselves and a big double bed upstairs. Things could be a lot worse, he said to himself, as he opened a bottle of sparkling wine. A whole lot worse in fact!

Joan's family had left them discreetly alone, assuming that they were only too glad to be together and it should have been a marvellous time, but it wasn't, and Matt was thoroughly disappointed. By the time he woke up on the second morning of what was supposed to be his honeymoon he was well and truly browned off. They'd made love a couple of times or, more to the point, *he* had made all the running. For all the feeling Joan had shown him, he might just as well have turned on his side and gone to sleep.

Later they took a bus ride up to Wimbledon Common and went into the pub to have a drink with Bill and Poppy, and Bob got on well with Matt. After a while they made their way home, in what Matt hoped was a happier frame of mind.

After a quiet lunch Matt led her upstairs. Loving and gentle though he was, he simply could not rouse her. Suddenly she burst into tears, and he pulled her close to his chest and let her sob her heart out. 'This is supposed t' be our honeymoon,' she mumbled. 'You'll be saying soon you wished you'd never married me. I am sorry.'

'Never mind,' he soothed. 'It's only t' be expected, what with the thought of us having to go to yer granddad's funeral tomorrow an' all.'

'*Are* you sorry you married me, Matt?'

''Course I ain't,' he declared. 'After all, I know what you can be like, remember? Just think, I've got that kind of loving to look forward to for the rest of me life now that I've made an honest woman of you.'

They lay together under the eiderdown and talked. 'It's just unfortunate that death got mingled up with our wedding plans. But think, Joan, despite losing your granddad and having to put up with all the miseries and shortages of this flipping war we've still had this time together, and I know some of me mates would have given their right arm for as much. By the time this war's over we'll look back on this and laugh. We'll have all our lives before us then, just the two of us, an' we'll plan our future together.'

Joan raised herself up on her elbow and stared down into her husband's face. 'Wait a minute! I think you're forgetting something. Not so much of the two of us! There'll be three of us by then.'

'Crikey, yes.' He laughed. 'And if it drags on for much longer and I get regular leave, who knows? We'll probably be on our way to making our own football team, time I get demobbed.'

'Bit ambitious, aren't you?' She giggled, feeling much better as she snuggled up to his bare chest.

'You'll get through it,' Matt told her softly, as she took delivery of yet another wreath.

Joan was doing her best to stay steady and composed, standing beside Matt to open the front door to what seemed an endless number of mourners. Her nan was weeping, her father constantly blowing his nose. Only Daphne was doing her bit, handing out glasses of sherry to the ladies and whisky to the men. Joan thought her mother looked older today, dressed in black, a neat little hat perched on her bright hair. You could tell she'd been crying, even though her face was covered by a thin black veil.

In church the vicar had had plenty of good things to say about Pops. He was well known and liked, having lived in the same road from the day he and Hester had got married. Everyone was thankful that the service at the graveside was brief: with the rain coming down in torrents, it was bleak and cold out there among the weatherbeaten headstones, even under an umbrella. Back at the house all the relatives, friends and neighbours had eaten ham salad with hot boiled potatoes, nibbled cake and drunk tea from a range of borrowed cups. Then they said their tearful goodbyes.

Soon only Hester, Bill, Daphne, Joan and Matt were left in the kitchen.

'I'll 'ave t' get going now,' Matt whispered to Joan, taking his battle-dress down from the hook in the hall.

Joan felt she didn't have the energy to get out of the chair. An awful numbing fatigue had engulfed her but somehow she had to make the effort.

'If you're going to the station with Matt, I'll come with you,' Bill Harvey said, looking at his daughter. 'Breath of fresh air will do me good.' He was thinking that she didn't look well enough to walk back on her own.

Matt guessed what he had in mind and was grateful. Joan got to her feet and slipped her arms into her coat, which Matt was holding. It was as if she was going through the motions like a child.

'Thank God the rain has stopped,' Matt murmured, as the three of them set off.

Standing on the platform Joan clung to Matt, dry-eyed, which worried him more than if she had shed floods of tears. 'I'll be back as soon as I can. It won't be long. I promise.' He kissed her gently, and pushed her towards her father. Then he shook hands with Bill, who was thinking how easy it was to make a promise: who, in times like these, could promise anything?

Joan and her father stood side by side, watching the guard slam the carriage doors and wave his green flag. The train looked awful: grey with dust, its windows criss-crossed with sticky tape to prevent flying splinters if and when a bomb dropped close. Joan tucked her hand through her father's arm and sighed. 'Everything, no matter where you look, is so shabby,' she said.

'I'm going to buy us both a drink,' Bill decided. 'Give your mother and nan time to clear up a bit.' Doing his best to smile, he walked her across to the station bar and ordered a pint for himself and a brandy for Joan.

'Sorry, we've no spirits whatsoever,' the stout barmaid told him.

'Pity. We've just come from a funeral and my daughter could use a pick-me-up,' Bill answered her.

'Truly, we haven't a drop.' Then, almost as an afterthought she turned to look at Joan and said, 'How about a nice drop of port? That'd warm you up.'

'Yes.' Joan managed a weak smile. 'Yes, please, that would be nice.'

It was warm and crowded in the bar and they made their way over to stand against the wall.

'Cheer up, my love,' Bill said, wiping the froth from his mouth on the back of his hand. 'Things will work out for you an' Matt, you'll see.'

'I suppose so,' Joan answered, sounding unconvinced.

'We'll find you a nice place to live, somewhere near to your mother an' me,' he promised. 'You'll stay with us, of course, but you can spend your time making a nice home for Matt and the baby so that it's all ready by the time this wretched war is over.' Then he chided himself. What had he thought when he'd heard Matt make her a promise? Now he, too, was doing the same thing, telling her they'd find her a place of her own. With all the bombing, streets and streets of houses flattened to the ground, he'd have to admit that it would be virtually impossible.

Matt's thoughts were much the same, as he listened to the iron wheels going clickety-clack on the railway track. Over and over again he had wondered how to get them a place of their own. More so now Joan was expecting and . . . boy, oh, boy, she's my wife, Mrs Mathew Pearson. Funny that, not a single soul had mentioned it. What a wedding! They had had a few flowers and a cake of sorts, but no presents, no telegrams wishing them well. No one had thrown confetti and, more to the point, his parents hadn't been there. Poor Joan, she must feel cheated. Maybe not at this moment, but there would come a time. Oh, yes, that was a safe bet. The time would come when she would realize that their wedding day had been a sham: nothing to look back on, no mementoes, not even a photograph of the bride and groom. God! His mother had been right: they'd look back on that day and have a great many regrets.

We'll do it all over again, when this bloody war is over. Now he was making a promise to himself and, God willing, it was one he would keep. And it won't be in the south or in no ruddy register office. Wait till I see me mum again. I'm going t' let her know how right she was, and how bad things were, and that this time I'll let her make all the arrangements. He was laughing to himself now: if his mother had her way there would be a right ding-dong. Well, that would be fine by him. Let the whole of the East End turn up, he wouldn't care, because next time he was going to make sure that Joan had the works.

And to make sure his mum was happy, he'd see to it that it was the biggest and noisiest ding-dong Whitechapel had ever seen.

Chapter Five

BEING A MARRIED woman didn't change Joan's life to any great extent. She still lived at home, still worked at the Fox and Hounds and slept there when she was doing a late shift.

Was she happy? Was she looking forward to having the baby? These were questions she constantly asked herself. As for being a good mother, she felt far from confident about that, although she put on a brave face, especially when her nan was around.

Matt and his brigade were now in what he described as a holding unit out at Hassocks on the south coast. First off he had suggested that Joan come and stay down there in one of the local pubs so that they could meet, even if it was only for an hour at a time, but Bill Harvey was dead against that idea. He felt that quite soon now the war was going to change, and that most of the troops left in England would be on the move. You only had to listen to the wireless or read the papers, he said, to get the feeling that something was about to take place. Hoardings all over the place had been scrawled with the demand 'Second Front Now'.

'The last thing we want is for you to be stranded in some out-of-the-way village when the baby is born,' was how he stated his case.

'But I'm only four months gone,' had been Joan's reply. But in her heart she knew her father was right: she didn't want to be in a pub or a bed-and-breakfast guest-house where she wouldn't know anyone or have anything to do, except wait and hope that she might be able to spend a little time with Matt.

Instead she wrote long letters to him. She told him how her nan was knitting and sewing enough clothes for four babies. How her mother thought that Joanie being pregnant had been a Godsend to Hester. 'She misses my granddad like mad, but at least she's thrilled to think that very soon there will be a baby in the house. Neighbours, too, are very kind. Old Granny Wallace, you know her, lives on the corner opposite the paper shop, well, she's crocheting a shawl for us which my mum says will do for the christening. It's already half finished and she has shown it to me. I can't believe how lovely it is. So fine and delicate. It makes you wonder how the old lady can see to do such work, and as to where she found the silk and the wool, well, my mother says I am not to ask.'

One thing really did please Joan, and that was that Matt wrote to her just as regularly as she did to him. He always wanted to know if she was keeping well, and telling her how proud he was that they were going to be parents. His last letter, though, had frightened her. It was as if he was warning her about something: 'Joan, dear,' he wrote, 'please do me a favour and go up and see my mum and dad. They may have grandchildren already but they really are pleased about our news. Well, me mum is now that she has got used to the idea and, as I see it, you two did get on really well in the short time you stayed with her.'

It wasn't much to ask, Joan decided, and she had been feeling a bit guilty because she had never been in touch with Amy Pearson since she had spent those few days with her. And Amy had gone out of her way to make her welcome.

London was proving too much for Joan. The train ride from Wimbledon hadn't been too bad – folk still had time to help a pregnant woman. However, as she stood surveying the crowds she decided that getting on to a tram was going to be far too difficult and that for once she was going to be extravagant and take a taxi. She got out at the top of the road – she didn't want Matt's family to think she was show-ing off – and walked slowly down it towards the house. She was feeling lonely, because the last time she had been here Matt had been with her, and even a bit miserable, not know-ing what kind of a reception she would get. She raised her head at the sound of running feet. It was the two boys, Teddy and Jack.

''Allo, Joan, come t' see our gran, 'ave yer?' Teddy asked, giving her a cheeky grin.

Before she could answer little Jack piped up, 'Cos she ain't in. She's gone to a jumble sale with me mum an' our aunt Laura.'

Now Joan didn't know what to do. She looked at the chil-dren. Both of them looked as if they could do with a good wash. Their hair hadn't been combed. Teddy's jacket was patched and threadbare and the short trousers Jack was wearing were miles too big for him. Yet for all that they both seemed as happy as a pair of larks and as fit as fleas.

'Never mind,' Teddy said kindly, 'the front door's open an' I'll come indoors an' make yer a nice cuppa tea.'

Joan could have kissed him. As she worked her way down the cluttered hallway she had to step over two little girls, whose names she didn't know, and she couldn't remember if she'd seen them before or not. 'They're our cousins,' Jack informed her. 'Our aunt Laura's their mum.'

Teddy plumped up the cushions in the big old armchair set nearest to the scrubbed-topped kitchen table saying, 'Sit in me granddad's chair. I won't be long with the tea.' Then, grabbing his young brother by the arm, he spoke quickly: 'You can set the cups out and see if there's any bread in the bin an' if there is get it out an' the marge an' the jam – that's if there's any of that either.'

Joan had to smother a smile. He was really trying: she was getting the right royal treatment.

Teddy came back with a quart bottle half full of milk and set it down on the table. 'Can't find no sugar,' he said, shaking his head.

'Not to worry,' Joan told him, 'all my family gave up taking sugar in their tea soon after the war started. Just as well, cos it's like gold-dust now, isn't it?'

Young Jack was doing his best to set out the tea things, but every now and then he paused to dart a mischievous grin at Joan from under his long fair eyelashes. Soon Teddy was pouring tea from the big brown teapot into what she supposed must be one of their grandmother's best cups.

Needing to talk, Joan asked Teddy, 'How come you two are still in London? I thought that all children were evacuated about three years ago when the air-raids were so heavy.'

'We was.' This forthright statement had come from Jack.

'What do you mean, you was?' She grinned at the small boy.

For a moment there was silence in the room. Then Teddy said, very softly, 'It was awful. They put labels on us, tied them on with string, and put us all on a train, an' when we got there they separated us. Bruvvers an' sisters, it didn't matter to them, they didn't care. Jack was only a little tiddler an' the last thing me mum said t' me was I 'ad to keep 'old of him an' look after him. I couldn't. They took 'im away. Them people didn't like us an' we didn't like them. All the kids in our street came 'ome once I let me mum know what was going on.'

'Yeah, an' when we come, me mum said we ain't got t' go away no more.' Jack sounded as if he'd scored a victory.

As she listened Joan felt that Jack was old beyond his years. They both were, come to that. She sighed inwardly. Poor kids! Despite the terrors of indiscriminate bombing they had made up their own minds that there was no place like home and that no foster-parents could make up for their own mothers and fathers.

'What the 'ell is going on in 'ere?' Amy pushed open the kitchen door and beamed with delight when she spied Joan.

'I made tea for 'er,' Teddy said proudly.

'Yeah, an' I laid the table, but I couldn't find anything t' put on the bread,' Jack added.

Watching Joan try to suppress her amusement, Amy Pearson said, 'By God, it's good t' see yer, gal. Sorry I wasn't in. We've been to see what we could get in the way of clothes over at the church 'all. Me two girls 'ave stopped off t' do a bit of shopping. They'll bring in something an' I'll soon 'ave a meal on the go.'

Then flopping her heavy body down on to a chair she grumbled, 'If only me blinking legs wouldn't swell up so much I'd be able to get out an' about a bit more. Still, we've done all right today. Got a load of stuff for the kids and ain't 'ad to part with a single coupon.' So saying she tipped a sackful of clothes out on to the rug that lay in front of the fireplace.

Most of the jerseys, shirts and even a few pretty little dresses seemed clean and in good repair to Joan, who was flabbergasted when Amy, smiling broadly, said, 'Whole lot cost me one and tenpence.'

'You're having me on, Amy. You must have paid out more than that.'

'Gawd's truth, love, and if I'd known you were 'ere I'd 'ave been first in the queue for the baby clothes. Still, I'll keep me eyes peeled. How much longer, d'yer know?'

'The end of November, the clinic reckons, but they can't be sure, can they?'

Amy Pearson threw back her head and let out a great belly laugh. 'I didn't need no clinic to tell me no date. It were my Ernie! If he were passionate in a certain kind of way I marked it off on the calendar an', sure as eggs is eggs, it turned out right every time. Better watch out for our Mathew. Who knows? He might take after his ole man.'

The expression on Joan's face set Amy off again. And she was still laughing and clutching her sides when her two daughters came back each carrying a basket of shopping.

'Oh, it's our Matt's wife.' Bertha greeted Joan with a smile. 'What brings you 'ere?'

'Well, I haven't been in touch, and I thought it was about time I came an' thanked your mum for having me to stay when Matt was on leave last time.'

'Never got invited to the wedding, did we?' Laura's voice held a touch of harshness.

'No, I'm sorry. Wasn't much of a wedding because my granddad died and we had to bury him two days after we got married.'

'Oh, we never knew nothing about that, did we, Mum?'

'Well, as a matter of fact Matt did write to yer dad an' me at the time but, you know, I was feeling well out of sorts with the pair of them so I kept quiet. Still, that's water under the bridge now, an' as Matt says this war can't last for ever an' then he swears he's gonna show us.'

Joan was wondering what her mother-in-law meant by 'show' them when Bertha cut in, 'As long as you're all right, love, and the baby arrives safe an' sound, what does it matter 'ow yer got wed?'

Joan felt a debt of gratitude to the mother of the two boys, who had worked their charm on her. Even the children had their hearts in the right place. They were all loyal to each other and to the family. At that moment she felt she might have ended up with far less loving folk than Matt's lot.

'Any luck?' Amy asked her two daughters, changing the subject.

'Not too bad, I suppose,' Laura answered, smiling at Joan for the first time. 'We won't be able to produce a feast but we can run to sausages and mash if that'll suit you?'

Joan felt it was up to her to answer and she said, 'That would be a treat, but only if you're sure there's enough to go round cos I can easily get a meal when I get home.'

Bertha and Laura were unpacking their baskets and placing the shopping on to the table, but at this they stopped, turned their heads and stared at their sister-in-law. 'Send you 'ome with nothing inside yer? Yer don't know our mum very well yet, do yer?' was what Bertha said.

'I'm glad it's sausages for me dinner, I like them best. You will an' all, Joan. They're luvverly.' This statement, from young Jack, had them all laughing.

'Mind you,' his grandmother remarked, 'Gawd above knows what goes inter sausages today. Gone are the times when you could say whether you wanted pork or beef. Still, if you stopped to think about 'alf of what we've ate since this war started you'd never sleep nights.'

'Oh, Mother, give over, and get that big frying-pan going before you put all of us off our meal.' Bertha reached into a paper bag and produced two sticky buns. 'Take these out to the passage, one each for the girls, and tell them dinner won't be long,' she said to Teddy. Jack's eyebrows were raised but before he had a chance to complain his mother was holding out two more buns. 'Now, would I leave you an' Teddy out?' She grinned. 'You'd make me life a misery for the rest of the day if I did, I know that for a fact.'

Then Bertha licked her fingers, pushed her permed hair back from her forehead and apologized that there weren't any buns for the adults.

'Never mind,' Laura sounded apologetic too, 'I'll make a fresh pot of tea an' we did manage to get a packet of short-cake biscuits. We can 'ave them with a cuppa while the potatoes are cooking.'

Joan was glad suddenly that she had made the effort and come up to Whitechapel. It wasn't possible to feel down in the dumps – not with children playing with their dolls out in the hallway, two cheeky lads munching away at sticky buns and three women who were willing to accept her as Matt's wife, even if they had never been invited to the wedding. All in all she had a very pleasant day.

Matt's two sisters came with her to the railway station where they kissed her and said they hoped to see her again soon. If only there hadn't been a war, she was thinking, as she settled into a corner seat of the carriage, maybe she and Matt would have settled down in one of those little terraced houses and their baby would have loads of cousins to play with. But, there again, if it hadn't been for the war and Matt being in the Army, the chances are they never would have met. It was no good thinking of what might have been, she scolded herself, trying to be sensible. There *was* a war and there was nothing she could do about it. But, oh, how she wished that she and Matt could be together. She missed him so much, and more so today, having been in his home and he not there. Nothing had gone right from the moment her granddad had died. If only she and Matt could have had a honeymoon. Just a short while away somewhere on their own. All the way home, she thought of what a difference that would have made, no matter how hard she tried to think of other things.

Chapter Six

SEVERAL THINGS WERE worrying Joan. First, the doctor at the clinic hadn't thought it advisable for her to have her baby at home. Second, the two hospitals in their locality, the Wilson just up the green from the Cricketer's at Mitcham, and the Nelson Hospital at Merton Park had no maternity facilities. The doctor had decided that she would reserve a place for Mrs Joan Pearson at Epsom Hospital in Surrey. A determined woman, she hadn't bothered to ask Joan how she felt about it.

'Epsom!' her father had exclaimed. 'That's ruddy miles away! An' how are we supposed to get you there? What if we should have an air-raid at the same time?'

He was a darling, was her dad. He had got his post-office savings book out straight away, scanned it carefully and declared that, his finances being rather good, his first grand-child was going to be born in a private nursing-home.

He had been as good as his word. Her dad had gone off on his own and God alone knew how many inquiries he had made or how many nursing-homes he had visited. Then came the day when he was home grinning like a Cheshire cat. 'I've found the very place. No, don't start having a go at me,' he said, ignoring Joan but facing his wife and his mother-in-law squarely. 'I've not committed myself or Joan to anything as yet, but I'll tell you this, here an' now, you can walk the streets of London till your feet are raw and you won't find a cleaner, more organized private place for our Joanie to have her baby than the Haven nursing-home.'

The three generations looked at each other and had a job to control their amusement. Fancy, a great big bloke like Bill Harvey traipsing in and out of different nursing-homes telling the proprietor that he wanted only the best for his daughter and his first grandchild.

'And what's more,' he went on, 'I've made an appointment for all four of us to go and see the place tomorrow afternoon.'

Three o'clock sharp, and they were there, standing on a grassy verge that overlooked the railway line in Wimbledon. The Haven, a large, detached, double-fronted building, stood behind them. Hester, Daphne and Joan had all made a great effort, and Bill was well aware that he had three well-turned-out attractive women with him as he opened the large iron gate and let them into the attractive grounds in which the nursing-home stood.

It was the first time Joan had been inside a hospital, and as she walked down the corridor, which smelt of disinfectant and floor polish, she felt frightened.

'Good afternoon, Mr Harvey. This is your daughter, I presume.'

Bill made all the introductions and by then Joan was feeling more relaxed.

One of the reasons that Grace Medwin had made such a success of her chosen career was that she had developed the ability to summarize a situation quickly and thereby put folk at ease. 'You'd like to see over the place,' she turned her attention to Joan, 'so we'll start with the day room, and by the time we've finished our tour I'm sure you will all be ready for some tea.'

Mrs Medwin looked and sounded like a very superior person, and the clothes she wore were both expensive and practical. The jacket of her navy blue suit covered a white cotton blouse with pin-tucks that ran straight from the points of her starched collar to the nursing belt that was buckled around her waist. Her light brown hair hung, shining and clean, to her shoulders, and her clear-skinned face was devoid of makeup. 'I am a qualified midwife,' she said to Joan, who was gazing in amazement at the comfortable lounge and the beautiful gardens that lay beyond. Then, turning to Bill, she said, 'I'd like to put your mind at rest on one score. You see that drab brick building over to your left, the one that has the steep slope leading down to its double doors?' Bill stepped nearer to the french windows, looked and nodded. 'That is our reinforced air-raid shelter, which is equipped to handle any emergency. Let's hope we shall have no need of it since the air-raids have, thankfully, become a thing of the past.'

Bill almost said, 'I wouldn't put my money on it,' but thought better, and Mrs Medwin went on, 'We always have at least two porters on duty, day and night. If need be, they can push trolleys down there so that our young mothers can rest easily and have their babies delivered in safety.'

Almost reluctantly Joan's mother and grandmother walked forward to take a look.

'Next I will show you the bedrooms. Every mother has a room to herself and a cot for the baby is positioned by the side of the bed, though we do have a nursery for the odd occasion when Baby may be a bit restless and Mother needs her sleep. We have three resident midwives and two doctors on call for emergencies. Do you have your own doctor,' she asked Joan, 'or have you just been attending a clinic?'

'I've been seeing the lady doctor at the clinic quite regularly,' Joan said. 'Is that all right?'

'Perfectly,' Mrs Medwin answered, as she threw open the door to a bedroom. It had pretty curtains at the windows and a high bed stood in the centre, covered with a snow-white bedspread and a mound of pillows. A large, well-padded armchair was set to look out over the gardens and a low chair with an upholstered high back was set beside a cot adorned with yellow-dotted white muslin frills. Two lovely teddy bears sat side by side on the window-sill. One bear had a pale blue silk bow-tie and the other's was pink.

'I don't think we need to show you the labour ward or the delivery room yet,' Mrs Medwin said softly to Joan. 'I think there will be time enough for that later.'

The tour ended in Mrs Medwin's sitting room, a charming room that, again, spoke of the good taste of the owner of this nursing-home. While the elders ate scones and jam and drank their tea, Joan was thinking that her father's decision to book her into this place had not only been a kind and generous act but a wise one too. She hadn't exactly been looking forward to giving birth. Once she had her baby in her arms everything would be wonderful but the actual birth terrified her. Knowing that she would be in safe hands here made all the difference. She suddenly felt optimistic, as if something marvellous was just about to happen.

She couldn't wait to get home and write a letter to Matt, telling him all about the arrangements her dad had made.

Mrs Medwin wasn't the only one to make the wrong assumption that raids from German planes were no longer a serious threat. When summer arrived so did the planes – in a more frightening form: flying bombs, planes with no pilots. Mostly there was no time to sound the warning sirens. The population of England, and London in particular, stood still in broad daylight, watching helplessly. There was no defence against these planes, which were clearly visible, with flames shooting out of the tail. While the engine could be heard you were safe, but the minute it cut out the silence struck terror into the bravest heart. Young and old alike prayed, Please, God, don't let it come down here. Then the engine would cut out and the plane would dive, dropping like a stone, exploding on a hospital, a school, on a shop, factory or playing-field. The massacre was horrifying.

During the first few days in June everyone was living on a knife's edge. The news on the wireless hinted at happenings yet gave no real information. The weather report was awful: strong winds, heavy rain and rough seas.

Then came the breakthrough: the weather had improved so the second front had been launched. Every household had the wireless constantly tuned in.

American, British and Canadian troops landed on the coast of Normandy on 6 June under General Eisenhower and General Montgomery. Allied planners had kept the Germans guessing as to where the actual landing would take place, which meant that they had had no choice but to position major defences along the whole of the northern coast of France. Casualties were still high, and Normandy suffered heavy damage in the battles that followed. Once the Allied beachheads had been established, the build-up of troops, tanks and artillery was rapid. The German defences were breached and Allied forces broke through into the Normandy countryside.

Day by day the mood of the British people grew lighter. Maybe, just maybe, the end of this terrible war was in sight. One evening, the reader of the nine o'clock news sounded triumphant: a great bonus of the D-Day landings was that Allied troops had discovered and overrun the launching sites of the flying bombs.

As the news improved the long bright days of summer boosted everyone's morale. Even letters from Matt arrived more regularly. During the time when he had not been able to write, Joan had worried herself sick. She knew she had been grumpy, difficult to live with, but as Daphne said to Bill, ''Tis only t' be expected. She's put on such a lot of weight, can't go dancing, and when me an' her gran took her t' the pictures the other night we had to get up an' come out before the end of the film. She just couldn't get comfortable. Fidget, fidget all the time, till the folk behind us complained.'

'I wish she'd give up her job,' her father said. 'Serving behind a bar is not what a pregnant girl should be doing.'

'Oh, give over, Bill. She's only doing three days a week an' no late turns. Bob an' Poppy won't let no harm come to her, and it does get her out of the house and lets her meet people.'

'Yeah, I know all that, but she still has to serve a lot of men and I don't think she should be doing that. Not in her condition.'

Daphne struggled to hold her temper in check. 'She not your little girl any more, she's a married woman, and if she wants to work it's not up to us to stop her. It takes her mind off things and keeps her going.'

'She's so young,' Bill protested.

That made Daphne laugh. 'Not so young that she hasn't found out how many beans make five. Anyway, she'll have to give up working soon, so why not let her make the most of it while she's able?'

'Suppose I don't have any choice in the matter, do I? But with Matt away and not much likelihood of him getting leave before the baby's born, I still feel responsible for her.'

'She'll be fine, you'll see, and you'll be a granddad before you know it.' Daphne grinned. 'Then you'll have two to worry about.'

One afternoon when she got home and found not one letter from Matt but two Joan's heart missed a beat. Her gran was out, doing her bit for the war effort (three afternoons a week she helped out at the Wilson hospital), and her mum was busy making pastry. Daphne shook the flour off her hands and moaned about the shortage of decent margarine and the fact that they hadn't seen a fresh egg for the last three weeks. 'This ruddy dried egg's no flipping good for baking, and as for the marge it's more like cart grease than stuff you're supposed to put on bread.'

'Never mind, Mum. You still manage to turn out real good pies, and the cakes you make don't hang about, do they?'

Daphne laughed. 'I said as much t' yer father on Sunday afternoon when he said that there wasn't much jam in the sponge. Know what he said? "You eat anything if you're hungry enough."'

'Oh, Mum, you know darn well he was teasing you.'

'Yeah, I know, but cooking doesn't give me the pleasure it used to. Anyway, why are you sitting there staring at your letters? Why don't you open them, see what Matt has to say?'

'I'll make us a cup of tea first,' Joan answered, thinking that she'd rather be on her own to read them.

Having gone through the motions, she set a cup down on the far end of the table to where her mother was working, saying, 'Drink it while it's hot, Mum. I'm going to take mine upstairs, maybe rest my legs for a bit.'

Daphne sighed heavily. Joan was such a good-hearted girl, but she tired so easily these days. She was getting so big too – maybe she was carrying twins. This should be such a happy time, but instead Matt was far away and Joan was doing her best to put on a brave face even when she didn't feel so great. Daphne found herself hoping that Matt would prove a good husband and father. Got to get this ruddy war over first and then perhaps he and thousands more of the young men who had been snatched away from their families would be given the chance to prove themselves. They might only have been boys when they were called up but it was a ten to one bet that those lucky enough to come home would be a lot older and certainly a lot wiser.

Upstairs Joan found it pleasant in her bedroom, even though the window-panes were covered with the inevitable sticky tape. She wondered what it would be like when the war ended and all the boarding and this horrible brown tape was stripped off. Homes, hospitals, workplaces and public transport would once again be allowed to let in the daylight. Wouldn't it be nice not to have to shut out the sunlight during the day and black out all the windows every evening? Joan turned down the counterpane, lay on the bed and tucked the eiderdown over her legs.

The first letter had been written three weeks ago and was very short, merely asking if she was keeping well, and saying that he hadn't time to write to his mum and dad and would she let them know that he was all right? He had ended by saying he loved her very much.

The second letter was, oh, so different: 'I do miss you, Joan, and how I wish I were going to be with you when our baby is born,' was how it began. A warm glow spread through her, she closed her eyes and hugged her pillow. Oh, Matt, you don't wish that half as much as I do. They seemed to have had such a short while together and she hadn't been very nice to him directly after the wedding. Losing Pops like that hadn't helped. If only Matt had been given more leave. And if only they hadn't been so headstrong they wouldn't have had to have such a rushed wedding. She read on. 'I love you so much, and just you wait and see, Joan, we'll have a home of our own as soon as we can and, like you reminded me, there will be three of us, and like I told you then, we'll do our best to see that our first baby is not our last. Just keep on loving me, please.'

Tears welled up in her eyes, she placed her two hands over the bulge in her stomach and sighed. This blinking rotten war, the separations it caused, the loneliness, the loss of young men's lives, to say nothing of all the civilians that were being killed in the air-raids. It seemed as if there was no end to it. Surely it couldn't go on for much longer.

'Oh, Matt,' she cried, burying her face in the pillow so that her mother wouldn't hear her sobs.

Later she went into the bathroom, rinsed her face and

hands under the cold tap and went downstairs to help her mother prepare their evening meal. Her dad came home, bringing her a rare bar of milk chocolate, and her nan, who joined them most days for her dinner, showed her yet another matinée coat she had made for the baby. But, through all their efforts at cheerful conversation, Joan's thoughts were miles away with her husband. Before she went to bed that night she had decided that she really should go up to Whitechapel again.

Chapter Seven

TIME HAD PASSED so quickly, yet the days now seemed to drag. Joan didn't know what to do with herself. She was bored. As soon as August had come, her father had insisted she give up her job and stay at home. In herself she felt remarkably well. Every day she went for a walk. Sometimes she took the bus up to Wimbledon Hill, sat for a while on the common then went into the pub to see Poppy and Bob. But she felt useless: there wasn't a thing she was allowed to do at home – both her mum and her nan were treating her as if she were the only woman in the world waiting to give birth.

Breakfast was over, and Joan was in the house on her own. She stood looking out of the window. It was now the last week in October and the weather looked good, but she knew it wouldn't be very warm even though the sun was shining.

She was considering her options. Yesterday she had received a parcel that contained gifts not only from Amy, her mother-in-law, but also from Laura and Bertha, her two sisters-in-law. They had sent some lovely things for the baby, and although she was grateful she felt guilty. She had written quite regularly to Amy, never omitting to let her know when she received a letter from Matt, but she had failed to keep her promise and pay them a visit.

'I'll go today,' she declared. 'In fact, I'll go right now.' She knew that if she waited until her mother or her nan came back from doing the shopping they would have a hundred and one reasons why she shouldn't travel. 'You're nearing yer time, only three or four weeks to go . . . You must be mad – the doctor at the Haven told you only last week that you should take things easy now.'

When she got outside it was colder than she'd thought so, very rashly, Joan flagged down a taxi that happened to be passing. 'Wimbledon station, please.' She smiled at the driver. Once there he climbed down from his cab, opened the door and helped Joan to alight. That thoughtful gesture was only the first she encountered on her journey. Folk smiled at her, made sure she had a seat both on the train and on the tram. The jungle of London's back streets were showing signs of being war-torn, but she was very glad she had made the effort she decided as she walked slowly down the road towards her mother-in-law's house.

The street door stood wide open and Joan called loudly, 'Anyone at home?'

''Allo, Joan, my love.' Amy sounded surprised but pleased as she heaved her great bulk up the passage. 'Christ,' she said, eyeing Joan from top to toe, 'you ain't 'alf a size, but you look marvellous.'

And she was right. Despite the cold weather, Joan

bloomed with health. Her skin glowed, her fine cheekbones had a lot more flesh on them, and her long auburn hair, tucked into a French pleat at the back and piled high on top, shone like amber gold.

'And rationing hasn't made you any thinner,' Joan teased, as she kissed Amy's cheek.

'Aw, Gor blimey, don't you start! I 'ave enough of that from my lot – an' any'ow, should you be 'ere? I take it you've travelled on yer own.'

'Don't you get on to me,' Joan pleaded. 'I made my mind up on the spur of the moment cos if I'd waited to tell my mum I know she would have kicked up ructions. Besides, I wanted to see you all to say thanks for the parcel. I'm not an invalid, you know.' The look that Joan gave Amy defied her to say otherwise.

In spite of her misgivings Amy had to smile: Joan's determination was something else. 'Anyway, let's get you inside, the kettle's on.'

Now it was Joan's turn to smile. When wasn't the kettle on in this house?

As she walked through the kitchen door the heat hit her. What a lovely sight! The fire was roaring away, the darting flames reflected in the big mirror that hung on the opposite wall. Then Joan stood still and stared. The gas jet was alight, but that was the only means of light. The window was boarded over with planks. 'Whatever happened?' she asked, nodding towards the window.

'Laundry at the back of us got a direct hit from one of them doodlebugs an' we caught a lot of the blast.' Seeing the look of horror on Joan's face, Amy said quickly, 'We're the lucky ones. No one in the street has any glass left but no one was killed. It was 'alf past eight in the morning, girls 'ad just started work. Wasn't anyone got out alive. Had a mass funeral. Terrible, it was.'

This was said so sadly that Joan couldn't think of a reply – nothing would sound right in the face of such a disaster.

When Matt's two sisters came in Amy and Joan were munching hot toast and drinking tea from giant mugs. 'We're going shopping down Chapel Street market if you feel up t' coming with us,' Laura announced. 'Word was down the corner shop that there's not only fish about but some decent rabbits as well.'

'It's half past twelve now so I don't suppose we'll be long,' Bertha said, smiling at Joan. 'Be nice to 'ave yer company, catch up on all your news.'

'Well, make sure you don't keep 'er out too long,' their mother instructed. 'She'll 'ave to catch an early train back or else 'er folks'll be worrying themselves sick.'

The three young women set off. They had barely got among the stalls when Joan was knocked flying. She had seen the three children on skates riding round and round in a circle but hadn't been quick enough to get out of their way as they made a spurt to dash off. All her insides went taut. I don't know which way to turn, was her last thought as she felt her feet leave the ground. She wanted to be sick. 'Oh, my back,' she murmured, as Bertha and Laura bent over her. The young boy who had bashed into her kept saying how sorry he was.

Joan was trying hard to sit up, gasping for air.

'I wouldn't try t' move 'er,' one burly stall-holder advised.

'No, I'll go in t' the butcher's an' get them to phone for an ambulance,' his mate called.

The ambulancemen were kindness itself, and Bertha went with her to the hospital while Laura did their shopping before making her way home to tell her mother what had happened. All kinds of thoughts were buzzing through Joan's head. Was her baby all right? She dreaded to think what her parents and her nan were going to say.

The ambulanceman looked at her and grabbed a bowl. Just in time. To Joan's embarrassment, she was violently sick.

'How badly is she hurt?' Fear was making Daphne raise her voice.

'Please,' the staff nurse begged, 'Mr and Mrs Harvey, sit down and try to calm yourselves. Your daughter has been well looked after and at the moment she is sleeping. I'll try to get a doctor or sister to come and have a word with you.' Sensing that the mother of Mrs Pearson might prove difficult she allowed no argument: with a swish of her starched uniform she turned quickly and left the office.

Bill Harvey was afraid, of course he was, and he fully agreed that Joan had done a daft thing in coming up to London when she was so near to having her baby. Having said that, he began to feel that if his wife didn't give over and stay quiet for a few minutes he would cheerfully strangle her.

The news that Joan was in hospital had knocked them both for six and it hadn't done Hester much good either. Bill was glad that he had managed to get her to stay at home: she had convinced herself that Joan was going to lose the baby and she was the last person he wanted around at this moment. He was having enough trouble with Daphne.

They'd got to the hospital in record time, thanks to his neighbour's offer to run them up in his van. A policeman had come to the house with the news that Joan had had an accident in Chapel Street market, and from the moment he had left Daphne had gone on and on: 'That daughter of ours hasn't got the sense she was born with. Fancy going off like that! Just a scribbled note to say where she'd gone and that she'd be back some time tonight. And what about those in-laws of hers? What sort of people are they? We wouldn't know cos we've never been given the opportunity to meet them. What were they thinking of, dragging our girl round markets in her condition?'

Bill was just about to threaten his wife that if she didn't shut up . . . when, thank God, the nurse was back, and with her a sister in a dark navy blue uniform, and a wide winged starched headdress. The sister smiled, but the smile only reached her lips, not her eyes in which there was no friendliness. 'As far as the doctor can tell at the moment, your daughter has suffered no ill effects from her fall.' Stern was the only way to describe her tone. 'She has a few bumps and bruises and a very nasty headache, for which she has been given something, and my nurse has already told you she is sleeping peacefully.'

Daphne was taken aback. It was like looking at and listening to a headmistress.

It was Bill who said softly, 'Two questions, please, Sister. Is the baby going to be all right and may we take our daughter home?'

Ignoring the first question the woman spat out, 'Certainly not. A pregnant woman is knocked down by boys on skates and you think she doesn't need careful monitoring?' Not waiting for Bill's reply she hurried on, 'Mrs Pearson will be kept in for at least forty-eight hours. You may take a peep at her before you leave and Nurse will give you a list of our

visiting hours, which we adhere to strictly. Only two visitors
allowed at any one time at the patient's bedside.' With that
she was gone, and for a full minute you could have cut the
silence with a knife.

The nurse moved first. With a kindly gesture she touched
Daphne's arm, looked across at Bill and nodded towards
the doorway, saying, 'If you'd like to come with me.'

It was coming up to five o'clock in the evening and two
men in brown overalls were walking the long ward placing
the wooden blackout boards against every window. Joan
had been settled in the first bed. 'Just so that we may
keep an eye on her from the office,' the nurse explained,
and then, as if she felt she needed to comfort them in
some way, she added, 'Come back tomorrow. She'll be
awake then, and you'll be able to see for yourselves that
she's all right. I'll leave you to have five minutes with her
now.'

As he stared down at his daughter Bill felt choked, but
he managed to murmur, 'Thank you.'

'She don't look all right to me,' Daphne said.

Because her voice was shaky Bill answered her gently.
'Please, love, leave it for now. Let her sleep. Tomorrow everything will seem better.'

'You don't know that,' she mumbled. 'If she has to be in
hospital why can't it be nearer home? Oh, I can't just go
away and leave her here.'

Bill felt exactly the same way. He leant over the bed.
Joan's face was deathly white but there wasn't a mark on
it, which he thought must be a good sign. Her hair looked
a bit untidy, and against the whiteness of the pillows it was
a deep chestnut. He wanted to tell her she looked a proper
copper knob. He wanted to tell her that he'd lift her up in

his arms and take her home. He wanted to tell her that he'd booked a place for her to have the baby in a lovely nursing-home near to where they lived, and that he didn't want to go away and leave her here in this long drab-looking ward of a big London hospital. But he couldn't tell her anything. All he could do was gently stroke a few strands of her hair back from her forehead and place his lips there in a soft kiss. Joan never stirred.

Her mother did the same. Only she, too, felt so helpless she couldn't control the tears that were trickling down her cheeks. She was praying to God that her daughter would be all right, as her husband put his arm around her shoulders and led her away.

When Bill and Daphne got back from the hospital it seemed as if half the street was gathered in her living room, keeping Hester company and all anxious for news of Joan.

Next day, at three o'clock sharp, Joan's parents and her grandmother were waiting in the corridor outside the ward that Joan was in. A very young nurse removed the screens that covered the glass doors from the inside and bolted the two doors back against the wall.

'Two visitors only to each bed, and the bell will ring at ten minutes to four to warn you that visiting time ends at four o'clock.' She was a pretty girl and her words were recited in a sing-song voice, evidently she was tired of repeating them day after day.

'Only one hour's visiting time?' Hester was appalled.

'You go on in with Daffy first,' Bill insisted. He wasn't going to incur his mother-in-law's wrath by telling her she had to wait out here in the corridor.

'Oh, my darling, you look so much better.' Daphne's face

was wreathed in smiles when she saw that her daughter was sitting up, propped by a mound of pillows, and looking hardly affected at all by her fall.

Hester was a different matter. She stepped forward to kiss Joan and burst into tears.

'Don't get so upset,' Joan implored, wriggling to get herself comfortable in the narrow bed. 'I'm fine, Nan, really I am. Doctor said another twenty-four hours to be on the safe side and then I can come home.'

'Oh, my love,' Hester sniffed, 'whatever got into you? Going off like that! The sooner we get you home where we can keep an eye on you the better. I'm not going to let you out of my sight till that baby's born.'

Joan sighed inwardly. What have I let myself in for? she wondered. There was something she had to ask her father. She hoped against hope that she'd be able to get him on his own because the request she was going to make wouldn't please her mother and it would upset her nan even more.

'Tea or a glass of milk?' a rosy-faced ward orderly asked Joan, as her two visitors sat one each side of the bed.

'Tea, please, no sugar.'

'One or two slices of bread, an' would you like jam or fish-paste?'

'One slice, please, and a little jam.'

'Is that all they give you for your tea?' Hester sounded indignant and Joan wasn't sorry when her mother suggested they walk down to the hospital shop and buy her a bottle of orange squash. 'We'll send your dad in to keep you company while we're gone.'

Thank God for that, Joan thought, then smiled broadly as she watched him step inside the ward and come to the side of her bed.

'And how's my old sleepyhead?' he asked, taking both her hands between his own. 'You didn't even open an eye when we were here yesterday.'

'Oh, Dad, I am sorry I've been so much trouble, and now while we're on our own I want to ask you a favour.'

'Pet, you're not to upset yourself, and whatever it is if I can do it you know full well I will.'

'Dad . . . there's an hour's visiting tonight, isn't there?'

'Yes. Why? Are you worried we won't come back?'

'No, Dad, that's not it at all. I can't tell Mum or Nan but Staff Nurse said that Matt's sisters rang up and when they were told you were visiting me this afternoon they said they'd come and bring their mum to see me tonight. They're ever so worried, Dad. I think they blame themselves for taking me to the market when they were only being kind.'

Her dad patted her hand. 'Don't fuss yourself. I understand, truly I do. I'll think of something to tell your mother. We won't come tonight but we'll be back tomorrow, hopefully to take you home with us.'

'Oh, Dad, you're great, you really are.' Joan sighed with relief. It was difficult playing peacemaker with both sets of parents.

'Well, I've got a great daughter, and I can't wait to see whether you're going to present me with a granddaughter or a grandson. I'm so pleased you'll be having the baby at the Haven. Their visiting rules are a lot less strict, so Mrs Medwin tells me.'

Joan breathed another sigh, laid her head back against the pillow and closed her eyes. She was surprised at how tired she felt.

'I brought you two magazines and a tin of fruit drops,'

her father whispered, as the warning bell sounded. 'I'd better go now and let your mum an' your nan come in to say goodbye.' Then he put his arm across the top of the pillow and told her, 'I'll be here to fetch you tomorrow. We all love you – you know that, don't you? Get some rest now.'

Joan sat up to put her arms around her father's neck. It was a touching moment, when neither of them could say a word.

It was much the same when her mum and her nan gave her a cuddle, and as Joan watched them wave goodbye she was telling herself she was a lucky young woman to have such a caring family.

It was close on midnight, and Joan hadn't been able to get to sleep. She had refused the nurse's offer to ring a doctor and ask permission for her to have a sleeping pill. It was difficult to turn over: the great swelling of her stomach kept the bedclothes high, and although she had heard several of the other patients complain of how cold the ward was she was sweating profusely and the pain in her back was driving her mad.

'Here, I've brought you a cup of milky Horlicks. It might help you sleep.' It was the same two nurses on duty as on the previous night, and this one in particular seemed very friendly.

'Thanks ever so much, but I think I need to go to the toilet before I drink it.' Joan had already pushed back the bedclothes when the nurse said, 'Stay where you are, I'll get a bedpan.'

'No, please, I think I need to do more than just wee and I can't go on a bedpan, really I can't. Please, let me get to the toilet.'

'Well,' the nurse sounded reluctant, 'I'll fetch a wheel-chair. Wait just a minute.'

Joan felt so thankful as she waited. Bedpans were horrible. Turning back the top sheet still further she swung her legs over the side of the bed as the nurse reappeared with the chair. Her feet touched the cold floor and she stood up only to gasp in amazement. A terrific pain had settled in her lower back and she was wetting herself. She had no control – the wee was running everywhere around her feet. 'Oh, I'm so sorry,' she murmured, as it ran down her legs and splashed on to the wooden floor. Never could she remember having felt so embarrassed.

The kindly nurse grinned. 'Not to worry but I'd better get you back into bed and alert the maternity unit. Your waters have just broken.'

'What?' No one had warned her of anything like this. 'Does that mean that the baby's coming?'

Now they were joined by the second night nurse. 'Not as easily as all that, I wouldn't think, but by this time tomorrow I'd say your baby will be a few hours old.' They were laying dry towels on the bed and lifting Joan's legs back up.

'I can't have my baby, not here,' she moaned. 'I'm booked into a nursing-home – my dad's paying for it all. Oh, please, can't I go home?'

The nurses looked at each other and laughed. 'You've left it a bit late for that,' they said. 'You have no say in the matter now. He or she has decided it's time to come into this world and you can't stop it. So, be a good girl, we'll have the porters here with a trolley and you'll be whisked off to the mother-and-baby unit.'

Joan didn't get a chance to answer because she was doubled up in pain.

It wasn't until an hour later that the full extent of what the doctor was telling her sank in: 'I'd say another couple of hours then the labour pains will increase and you'll be ready to give birth. Would you like a hot drink now?'

The pain would increase? She'd never be able to stand it. Whatever had she done to deserve this?

She was in a small, very shiny clinical room, which they told her was the labour ward. A doctor and a midwife had placed cold instruments on her swollen tummy and listened to the baby's heartbeat, or so they'd told her. The bed she lay on was very high, and more than once she'd been afraid that, as the pains came and went, she would fall off. This was a nightmare, nothing short of a living nightmare. What was she doing here? Did her mum and dad know what was happening? What about Matt? Several children, he'd said he wanted. Well, *he* could have them! If he thought for one moment that she was ever going to put herself through all this again he couldn't be more wrong.

Oh, oh, oh. She bit her bottom lip until it bled. Where is everybody? How can they come and look and say, 'You're doing fine, Mrs Pearson,' then go away and leave me all on my own? After all the trouble to which her father had gone in finding the Haven nursing-home! Now here she was, miles from home, in a place where no one seemed to have any time for her. Her dad would be upset about this. Oh, it wasn't fair. Somebody, anybody, help me. Please help me. Her hair was lank and wet and she was sweating like a pig. She smelt horrible. I know I do, she told herself, wiping her face on the corner of the sheet.

'I'm the senior midwife in this hospital, Mrs Pearson. This is your first baby, isn't it?'

A stoutish nurse was leaning over the bed, and Joan

thought she'd never been more glad to see anyone in her whole life. 'Yes,' she said, through gritted teeth, as yet another pain tore through her. Reaching out she grabbed the midwife's hand and, like a small child, she pleaded, 'Please, don't leave me on my own. I'm frightened, I'm not supposed to be here . . .' She doubled up her knees, dug her fingers into the arm of this nurse and just yelled. It was unbearable – her voice was now one long terrifying scream.

'All right, Mrs Pearson, all right. Just be a good girl and try to relax. Baby is just telling us it's time to begin work.' The midwife moved to the end of the bed, and as she did so the door opened and a doctor and another nurse came into the room.

There was a hurried discussion. Joan caught the words 'First baby, very large, mother has small pelvis.' Now there were other sounds. A trolley was dragged across the floor. A machine was placed near the bed. The doctor put on a face mask. 'Bend your knees up, Mrs Pearson,' he ordered, pulling a long metal arm that held a strong electric light down from the ceiling. He switched it on and manoeuvred it into position so that the beam would be directed between Joan's legs.

From that moment on Joan lost all sense of time. She ached from head to toe. She was sopping wet, yet her mouth was as dry as a bone – oh, she'd give the world for a drink. The pains were coming more frequently now, and each one left her feeling shattered.

'Push,' she was ordered, time and again. 'Almost there, great big push this time.'

'We've got the head, come on, push.'

'Well done, Mrs Pearson. You have a lovely baby boy.'

Again she caught snatches of their whispering: 'Still bleeding heavily, badly torn. I'll have to put in a few stitches.'

Joan heaved a huge sigh, but didn't get the chance to tell them she wanted to hold her baby, because at that moment there was an awful roaring sound, followed by an almighty thump. The bed on which she was lying felt as if it rose up then fell down heavily. The whole room seemed to rock as instruments rattled to the floor. The blackout board clattered down from the window – it sounded as if it were raining broken glass. Then all the lights went out.

The doctor swore loudly and even the midwife let out a scream. All Joan could think was that if it was a bomb it must have landed very close to this hospital, and she prayed as she never had before that she and her baby would soon be safely at home. She wanted her parents, she wanted her nan, and most of all she wanted and needed Matt. At the same time she was asking, Why, oh why did I come to the East End? It was so dark and there didn't seemed to be enough air: she was fighting for breath. She felt, rather than saw, the doctor lean over her, his voice reassuring as he said, 'Everything is under control, Mrs Pearson. The nurses are fetching torches, everything is fine. I'm going to give you an injection. You'll be able to have a little sleep while I clean you up.'

'But I haven't even seen my baby yet,' she protested.

She felt a scratch on the back of her hand and then she was falling. It was dark, oh, so very dark, and the ground was a long, long way down. Then she was oblivious to everything.

London was experiencing another type of bombing, this time from huge rockets, and such were the explosions that they caused deadly damage and the blast was felt for miles around. Patients were being brought into the hospital. Bodies were being transported to the morgues, and rumours were adding fuel to the fires.

It was 2 November 1944. In the early hours of the morning, amid all the turmoil of London's first rocket raid Joan Pearson had given birth to her first baby, a boy. The nursing staff were clearing up, the baby had already been washed and taken to the nursery. Joan had received four stitches to her insides, and was now lying unconscious on a trolley, waiting for a porter to take her back to the ward.

The midwife was filling in her notes when she looked up as the other nurse remarked, 'No wonder she was so frightened. She's only eighteen, nineteen on Christmas Day, according to her notes.'

'That's if she lives that long,' came the blunt reply.

Startled, the homely midwife looked up. 'She's not that bad, a bit torn about but that's because the baby was so big, nigh on nine pounds.'

'I didn't mean it like that,' the nurse added quickly. 'Who knows how many of us will be here to see Christmas? By the look of the bodies they're taking downstairs I'd say Hitler really has thought up something terrifying for us this time. From what the air-raid wardens are saying, we're not going to get any warning from these rocket-type bombs.'

'Oh, come on, lass. Don't start thinking along those lines. Best thing to do is live your life from day to day.'

'That's all very well, but if there's no telling when or where these new bombs are coming over then it stands to reason we aren't going to have any defence against them, doesn't it?'

The older midwife stared at the young nurse. What an attitude to adopt. Oh dear. She sighed sadly to herself. This war had an awful lot to answer for. It was certainly putting old heads on young shoulders.

Chapter Eight

———

JOAN LAID HER baby son down in her father's armchair, looked round the room at all the smiling faces there to welcome her, and decided she was never going to leave home again. At least, not for a very long time. Tears of happiness welled in her eyes. This was the first time she had felt safe since the blast from the rocket that had exploded so near to where she lay in hospital.

They say that in the wake of evil good can follow. Well, it certainly had in this case.

She had her darling baby son. He was gorgeous. Round chubby face, a dimple in his chin where the angels had kissed him. Fat little hands, long fingers each with a perfectly formed pink nail. Not very much hair but what there was showed signs of being dark like his father's. Skin like silk. Each time Joan guided his little mouth to her nipple and held him close to her breast her wonderment knew no bounds. He was perfect. Warm, soft, sweet-smelling, oh, she was so lucky. Hard to believe that she and Matt had made this tiny human being.

Everyone argued about what name he was to be given. Hester had said, 'Call him Edward after your grandfather,' but that didn't seem fair to Matt or his family.

William, Daphne wanted, 'After your dad,' she pleaded. Peggy Watson had suggested Geoffrey or Stuart – Sees too many films, does my friend Peggy, Joan had decided. In the end she had learnt from her mother-in-law that Matt's father's second name was James, and as her own father was named William James, she made the decision herself. Pushing the lovely high perambulator that had been Hester's gift she had set off for the council offices. Taking the baby in with her – she couldn't bear to leave him outside in his pram – she waited her turn. James Mathew Pearson, she registered him.

So the days passed. She wrote proudly to Matt, every letter giving him the tiniest scrap of information as to how his son was doing. She still missed him terribly, was wishing they could go to the pictures together or up on the common, arguing over who was going to push the pram. He was missing so much. Jamie, as everyone seemed to call him, now gurgled, looked at his own fingers and wiggled his toes when at bath-time she tickled the soles of his tiny feet. Matt wrote when he could. The end of the war which had seemed so close in June, had not come about. People were disheartened again.

The rockets were different from anything anyone had remotely imagined. Reports were that they could be launched from anywhere and that they travelled at 3,600 miles per hour – several times the speed of sound. Once launched they could not be intercepted and arrived without warning. There was even talk of children being evacuated from London again.

Christmas was upon them. Shortages made decent presents almost impossible, but parcels were sent and exchanged between Matt's family and Joan's, although as yet Amy had not seen her new grandson.

Joan had to admit that theirs had been a happy Christmas Day. Just watching her father lying flat on his stomach holding up toys and shaking rattles to make Jamie smile, not to mention the silly faces he pulled, was enough to make her, her mother and Nan, sigh with contentment. Though the awful thought was always in everyone's mind: how many more Christmases would be spent with families separated, young men, sons and fathers in different parts of the world?

On Christmas night, before Joan lay down to sleep, she had added a postscript to the letter she'd written earlier that day: 'Roll on peacetime and we can be a proper family with a home of our own, please, God.'

Days later, when Mathew Pearson received that letter, he had to turn away from his mates – He was a soldier, fighting for his country. At that moment all he wanted was to be with his Joan, and to look down on his baby son. Even perhaps to hold him. The writing on the letter was blurred now because his eyes were brimming with tears.

One week later it was New Year's day: 1 January 1945. Still the war dragged on. Matt had written that there was a slight possibility he'd get seven days' leave, and ever since Joan had lived on that hope.

For reasons best known to the British Army, no leave was granted at that time. The days were dark and bitterly cold; even the weather seemed as if it were against everyone. There was a terrible shortage of coal, and one Monday morning, when Bill Harvey was on a later shift, he declared that he was borrowing a barrow from the corner shop to go up to the coal yards at Tooting Junction with two mates in the hope that they would be allowed to buy a few sackfuls.

Three hours passed, then Joan, Daphne and Hester heard a commotion out in the street. Running to the front door, Joan turned and called, 'Come on out here, Mum! This you've got to see!'

Mother and daughter plus several female neighbours fell about laughing. 'Talk about the Black and White Minstrels,' one cheeky young housewife yelled from across the road.

Joan's dad was walking down the front path of old Granny Seymour's house, folding up a dusty coal-sack as he came. He looked every inch a cross between a chimney-sweep and a coal-miner just up from the pits, and his two mates were just as bad. Between them they had a wheel-barrow, an old pram that had a wobbly wheel, and what looked liked a bicycle with a home-made side-car attached to it. All three vehicles were loaded with half-filled sacks of coal. Well, there was as much dust as actual coal. Three more houses received a quick delivery, two where just a single elderly person lived, and the third was the home of a young mother with three children whose husband was away in the Army. When all this was finished, and the men prepared to take the remaining sacks into their own homes, a roar of thanks and applause went up from those who had been watching.

Inside the Harvey household poor Bill was dispatched to the scullery and told to strip all his clothes off. Daphne was adamant that she wasn't having him traipsing through her house shedding coal-dust.

'It's all right, Dad,' Joan laughed, 'I'll run you a bath, but

I'll have to bring you up a couple of kettles of hot water cos the fire's been nearly out and the back boiler hasn't been able to heat the water.'

Bill didn't find that funny: he ached in every limb, had coal-dust in every pore, and all the thanks he was getting for having trudged all the way to Tooting Junction and back was a cold bath!

The weeks did pass. Spring was a certainty, and suddenly the day started with the sound of raised, joyful voices. It was 8 May and on all sides could be heard, 'THE WAR IS OVER. Really it is. No, I'm not making it up.' It was difficult for people to comprehend that the day they had waited for so long had finally arrived.

'Germany has surrendered unconditionally.' The words echoed again and again, and folk everywhere sent up silent prayers of thanks.

Bonfires were lit and allowed to burn all night. Who cared now if the flames could be seen from the sky? For the first time in six years, folk felt they were entitled to laugh, sing, shout and cry with relief. Many thanked God that their menfolk had come safely through this awful war and would soon be coming home.

For others it was a sad time, a time to mourn again the loved ones they had lost, men *and* women who would never again walk into their homes. No amount of celebration could ease the pain of those folk.

Now came the demolition. Unsafe buildings had to be razed to the ground. Some whole streets had to be totally pulled down. All this left ugly bare sites throughout the length and breadth of the country, and a great shortage of houses for married men returning home from the forces. The joyful part was the removal of boarding from all the window-frames and hundred of sandbags being taken away from the outside of buildings.

Ten months passed before Matt finally got leave, but at last he was coming home to his son, who was already sixteen months old.

On this bitterly cold day in March, dressed in her winter coat, with a navy blue velvet collar, her hair freshly washed and set, Joan paced the platform of Wimbledon station in a fever. She was longing to see her husband again, yet terrified as to how they would react to each other after so long a separation. Should she have brought Jamie with her? Would Mathew be cross because she hadn't? How would Jamie react to a father who was a stranger to him?

Whistles and bursts of steam heralded the train's arrival.

She saw him! His head and shoulders were hanging out of the carriage window.

The train came into the station and shuddered to a halt. Throwing caution to the wind she ran. The moment they neared each other he dropped his kit-bag and she was safe, held close in his strong, muscular arms.

'Oh, Joanie,' he murmured, 'I've longed for this moment for so long.'

Regardless of the crowds heading for the barriers, the WVS women who were manning the tea-wagons, the train guard and the porters, they stood clinging to each other. This was their moment and they savoured it to the full.

When at last Matt released her, Joan cried, 'I still can't believe it.' Putting out a hand she touched the lean lines of his face. 'It really is you, Matt.' Suddenly she felt shy. This man, she knew, was a very different person from the easy-going lad Mathew Pearson had been the last time she saw him.

Then again she was different too: a young girl who hadn't really known her own mind when he'd left her, now a mother. 'Let's go home, Matt,' she said, with a sob in her voice.

It was another four months before Matt was finally released from the Army, and during all that time Joan stayed on at her parents' home. When Matt was on leave, it was far from the ideal situation, and worse when it looked like becoming permanent. Sleeping with Jamie in a cot beside their own bed in a room next door to her parents', Joan was embarrassed by Matt's passionate lovemaking. 'These walls are paper thin,' she would complain, which Matt would have ignored but not Joan.

That was only one of the problems that stared them in the face. Civvy Street wasn't all that men returning home had imagined it would be. Matt, like hundreds more, needed a job. His preference was to be in the East End of London, to be near to and work with his brothers, his father and his mates. And for him that was no problem: his old manager eagerly offered him his job back in the timber yards. There was also an offer, secured by his father, from the Port of London, and yet another came through his eldest brother Stan, who was employed on Butler's private riverside wharf.

There were no such offers of employment floating around Merton Park and Wimbledon where they were living, not by Matt's choice.

The final offer came from Matt's mother. She had had a word with the landlord and he had a two-bedroomed house coming vacant in Bull Yard at the end of the week. After she'd made this important announcement, there had been a dramatic pause and then, with all eyes on her, Amy had burst out, 'I've paid him a month's rent in advance, got him t' give me a rent book with Matt's name on it. Did it before 'e 'ad a chance to change his mind. Wasn't gonna let the bugger slip off the 'ook if he got a better offer. That much yer can forget about. Never did get round to giving the pair of yer a wedding present so me an' yer dad went 'alf each an' that'll give yer a bit of time to get on yer feet before you 'ave to start paying rent.'

Sitting in her mother-in-law's living room, which was crowded with various members of the family and Jamie on the lino being petted and fussed over by half a dozen kids, Joan did not know what to think, let alone say. To *her* the offer was a death knell. 'Why, that's marvellous, Mum. Bull Yard, that's not ten minutes from 'ere. You've saved our bacon,' Matt cried. Then, to Joan's dismay, he added, 'Joan's pregnant again an' we couldn't 'ave stayed in her folks' house much longer. Bad enough with one baby, never mind two.'

Joan felt herself flush a deep red. If looks could have killed, at that moment Mathew would have been stone dead. Bad enough that he was thrilled his mother had rented them a house, never mind that it was in an area she had no wish to live in, that it was miles away from her friends and family – and, what's more, that it was a place she had never set eyes on. She'd never been inside the front door and here was Matt accepting the offer and being grateful. And to top it he had blurted out that she was pregnant again. She hadn't even told her parents yet, or her nan.

She thought they had had problems before, but now they were really beginning.

Ten days later, a stern-faced Bill Harvey stood out in the street beside a tearful Daphne and Hester, and watched as

Jamie was handed up to Joan. Matt had hired an open-backed truck, which was now loaded with odd items of secondhand furniture, rolls of linoleum, several rugs, boxes of china, cooking utensils and a hamper packed with bed-linen. 'At least they've got the basic necessities,' Hester said to her daughter.

Daphne was lost for words. She had spent the last three days helping Joan to clean and decorate the small terraced house in Bull Yard, which was now to become her daughter's home. The whole area was appalling. At least, in her opinion it was.

Nearby, whole families lived on barges on the Thames, more children than you could count, scraggy-looking dogs and cats, and the adults, as well as the kiddies, looked none too clean. Was that the type of child Jamie was going to grow up with? Go to school with? If, indeed, those families ever sent their children to school. And that wasn't the worst of it: Bull Yard was narrow and dark, with houses only on one side of the road while on the opposite side stood a huge warehouse. From the windows of the house her daughter would be living in, you looked out on nothing but a great wall of sooty bricks. The most terrifying sight, although she had to admit it was magnificent, was a giant passenger liner at the bottom of the yard. At least, the ship's middle section was visible above the brick wall that formed the end of Bull Yard. It straddled the whole width of the Yard. The great ship was in dry dock, towering over the small houses and the children playing in the street. At least three of her decks and two mighty funnels were visible from Joan's doorstep.

Matt didn't give two hoots that his in-laws disapproved of his taking Joan and the baby to live in the East End of London. 'We have our own front door, our own bedroom and, most important, plenty of privacy,' he told her repeatedly, always giving her a cheeky grin.

Joan did her best to settle down in her new surroundings – at least, she thought she did. Matt didn't agree. Only this morning, before Stan had picked him up to go to work, Matt had yelled that she didn't put herself about enough and didn't mix with his family as much as she should.

Left on her own at only seven o'clock in the morning, another long, lonely day stretched out in front of her. Closing the front door behind him, Joan ran her fingers through her hair, then went back to the kitchen to clear away the breakfast things. She felt miserable and frustrated. She knew the rows were partly her own fault, but her idea of a good weekend was not going from pub to pub, watching the men play darts or snooker and listening to the women gossip. In her whole life she had not felt quite as she did now, so agitated with her temper on such a tight rein. Normally she was calm, in control.

But her world had never been turned upside down before.

Only weeks to go and she would have another baby to care for, and that meant more washing. There was nowhere to hang a washing line, except out in the street, and Joan couldn't bring herself to do that.

With a heavy sigh, she poured boiling water from the kettle into a bowl and began to wash up. Thank God Jamie was blessed with a sunny disposition and a cheerful personality. For one so young he was great company. Funny thing was, Matt didn't take much notice of him. All he ever said was it would be great when he could take him to the speedway and to football matches. 'And to pubs,' was what Joan always felt tempted to add. Maybe she should feel grateful that she was about to have another baby: he or she would be company for Jamie. But money was so short, or at least it was for household goods, baby clothes and things like that.

Matt gave her five pounds a week, and that wasn't too bad as far as food went – she had to make sure there was plenty on the table or there would have been ructions. But there was never any money left over, at least not where she was concerned, at any rate. Friday night, Saturday and Sunday Matt spent freely, and to give him his due she could have had anything she asked for when they went out, just so long as it came in a glass and was handed over the bar of one of the numerous public houses that the Pearson family and their mates seemed to spend half their lives in.

By the time she was heavy with this second baby Joan was listless. She had tried to change a good many things in her day-to-day life but it was useless. She would just have to put up with it, was the conclusion she had reached. She no longer hoped that Matt would change, for she'd realized that that was like asking for the top brick off the chimney.

Her first daughter was born in the same hospital as Jamie, just six days after Jamie's second birthday. Less than five months later when she realized that she was pregnant once more Joan gave up worrying. She got by, taking each day as it came, coping with whatever life threw at her. But only just.

Her second daughter was born at home, in the upstairs front bedroom with only an elderly midwife in attendance. After that birth, to the horror of her parents and her grandmother, she let herself go. She hadn't argued when her in-laws suggested that the first girl be given the posh name of Margaret, although she had thought that inevitably she would be called Maggie. And Joan had been right. She hadn't protested either when the midwife had declared her second girl as sweet as a rose, and Matt had decided that that should be her name.

She kept the children clean and tidy, no complaints there, and she cooked good, hearty meals and kept the house as clean as possible against all the odds of London dirt and grime. As to herself, it was as if she had given up all hope of ever having a better life.

The funny thing was, Matt adored his two daughters. They were lovely little girls, as alike as two peas in a pod, so pretty with light auburn hair and the same colouring and beautiful skin as Joan, her mother and grandmother still boasted. They had cherubic faces, covered in freckles, and were always laughing and into mischief. They were certainly their daddy's girls, and Matt spoilt them rotten.

Jamie was different: very protective of his sisters but quieter in every respect. He was doing well at school. His teachers were pleased with his work, and Joan was thrilled with his reports.

Matt wasn't: he believed he should be out and about, roughing it with other boys, even getting into trouble around the dockyards. That was what boys did, not sit hour after hour with their nose stuck in a book. Matt never looked at a book, and the fact that Jamie liked to read was becoming an obsession with his father.

Joan often thought that at times Matt made life so difficult.

Of course, looking back she had known there were two sides to his character when she married him. To say he was outspoken would be putting it mildly. And he had to have everything his way, no matter what. If his brothers were going to the pub, then Matt went with them. Nothing was allowed to stand in his way, especially if there was a darts match to be played.

On a day when she wasn't feeling too washed out, Joan would tell herself that, when all was said and done, Matt was a good husband and she could have done worse. Oh, yes, as her mother-in-law was fond of telling her when she complained, much worse.

So the time went on and as a family they muddled through, until Jamie came to sit his eleven-plus examination. The boy tried so hard. He could please most people but hardly ever his father. He did go to football matches with his dad and every single week to the speedway. He was enthusiastic about motorbikes but not nearly as keen as Matt.

Joan listened to their conversations and her heart ached for her son. Matt taunted him, she didn't know why. His mind was set on Jamie leaving school at the earliest possible age and going to work with one of his uncles or with himself. Schooling got you nowhere, was Matt's view and he wouldn't change it for anyone. Good, hard work was what paid dividends, according to him, and despite all Joan's pleading, he would never give Jamie any encouragement when it came to academic subjects.

Ah, well, she sighed, trying hard to put it out of her mind, if things don't alter, they'll stay as they are.

Chapter Nine

THERE WERE TIMES when Joan felt the whole world was changing around her yet, try as she would, her life never did, from one year's end to the next. Well, not for the better, it didn't. There had been that letter from the council, which had arrived more than a month ago stating that the houses in Bull Yard were due for demolition and that they would be advised as to where the tenants were to be relocated.

Not rehoused! Oh, no. Relocated, as if they were pieces of machinery.

Matt said houses in Bull Yard were nothing whatsoever to do with the council, to burn the letter and not to worry about it. She couldn't help but worry, and more so since her next-door neighbours on both sides had told her about their visit to the town hall.

'Definitely going to be in one of the new blocks of flats up near the Angel, Islington,' was what Doris Shepherd insisted she'd been told, while on the other hand May Brown said her information had been along the same lines but in a different area. Either way, Joan dreaded to think how she was going to cope in any of these new high-rise blocks of flats. How could she keep an eye on her children if they were playing out on the street and she was indoors up several flights of stairs? Her sisters-in-law had thrown in their opinion. According to them, she and Matt should count themselves lucky that they'd probably be getting a three-bedroom flat with a proper bathroom and a modern kitchen.

An indoor lavatory would be a dream come true. So would a nice bathroom – now she had to drag the tin bath in from the yard. Apart from those two factors, though, Joan was convinced that if they were rehoused in any one of those horrible cement columns with windows, it would be a change, all right, but a change for the worse. Still it had been quite a while since the letter had arrived, so it was still a case of wait and see.

As usual, at this time in the morning, she was alone. Jamie had left home at a quarter past eight – he liked to get to school early – and the two girls had left home at twenty to nine because the junior school they went to was only a five-minute walk from the house. She was bored. How long would it take her to make the beds and put a duster round the rooms? And then what?

How often she wished she had a reason every day to leave this dismal house – to go out to work. Any job would do, just so long as it brought her into contact with people. People who would talk about something other than what was on sale up the market or which pub they were all going to on Saturday evening. Besides the company, a little cash she could call her own wouldn't go amiss.

What had Matt to say when she broached this subject?

'You can forget it! No wife of mine is going out to work.

A woman should be at home, looking after the kids and keeping the place nice.' He should have added, 'And have my dinner on the table at whatever time I tell you I want it, and a clean shirt and jacket laid out on the bed on the nights I play snooker or darts.'

Matt had been like a dog with a bone. He just wouldn't let the matter drop. 'I can just hear my mates talking among themselves, sniggering behind my back cos my wife 'as t' work to help support my kids.'

'You and I both know that's not the reason I'd like to go out to work,' she had pleaded.

'Maybe not, Joan, but I'm telling yer, that's what they'll think. Just you remember that I'm the man in this house and I pay for the food that goes on our table, and I make the decisions, not you.'

She had tried so hard to stand her ground with Matt, asking, 'Why does it matter what people think?'

'Leave it. I don't want to 'ear another word.' And with that he had brought his fist down on the table so hard that all the dishes had rattled.

She had been too frightened to pursue the matter any further, but that didn't stop her from thinking that because Matt had married her he had no right to control her, as he seemed to believe. In the end she had given in: arguing with him was like bashing her head against a brick wall.

So much was happening outside her little world. Every time she picked up a paper or saw the news at the cinema she wished she could be a part of it all. Take television: Matt had gone spare when she suggested they might rent one, yet if folk were to be believed you could sit in your own home and watch a film, see big dance bands and hear plays. There was talk of major sports such as football being televised. If that came about then Matt would be first in the queue. Another thing: telephones in private houses weren't rare now – her own mum and dad had one. She'd have to live a long time before one would be installed in this house. Asking for a new pair of curtains was like asking for the crown jewels, never mind a telephone.

Slowly she climbed the narrow flight of stairs. These walls hadn't seen a coat of paint in all the ten years they'd lived here. Matt's view on that was that there was a major crack running right through the middle wall of the house and that things were best left untouched. Ah, well, nobody had everything they wanted in this life.

Maggie and Rosie had both been cross with her last week because she wouldn't buy them each an Elvis Presley record. She'd never heard of him until Laura, her sister-in-law, explained that he was a truck-driver in America who had shot to fame and become the king of rock 'n' roll. Needless to say, Matt had given in to the girls. He'd bought records for both girls, and now Joan knew the words of both songs off by heart, because the girls played them endlessly.

She began by pulling the bedclothes off the twin beds in the room the girls shared. She wished they had a garden, instead of just a yard that was only slightly bigger than the shed that housed the lavatory. Oh, well, it would get her out of the house if she took the sheets up to the wash-house. At least other women would be there to talk to.

Stripping the cases off the pillows her eye caught sight of a poster on the wall of Princess Margaret. The girls always reckoned they had been named Margaret and Rose because they were the two names given to the Princess. It wasn't true. At the time the thought had never entered her head. Nevertheless she did not disillusion her daughters, rather she encouraged them to follow the life of Princess Margaret and, indeed, the whole of the Royal Family. Gazing again at the picture, which had been cut from a magazine, she felt sad for Princess Margaret. She and that Group Captain Peter Townsend had appeared to be so much in love with one another. Now it was all off. The announcement had come on the wireless: the Princess had decided not to marry him because he was divorced. Such a shame. Joan felt she had been pressured into making that decision and not for the first time wondered why individuals weren't allowed to make up their own minds.

With the upstairs two bedrooms sorted, she came down, her arms full of dirty sheets, which she dumped in the passage. Now to see to Jamie's bed. She couldn't say bedroom cos the poor boy didn't have one. Until Rosie was born, when Maggie had slept in the big bedroom with Matt and herself, Jamie had had the other. With the coming of Rosie, Matt had decided that two beds in the small room was best for the girls, and Jamie got a Put-U-Up in the front room.

As Joan pushed open the door she smiled to herself: she was proud of this room. It was one battle with Matt she had won. The focal point of the room was the fireplace and she made sure that every Sunday a fire was lit in the hearth and they had their Sunday tea in there and spent the evening in comfort. Six days a week was quite enough to live in the kitchen. Matt had argued that most folk lit a fire in the front room only on high days and holidays. The tiled surround was surmounted by a heavy wooden mantelpiece. On this stood a small clock, two brass candlesticks and a framed photograph of each of the three children. The hearth was protected by a heavy brass fender, her pride and joy. She cleaned it regularly every Friday and it glittered like gold in the dancing flames of the fire. Two brown corded-velvet armchairs stood at each side of the fireplace, and the brown and fawn tweedy-looking settee was placed beneath the window. This was what served, when folded down, as a bed for Jamie.

He was a good lad: he never failed to leave the room fairly tidy.

The minute his father left the house of a morning, at about seven o'clock, Jamie was up, washing and dressing in the scullery. His clothes were kept in half of the wardrobe that held hers and she had managed to find him a tiny chest of drawers, which just about fitted against the wall of the small landing. It wasn't the best of situations but, as always, Matt disputed that his son was hard-done-by. As a young lad himself, he'd had to share a bed with two of his brothers and he considered Jamie lucky to have a bed to himself.

Looking up the passage to the front door Joan saw that some post was lying on the mat. Postman must have been late today, she thought, bending to pick it up. One letter was for Mr M. Pearson, probably setting a date for yet another darts match, and there was a postcard from her mother, which she read at a glance. 'Coming up to visit you tomorrow. Bringing your nan with me. Expect us about 11 o'clock. Love, Mum.'

That set her brain ticking over. Whatever could it mean? How many times had her parents been to visit them since they'd lived in this house? Three, maybe four times at most. She went home, as she still referred to it in her own mind, as often as she could, always taking the children with her. Never once had Matt accompanied her. God, she could remember the time when the children had had half-term and once during the long summer holidays when she had dared to suggest that she and the children spend a couple of weeks down at Merton Park and that Matt could come and stay at weekends. She might just as well have been suggesting that they fly to the moon, for all the notice Matt took of her. Her place was here, in the home that *he* provided. And nothing she'd been able to think of had shifted him.

Well, this certainly was giving her something to think about now.

She popped the card into her bag, packed the laundry into the special sack she kept for that purpose, changed her shoes, donned her coat and set off for the wash-house, which was in the next street. On one corner of Bull Yard there stood a big red pillarbox and on the opposite corner there was a metal rubbish bin.

The thought came into her head, Get rid of that card.

Why should I? she questioned herself. Because if, for any reason, Matt should find it and read it, he would want some answers and want them quick. It was ten to one he'd convince himself something was going on that he should know about. She wouldn't be able to tell him a thing because she had nothing to tell. She couldn't fathom why her mum and her nan were coming up to visit her, but Matt wouldn't take that for gospel truth and he'd more than likely finish up belting her round the head again. He was becoming too fond of doing that and the last blow had given her a headache that lasted for days. So, having reasoned all that out with herself, Joan crossed to the other side of the street, propped the sack of bed-linen against the wall, took the postcard out of her handbag and tore it into strips. With a slight smile she pushed the pieces down into the litter-bin. Time enough to tell Matt after the visit. Then she would swear her life away that it had been a total surprise, them coming to see her after all this time. Well, it was, wasn't it? She didn't tell lies. Well, maybe white ones when it suited her.

It had turned half past eleven. I stayed too long chatting, Joan was saying to herself, as she hurried down Bull Yard carrying her sack of damp washing. The girls will be home for their lunch soon and I meant to iron a load of this wash-ing before then. Jamie always had his mid-day meal at school and Matt at work, so she and the girls only had a snack and she cooked the main dinner at night.

Having finished laying the table for three, Joan set the big pan of soup nearer to the hot-plate of the range and began to cut thick slices from the new loaf of bread she had bought at the Jewish bakery. Nobody made bread better than Mr Isaacs did. She grinned and smothered butter on a slice and munched it contentedly. She heard the front door bang open and two voices calling, 'Mum, Mum, there's a man here says he wants to talk to you.'

Maggie and Rosie came flying down the passage and flung themselves at their mother. Joan bent down, kissed the tops of their heads and hugged them both to her. Then she raised her face and smiled at the gentleman standing on her top step. He was tall, well-built and, with the heavy overcoat he was wearing, broad-shouldered. Very masculine, she decided. He wore a trilby hat, which he removed, showing blond hair, a fair complexion and friendly grey eyes.

'Mrs Pearson?' he asked.

'Yes.'

'Mr Stevens, your housing officer.' He smiled, holding

out his hand for Joan to shake, which she did, without enthusiasm. 'We don't have a housing officer,' she told him firmly. 'All these houses in Bull Yard are privately owned.'

'Not any more.' He shook his head to emphasize what he was telling her. 'Several properties in this area have been acquired by the council under a compulsory-purchase act and are now due to be demolished.'

'Oh, yes, and where does that leave us?'

'We have a duty to rehouse every tenant. You were sent a letter laying out all the facts and offering further information and advice if you cared to visit the town hall.'

'We did get the letter but my husband said at the time that we were protected by our landlord.'

'Well, Mrs Pearson, your husband has got it wrong.'

Quick as a flash, Joan flung at him, 'Come back when he's home and try telling *him* that! Anyway, I haven't the time to chat to you now. I have to give my girls their meal and get them back to school.'

She was half-way to closing the street door when he thrust out his arm and said, 'Just one minute and then I'll leave you. The point of my being here now is to invite you to view a few of the flats that we shall be offering you as alternative accommodation. Sorry it's such short notice, but if you wish to take me up on the offer could you be outside Whitechapel Underground station at two thirty this afternoon? A colleague and I will be there to meet a group of you.'

Well, that was a turn-up for the books!

Joan still hadn't made up her mind if she was going. It was as she stood at her front gate, seeing the girls off back to school, that it was made up for her. Doris Shepherd opened her front door and called, 'Shall we walk up together?' And when Joan didn't answer straight away, she added, 'You are gonna come along and see what's on offer? I thought it was just as well for some of us t' be nosy. May Brown isn't in, she's working today, so I'll 'ave t' tell her about this Mr Stevens ternight.' She looked at Joan urgently and repeated, 'You are gonna come?'

'Yes, all right, Doris, I'll walk up there with you. Give me a shout when you're ready t' go.'

The Whitechapel Road, with its wide pavements, still delighted Joan. She had never got used to the traders, their stalls and their barrows. They whipped fruit from the stall to the scales and into a paper bag all in one swift movement. Vegetables were ladled up in a brass scoop, weighed, and shot straight into the customer's shopping bag. No dithering as to the cost. These men had been brought up on mental arithmetic. 'That lot'll cost yer five an' six, me ole darlin'. Six bob? 'Old on, I'll get yer a tanner change.'

After all this time their chatter still made her smile.

When they arrived at the tube station Mr Stevens was there. Only three women besides themselves had bothered to turn up, and Mr Stevens introduced his assistant as Marie Wilkinson. She looked to be in her early twenties, and had long dark hair tied back in a plait.

'What are you going t' do if we don't like any of the places you're offering? We could refuse to move, you know,' Doris Shepherd asked as they reached the entrance of the first block of flats they were about to view.

Without any hesitation the young woman snapped, 'We'd apply for an order to evict you.'

'Well, thanks a bunch.'

And all four other women joined Doris in her condemnation.

'That's great that is.'

'Take what you offer or else.'

'Never mind what we want, just chuck us out in the streets.'

'Big-hearted – is that what they call you, Miss, down at the town hall?'

'Now, now, ladies, please, Miss Wilkinson was merely pointing out that we must find somewhere to suit each and every one of you.' Mr Stevens had his job cut out, trying to be a peacemaker.

The foyer of the flats smelt of new paint. Already several families were living there but they had only been moved in recently, according to Mr Stevens.

Joan looked across at Doris and knew they shared a sense of dismay. There was a clutter of toys. Two bicycles and a pushchair that had lost a wheel lay side by side, and a sack of rubbish had burst, spilling empty baked-bean tins and wet newspaper over the floor. But it was the walls that were so appalling: somebody had written in bright red wobbly letters every swear word you could think of and the name of a girl who apparently gave her favours for free.

'What are you going to do about that?' one woman asked, pointing to the graffiti on the walls.

'We're not sure yet,' Mr Stevens answered, keeping his voice low.

'Typical council attitude,' the woman said, tossing her head.

They split into two groups to ride up in the lift to the seventh floor.

There Miss Wilkinson put a key into a lock and flung open the door on to an empty set of rooms. The view from the wide, uncurtained windows was fantastic: out over the rooftops of London, and in the distance the mighty Thames winding its way ever onwards. The kitchen had cupboards fitted to the walls, and in a corner stood a shiny but tinny-looking gas-stove. 'Cost a fortune to feed the meter and cook by that thing,' a woman said, nodding in disgust.

The bathroom! And, oh, the toilet! Sheer joy. Three bedrooms. Jamie would get a room of his own. Joan was almost convinced. Tempted for sure.

The door to the flat had been left open, and Miss Wilkinson could be heard arguing with a group of boys who had been standing on the landing when they had arrived.

'And who the fucking 'ell is gonna make us do it?' the lads were jeering at her.

Joan took a step backwards, while Doris Shepherd went forward and was peering down over the railings of the balcony. 'Blimey, it's a damn long way down. I've got four kids. What am I supposed t' do with them if we lived up here?' she asked of no one in particular.

'Chuck 'em over the bloody balcony if they git on yer nerves, missus,' grinned the tallest of the five lads.

'Yeah, then yer can always go down and scrape 'em up like a load of strawberry jam,' his mate volunteered.

Mr Stevens wasn't at all pleased at the way things were going, and he wasn't surprised when the oldest woman in the group said, 'I've seen more than enough for one day, thank you very much. If you can't come up with something better than these flats then I'll stay where I am, compulsory-purchase order or not. Wild horses wouldn't drag me from my little house to live 'alf-way up to the sky with nothing but riff-raff for neighbours.'

A set of heads nodded agreement as the group walked towards the lift.

'I'll see you back at the office,' Marie Wilkinson called to Mr Stevens as, without so much as a goodbye, she ran off, dodging between the groups of children playing hopscotch outside the entrance to the flats.

Doris and Joan both shook Mr Stevens's hand. If anything, they felt sorry for him: he was only trying to do his job. Blooming difficult job it was an' all, they agreed, as they set off to walk home.

'I've got a feeling we haven't seen the last of him,' Joan muttered sadly.

'No. You're probably right,' Doris reluctantly concurred.

Chapter Ten

JOAN HAD BEEN up since the crack of dawn. She had even walked the short distance to school with her two girls. It was a lovely day, considering it was late October, sunny but bitterly cold. One of those days that so often occur in the autumn, just before winter sets in.

In her kitchen all was ready for her mum and her nan. The air was fragrant with the smell of freshly baked pies, and on the dresser she had set two fruit cakes to cool before she took them out of the tins. She had filled one of the pies with Bramley apples and the smell of cloves and cinnamon was strong.

She was washing and drying all of her cooking utensils. It was still only ten o'clock and she wasn't expecting her visitors until after eleven so she glanced up in surprise when she heard the front door open. Her mother walked in, followed by her nan. God, they were a sight for sore eyes! They both looked as if they'd just stepped out of a band-box. Smart and trim down to the last detail, they could easily have passed for sisters rather than mother and daughter.

'You're nice an' early,' Joan said to her mother, as she threw her arms about her. 'Hallo, Nan. Cor, don't you look posh! New winter coat, is it? Come on over to the fire, take your coats off. I'll make a pot of tea.'

'Joan,' her mother laughed, 'will you please stop talking for a minute and give us a chance to get inside the door?'

The kettle was hissing and steaming on the range, as it always was in winter, and Joan spooned tea into her enamel teapot, then filled it with boiling water. She placed it on the table beside a tray she had already set with her best cups and saucers, seated herself and looked across to where her mother and her nan were now sitting, one each side of the fire.

'I suppose Dad's working,' she said. Then, without waiting for a reply, she pressed on, 'I'm dying to know what's brought you two up to see me.'

Daphne flushed, but she did not reply since this trip and the reason for it had been her mother's idea. Not that she hadn't gone along with it. She had. Wholeheartedly.

'I'm about to poke my nose into your business,' Hester volunteered. 'I've been worried sick since you wrote and told us you were probably going to have to get out of this house and be rehoused in a flat. I want you to know that I can get you a house in Morden.'

'I see.' Joan sat up straighter and stared hard at her grandmother. All kinds of thoughts were buzzing around in her head. Morden, in Surrey, was near to where her parents lived and such a nice place. It would be like living in the country. She then sighed the deepest of sighs and murmured, 'Matt would never go for it.'

'You haven't heard what I've got to say. I want you to listen to me,' Hester said, leaning forward, fixing her eyes on Joan's.

'All right,' Joan said, putting her cup down on the saucer, instantly aware of her nan's stern tone.

'We, your mum an' dad as well as myself, feel you're facing a serious problem and it's about time you let us help you. It came about like this. A young woman I've worked with up at the hospital for some time now told me she was taking her mother to live with her for reasons that I won't go into now. She also said she was putting her mother's house on the market but was complaining at how much of the sale price would get eaten up in the estate agent's fee and how much better it would be if she could find a private buyer. That's when the idea came to me. It would solve all your problems.'

'Problems?' Joan's voice was little more than a whisper. 'We've not got more than most.'

'Come on, now, Joan, don't play dumb with me. You've let yourself go downhill badly these past few years, which is one signal that everything is not exactly right. And we don't see anywhere near enough of you and the children.'

Joan noticed her nan did not include Matt.

'Nan, we've no money to buy a house.'

'I've nowhere near finished telling you why I've come here today, so please, Joan, be patient. When your grand-father died he hadn't made a will. He hadn't got a lot of savings but he did have a lump sum due from his employers and quite a hefty amount from an insurance policy. I also draw a pension from his firm. I don't go out to work because I need the money. I do it to get me out of the house and to meet people.'

Joan smiled, knowing exactly what her nan meant.

'I want you to have some of your granddad's money. It's what he would have wanted, and you know that's true. I got this young friend of mine to invite me home to meet her mother. The youngsters are not selling her house just to get the money. I made sure of that. She'd only be moving a few streets away, still near enough to visit her friends, and the money from the sale of her house is going to go towards building a self-contained apartment on the back of her daughter's house. The mother won't feel so lonely, she'll have her own place still, and an income from the money remaining from the sale.'

Hester paused for breath and Daphne moved her chair away from the fire, saying, 'I've soon got warm in here. Is there any more tea left in that pot?'

Joan jumped to her feet. 'Oh, Mum, I am sorry. I've been so intent on what Nan's been saying that I've not offered you anything to eat.'

Daphne waved away her protests. 'I'll see to the tea and you hear your gran out. Time enough then for you to feed us.'

Hester took a deep breath. 'The asking price for this house is eight hundred pounds.' She had to stop talking because Joan had gasped so loudly. 'Sounds a lot, doesn't it? But, as a gift from your granddad, we could pay one hundred pounds down, and from what I've learnt, the repayments over fifteen or twenty years would be about four pounds twelve shillings a month. Also out of your granddad's money I would be able to pay all your legal fees and the removal costs.'

'Oh, Nan! You make it all sound so easy. But where would Matt get a job? That was the main reason we had to come and live in the East End in the first place.'

'Things are different now. Your dad has made enquiries and the best and quickest way would be for Matt to keep his job and get the tube straight up from Morden station.'

'If only it were that simple.' Joan felt tears burn the backs of her eyes. 'I'll see about some lunch now. The girls will be in any minute – they didn't want to go to school this morning when I told them you were coming.'

'How about Jamie? Will he be coming home?' Hester asked hopefully.

'No, he's got further to come so he has school dinners.'

Between them Daphne and Joan soon had the table laid. Potatoes and a saucepan of mixed pot-herbs had been slowly simmering on the back of the range, and in the slow oven to the side there was a golden-topped steak and kidney pie. Daphne was stirring the gravy when the door burst open and Rosie ran into the kitchen, followed more sedately by Maggie.

'You did come, Gran, you an' all, Nan,' Rosie yelled, throwing her school hat and scarf on a chair. Her coat followed, and she flung herself at Hester.

Maggie, who was taking off her own coat, said, 'I can't believe you've both come. Wish Granddad was here too.' She kissed them both in turn.

Daphne looked at her two lovely granddaughters and her heart ached. They were growing up so quickly and what her mother had said was true: they didn't see them very often, and when Joan did bring them down to Merton Park they were never allowed to stay for a few days.

Hester's thoughts were running along the same lines. There were four generations of females in this kitchen. Maggie was nine with huge green eyes like her mother's and bright red-gold hair. Her sister, seven-year-old Rosie, was a bit of a scatterbrain, but her winning smiles and fanciful chatter endeared her to everyone. In fact, we all have the same colouring, the same build and the same friendly nature, she was thinking, as she looked from one to the other.

Now she was praying hard. She had spent a few sleepless nights, pondering whether or not it was right for her to interfere in Joan and Matt's lives. Pops had settled the question for her. Oh, yes, if she said that aloud to anyone they would have thought she was mad because, of course, he was dead. But there was times, especially when she needed him, that he was never far away and talk to him she did. Out loud at times. She spent so many hours on her own. She was lucky, and she realized it only too well, to have Daphne and Bill living only doors away, but she didn't impose and when she wanted advice she felt somehow that it was Pops who gave it to her. And despite all the arguments that Matt would put up, she was going to do her damnedest to see that Joan and her lovely children didn't end up in a tenement flat.

After a happy, jolly lunchtime, Daphne and Hester walked the two girls back to school. There were hugs and kisses at the gate, promises that they would see them soon. 'Your granddad has sent you and Jamie some pocket money, and we'll leave it with your mum,' their gran called after them.

Maggie stopped dead in her tracks, turned and came back. 'Aren't you going to be here this afternoon when we get home?'

Daphne shook her head. 'No, love, we're going to get the train before the rush-hour starts. Besides, it gets dark so early and your granddad would start to worry if we weren't home when he gets in from work.'

Maggie looked thoughtful for a moment. 'I see.' She reached up and planted another kiss on Daphne's cheek. 'That one's for Granddad. Tell him we all love him.'

Daphne was too choked to answer. She nodded and waved at Rosie, who was standing still, waiting for her sister.

Time was getting short, and Hester felt she still hadn't made her point. They were hardly inside the house before she began again. 'Would you like to hear about the house, Joan?'

Joan laid aside the tea-towel she had been using to dry the lunchtime dishes, and turned to face her nan. 'What would be the point? I'm sure it must be a nice house but what chance do I have of ever getting out of here and going to live in Surrey?'

'If Pops were here, d'you know what he would say?'

Joan shook her head.

'Don't be such a pessimist, that's what he'd say. He'd also tell you that in this life, if you want something bad enough and you try hard enough, you'll get it in the end.'

'Sounds lovely when you say it, Nan. But how do I convince Matt – and, more to the point, his family? Because believe you me, Nan, the Pearson family will have a great deal to say about whether or not their beloved Matt moves away to the other side of the river.'

'We'll cross that bridge when we come to it,' Hester said, knowing she was beginning to sound cross. 'Now, listen, these houses I'm talking about were built not long before the war started. This one in particular is very close to Ravensbury Park. It has three bedrooms, well, two fair-size ones and a box room, which is still big enough for a single bed, a bathroom and a separate toilet all on the first floor. Downstairs there's a sitting room, a dining room, and a big kitchen. Half-way up the stairs, there's a window and on the window-sill my friend's mother had a beautiful trailing plant. There was a light, airy feeling about the whole of the house. It had a happy atmosphere. But,' and here Hester paused and stared straight at Joan, 'I've saved the best bit till last. There's a long back garden, which borders on to the park. The lady has most of it laid to grass but there's rose bushes and two trees down at the bottom.'

'Oh, Nan,' Joan moaned, 'how I wish!' But what she was asking herself was, could I convince Matt? She was sure he could afford the monthly repayments on this house. He was better off than he let on to her. She was convinced of that.

Immediately after they had come to live in Bull Yard he had gone to work with his brother Stan, and eventually, after talking about it for ages, they had set up on their own. He no longer worked in the timber yards and he had given the dockyards a try but working with his father hadn't suited him at all well. Stan did most of the costing and the paper-work while, as far as she could make out because Pearson men did not discuss business with their womenfolk, Matt acted as the foreman when they were busy with local projects.

Joan smiled at her nan. 'Seems ever so strange that I got your postcard yesterday saying you were coming today and yesterday afternoon I went to view a flat.'

'Oh, Joan,' her mother exclaimed sadly, 'so it's come about, even though Matt said they wouldn't be able to get you out of this house.'

'Afraid so, Mum. A council officer called here yesterday morning and when Doris Shepherd, from next door, and I told him these were privately owned houses he soon put us right. Said there had been a compulsory-purchase order on most of the properties around here. Clearance of the whole site was how he put it.'

'And how was the flat?' Hester asked.

Joan resisted the urge to swear. 'Nothing wrong with the flat – the inside could be made into a very nice home. Trouble was the area, the kind of people who are already living there, and the fact that the one we were shown was on the seventh floor and there were five more floors above that.'

'Oh, my Lord!' Hester gasped, striving not to show how horrified she was. 'Tell you what, bring the children down for the day on Saturday. We'll leave them with your father and I'll ask my friend if her mother will let you look over the house. See what you think of it. Then we'll see what we can do.'

Can you work a miracle? was what Joan was wondering, as she walked back home from seeing her mum and her nan board a tram to take them to the railway station.

She was so lost in thought that she almost jumped out of her skin when she walked into her kitchen and saw her mother-in-law and her sister-in-law seated at her kitchen table. 'Hallo, Amy, Bertha,' she said.

'Knew the key was on a string so we let ourselves in when Doris next door said you'd gone to the tram stop with your mum and your nan,' Amy told her.

Well, I'll be blowed. Everyone knows everybody else's business around here before it even happens, Joan thought, as she made tea for her second lot of visitors. Setting out her best cups again Joan placed what was left of the cakes she had made in the centre of the table, picked up a long-bladed knife and cut some slices. 'They're both recipes that you've given me over the years, Amy, but I never think my cakes turn out as well as yours do.' She smiled as she slid two slices on to pretty plates and set one in front of Bertha and the other for Amy.

First sipping her tea then nibbling her cake, Amy nodded in approval before she said, 'We 'eard you'd been to view a flat yesterday. Is that's why yer mum came up today?'

Once again Joan was astounded. Talk about bush telegraph!

'How could my mum possibly know that I went to see a flat?'

'They're on the telephone, aren't they?'

'Yes, but I hardly ever phone them.'

'So why did they come? 'Tain't often they do.'

Joan knew her mother-in-law had her trapped. She couldn't think of a plausible story on the spur of the moment, and she could hardly tell her to mind her own business. 'My nan has a friend who has a house for sale and she thought it might do for Matt and me. It has three bedrooms so it would be ideal for the children.'

'And I suppose this 'ouse is on the other side of the river, near to your parents?' Amy retorted swiftly.

'What difference does that make?' Joan protested indignantly.

Amy pretended to sigh. 'Matt is an East-End boy, his work is here. What would he do if he lived down south?'

Joan's temper was rising, though she was striving to keep it under control. 'There are such things as trains and buses, but that's not the point you're trying to make, is it, Amy?'

The air was heavy with silence. Joan shot a glance at Bertha, who merely shrugged her shoulders.

She had another try. 'You mean Matt wouldn't be able to make constant visits to you or go out night after night with his brothers and their mates. Well, think about me for a change. I've had to put up with being so far away from my folk ever since we got married.'

Amy shook her head. 'You don't understand, lass. That's the way of it in our working-class world. The men work 'ard, take care of all the bills and see that there's always plenty of grub on the table. In return for that you surely can't begrudge them a few pints, a game of darts or snooker, a laugh or two in male company?'

'No, of course I don't. But there are times when I would like to go out with my husband. Do things together. Take the children to see my parents a bit more often.'

'But Matt offers yer to come out every weekend and you used to. Now you don't. Too rowdy for you, are we?'

Joan's face tightened in annoyance, and she spoke the next words in haste. 'What I would like is to be allowed to get a job. Do something useful, meet people and have a bit of money to call my own.'

'Do what? My sons would never agree to their wives going out to work!' Amy exclaimed, sounding horrified. 'It would make Matt feel less of a man. Whatever would people think? I think it's downright terrible that you should even think of such a thing. Matt works 'ard. Neither you nor his three kids go short. You ought to think about appreciating him a bit more.'

Joan stared at her mother-in-law in utter astonishment. This was 1955 and she was talking as if they were still in the Dark Ages. What she almost yelled in reply was, 'I don't give a damn what people think!' Instead she bit back the words and took a deep breath.

Suddenly she felt she was fighting a losing battle. She had often thought that Amy regarded her as standoffish, even a snob, but what could she do about it? True, she came from a different background, but she had done her best to adapt herself to their way of life. Oh, I have, I have, she was saying over and over in her mind, but a damn lot of good it seems to have done me. She turned to look at Bertha. Now, she had always been her friend. Both she and Laura had been kind to her. You could say they had initiated her into the ways of the East End. It wasn't their fault that she hadn't knuckled down and acted as if she had been born there. She and Bertha now exchanged a knowing glance.

Joan jumped to her feet and made sure she was smiling when she looked at Amy and said, 'I'll make a fresh brew, shall I?'

She felt relieved when Amy shot her an answering grin, which let her know that she had had her say and as long as Joan took her words to heart they could go on being friends.

Well, it was all to the good to let her think she had won the day . . . But she can talk till she's blue in the face! I'm still going to do whatever it takes to make Matt come round to my way of thinking. Moving to Surrey *had* to be a good move for all of them.

This was one time when she was going to have things done her way or she'd know the reason why.

Chapter Eleven

JOAN WAS TERRIFIED. She and Matt were standing in the entrance to Manor Park Court, which was another block of flats they had gone to view. Only yards away men and boys were fighting, their voices loud in anger, fists flying, language disgusting. She had the feeling that Matt was about to dash forward to help what looked like a woman lying on the floor surrounded by not only burly-looking men but several teenage boys, who were leaving the fighting to the men but were kicking the woman's body.

Matt pushed Joan backwards but then she screamed: knives were flashing. 'Christ, this is getting positively dangerous,' she heard Matt mutter. The sound of sirens filled the air, blue lights were flashing, and from every direction police cars were screeching to a halt.

Matt stopped dead. He turned, grabbed her arm and hissed into her ear, 'For Christ's sake, let's get out of here.'

Her feet barely touched the ground as he propelled her along. Within minutes they were outside a pub and for once

Matt walked past the public bar and pushed open the door to the saloon. He practically pushed Joan down on to a seat and said, 'What do you want? Beer or a short?'

Joan did her best to smile. 'I think I need a whisky tonight, please, Matt.'

He returned with a tray that held two double whiskies, a dry ginger for Joan and a pint of beer for himself. He flopped down beside her and lit a cigarette. He drew heavily on it, letting the smoke go deep into his lungs, then tossed a third of the whisky down his throat before taking a sip of his beer.

Not a word had passed between them when the double doors were pushed open and three men made for the bar. Joan didn't know where to look. One – he was hardly more than a boy – had blood streaming from a cut to the side of his head. A second man was holding out his hands to his mates, both fists bloody. The third man was smartly dressed and had obviously not been involved in the fight, but as he glanced towards where she and Matt were sitting Joan was scared. The fierce look in his eyes sent a chill right through her.

It was Saturday night, and all Joan could think now was, I shouldn't be here, I should have gone home today. Gone with my nan to view that house.

Matt had put a stop to her plans. He wouldn't even let her finish telling him the details of the house. The very next morning, at seven o'clock, Mr Stevens, the housing officer, had again appeared on their doorstep. The long and short of his visit was a declaration that he had been ordered to deliver in person. It stated quite plainly that all tenants had until 21 January 1956 to relocate into alternative housing or face being evicted on to the streets. Mr Stevens had also handed Matt three addresses of flats from which he could take his choice.

Faced with such an ultimatum Matt agreed they would have to start looking at whatever was on offer. On Saturday evening he had grudgingly agreed to go with her and view the first of the three addresses on the list.

For days afterwards Joan asked herself if that fight and the police raid had been a lucky break. Depends on which side of the fence you were standing, she would answer, feeling grateful at the same time.

It was Matt who broke the silence. 'Could 'ave got me brains bashed in there, couldn't I? If the villains hadn't have copped me one it's dead sure the coppers would 'ave.'

Joan didn't answer. Her insides were still wobbly and she was having a job keeping her hands from trembling.

'Was the flat you and Mrs Shepherd looked at just as bad?' he ventured.

Joan shrugged. 'What d'you mean, "just as bad"? We haven't yet looked at anywhere else. I told you, the flat itself was all right. Very nice, in fact, but it was on the seventh floor and there were gangs of lads hanging about. Anyway, that one isn't on the list Mr Stevens gave you so I suppose it's gone.'

'Oh, yeah, had a queue lining up for it I've no doubt.'

Joan was irritated by his sarcastic tone. 'The one we were about to see just now was on the eighth floor.'

Matt raised his eyebrows. 'All I can say is it's a jolly good job we weren't stuck up there when the police arrived. Bloody council! You'd think that for families with kids they'd come up with something better than a flat in a skyscraper block. They've no right to chuck us out of our houses then treat us as if we're nothing. Damn town-hall wallies, they always were full of bullshit.'

Matt was spoiling for a fight, and Joan didn't know what to say. If she dared to tell him it wasn't her fault, he'd only come back with 'Then whose bloody fault is it?' Because say what you like, plead all you like, there was no way that Matt was going to accept that the blame for any of this might be laid at his door.

Then, out of the blue, his attitude changed. 'Drink up, love. I'll get us another drink, and then I think I'd better have a talk with you.'

She drained the remains of her whisky and dry ginger and for once did not argue. She felt she could well use another drink.

Matt came back, set down the drinks then looked at his watch. 'I'm supposed to be meeting Stan and a client at the Flying Horse at six but it's ten past now so I think I'll give him a quick ring t' tell him I'm not gonna be able t' make it. I'll be back in a minute.' He made for the telephone box, which he'd said the barman had told him was outside in one of the corridors. He was letting his brother down to stay with her! Wonders would never cease. Why had his mood changed so rapidly? What was he going to talk to her about? Couldn't be anything to do with the Pearson family or the whole lot of them would be here to join in the discussion.

Both of them were shaken by what had happened at the block of flats. As Matt had said, fights on a Saturday night were nothing out of the ordinary when the pubs were turning out, but so early in the evening and in an area where the council expected folk with children to live, oh, no, that's not on. And the fact that it wasn't a bloke on the receiving end but a woman! No way did a gang of blokes set about one woman. That wasn't on either.

Joan soon began to realize that it was warm in this pub.

She pulled off her woollen scarf and unbuttoned her coat, then settled back to wait for Matt.

When he returned, he took a long drink of his beer, lit another cigarette and said, 'Tell me some more about this house your nan was on about.'

Had she heard right? Don't be sarcastic, she chided herself, and don't make it any harder for him than it already is. 'It sounded nice, and there was a garden,' she replied, giving him a little smile.

'Can't live in a garden.'

'No, but be great for the kids, and just to have somewhere to hang my washing out. You could grow a whole load of vegetables.'

Matt made a face. 'Hmm, that's what you think. Plenty of barrow-boys sell veg without me breaking my back digging for hours on end.' He drew on his Woodbine, blew out the smoke, then flashed her one of his cheeky grins. 'Had a talk with Stan this dinner-time. He reckons I'm a jammy bugger and that I'd be daft not to go for your nan's offer.'

Joan was silent for a moment. She was too busy sending up a silent prayer of thanks for brother Stan. Then she said, 'Really? He's the last person I'd have thought would encourage you to move away from the East End.'

'Yeah, me too. Thought he was taking the mick at first. Then when I realized he was serious I put up all sorts of reasons why the whole idea was sheer madness.'

'Tell me, Matt, what were those reasons?' Joan was sorry the minute the words were out of her mouth. She didn't want to hear all his negative arguments. She should have kept her mouth shut.

'How the 'ell I was gonna get to an' from work for a

start?' He smiled at the despondent look on her face. Then, to Joan's amazement, he threw back his head and gave a great belly laugh. Minutes passed before he said, 'Guess what his answer was. Go on, take a guess.'

'Same as my dad said, I suppose. Use the Underground. The house is only about five minutes' walk from Morden station.'

Matt was still laughing. 'Never in yer life! "Buy yerself a car, yer great big dope," is what he yelled at me.'

Talk about surprises! This evening was turning out to be something else! First off she was having a drink with her husband, just the two of them. No Pearson clan, where the men grouped on one side of the bar, the women on the other. And they were actually talking to each other. Just the two of them. No Amy to put in her two-pennyworth. *And* they were smiling. *And*, best of all, there was hope!

Suddenly Joan was laughing fit to bust.

'Now what's tickled you?' Matt asked, thinking it was a long time since he had seen his wife look so happy and, more to the point, she looked so nice tonight. She'd taken pains over what she wore and her hair, which these days was usually just dragged back and tied with a piece of tape, was shiny clean and piled up high in a tight bunch of curls.

'Sounds as if things might be going to get better and better,' Joan said, still smiling. 'Not only are you asking about the house but now you're considering buying a car.'

''Old yer 'orses,' Matt told her sternly. He wasn't about to give in that easily. If, and it was still a big if, anything was to come of Hester's proposition then at least it had to seem that the final decision had been his. He'd make damn sure of that! He wasn't going to let all the womenfolk believe they had ordered him to change his way of life. 'I ain't said anything was gonna 'appen. Not yet I 'aven't.'

Joan kept quiet. All right, he was making out that he was chastising her but only mildly.

Now he was on his feet, empty glasses in his hand. 'Do you want another drink?' His voice was quite soft.

'No more for me, my head's swimming already.'

Matt made for the bar, and she could hear him whistling under his breath. The evening that had begun so disastrously was turning out to be . . . oh, she couldn't find words to explain it even to herself. Matt had been adamant. No, he wouldn't move, especially not south of the river, and nothing she could say or do would shift him. Now listen to him! Oh, if only it could come about.

Most of it would be down to her nan and Pops. Mustn't forget Pops. How she wished she could still run to him, tell him how grateful she was. And how much she still missed him. She hadn't had her last surprise of the day.

'I'll finish this drink and then I'll take you home. We're not bothering to look at any flats tonight,' Matt said, giving her a kind of sheepish look. 'But before we leave 'ere I want yer t' do something for me.'

'Oh, yeah?' she answered, grinning cheekily.

'Behave yerself, Joan,' he muttered, but even he couldn't keep the grin off his face.

Pushing a handful of coppers towards her he said, 'Go and phone your mum an' dad. Tell them I'm gonna borrow a car an' bring you and the kids down for the day termorrer. Ask 'em if that'll be all right.'

Well, if he'd said he was going to sprouts wings and fly she couldn't have been more surprised. 'Oh, Matt,' she muttered, throwing her arms around him, 'I don't know how to say thank you.'

His mouth twitched and he burst out laughing. 'I'll show you a way later,' he whispered in her ear.

The time was getting on and by now most of the seats in the bar were taken. Several customers were looking at the pair of them as if they'd gone mad. Joan picked up the pennies and went to make that oh-so-important telephone call. Then a sudden thought hit her. So hard it was like a bolt out of the blue.

If events did turn out favourably, and she, Matt and children ended up living in Morden, Surrey, what would her mother-in-law have to say about it all?

She shook her head hard. Didn't bear thinking about.

Later, going home with Matt, she was aware that the events of this evening had encouraged him to have second thoughts about Hester's kind suggestion. That and his brother Stan's sensible comments. All being well, in the not too distant future, her life should take a turn for the better. Right until the moment they reached their front door she kept her fingers crossed.

BOOK TWO

MORDEN, SURREY, 1964

Chapter Twelve

'FLAMING JUNE' WAS absolutely the right description for it and into the second week the weather was glorious. It was going to be another long, sunny weekend, the kind that made you want to stay outdoors for ever, Joan was thinking. She glanced over to where her two daughters were sitting on the lawn eating their midday snack. They could still almost pass for twins and were so like her, except that their golden reddish hair was nowhere near as unruly as hers. She felt so lucky. She had everything anyone could ask for: a husband she loved, and who loved her, a safe, secure life, and three wonderful children. What a difference moving out of the East End had made, but where had all the years gone?

Her beloved Jamie would be twenty in November, and in the same month Meg (as Margaret had preferred to be called, rather than Maggie, since she started working in a solicitor's office) would be eighteen, while young Rosie had turned sixteen and was working for the Water Board. Those two girls were absolute gems. And just sitting there watching them on this Saturday morning she could feel the strength of the bond between them. Another blessing was that they both adored their big brother.

This house in which they lived, thanks to her nan, wasn't elaborate, but it was roomy and comfortable, in a nice area. Hardly a day passed that she didn't count her blessings and feel grateful. How different all their lives might have been if they had moved into a flat in one of those high-rise tenements when they were evicted from Bull Yard.

As her mum and dad, who were now frequent visitors, were fond of saying, she had turned this house into a lovely home. Her reward was that Jamie and the girls brought their friends home. She had overheard one girl ask whether their mum would mind them coming without notice and Rosie's answer had been, 'Oh, no, our Mum's OK,' which was high praise from a sixteen-year-old.

Jamie, having got himself eight O levels and three A levels, was at university. That was one thing she and Matt still disagreed on. According to Matt, Jamie should be out in the world earning his own living. Her one big fear was that their son would give in to his father's complaints and leave university before he had his degree in economics. Still, Matt had given way on quite a few things, even going so far as to buy Jamie a motorbike on his eighteenth birthday. She smiled, remembering how frightened she'd been the first time he had roared up the road on it. If anything were to happen to him she didn't know what she would do. She said a prayer for his safety every time he left the house to ride that bike. She couldn't begin to imagine life without him.

She loved her girls with every fibre of her being but, she had to be honest, Jamie was the light of her life. She shuddered, remembering the night he had been born. The memories had never dimmed. Both she and her baby could so easily have been killed. Her labour had been long and hard. She had never felt so lonely. So cheated. Because, of course, if things had gone according to the plans her father had made, Jamie would have been born in a quiet nursing-home in Wimbledon, not in a London hospital so near to where a German rocket had landed. But in the end, they were both safe and he was perfect.

Maybe it was because of the danger they had shared that night that they were so close. It still startled her sometimes when he walked into the house. He was so strikingly good-looking, so mature, at six foot two not quite as tall as his father, with Matt's dark hair, and the most gorgeous big blue eyes. She'd wondered about that when he had been born because her own eyes were green and Matt's a deep brown. 'Most babies have blue eyes to begin with,' one of the nurses had told her. 'They change colour later on.' Jamie's never had. He was always on the go, thinking ahead to what he wanted to do next, yet always thoughtful of others. And Joan was particularly pleased about the bond that had grown between her father and her son.

Jamie had been eleven years old when they had moved to Morden and until then had not known his grandfather well. Now it was a different story. When Jamie played rugby, Bill Harvey was on the touchline. They went swimming together and Joan often thought that her father would have given the world to be young enough to own a motorbike and roar off into the wind beside his grandson. Fishing was another sore point with Matt: 'Sheer waste of time. Asking to catch yer death of cold. So boring, sitting silent on a riverbank for hours on end,' he would say, and those were only a few of the arguments he threw at his father-in-law and his son. But nothing, least of all the weather, deterred Bill or Jamie. Fishing was high on their list of priorities.

It was a shame, really, that Matt didn't spend more time with Jamie, while he would go to the ends of the earth for his two girls. He spoilt them both rotten and always had, right from the beginning. As her nan was fond of telling her, that was the way it always was. Fathers spoil their daughters and each and every mother thinks her son is a gift from God, especially if he happens to be an only son. If that was true then Joan was no exception.

Matt was working this morning, which was unusual for him on a Saturday. He said that, more than likely, he would be home this afternoon but that this evening he was play-ing darts. She wished that Matt didn't spend so many Saturday nights in the East End, but she never argued the point: it was a chance for him to relax and catch up with what all his family were doing. She knew she'd be more than welcome to join him but doing the round of the pubs still didn't appeal to her.

As it was so warm, Joan was thinking about making a picnic dinner, with a few hot dishes and some salad they could eat in the garden. She'd have it ready early just in case Matt came home. 'What are you two planning to do with the rest of the day?' she called across to her daughters.

'Haven't quite decided,' Meg answered.

'Tennis first. We've promised to play doubles,' Rosie reminded her sister. 'Then I'd like to go swimming.'

'Rather you than me.' Their mother smiled. 'At least, the tennis bit. It's too hot. Who's making up the foursome?'

'Mary and Linsey. Their dad said he'd drive us to the

courts, and then I expect he'll have a drink in the club-house while we play. He'll take us to the baths too.' Meg offered the information with a knowing look.

'It's kind of Mr Chapman to run all you girls here, there and everywhere. I don't know him all that well but I've always had the feeling he's a nice man,' Joan said.

'It gives him something to do,' Rosie said, sounding like a thoughtless kid.

'How do you know he's nothing more important to do with his time?' Joan was quite shocked.

'Oh, Mum,' Meg exclaimed, 'you know very well his wife went off with another man.'

But that had happened over two years ago, Joan remembered. At the time it had come as quite a shock because everyone had thought of the Chapmans as an ideal happy family. Since then everyone who knew of the situation had been impressed by how well John Chapman had coped with his two daughters, and how much he did with them.

There had been just one time when he had admitted to Matt that it wasn't easy. He made no secret of the fact that he had loved his wife deeply and had been badly hurt when the truth came to light that she'd been seeing this other fellow for more than two years before she left him.

Linsey was the same age as Meg, and Mary was just a year younger than Rosie.

'Mary says she wishes her dad would find himself another ladyfriend,' Rosie piped up.

'Well, I've never heard her say anything of the sort,' Meg rebuked her sister. 'Her dad likes taking them both out and about and he's always pleased for us to join them.'

'Well, I think you two are very lucky,' their mother told them as she stood up, leaving her book on the garden table, and collected the empty glasses. 'I'm going indoors to make another jug of lemonade.'

'Mum,' Meg called after her, 'which weekend did you say Jamie would be coming home?'

'Not for three weeks yet. He said he's trying to swot up for the summer exams.'

'Oh, that's a pity. Linsey's having a party a fortnight today and I was hoping Jamie would be home and perhaps bring a friend with him.'

'Well, he'll phone tomorrow. You know he always does on Sundays. Talk to him about it then.'

As Joan neared the house the phone rang. She hurried through the kitchen to answer it, placing the empty glasses on the draining-board as she went.

'It's only me,' Matt said, as she lifted the receiver. 'Shan't 'ave time to come 'ome. Big match tonight, starts early, so I'll grab a bite at me mother's. I'm sorry, love. Still, you've got the girls for company. Why don't you go to the pictures with them?'

Joan wasn't surprised that he wasn't going to come home, and she certainly wasn't going to debate whether girls of sixteen and nearly eighteen would want to go out with their mother on a Saturday evening. Instead she said quietly, 'It's all right. Hope your team wins the darts match. But before you go, Matt, will you please do something for me? Make sure you remind your mother that we've booked the Crown for Jamie and Meg's birthday do, and ask her to let the rest of the family know.' She heard Matt sigh heavily. 'Oh, for God's sake, Joan, it's months away. Even I'm getting tired of hearing you go on an' on about it.'

'All right, all right, but make sure you tell your mum. I'll be up to see her next Sunday, not tomorrow, a week from tomorrow, and I'll give her all the details then.'

'Yeah, I'll tell her, an' if it'll make you 'appy I'll check with Stan just t' make sure he's got the date OK.'

'Thanks, Matt.'

'See yer later, then. Don't wait up if you're ready for bed cos I'm sure to be late.'

'Is that Dad?' Rosie yelled, her face lighting up as she ran through the hall.

'Yes,' Joan said, handing the phone to her youngest daughter, knowing she'd want to chat to her dad.

As she walked to the kitchen and set about squeezing a couple of lemons Joan was in a thoughtful mood. For a year after they had moved out of the East End, relations between herself and her mother-in-law had been strained, to say the least. Amy Pearson, the respectable, warm, kind-hearted mother of six, dependable, honest and generous to a fault, was stubborn as a mule.

There were times when Joan had to feel sorry for her, probably because it was Matt and she who had started the ball rolling and put the idea in the heads of his brothers and sisters. Whatever the reason, only two of Amy's children, Stan and Bertha, now lived within walking distance of the family home. Added to that, in 1958 Matt's father had died suddenly of a severe heart-attack. It had all left Amy feeling lonely and, perhaps, unwanted. Laura and her tribe had moved to Southend, and although she got a train up to Fenchurch Street station and called in on her mother from time to time, Bertha had confided to Joan that Amy had not set eyes on either of Laura's children from the day they had moved out of London.

The same could not be said of Joan's children. Thankfully

she had no problems on that score. Jamie thought the world of his gran and whenever he was in London he never failed to call in and see her. As for Meg and Rosie, she had taken them regularly to visit their gran. When Joan planned river trips, outings to Greenwich or to the Tower – the girls loved the Beefeaters – and to the museums she always asked Amy if she wanted to accompany them. Sometimes she did, if not too much walking was involved. However, if her legs were playing her up they'd set off without her, knowing that by the time they got back Amy would have a feast of a tea all ready for them.

Now shrieks of merriment were coming from upstairs as her two girls got ready for an energetic afternoon. Joan liked weekends best when Jamie came home and brought a couple of mates with him. They were precious days. The house really came alive: the lads would be boisterous, and they teased the girls unmercifully, but their laughter was good to hear.

She was about to go back out into the garden, carrying a tray of clean glasses, the jug of lemonade and a plate of butter shortbread she had made earlier that day when Meg came down the stairs, followed by Rosie. Meg looked particularly grown-up, in her pleated white tennis skirt, a pale blue jumper, with a V-neck and short sleeves, and her shoulder-length hair loose and shiny. She had grown into a real beauty.

Her eyes turned to Rosie, her baby, but there was nothing babyish about her today. Oh, why did they have to grow up so quickly? Rosie was wearing white linen shorts, a pink top and a little bit of makeup but she still looked clean, healthy and young. 'Well! You've both gone to a lot of trouble. Meeting someone special, are you?'

'Depends if there's four good-looking guys at the tennis club this afternoon.' Meg grinned. 'There's four of us so it's a case of take one, take us all.'

'Are you coming back for your dinner?' Joan asked.

'Not unless you want us to. Mr Chapman said we could eat at his house or maybe he'd treat us all to fish an' chips.'

'Oh.' Joan saw a lonely evening stretching before her, but before she had a chance to reply they heard a car draw up outside the house and the sound of a horn. Both girls kissed her, picked up their tennis racquets and raced off.

'Hey, wait a minute! What about these bags? I suppose they hold your swimming things, don't they?'

'Oh, yes, ta, Mum.'

'It's very kind of you to give up your time like this,' Joan said to John Chapman, as she leant through the driver's window.

'My pleasure,' he assured her. 'And please don't worry, I'll make sure they're all right and I'll have them home by, say, nine o'clock. Is that all right by you?'

'Yes, that's fine, thanks again.' She straightened up and stepped back, and all four girls waved as the car moved off.

It was just two thirty.

Joan walked slowly into the house. She felt lonely. It was stupid: she was a grown woman and she couldn't keep her children tied to her apron-strings for ever. And there was nothing stopping her from going up to London and spending the evening with her husband and his mates. Except that she didn't like sitting in a pub for hours on end.

In the months that followed there wasn't time for any of them to think about much except the coming double birthday party. There were days when tempers flared and Joan felt she had an enormous task in trying to please both adults and children. And that wasn't counting Matt. Londoners were renowned for their parties, and over the years Joan had attended quite a few hosted by the Pearsons. This was the first one she had organized on her own. For several reasons she had felt compelled to do it. On 2 November Jamie was to be twenty years old. No longer a teenager. Six days later, on the eighth, Meg would be eighteen and, these days, folk tended to regard that as coming-of-age. When she had first suggested the idea of a double party to their father, Matt had been as defeatist as ever. 'Ten t' one they'll both want another do when they really do come of age! Wait till Jamie is twenty-one – you'll see! And our Maggie will be just as eager for another party in three years' time,' he had declared.

Joan had pushed that thought to the back of her mind and gone ahead.

Now the day had dawned.

The room they had hired ran the full length of all three bars that were open to the public down below. A special bar, with two barmen, had been set up for this evening and Matt had placed a generous amount of money with the land-lord of the Crown so that all drinks were free to their guests. He and Joan had also had the forethought to book several rooms in and about the pub for those who were too tired or drunk to travel home that night.

Fifty-four relations and friends had sat down to a four-course meal, and now they were on to the speeches. First, Matt had stood up and praised his children to the high heavens, even going so far as to thank their mother for all her devotion over the years. Brother Stan made a point of thanking Joan for all the hard work and effort that he knew had gone into making this evening such a great success.

Then Amy was on her feet. Wonder upon wonders, she had something she needed to say. ''Andsome is as 'andsome does,' she declared. 'Well, I think you'd go a long way to find a better-looking lad than our Jamie and a kinder one, come to that. I'm not going to tell yer that I always agreed with the way his mother was bringing him up cos I didn't. Bit posh, like, for me, giving him big ideas, getting above his station and looking down on us as 'is relations. Now, I'm telling all of you, I was wrong. Yes, you can snigger, and laugh all yer like, cos I know what you're all thinking. It's gotta be a first, Amy Pearson admitting that she was in the wrong. But I freely admit I was. Our Jamie 'as turned out a smasher, an' I for one am dead proud of him. For all his schooling he's not a snob. Turns up on my doorstep, brings his mates as well, ain't ashamed of me or of where I live, and eats my bread-pudding like it's going out of fashion. And his sisters are all right an' all. The pair of them 'ave always had time for their old gran, so I'd like to take this chance and give a vote of thanks to their mother, my daughter-in-law. She's done a damn good job.'

It was impossible to say who was the most embarrassed, Jamie or his mother, yet when they looked at each other their pride was apparent. Praise from Amy Pearson was something that not many people received.

Matt asked his father-in-law if he wanted to say a few words, but Bill Harvey shook his head and smiled broadly. 'How on earth could I follow your mother? Leave it be. Amy was the star turn tonight.' That brought forth not only laughter but a standing ovation, which Amy had *not* bargained for.

Now the hall was filling up with extra young friends who had been invited for the evening, and the revelling began. Unrestrained by their elders, the youngsters took to the floor and the singing and dancing continued until midnight.

'I reckon we ought t' meet 'ere for a drink at lunchtime,' Stan said, beaming round at members of his family. 'One for the road to round off this smashing weekend.'

There was a general nodding of agreement as everyone moved towards the door.

Matt stood where he was with his arm round his wife. 'Did you see the girls and lads that went off with our three? Suppose they're all going to kip down at our place.'

'You don't mind, do you? But I expect you're right, we'll probably have to step over bodies lying on the floor when we get in. But it all went off very well, don't you think?'

'Oh, not bad,' he teased her, and then grew serious. 'You've done a fine job, in more ways than one. Even me mother said you 'ave.'

They were both still laughing when he added, 'Come on, let's go 'ome.'

Chapter Thirteen

JOAN FELT AS though her life had been transformed. Christmas had been a wonderful time with just her, Matt and the children, and not once had Matt shown he was restless. On Boxing Day they had gone to her parents, and Matt had been the life and soul of the party. Even Hester said it had been a joy to have him around. They had spent the weekend in the East End, staying at Amy's house and having one evening with Bertha and her family, and the other at Stan's.

Now it was January, a new year, a new beginning.

Jamie had got himself a part-time job, of which his father heartily approved, because his grant didn't stretch to cover his expenses. He came home as often as he could and Joan teased him that the main reason was to show off his beloved motorbike. Both Meg and Rosie worked locally, sometimes popping in at lunchtime for a snack, and she had the feeling that Rosie had a boyfriend. In fact, it was more than a feeling. She knew. Rosie was taking so much time and care over her hair, her makeup and her appearance that it was obvious she was trying to impress someone special.

Meg had been courting for some while now but had only brought Brian Clarke home regularly since the night of her birthday party. There were days now when she'd say, 'I won't be in for dinner tonight,' and her father would tease her. Joan wondered how long it would be before they announced their engagement. Not too long, she hoped, and smiled to herself at the thought of making her daughter's wedding dress with the help of her mother and, of course, her nan.

Brian worked for Macdonald and Partners, chartered accountants, whose offices were housed in the same block where Meg worked. It seemed he had a good job, which mattered to Matt. Joan didn't mind what he did for a living, as long as he was fit and healthy and would make Meg happy.

Joan had the front door open, her purse was in the bottom of the shopping basket and she had pulled on her gloves then flung the end of her long scarf over her left shoulder. These January winds were biting cold. She was wondering what meat to buy for dinner that evening and was about to close the door when the shrill ring of the telephone made her hesitate. Should she answer it? It was probably one of the women from the Guild who would want to chat for half an hour and she hadn't the time to waste. But she decided she had better find out who it was.

'Mrs Pearson?'

'Yes.' Joan felt a little apprehensive: she didn't recognize the voice.

'Is your husband at home?'

What the hell had that got to do with this frosty-sounding woman on the other end of the line? 'No, he isn't at the moment. Can I help you?'

'I'm Miss Reid, secretary to Mr Clive Richardson, who would like to have a word with you. Will you hold the line, please?'

Really, this was ridiculous! Who was this Mr Richardson and what could he possibly want with her?

She didn't have long to wait before she found out.

'Good morning, Mrs Pearson. I am a partner in the firm of Richardson and Bentley, solicitors and commissioners for oaths. Would it be possible to make an appointment to see you and your husband? I will come to your house, if that is all right with you. You tell me when it would be convenient.'

The voice was educated but Joan still felt . . . She couldn't put it into words. 'Would you mind telling me what this is about?'

'Nothing for you to worry about, Mrs Pearson. I do want to reassure you on that score. But it is not anything we should discuss over the telephone. I'm sorry.'

'I can give you my husband's business number. Perhaps you should call him.'

'I know I'm treading on eggshells but I really do have to meet both of you face to face. You could come here to this office, in High Holborn, but I do urge you to let me visit you at home in the first instance. It would be better all round. Just say what day is best for you.'

In the first instance? A sense of urgency came over Joan. She had to find out what this was all about so she said promptly, 'Tomorrow morning, I'll ask my husband to go in to work at a later time, so come as early as you like.'

'Shall we say nine thirty, then?'

'Yes, that will be fine,' Joan murmured. By then the girls would have left for work.

'Thank you, Mrs Pearson. Goodbye.'

Joan did her shopping slowly. Her mind was muzzy, almost as if she had had too much to drink the night before. The man had been nice, very polite. But why all the mystery? The day dragged and she couldn't settle to anything. She made herself another cup of coffee, the second since she had got back from the shops. She could phone Matt at work, but what good would that do? He'd worry just as much as she was. Probably a whole lot more. And he would demand answers – probably look up the address of Richardson and Bentley and go tearing up there making a scene.

Suddenly she frowned. What if Matt was in trouble? Had he and Stan got into money difficulties?

Never had she been so relieved as when she heard her husband's key in the lock of the front door that evening.

She didn't give him time to get his overcoat off, just blurted out the essential parts of the telephone conversation in disjointed sentences.

'Oh, for God's sake,' Matt protested, 'the bloke's 'aving you on. Collecting for some charity or other, I bet.'

'Well, it didn't sound anything like that t' me,' Joan said. 'Honest, Matt, he sounded really serious. I can't tell you why cos I don't know myself but he frightened me. It was nothing he said, it was just a feeling I got that it wasn't good news he was coming to see us about.'

Matt laughed. 'Well, I'll make short shrift of him. I'll

give him just five minutes and then he'll be out of that door a damn sight quicker than he came in. Come on, love, I'll pour us both a drink so put it out of yer mind till termorrow.'

Easier said than done, Joan thought, as she tossed and turned in bed that night.

Clive Richardson rang the doorbell on the dot of nine thirty. He was about five foot ten inches tall, immaculate in his navy blue Crombie overcoat with his briefcase in his hand. Matt towered five inches above him as they shook hands.

'Thank you for allowing me to come to your home,' he said pleasantly, as Joan took his coat and Matt pointed him to an armchair.

'Just tell us why you felt it was so important,' Matt said, in what, for him, was quite a courteous tone.

Mr Richardson set his briefcase across his knees, clicked open the lock, took out three or four typewritten pages and was about to speak when Matt said, 'I might as well tell you, if this is anything to do with business I won't take kindly to you involving my wife. So let's 'ave it out in the open. Does she need to stay in the room or not?'

Clive Richardson sighed. He hadn't expected this to be easy. 'Mr Pearson,' he began, 'I am here as a lawyer, not an investigator. This is a very personal matter that concerns both of you. I know you will find it painful and I can't help wishing that this particular job had fallen to someone else. So as I can think of no way with which to soften the blow I will get to the point.'

Joan was really frightened now. Her eyes were fixed on the stranger.

'We have taken instruction from a firm in the United States of America who are representing a family whose son was born in a hospital in Whitechapel during the early hours of the second of November 1944. You also have a son, I believe, born in the same hospital round about the same time on the same day. Is that correct?'

Joan's hands flew to her mouth. She still had no idea why the man was sitting in her front room: all she knew was it concerned Jamie and the man had said his news would be painful.

'Yes, that's right,' Matt answered, his voice rising. 'What the hell 'as that t' do with an American family?'

Matt would have gone on, swearing like a trooper more than likely, but suddenly he realized that this solicitor was having a hard time. The man was tense: his knuckles were white as he gripped the handle of his briefcase. He was about to offer him a shot of whisky or maybe a brandy but decided this matter had to be got to the bottom of before a drink of any kind was brought out.

Clive Richardson looked from one to the other then back to Matt. 'I am so sorry. I have never, in all the years I have been in practice, had to deal with anything even approaching this. The American family in question had a family crisis. A relative needed a blood transfusion and it was only then that it came to light that their son, whom they had raised for nearly twenty years, was not their own flesh and blood. Wheels were set in motion. Hospital records were checked and it was discovered that a German rocket had been launched that night which fell close to the hospital in which this mother had given birth to her baby. The blast was so great that it caused windows of this hospital to be blown in and the electricity to fail.'

Clive Richardson paused. He could not bear to look at Joan, whose face was deathly white, but he knew he had to press on.

'During the chaos that followed two newborn babies were taken to the nursery.' He paused and swallowed. 'There is reason to believe that a mistake was made and that these two babies, both male, were wrongly tagged.'

Joan was drawing in great gulps of air. She felt sick.

Matt jumped up from the settee where he had been sitting next to her. 'What? What the bloody 'ell are you going on about? After all these years you expect us t' believe a cock-an'-bull story like that? Get out. Go on, take yer damn papers and get out of our house.'

All kinds of emotions were ripping through Joan. She was so angry with this man that if she had had any weapon in her hand she felt she would have struck him with it. How dare he come here to tell her that maybe Jamie wasn't her son! For that was what he was trying to say, wasn't it?

She was his mother. She'd breastfed him, nursed him for hours on end, cared for him through measles, mumps, chicken-pox and every other ailment kids get. Did he really believe I wouldn't have known he was someone else's child? My God! She was so angry. But, more than that, she was desperately afraid.

'Wait.' Just the one word came out of her mouth, and even that was a dry, harsh sound.

'Take your time, Mrs Pearson,' Clive Richardson said. 'Ask me any questions you like. If I have the answers I'll tell you, and if not I shall do my best to find them.'

By now tears were burning her eyes. Impatiently she brushed them away. 'I don't believe one word you said, and whoever sent you here is wicked. No, more than wicked. They must be downright evil to think up such a story. But before you go, tell me just one thing. What was an American woman doing having her baby in Whitechapel in 1944?'

She shuddered, and Matt was by her side in an instant. 'It's all right, love. We'll get to the bottom of this rubbish and, by God, I'll see some bugger pays for starting this rumour.'

'Oh, Matt, what if we have to tell Jamie?'

Even burly, street-wise Matt was appalled at the very thought, and the anguish that came through as his wife spoke those few terrible words was something he wouldn't forget if he lived to be a hundred. He couldn't let this happen. If it was true it would kill Joan. But it wasn't true. It couldn't be, because if it was the consequences would be too awful even to think about. Gently he pushed Joan back on to the settee and looked at the intruder.

His mood changed abruptly. Whoever had thought up this scam, Clive Richardson was in no way to blame: the poor man looked green around the gills. 'I'll stick the coffee-pot on and get the brandy bottle,' he muttered, and made for the door.

Silence hung heavy between Joan and the solicitor, and it wasn't broken until all three were sipping coffee. Both men had tossed down their brandy in one gulp. Joan hated the taste but she had drunk hers too.

'Mrs Pearson, perhaps you'll let me answer your question now.'

Almost apologetic, Joan said, 'I didn't think you knew the reason.'

'I have to tell you, the research has been thorough. The

mother was not an American. She was a London girl married to an American soldier. After her baby boy was born she lived with her parents in Stepney for two years.'

He waited, allowing that information to sink in, before explaining further. 'Many thousands of American soldiers had fallen in love with British girls. Some eventually married them and in 1946 they became known as GI brides when transatlantic liners took them to their new homes in the USA. That is what happened in this case. For some of the brides the experience was less desirable than they had expected. Fortunately for this mother, the father of her child came from a good family and until now it would seem that life has been good to both her and her husband. Very good indeed, from what we've been led to believe. They have two more children.'

Joan was startled to find herself becoming interested in what Clive Richardson was saying. Quickly she covered her ears with her hands. 'I don't want to hear about them. Not their names or where they live or what they do for a living. Nothing. Do you hear me? They, them, their kids, *I don't want to know.*'

'I agree,' Matt shouted. 'You can't just come here out of the blue and tell us the son we've had for twenty-odd years is not our son. Things like that don't 'appen.' His voice was hoarse and his cheeks were flaming. 'It's enough to scare the life out of my wife.'

'I just can't apologize enough,' Clive Richardson said quietly, 'but it did happen. The law firm we have taken our orders from have made extensive investigations and so have we. Without a doubt we have established that there were just two male infants born that night within minutes of each other. What happened after their birth was a tragic accident, one which came about because of the war. With broken glass and falling debris in the hospital, plus the fact that the electricity had failed, a mistake was made and at whose door the blame is to be laid is very uncertain to say the least.'

Matt was having a job to breathe now. His hands were knotted into tight fists. Trying hard to control his temper he got to his feet and said, 'That's enough, Mr Richardson. My wife has told you, and I'm telling you now, we don't want to hear any more.'

Now Mr Richardson looked tense again. 'There is a simple way for us to get at the truth.'

'Oh, yeah? Pay them off! Is that what this 'as been all about? Cos if it is I'll see the buggers damned first,' Matt yelled at him.

'That is not what I am suggesting. All you need to do is have a blood test, you, Mrs Pearson and your son. The results would be conclusive.'

Matt went mad. 'Oh, he's *our* son again now, is he? Thanks for bloody nothing. If you think we're going up to the university where our boy is to drag him out and say, "Oh, come on 'ome, son, cos we're all gonna get a blood test t' make sure you know just who your parents are," then I'm telling you, man, you're barking up the wrong tree.'

Mr Richardson shook his head sadly. 'The other family could insist. They could apply to the courts for an order.'

Joan covered her mouth with her handkerchief and ran out into the kitchen. Bending low over the sink she vomited until there was nothing left to bring up. Her heart was hammering, her head spinning. What was the object of all this? What did this American family want? Did they expect to exchange sons? How ridiculous. Would they have to tell Jamie he had to go and live in America then wait for a replacement to walk through the door?

She'd never be able to broach this subject with him. How could she? Where would she begin? Tell him that he wasn't and never had been her son? She couldn't begin to imagine the look on his face – and as to what his reaction would be . . . Dear God, it was a living nightmare.

Matt appeared in the doorway. 'You all right, love?' Then he added, 'Silly blooming question cos you're not. I'm gonna tell this bloke to leave now and then you can go an' 'ave a lie down.'

Minutes later as Matt held the front door wide open, Clive Richardson gave him a long, sorrowful look. 'Goodbye, Mr Pearson. I am sorry your wife is so upset, but I have to say you have not seen the last of me. This matter will have to be thrashed out. With or without your permission.'

As Matt closed the door he was striving to convince himself that he would be able to sort this out. Nobody could just walk into their house with a story such as the one Clive Richardson had come up with and be allowed to get away with it. Look what it had done to Joan already! If he didn't put a stop to it straight away it would turn their whole lives upside down. At that moment he caught sight of his reflection in the hall mirror. 'Jesus Christ, by the look of me I've aged ten years this morning,' he muttered to himself. 'It feels like it an' all!'

Before going in to comfort his wife he had to stand still and take several deep breaths. What could he possibly say to ease her mind? Somehow he had to find words that would make her feel less afraid. But how? He couldn't even convince himself that the facts that had been laid out for them were untrue.

The sad part was that in his heart he knew only too well that Clive Richardson had just spoken the truth.

They certainly hadn't heard or seen the last of him.

Chapter Fourteen

JOAN WAS SITTING in her bedroom, staring out of the window. Her hands were clenched in her lap and her head ached. Jamie would be home this morning and somehow she was going to have to tell him about Richardson and Bentley, solicitors, and why they were now deeply involved in their lives.

On Christmas Day she had turned thirty-nine. Before Clive Richardson had paid them a visit she would have said she didn't look her age. Like her mother and grandmother she kept herself trim and smart, but these past weeks had aged her. It had taken Richardson and Bentley a great deal of effort to persuade Matt and her to submit to blood tests. Now over the weekend they had suggested that, on some pretext or other, they get their son to do the same.

With that thought foremost in her mind Joan sighed. This was such a dreadful situation. How was Jamie going to feel to be told that maybe she wasn't his mother or Matt his father? They were not going to be able to put it off any longer. If they didn't persuade him to take a blood test while he was at home, the solicitors had threatened that they would deal with him personally.

Joan got to her feet and pressed her head against the window-pane, her eyes now too blurred with tears to see anything outside, her shoulders shaking.

She was sick with worry. Matt was, too, and not just with worry but with rage. His temper got worse every day. He had refused to be there when she spoke to Jamie and there was no reasoning with him.

She heard the motorbike before she saw him. She didn't move, just listened as he parked it, let himself into the house and went from room to room. Finally, from the foot of the stairs, she heard him call, 'Isn't anyone at home? Mum, are you upstairs?'

She came out of the room, rubbing hard at her face with her handkerchief. Then she smiled. 'Oh, Jamie, it is good to see you. I'll come down, make some coffee and get you something to eat.'

Her foot was only on the first tread when he reached her. 'Hugs and my kiss first,' he declared, wrapping his arms around her and practically lifting her feet off the floor. 'Oh, Mum, it's going to be a great weekend. I've invited David and Ken to come for the day on Sunday, hope that's all right. Where is everyone? Oh, the girls are at work I suppose?'

'Wait, wait,' his mother implored him. 'Let's go downstairs and you can get those outdoor clothes off while I make the coffee and then we'll talk.'

Jamie turned and walked slowly down to the hall. He waited until his mother was standing beside him, then, staring into her eyes, he said, 'Something's wrong. You've been crying. Come on, Mum, tell me, what's the matter?'

I can't tell him, Joan thought. No, I can't do it. His father should be here. He should be the one to tell him. He won't, though, will he? And it'll be a thousand times worse if strangers get him to one side and say calmly, 'Your parents are not who you thought they were. They're a different couple altogether. They don't even live in this country.'

Jamie felt the tension. It alarmed him. 'Whatever is it? Has Meg or Rosie had an accident? It's not Dad, is it?'

'No, Jamie, nothing like that. Please, let's go into the kitchen. Perhaps if we have a hot drink I'll find it easier to tell you.'

Jamie sighed heavily. 'All right. I'll get my things off while you put the kettle on, and then I want to know whatever it is.'

Like a robot, she set about doing everything just right. Cups, saucers, sugar-bowl, jug of cream from the fridge. 'Are you starving?' she asked.

'No, Mum. Just coffee will be fine.'

When they were seated opposite each other she poured coffee into each of their cups. Jamie added two spoonfuls of brown sugar and dribbled cream over the back of his teaspoon watching it make an ever-increasing circle on top of his coffee. 'You're not well, are you, Mum? Have you been to the doctor's?'

He sounded so concerned that her heart ached even more. 'I'm all right, truly I am, but I want you to listen to what I have to tell you,' she began, trying to keep her voice steady. 'You've heard me tell you often enough about the night you were born, haven't you?'

'Gosh, yes. I've even told that story myself. We were lucky to come through that night, so you've always impressed on me.'

'That's very true. It was an awful night. That German rocket caused so much destruction, and what followed in the hospital was chaos.'

Jamie was holding his cup in both hands and had been sipping his coffee. Now, very precisely, he lowered the cup to the saucer. Then he raised his head and looked straight into Joan's eyes, and said, 'Get to the point, Mum.'

She sighed softly. 'I suppose I better had.'

Jamie kept his eyes on her. It broke her heart just looking into them. Such beautiful eyes, not green like hers, not brown like Matt's, but a deep, deep blue.

'Two boy babies were born that night,' she whispered. 'You were one of them. The other mother was married to an American soldier and when her baby son was two years old she went to the USA to live. Recently your father and I have had a visit from a firm of solicitors acting for an American family who have reason to believe that in all the hectic goings-on in the hospital the night you were born there was a mix-up.'

Jamie didn't move. The silence just went on and on. Eventually he cleared his throat. 'If you're trying to say what I think you are, then something is terribly wrong.'

'Don't I know it?' she muttered, and burst into tears. She reached across the table and took his hand between both of hers. 'Oh, Jamie, I'd give the world for this not to be happening. The solicitors have practically forced your father and me to take a blood test. They said they'd get a court order if we didn't agree. And now they want you to do the same.'

'Mum, stop crying, please. That's no problem. I'll do as they ask and surely that will prove conclusively that they're barking up the wrong tree. Now, try and be calm and start at the beginning. Wait. First tell me what Dad had to say about this.'

Joan wiped her eyes and even managed a laugh. 'Can't you guess? "Load of old cobblers!" He said it must be a scam to get money out of him. He'd get to the bottom of this, he said, and when he did he'd commit murder. If anyone could even think that he didn't know his own son after twenty years then they ought to be locked up in a lunatic asylum.'

'Good old Dad. Now tell me everything, right from the beginning. Please.'

Slowly, and as calmly as she could, Joan went back to that first telephone call, how she had felt apprehensive right from that very moment. She told him the events in the order they had taken place.

Jamie looked shattered. 'It's so crazy. Can it be true? Perhaps Dad is right and someone hopes to gain from this, though it's hard to see how.'

'Well, according to Clive Richardson, the lad in America has been proved beyond all doubt not to be the other couple's son.'

'Even so, what is it they want? Do you know the name of this family? Their circumstances?'

'We have been told that they have two other children and that the family is pretty well off. All the main details I wouldn't listen to. I don't want to know who they are, where they live or anything about the lives they lead.'

She couldn't add that at the back of her mind was the awful thought that if she were to listen to all the facts about this family she might have to admit that they had been bringing up a son to whom she had given birth. That would mean she believed their claim. Never in a million years was she even going to give half a thought to the idea that this dearest boy, who was sitting opposite her now, was not her own flesh and blood. She cringed inwardly at the thought. He was the light of her life. After all the intimate details of bringing up a child to manhood, you just didn't take as gospel the words of a solicitor who came along and to put it bluntly said, 'Oh, sorry, but you've had the wrong boy right from the start. Please change over with a family that lives thousands of miles away in America.'

What about this American family? How had they felt when a simple blood test apparently proved beyond doubt that their son, whom they also had brought up for twenty years, was *not* their own boy? Had they stopped loving him? Did they really want to make an exchange now? Or perhaps, since they were well off, they thought they could entice Jamie to become part of their family, thereby gaining another son while she and Matt lost out. Could folk really be that cruel?

What if she and Matt had found out first? I wouldn't have told a soul! Least I don't think I would have. What good would it have done? Just bring heartaches all round. Why had they engaged an English firm to sort this matter out? As yet, no one had said what they hoped to achieve by getting at the truth.

Jamie refilled their coffee cups. Then he said, 'I rather fancy we're going to have to listen to a lot more facts whether we want to or not, before this farce can be brought to an end.'

Joan drew in a long breath. 'Son, are you saying that this could turn out to be rubbish?'

'Probably. It's too ridiculous to be true. You'd have known over all these years if I wasn't the son you gave birth to. Wouldn't you?'

'Oh, Jamie, that's exactly what I've been saying all along – when you cut your first tooth, took your first steps on your first birthday because we'd bought you a wooden horse on wheels. You grabbed the handle, stood up and tottered along the narrow passage we had in our house at the time. Every illness. The worst was when you had whooping-cough – I hardly had you out of my arms for days and days because that cough racked your little body so much.' She ended on a sob and when she could bring herself to look at her son she saw that he was crying. She got to her feet, came around the table and drew him into her arms. Holding each other tightly, her head buried in his chest, they shed tears that came right from the heart.

They didn't hear Matt come home. Quietly he opened the door to the kitchen. The sight of his wife and son clinging together, both crying their hearts out, met his eyes. If he had the rotten person responsible for this in his house right now he would kill the bastard. 'With my bare hands I would, and bugger the consequences,' he muttered.

It took a minute or two for him to control his temper. When he spoke his voice was filled with emotion. 'I guess you've told him. I've brought a drop of brandy for us. I'm sure you two need it.' Then he watched his son break free of his mother, swipe the tears from his eyes and turn to face him.

'I know, lad, I should 'ave been 'ere.' He opened his arms and, without hesitating, Jamie went into them. 'I'm so sorry, son.' Now there were tears running down the cheeks of Matt Pearson, a sight his wife had never seen in all the years she had been married to him. Moving his big hands gently up and down Jamie's back, his father whispered, 'We'll get this bloody mess sorted. You take the test – that'll show 'em.

You're a Pearson through an' through, an' I'm not gonna 'ave anyone tell me different.'

'I'm sorry, too, Dad. I shouldn't be crying like this – but to come home and hear that solicitors are saying my real parents are in America! Well . . . How could they do that to their own son? What must that lad be feeling like? Don't they want him any more now they've found out he's the wrong blood group?'

'God knows, son!' Matt's heart was doing somersaults. Jamie's shoulders were heaving and sobs were racking his body. 'Go on, son, get it out of yer system. It's not a sin for a man to cry. Jesus Christ, I saw enough men cry when I was in the Army during the war.'

Four days later, long drawn out days. Some spent mostly in silence, others when they talked until their heads ached, going over and over every single detail. Now Joan, Matt and Jamie sat facing a doctor, who was sitting behind his desk.

The doctor turned his gaze away from the three to look out of the window to where ambulances were unloading patients. He wasn't sure whether it was worse to have to tell parents that a child had died or to give them the information he was about to impart. Never had he come across such a case before. It did happen, he knew, he'd heard of such cases, but after twenty years for such a thing to come to light! A catastrophe, nothing less, for each and every person involved.

Matt was the first to break the unbearable silence. 'Doctor, we'd rather you just spat it out. You 'ave got the results there in front of you, 'aven't you?'

The doctor was a young man and he was considering how to be kind, how to wrap it up in some way. He picked up a fountain pen and twiddled it between his fingers, lifted a paperweight. Then he took a deep breath and let it out slowly.

'You have to tell us one way or another,' Joan said.

'Yes, I'm afraid I must.' His voice was barely more than a whisper. 'I have the results of the blood taken from all three of you now. I am so sorry, but they do prove that James cannot be your son.'

This must be what they mean when they say, 'It hasn't registered yet,' Joan thought, as she sat in Matt's car staring at the back of her son's and her husband's heads. But the terrible truth had been admitted at last.

Jamie was not her son. Neither was Matt his father. Inside her head a voice was screaming, *What are we going to do? What are we going to do?* She wasn't shedding tears. She had none left to shed.

Chapter Fifteen

JOAN SHIVERED AS she pulled the string through the letter-box, found the key on the end and used it to open the front door of her mother-in-law's house. She walked down the narrow passageway, the smell of Mansion polish in her nostrils. When she pushed open the kitchen door the warm aroma of baking filled the air.

'Good God above!' Amy Pearson cried, appearing from the scullery dusting flour from her hands and running them down the front of her spotless white overall. 'You're a sight for sore eyes an' no mistake. But what's brought you 'ere? Oh, never mind, I'm that pleased t' see yer. I'll put the kettle on.'

Joan gave her a grateful look. 'I asked Matt what days you were home.'

'Well, he got it right for once. Sit yerself down, I'll see to the tea.'

Amy lifted the big black kettle from the hob and went into the scullery.

Joan took off her coat, sat down and looked around the familiar room. What a change! Over the past two years Amy had become a different woman. She had got herself a job down at the local police station. Three mornings a week she did an early shift cooking breakfast for the constables. At first she had been the butt of her sons' jokes. But she had shown them! Proved herself no end. Having something to do, meeting people and feeling wanted had made all the difference in the world to her. When most of her family had moved away it had shattered Amy. Living alone had left her feeling not exactly unwanted but un-needed. For a brief moment Joan smiled to herself, remembering all the arguments her mother-in-law had put up when she herself had wanted to get a job. Still, that was water under the bridge now. Everything and everyone seemed to have changed lately.

This kitchen was so . . . 'homely' was the word that sprang to Joan's mind. The same scrubbed table dominated the centre of the room but now it was covered with a dark green chenille cloth edged with long tassels. A cut-glass bowl filled with fresh fruit stood in the middle. Two fairly new armchairs were at either side of the fireplace, comfortable-looking with plump cushions and lace-edged linen headrests. The cooking range was well blackleaded, as it always had been even when the house had been crowded with adults and children. The mantelpiece was full of china knick-knacks, which Joan knew had been presents from her children when they were growing up. There was a memory in each and every one. This morning the fire burnt brightly and the brass fender shone. The big dresser still held an enormous amount of china and some of the huge old meat dishes, which Joan felt must be valuable.

Amy came back carrying a tray. She had set out her best cups and saucers and a plate of warm rock cakes. 'This is a surprise,' she said, and set the tray on the table. 'Don't very often get t' see you of a weekday. Though, if I tell the truth, I 'ave been 'alf lookin' for yer t' turn up.'

Joan flushed. 'So Matt has told you?'

'Not much,' said Amy quickly. 'He was in such a state the night he stayed 'ere. I blamed our Stan for letting him drink so much. He just needed someone t' talk to. I expect you do as well. My 'eart went out t' the pair of you when Matt told me. Mind you, it were only the bare bones of the matter he went on about and I didn't ask no questions. It weren't for me t' do that. You knew where I was if you wanted t' tell me, an' now you're 'ere it goes without saying that anything I can do to 'elp, you only 'ave t' say the word.'

'Oh, Amy,' Joan whimpered. Her mouth was dry and her hands were shaking.

'There, there,' Amy soothed her. 'Drink yer tea. It'll all come out in the wash and someone will 'ave t' pay for this mistake.'

'Amy, there is no mistake. It has been proved now that our Jamie does not have our blood group but he is a match for this American family and the same goes for the lad that they have had since birth.'

A few minutes passed before Amy spoke. 'Joan, I am so sorry for you and our Matt. Whatever can I advise you to do?'

'Nothing. There's nothing anyone can say or do that will alter the situation in any way whatsoever. We have to face it. The truth is that a mistake was made in 1944 and now two families have to face up to that fact.'

'Oh, God, what's this doing to our Jamie?' Amy fumbled for her handkerchief. Then she turned to Joan almost beseeching her, 'We won't lose 'im, will we?'

'I've asked myself the same question over and over again. I couldn't bear it if we did.'

'Can yer tell me how he's taken it?' Amy asked, tears running down her cheeks.

'I can't fathom him out.' Joan sighed. 'Even when there's just him and me he won't talk about it. When I move around his eyes never leave me. It's queer. Everything about Jamie at the moment seems queer.'

'Oh, this is all so dreadful. 'Ave this other family been in touch with you and Matt?'

'No, that's the strange part of it all. Mr Richardson, he's the solicitor that first contacted us, gave a letter to Jamie which was supposedly from the American family his firm are acting for. Jamie has never mentioned it. Whether he read it, destroyed it or if he's just put it away somewhere safe, I just don't know. I did ask him if it were a nice letter but he ignored me.'

Silence hung heavy between Amy and Joan. They were both at a loss for words. Then, more to herself than to Joan, Amy mumbled, 'What I can't make out is why they did it. What in hell's name are they after?'

'Me too,' Joan confessed. 'Listening to the men in posh suits, which is how Matt describes them, you'd think it was me and Matt that had done this family a terrible injustice. Wronged them something terrible. There's never a mention that the same tragedy has affected us too.'

'What about this other lad, the one that's supposed to be yours? Have they written to you about him, or has he contacted you?'

'No. According to what we've been told he's doing well and is truly considered their son.' Joan hesitated. 'Amy . . . that's partly my own fault. I refused to listen when the solicitors went on about who this family are, where they live and how prosperous they are. I felt . . . I can't find the words to describe it. I dunno, but if I can get anyone to understand I think it'll be you. I can't seem to get through to my own mum. She's too upset at the thought of losing Jamie.'

'Come 'ere.' Amy was on her feet. She had lost some weight since she'd been working but still had plump arms and a soft bosom. Pulling Joan close she patted her back as if she were a small child. Minutes later when they'd wiped away their tears, she said, very seriously, 'Joan, take your time. Tell me, if you can, just what's going through your mind. Maybe together we can get it sorted and if not, well, they do say a trouble shared is a trouble halved.'

'It's this feeling,' Joan began slowly, 'and if I let it take over then I'll be lost. If I let myself wholeheartedly believe that Jamie is not the baby I gave birth to, no longer anything to do with me, that he belongs on the other side of the ocean, then I don't want to go on living and that's hardly fair on Meg and Rosie. Nor on Matt, I suppose. But he gets so angry if I try to talk to him. If I were to listen to details of this family, how they live their daily lives and so forth, my imagination would have something to go on and I'm afraid it would run away with me. Would Jamie be better off with them? I keep asking myself that question. Could they give him much more than we can? They say that America is the land of milk and honey. Are Matt and I depriving him of things that should rightfully be his?'

'Joan, I do understand,' Amy said softly. 'I ain't never 'ad much t' give my lot but there's always been love. Every brick in this 'ouse can vouch for that. So, you listen t' me. Remember the party you gave just before Christmas?'

Joan half smiled and nodded.

'We couldn't 'ave known then that this bombshell was going to drop on you and Matt, could we? Course we didn't. But, looking back, it's as if I did 'ave that knowledge. I got t' me feet and I told everyone that there wasn't a bit of snobbery in our Jamie. He was our lad and he loved each and every one of us. Even his old gran who still lived in a two-up-an'-two-down 'ouse with a lavatory out in the back-yard. But did he mind? Never in yer life. He came t' see me cos he wanted to, *and* he brought his posh, well-dressed mates with him. And it wasn't t' take the mickey out of me neither. I never knew when they were coming, they just took me as they found me. Those lads came time an' time again *and* they never failed t' kiss me goodbye. So, I'm saying t' yer now, gal, you're misjudging that son of yours. Yes, I said it and I mean it. In your heart he's your son, he knows it, an' you an' Matt knows it. And don't you dare try an' tell me that Maggie and Rosie 'ave altered one iota in their feel-ings towards their brother. No blood test can wipe away twenty years of love and affection from bloody good parents. I don't care what no blooming doctor or solicitor has to say.'

'Oh, Amy, you're a tonic, you really are. I got up this morning and felt I'd go mad if I didn't talk to someone. Just couldn't wait to get on the train and come an' see you.'

'Well, you're 'ere now. You can stay all day, can't you?'

'Yes, I'll take you out for a bit of lunch, if you like,' Joan answered, sniffing away her tears.

'No, I've got plenty in the 'ouse. Now, if we go through this together we'll not only feel a whole lot better, we might even come up with an answer to what we can do about it.'

Joan doubted that. Hadn't she gone over and over it through the long hours of the night, from the very moment Clive Richardson had dropped it on them?

''Ow about a bacon sarnie? I've become a dab 'and at frying rashers, an' if they're good enough for the local coppers they ought t' suit you, my lady.'

Joan set a determined smile on her face. 'I mean it, Amy, you're better than a dose of salts. I'd love a sarnie. I'll come out and help you.'

'Where's Jamie now?' Amy asked, snipping the rind off half a dozen rashers of back bacon.

'He's gone back to university. He phoned us on Sunday, just as he always does, but he seemed so, well, distant. Meg and Rosie spoke to him – they're the only ones who don't seem to think this is a disaster. They were laughing fit to bust when they put the phone down.'

'There yer are, then. Those girls know he's their brother. He's loved them, teased them and looked out for them since the day they were born and no solicitor is gonna change that.'

'I heard them telling my dad much the same thing. Amy, you wouldn't believe how cut up he is over all this.'

'I can guess, love. I've seen the pair of them together. To your dad, Jamie's the son he never had and, being a grandfather, he's got time to devote to him. It takes some believing for all of us. Things like this only 'appen in books and plays and then not to ordinary folk. You said yer mum was taking it badly, what about Hester?'

'I couldn't bring myself to tell her. Left that to my dad.

Poor old Nan. She'll be seventy-five this year and she could have done without this shock.'

'Couldn't we all?' Amy muttered. 'Especially you an' Matt.' She was busy at the frying-pan. She'd laid out four thick slices of bread on a dish and said, 'Spread them for me, will you, love? You can 'ave butter or dripping, whichever yer prefer. It's pork dripping, lots of thick jelly on the bottom. I'll 'ave that – put plenty of salt an' pepper on it for me.'

Soon they were seated at each side of the fire. 'I'd forgotten just how good a bacon sandwich can be.' Joan smiled, munching away.

'I'm just so glad you decided t' come up 'ere today,' Amy said.

'So am I,' Joan answered. She stared out of the window. 'There are times when I feel guilty. I should be thinking about this other lad, the one that's supposed to be my son. How does he feel about me and Matt? But then I think, No, it's not true. Jamie's ours. It's not fair. We've been good parents. Why, oh, why did this have to be brought out into the open? What we didn't know wasn't hurting anyone.'

Poor Amy didn't know what to say or do. She frowned, then murmured, 'The whole thing is a right old cock-up.'

In spite of everything Joan had to smile. Trust Amy to call a spade a spade. Because if you went right back to the night that these two baby boys had been born that's where the trouble was started. And to coin Amy's phrase it had certainly turned out to be a right cock-up.

Later, on the way home, Joan was telling herself how much better she felt for having paid a visit to her mother-in-law. Rough and ready Amy might be, but she was the salt of the earth. She hadn't been able to solve any of their problems but just being with her, feeling the warmth of her love, had gone a long way to helping Joan feel that she hadn't got to cope all on her own.

Chapter Sixteen

In spite of her misgivings, Joan opened a padded envelope which had been forwarded to her by Clive Richardson, and took out what was obviously a wallet containing photographs. She placed it to one side without looking inside. Then she withdrew the letter. There were six pages, handwritten.

Breathing heavily she sat back in her chair and started to read.

3021 16th Avenue
Circle west
Kingston 32405
New York, USA

Dear Joan,
All things considered, I think we have to be on first-name terms, don't you? I have had more time to get my head around this situation, so I do know what

you are going through. Mixed-up feelings, eh? Where
to lay the blame? Asking, 'How can anyone have
done this to me?' Telling yourself over and over again
that you'll die if they take your son away from you.
I've spent the sleepless nights. Cried buckets of
tears. Blamed everyone and anyone. And still have
no answers.

The whole thing is so crazy. Think about it. We
must have seen each other in that hospital. Said
good-morning, maybe good-night. Looked at each
other's baby and admired, even maybe discussed
feeding problems. I do remember my breasts were
very sore and someone gave me a loan of a tube of
soothing cream. Could well have been you.

For nearly two years after having my baby I lived
with my mother, only a tram ride away from where
our babies were born. I understand you lived near
Wimbledon.

Then in 1946 I came to the States. What a journey that was! If the mix-up had taken place during
the voyage I could have understood. We GI brides
were jammed into cabins with tiered bunks, but the
babies were put into one huge nursery with Army
nurses to take care of them. Thank God Peter was
going on for two years old and I was able to keep
him with me. My mother chose the name Peter,
after my father who had died when I was very
young, though immediately we arrived in America
my in-laws called him Junior, and I'm afraid that has
stuck.

One thing I have come to be grateful for is that
both of our baby boys went to a decent loving

family. Mr Richardson has not only written to me, we've spoken a few times on the telephone. I wanted to know everything about you and your husband and was so pleased and, yes, relieved to be told that you were kind, loving people and that James is such a nice young man. It was a great comfort to learn that you both love him dearly, as we do Peter. Things could have been so very different. Especially for me.

I left my home, family and friends and brought my small son to live with strangers thousands of miles away. It wasn't easy at first. I was desperately homesick. But in so many ways I was extremely lucky. For a great number of the English brides, coming here was a disaster. My new family were well-off, but the conditions some young women encountered were truly bad. Some brides found their new home to be little more than a wooden shack, miles from anywhere and with none of the amenities we'd all taken for granted back home. Almost all toilets were outside and running water was not laid on because of the distance to run the pipes – all water had to be drawn from a well. However, on the other hand, food was so plentiful. After the British rationing almost every meal was like a banquet. But, like so many more war-time brides, I was so home-sick, I felt so lonely – day in, day out, I longed to be back in the East End of London. I missed the Thames and the busy life of the river. I missed the London voices, the Cockney accent. That sounds silly, doesn't it? But it's true. The American way of speaking took a long time to get used to.

I had more babies and that helped.

When I became pregnant again my husband, Joe, was really happy and not only his parents but all his relations (and there are plenty to contend with) seemed to take to me from then on. I have to say, though, I still felt so much closer to Peter. Not only was he my first-born, he was a reminder of London. My Cockney lad. Though you'd never think so to hear him speak. Junior won't have it. Likes to be told stories of England, but to him that is all they are, stories. He is an all-American boy, according to him and his father. Which is only natural, I suppose. He *has* grown up here, has experienced all the good things that America has to offer, been part of a large family whereas I was an only child.

Peter was eight years old, and Joe and I had had two more children, both girls, before my mother came over to visit us. It was her reaction to how we lived that set me thinking. Mum went on and on about grey British skies, the cold climate and how the damp English chill got right through to her bones. Our American home is very large and warm inside, and the sun shines outside, or at least it did while she was here. My memories of London had been rose-coloured. Her stories of poor housing and not too many jobs had me real- izing how lucky I was and what a wonderful chance Joe had given me and Peter. Not far from where we live is a tourist area. Peter and three of his cousins worked there one summer, when they were all about fourteen years old. Their fathers teach them from an early age that it is good to work. Peter enjoyed talking to British visitors and I suspect he boasted that he had been born in London.

He does say that, at some stage in his life, he would like to have a vacation in England. Now to the hard part.

How does Peter feel about you and your husband? I can't honestly answer that. He has always had a quick temper but since he has grown up it would take a hell of a lot to make him lose it. Since learning about his blood group he's been very quiet. Makes no comment. When questioned he gives no answers. We shall have to give it time.

How about James? Does he want to hear about us? Perhaps visit? How do you feel? Would you like to visit?

Writing this letter is probably the hardest thing I have ever had to do. But, then, it's doubtful that there has ever been a more heartbreaking situation.

If you will let me I'd like to keep in touch. We could write to each other about how we feel, about our sons, tell it as it happens. Don't know about you, though I'm pretty sure it must be the same, my heart aches just looking at Peter. For the first time in twenty years I do not know what to say to him. Joe feels the same. He said it is like walking on eggshells.

I hope you give it a try.

Put your feelings down on paper and send me a letter. Has to be better than doing everything through a law firm.

If you cannot bring yourself to write to me I will try to understand.

With all best wishes,

Yours,

Beryl Piviteaux.

PS

Peter is six foot two inches tall. Has dark hair with reddish tints, which the family have always said he got from his Polish grandfather. Big brown eyes. Is very intelligent. Kind and loving. Adores his two sisters.

When Joan had finished the letter her head was spinning. So many similarities! We both seem to have the same kind of feelings. Now I'm so mixed-up. One minute I didn't want to know, wasn't the least bit interested in that family. Now I feel guilty: this other mother wanted, *needed*, to know everything and anything about the boy to whom she had given birth. She wanted the truth, never mind how much it would hurt. I'm a coward, burying my head in the sand, telling myself that what I didn't know couldn't hurt me, instead of facing the fact that everything now had to be brought out into the open.

She folded the letter carefully and put it back in the envelope. She couldn't bring herself to look at the photos. Not yet. Not by herself. She'd wait until Matt came home and perhaps they could look at them together. Sighing again she scolded herself 'For God's sake, go and do something and stop feeling so sorry for yourself.'

Long past midnight Joan was still awake, turning things over and over in her mind. Matt had phoned to say he wasn't coming home that night. Very early business meeting on site in the morning, he said. He was spending the night at his mother's. Pity, she'd so badly wanted to share the letter with him. She couldn't show it to the girls. Not yet. Not before their father had been given a chance to read it.

She slipped out of bed, pulled on her dressing-gown, pushed her feet into her slippers and went downstairs. A cup of cocoa was in order, she decided. Waiting for the milk to come to the boil, her mind was on Beryl Piviteaux. For so long she had done her best to block out her and her family completely but now her attitude had changed. It had to! Wilfully disregarding this American family was no longer an option.

Like herself, Beryl had brought up a son for twenty years, had loved and cherished him, planned with such hopes for his future, which must seem so unsettled now. God alone knew, she and Jamie were close but Beryl had clung to Peter like a lifeline. She had been uprooted from the East End of London and transported to live thousands of miles away, in the midst of strangers, a totally different way of life. Joe, the husband, was among his own kith and kin but whom had that poor lass had to turn to in those early years? Was it any wonder that Peter was the love of her life? What had she called him in her letter? Her Cockney lad!

Bet she didn't even voice that thought out loud, not too often anyway. Not to all his American relatives. An all American boy is how his father saw him. As for Joe's family, seems they changed his name to Junior as soon as he arrived in the States. None of it could have been easy for Beryl.

The sound of the milk boiling over brought Joan's thoughts back to the present. She made her cocoa, wiped up the spilt milk from the top of the stove and sat down at the table. She sipped at her drink.

Jamie, my beautiful, gorgeous Jamie, isn't really mine! And poor Beryl's thoughts must be running along the same lines.

Again her mind returned to the similarities between them. She and Beryl were both only children. They had both given birth to one son and two daughters . . . God, what a mess! There was so much she wanted to say to Jamie. She wanted him to know that nothing would change, that he was still her son, Matt was still his father, Meg and Rosie were still his sisters, but how could she put into words things that she now knew were not true?

She folded her arms on the table and her head went down. Now she didn't bother to brush away her tears. She was crying not only for herself but for her girls, for Matt, her parents and even Hester, who stubbornly refused to accept the truth. She cried for the American family, and in particular Beryl, the mother who had brought up Peter, the baby to whom Joan had given birth.

'God help us all,' she murmured, then stayed still and truly wept for a long, long time.

Upstairs Meg turned over her pillow because it was damp with her tears. Her heart was thumping. She had heard her mother get up and go downstairs, had wondered whether to go after her and decided against it. What comfort could she offer? So much that had once seemed steadfast had changed.

Jamie was quiet, still loving, but distant. Was he frightened? Apprehensive as to who he was and where he belonged? He must feel as if the bottom had fallen out of his world. God knew, she would do anything to help her brother but what could she do? She was at a loss to know which way to turn.

Rosie had been distraught when Jamie had phoned to say he wouldn't be able to get home for a few weeks. 'He's gonna stay away! He's not going to come home any more!' she had sobbed. 'All because someone has told him he's not really our brother.'

It had taken Meg ages to soothe her, to reassure her sister that nothing would alter, that Jamie *was* their brother and *always* would be. She was now asking herself a question: who was going to reassure her?

Chapter Seventeen

HAVING SAID GOODBYE to his mates Jamie Pearson hurried out of the café. It was a quarter past two, he hadn't been home for three weeks and he wanted to be back in time for the family evening meal. As he walked to where his motorbike was parked he was wishing he didn't feel so nervous. For weeks now he had been saying to himself, I don't want to belong to another family. Couldn't anyone understand that he didn't? That he was more than happy being James Pearson? He had parents and grandparents who adored him and two sisters for whom he would go to the ends of the earth. Why in hell had someone had to come along and demand that he take that blood test?

He wasn't stupid. He knew it had to be true: he hadn't been brought into this world or fathered by the couple he'd always known as his mother and his father.

That was now a proven fact.

The amount of tests that had been done, nothing had

been left to chance. As the saying goes, if you wait long enough the truth *will* out.

But why now, after all these years?

To come barging into their home to tell *his* mother that the baby she'd given birth to was really in America. How many times had he been told the story of the night he'd been born. It was a miracle really that anyone in that hospital had survived and if – no, not if – a mix-up *had* occurred, no one could be blamed, not with all the chaos that must have been going on that night. Patients and staff alike must have been terrified.

As far as he could gather from the private talks he'd had with Clive Richardson, the other lad had led a good life. The parents seemed OK, loved their son and had provided well for him, so why on earth had they stirred up this hornets' nest? They had found out the truth by accident. Until then, no one had had any doubts or been unhappy within the families so why not leave well alone? He was certainly not bemoaning the fact that he should have been brought up in the USA. He'd been given every chance in life within a good, caring family and now he'd give the world not to have learnt that he didn't really belong to them.

What a mess! I'm James, known to everyone as Jamie, not Peter, with Polish ancestors. He climbed on to his bike, put on his helmet, tightened the straps beneath his chin, then sat for a while just staring into space. How could he look at his mother, knowing that he had no real claim to her? Until he had left home to go to university he could never remember a night when she hadn't kissed him good-night. As for his dad! They didn't always see eye to eye, especially on education, he was the rough and ready type who earned his living by sweat and toil, but that took nothing away from his good nature. In so many ways he was exactly like his mother, dear old Gran, the salt of the earth. She was the kind of person of whom you knew every little fault but loved them just the same.

Thinking of his dad brought back a memory that hurt. It was when they'd come out into the fresh air, having been told the results of the tests. Matt had been livid. Before they got into the car he had put his arms around Jamie, saying, 'You're my boy, aren't you? Always have been and always will be, and no damn stranger is gonna tell me different.'

It had taken a great effort on his part to get the words out but he had said, 'Of course I am, Dad.'

If only it could have been the truth!

It had been even worse with his granddad. They'd always been such good mates and now to be told that he was no relation was more than the old chap could take.

'This won't do,' Jamie muttered aloud. 'Staying away from home isn't going to solve anything. Besides, I miss them. Every single one of them.'

He kick-started the bike, the engine roared into life and he was away.

He was more than half-way home when the skies opened up and the rain fell in torrents. He shook his head to clear the water from his visor, and took his eyes off the road, just for a second. Then as he gripped his handlebars even tighter, he saw it. Too late. He leant right over to the left, hoping to take the bike swiftly to the near-side of the road and avoid the huge lorry negotiating the bend but it clipped his right leg and he went into a spin, skidding and slithering on the wet surface. The noise was deafening. He had no idea where it was coming from or where he was going. Then suddenly there was silence. At least, for Jamie there was.

Cars stopped, people got out and ran. One man shouted, 'I'll phone for an ambulance.'

'Won't do the bloke on the bike much good,' said someone.

A middle-aged man approached, saying he was a doctor. Two burly-looking workmen heaved Jamie's bike out of the way. The lad appeared to be unconscious, but having found a pulse the doctor spoke quietly and calmly: 'The ambulance will be here in a minute, son. Squeeze my hand if you can hear what I'm saying.'

There was no response.

One onlooker offered to remove Jamie's helmet.

The doctor raised his head, and very determinedly said, 'No, leave it until the ambulancemen arrive. They'll know better what to do.' He felt helpless. The lad was lying awkwardly with one leg twisted. There was a lot of blood on the road where he lay, and they wouldn't know what was wrong with his head until they could see more. The lorry driver had been lucky: apart from having had a nasty shock he appeared to be all right.

'Good God, they're taking for ever, aren't they?' said one of the men who had helped to move the bike.

'It just seems like that,' the doctor answered.

Then they heard the wail of the sirens, and finally the ambulance was there.

One ambulanceman knelt to check that there was still a pulse, and the other said, 'Best to get a drip into his arm,' to the doctor, who was cutting through the sleeve of

Jamie's leather jacket. Then, very carefully, the two ambulancemen slowly removed Jamie's helmet and gently
strapped padded boards and what looked like soft square
pillows under his head and around his face, which was
covered in blood.

Within twenty minutes the ambulance had sped off, its
sirens screaming.

By the time the six o'clock television news had finished,
Joan was worried. Jamie was always home by about four
thirty, five o'clock at the latest. She had done a roast, even
though it was a Saturday, because it was the one meal Jamie
said the university never had on the menu and it was still
his favourite. All the vegetables were dished up, the joint of
beef was on the side waiting for Matt to carve it and the
Yorkshire pudding batter was ready to go into the oven. She
liked the puddings to cook while they were eating their
starter; then she could carry them straight to the table and
show off just how much they had risen.

Meg was sitting on the settee talking to her boyfriend,
Brian Clarke. He had been invited to join them for dinner
because Meg had said she didn't want to go out this evening
as Jamie would be home. Rosie was sitting on the floor, her
head resting against her father's knees. Everything seemed
set for a happy family evening. Matt had brought some beer
and a bottle of brandy home with him, which said a lot
about how he felt to be seeing Jamie again. As a rule it took
a lot to keep Matt at home on a Saturday evening: he was
usually in the East End, touring the pubs with his brothers.

'It's foul out there,' he said, doing his best to calm Joan
down, who was pacing back and forth to the window. 'Jamie's
bound to be taking it carefully.'

By seven o'clock even he was worried.

Joan was just deciding that she had better feed them all and put Jamie's dinner in the hot cupboard to keep warm when the doorbell rang. She assumed it would be one of the lads with whom Rosie usually went to the community hall on a Saturday evening. As she was the only one on her feet she hurried to the front door. The sight of a policeman in uniform left her speechless and frightened.

'Mrs Pearson?'

'Yes.' It came out as a whisper, and fear gripped her.

'May I come in?' he asked, removing his helmet and undoing his drenched cape. 'I'll leave this in the porch, if that's all right,' he said. He wiped his feet on the doormat as Joan stepped aside.

'What's going on? What's 'appened?' Matt had appeared in the hallway. 'It's our boy, isn't it?' he asked, looking directly at the constable and placing a protective arm around his wife's shoulders.

'Yes, sir. I'm sorry to tell you that your son has been in an accident.'

'Oh, my God.' All the colour drained from Joan's face. 'Is he alive? Please tell us.'

'Yes, he is, but he was still unconscious when the ambulance got him to Kingston Hospital.'

'Kingston?' Matt queried. 'Then he wasn't too far from home. Can you tell us what happened – and how is he?'

'I know nothing of the accident, sir. I've only been told that your son has been seriously hurt and that you should get to the hospital.'

'Dear God,' Joan cried. 'What does "seriously hurt" mean? Just how bad is he?'

The constable looked uncomfortable. 'I'm sorry I can't

tell you more, I only know what I've been told. I've given you the message as it was given to me. I really think you should be getting to the hospital.'

'You're right,' Matt said, taking charge. 'I'll see you out then I'll get the car out of the garage. Thank you for coming. Yours is not an enviable job at a time like this.'

'I hope you get some good news when you arrive at the hospital. Goodnight, Mrs Pearson, goodnight, sir.' The policeman fixed his cape round his shoulders and headed out into the night.

Tears were streaming down Meg and Rosie's faces when their parents came back into the room. They had heard enough to know that their brother had been involved in a road accident and was now in hospital.

Matt was shoving his arms into his raincoat when he turned to Brian, saying, 'You'll stay 'ere with the girls till we get back, won't you?'

'Course I will, Mr Pearson, don't worry about them.'

'You'll ring as soon as you know anything, won't you, Dad?' Meg's voice was full of fear. Matt swallowed the lump that was nearly choking him and hugged his daughters in turn. 'The minute we know anything I'll be on that phone. Meg, you serve up the dinner – go on, never mind shaking your head, yer mother's gone to a lot of trouble and you three have to eat.' He turned to Brian. 'Give your folks a ring and tell them what's 'appened. They won't mind if you stay, will they?'

'Course they won't, Mr Pearson. I'll be here until you get back. And I do hope that you get some good news when you arrive at the hospital.'

Matt patted the lad's shoulder. 'Thanks, son,' he murmured, and headed for the door.

Joan pulled the belt of her coat tightly round her waist, tugged on her hat, pushed her handbag under one arm, kissed Meg, hugged Rosie, nodded to Brian and flew out after him.

Moments later they were on the way to Kingston. All the way Joan was praying, Please, God, let Jamie be all right, please don't take him from us.

Matt found a parking space near to the emergency entrance and together they ran into the building. The casualty area was ablaze with lights, and lots of people were sitting waiting, some with bandaged arms or legs. Further down was a corridor with a placard over the entrance that read, 'Treatment Area'. Matt took Joan's elbow and steered her towards the reception desk. His voice was gruff as he gave their names and asked to be directed to whichever ward his son had been taken to.

Joan's face was grey and she was trembling. The desk clerk felt sorry for her as she checked the surname and called a senior nurse. The nursing sister was efficient, yet her eyes showed that she cared as she led them both into a small private office. She made sure that they were sitting down before she began to speak. 'Your son has been taken straight to the operating theatre. He has a severe head injury. The doctors have decided to wait for a specialist. If you'd like to stay in here, where's it's quiet, one of them will come and talk to you both. He will be able to tell you more.' She went on, but Joan knew she wasn't taking in what was being said.

The sister left the room and shortly afterwards a middle-aged woman in a green overall came in bearing a tray of tea. Matt thanked her and took charge. He poured it out, then, remembering that he had once been told sweet tea was good for shock he ladled three heaped spoonfuls into one cup and stirred it well before handing it to Joan. She had taken several sips before she could bring herself to ask, 'Did the sister say that Jamie's head injury was serious?'

'Yes, she did,' he told her. 'She also said that if the surgeon does go ahead and operate it will take three to four hours, maybe longer. We just have to be patient and try not to panic.'

'I wish they'd let us see him,' Joan murmured softly. So many thoughts were going round and round in her head. Would her son end up brain-damaged? Would he die on the operating table before she had a chance to tell him she loved him? To let him know that no matter what any solicitors, doctors or members of that American family wrote or said to her he was, and always would be, her son, her one and only son. Oh, dear God, please, please, spare him. Don't take him from us. Not like this.

Matt felt at a loss. He could see that Joan was torturing herself. He took a deep breath. 'You just 'ave t' believe he'll pull through. Our Jamie's a tough nut, he won't give in, you'll see. Come on, love, drink yer tea.'

Joan was grateful that Matt was there. What if he'd been off on his usual Saturday-night binge with his brothers?

'I'm just going to find a telephone and ring the girls. I won't be long. You'll be all right? Though what the 'ell I'm going t' say t' them God only knows.' He left her and all Joan could think of was that her Jamie was lying on an operating table and the hospital staff wouldn't let her go to him.

Later, hand in hand, she and Matt walked the corridors and went outside to stand in the covered walkway feeling the cold air of the dark night. The rain continued to pour down relentlessly. When they returned, the sister approached them again. 'Mr Pearson, one of the doctors would like to see you both.'

'May we see our son now?' Joan's request was more of a plea.

'Just a little longer, Mrs Pearson. The doctor waiting for you will explain your son's condition. Give you all the details, well, as far as he is able.'

Joan turned quickly to stare at Matt and he was alarmed by the terrified look on her face. She hesitated, seemed unable to move, to put one foot in front of the other.

Matt grasped her arm. 'Come on. At least we'll know what's going on.'

They made their way down the corridor to where the doctor stood waiting. The very sight of him had Joan trembling from head to foot. He was still wearing what she took to be a surgical gown and a funny crumpled cap on his head. A mask had been pushed down to hang round his neck.

'Is our boy all right?' Joan blurted out. She had to know. Was Jamie alive and if so in what state?

The doctor directed his reply to Matt. 'Mr Pearson, your son has come through the operation. He's a well-built lad, strong constitution, which is all in his favour. His leg was broken, and he's suffered some internal bleeding. It's the head injury that was the problem, and we've done all we can for the time being. Now it's just a question of waiting. With such a head injury many a lad would not have made it this far. But James has, and that has to be a good sign, though I have to add there's a long way to go yet.'

'Thank you,' Matt said gruffly, holding out his hand to shake the doctor's. 'Will we be able to see him?'

'We'd rather he wasn't disturbed. We're going to keep him where we can monitor everything. Later on, maybe in the morning, he'll be transferred to a side ward.' He turned to Joan, who was staring into space, and wondered if she had taken in any of what he had said. 'Our main concern at the moment is his breathing, but that's to be expected with this type of injury. You can just take a peep at him. Don't be afraid of the tubes – he'll look so much better when you come back tomorrow.' The last sentence was spoken without conviction.

Nothing that anyone had said had prepared either Joan or Matt for what they saw when they went into the recovery room where Jamie lay. There was a breathing tube in his throat, and more tubes and machines seemed to be attached to all parts of the bed. His head was swathed in bandages. The small part of his face that was visible was so battered that Joan wasn't even sure it was Jamie who was lying there.

Matt was sobbing openly, but Joan took a deep breath and bent over Jamie, gently stroking his hand, which lay on top of the sheet. All she could think of was the night he'd been born. Both of them could so easily have died that night, but she had had him now for twenty glorious years. He was one of the best things that had ever happened to her. But suddenly everything was going wrong. How was it possible that so much could change so quickly? First to be told that he wasn't the boy to whom she had given birth and now this accident. Would he go out of her life for ever now? That couldn't happen. She wouldn't let it. He had to come home, be part of their lives. A big part: play pranks on his sisters, tease them, shout at them; leave his bedroom in such a mess that she would shout at him. I'll never have a go at you again, no matter what mess you make, she vowed silently. Just wake up and be well. Come back to us. Bring your girlfriends home, let me see you get married and have the joy of holding grandchildren who look just like you did as a baby.

Matt wiped his eyes and put out a hand to his wife. 'I'm going to take you 'ome now. We both need to get some rest and, anyway, the girls will be waiting up. We'll come back first thing in the morning.'

'All right.' She touched Jamie's hand.

Matt took his wife's arm and gently led her out of that strange, silent room. He helped her on with her coat and held her tight for several minutes. As he slowly released her he saw such deep sadness in her eyes that it frightened him. Never in all the years they had been together had he seen her suffering as she was at this moment.

'He doesn't deserve this,' Joan whispered.

Matt nodded but stayed silent. To himself he was agreeing, but he was also thinking that if everyone got their just deserts in life then where would we be?

Without thinking about it he found himself praying silently. Please, God, spare my son. I'll never ask for another thing if just this once you listen to me. I've not been the best of husbands but I can't stand to see my Joan suffer like this. And as to losing our son, it doesn't bear thinking about. Please let him pull through.

'How's Jamie?' Meg asked before they had set foot inside the door.

'Pretty poorly,' Matt told her. Then, doing his best to smile at his daughters, he added, 'But he's going to be OK. One of the doctors who helped operate on him said he's come through remarkably well. Now we have to wait and see.'

'I'm going to make us all some tea,' Rosie said.

Joan gave her a hug. Rosie was always so kind-hearted and thoughtful.

'I've left the car in the drive,' Matt said to Brian. 'I'll run you home.'

'If it's all the same to you, Mr Pearson, I'd like to stay here. I can kip down on your big sofa. I've already told my parents that I'd more than likely stay the night.'

Matt remembered something. 'Have you kids eaten anything?'

'Yes,' Meg answered softly. 'I dished up the dinner. Can I get you and Mum something, even if it's just a sandwich?'

'No, darling,' Joan answered quickly. She felt that food would choke her.

'Do you want anything, Dad?'

He shook his head. It wasn't fair: he should be looking after his family but he couldn't protect any of them from this.

Rosie's face was full of sadness. 'Our Jamie will be all right, won't he, Dad?'

Poor Matt. This was more than he could bear. It was as though an icy hand was touching his heart. He looked away from her. He couldn't lie to her and he didn't know the answer so he said nothing. Rosie stood beside him for a minute, then knelt down, placed her arms around his neck and cried. Yet somehow Matt felt comforted.

He heard Meg yawn. 'Come on, let's get you all to bed. Tomorrow everything will seem better.' He glanced across the room to where his wife was laying out a pillow and a blanket for Brian's makeshift bed. All tomorrows were uncertain, he thought, but none more so than this one.

Chapter Eighteen

BY TEN O'CLOCK on Sunday morning Joan and Matt were back at the hospital. For two hours they had sat in uncomfortable chairs in the waiting room. They hadn't been told much except that Jamie was holding his own, and so far they had not been allowed to see him. It didn't make sense to Joan, and Matt was getting more than a little irritated. It was a relief when, at last, a sister came and said the doctor had finished his rounds and would like to talk to them.

His first statement hit Joan like a fist in the face. Jamie's condition was so severe that he would have to stay in hospital for some time. But he had survived the operation well. It would be several days before they would know how complete his recovery would be.

Oh, my God! Joan's hands shook.

Matt wanted to put questions to the surgeon who had done the operation, but was told that was not possible.

Sister beckoned a young nurse and asked her to take them

along to spend a little time with Jamie, who had been moved into a side ward.

Joan stood beside the bed. She didn't dare look at Matt.

If anything, Jamie looked worse than he had last night. The top half of his face was free of bandages and both eyes were badly bruised. She clutched Matt's hand. Someone brought a chair and she sat down beside the bed.

Matt sat next to her, and his heart ached as he listened to his wife talking softly to their boy. 'Meg and Rosie send you all their love. Rosie said she got you that book you wanted from the library. Your dad is here . . . We both love you so much. Everyone does. We haven't told your gran yet. Can you imagine if she comes here to visit you?' Joan gave a foolish laugh, which she smothered. 'Knowing Amy, she'll want to take over. Only she can really take care of her Jamie. That's what she'll tell them.'

Hysterical laughter and tears were getting mixed as Joan continued to whisper, her face close to Jamie's bandaged head, without so much as a flicker of recognition from the still figure in the bed.

It was early afternoon when Matt went home. He had done his best to persuade Joan to go with him, but there was no budging her and the nurses said it was all right for her to stay. He said he would see that the girls were OK, have a bath, change his clothes and come back for her at about six o'clock.

Later, a young nurse suggested that Joan have a break. 'I'll walk with you, show you where the canteen is,' she offered. All the way there she chatted about how big and strong James was, and how that would help in his recovery.

'I can't see any of his hair,' Joan remarked, more to herself than to the nurse.

'That's because his head has been shaved.'

Once inside the cafeteria the nurse got Joan a cup of coffee and a packet of biscuits, then left her. Joan didn't hear anyone approach the table until she felt a hand on her shoulder. Looking up she saw John Chapman. He was the picture of health, wearing a dark grey suit and a crisp white shirt.

'Mary and Linsey told me the sad news. They've been to your house this morning and Meg and Rosie explained where you were, but they said Matt was with you.'

'He was. He's not long left, gone to see if the girls are all right.'

'Have you seen Jamie today?'

She nodded.

'How was he?'

Joan shrugged. 'Hard to tell. He hasn't come round yet.'

'Jamie's a strong lad. I'm sure he'll be all right.'

'Yeah. Maybe. Everyone keeps telling me he will be,' she said.

'You've drunk your coffee, but weren't you supposed to eat the biscuits?'

Joan tried to smile. 'They're too dry, they'd stick in my throat. Besides, I'm not the least bit hungry.' Then, changing the subject, she asked, 'What are you doing here on a Sunday afternoon?'

'Visiting a colleague. I've brought him a book. He's upstairs. Had a heart-attack, not allowed to get up. Now, tell me, when did you last eat?'

'I'm all right. Really. I just don't think I could eat just now.'

'You're going to have to try,' he told her, quietly but firmly. 'Come on, on your feet. Come to the counter and choose something hot. It need only be something light.'

Joan sighed. 'OK,' she said reluctantly.

At the counter he took a tray, leant forward and spoke quietly to a motherly woman, who was arranging an assortment of food. Then, turning to Joan, he smiled. 'You have a choice, poached egg on toast or scrambled egg.'

'A poached egg would be fine, thank you.'

'I'll bring it over to you when it's ready,' the assistant said.

John thanked her, then ushered Joan to a table, before going back to the counters. 'Don't know about you,' he said, 'but too much coffee makes me thirsty so I've bought tea for us both. You going to be mother?'

He chatted, Joan half listened, and then her meal was brought to her. It didn't seem right to her to be sitting here, eating hot food, talking to a neighbour with whom she had never been over-friendly. Jamie was lying unconscious, her girls were at home with no Sunday dinner, and Matt was having a hard job to cope with life at the moment. She managed to eat the egg and most of the toast, then laid down her knife and fork and thanked him.

John's quiet voice droned on as if in the far distance. She never realized her head had dropped forward and she had dozed off.

It was some time later when she woke with a start to find Matt watching her. There was no sign of John Chapman.

Matt looked at her for a long moment, not sure what to say to her, then glanced at his watch. He'd been to see Jamie. There was no change: he was in a deep coma. This was all too much for Matt: he needed a pint. In fact he needed several pints. What with the girls inconsolable, he was at his wits' end.

'Come on, Joan,' he pleaded, reaching a hand across the

table. 'I'll come with you to say goodnight to Jamie and then I'll take you home. You'll be all right with Meg and Rosie, won't you?'

'I don't understand,' she answered, rubbing the sleep from her eyes. 'Where are you going?'

'To see my mother. She must be very cut up about all this.'

Joan knew there was more to it than he was letting on. What he wanted was to go drinking with his brothers. Well, who could blame him? She wanted to ask him if he'd be home that night, but it would be late before he even got to his mother's and she knew what the answer would be.

It was ten o'clock on the Monday morning as Joan stood in her kitchen, trying to decide what to do next. She had come downstairs at seven and rung the hospital. Jamie was comfortable, whatever that meant, otherwise no change. She had been right in her assumption that Matt would stay up in the East End. He had probably had so much to drink that he would have been incapable of driving home. Like a zombie, she had made a pot of tea and taken a cup up to each of the girls' bedrooms, standing awhile gazing at their faces, which looked so peaceful while asleep. An early-morning kiss and cuddle had been a good start to the day. The three had breakfasted together, just cornflakes and toast, and she had promised to have a good dinner ready for them when they got home that evening. At the doorstep Rosie had turned back. The pitiful look on her young face made Joan's heart turn over. 'Mum,' she said, 'today please ask when we can visit Jamie.' Meg was nodding.

'I will. I promise. I do tell him all the time that you ask about him and send him your love.'

'But you said he can't hear what you're saying.' Rosie was on the verge of tears.

'We can't be sure of that,' her mother insisted. 'According to the staff nurse who was on duty last night, he might be able to hear everything. Perhaps it's just a matter of time until he responds.'

Rosie looked at her as she absorbed what her mother had said, then she asked another awkward question. 'Why didn't Dad come home last night?'

'By the time he got to your gran's it must have been late and I guess he went with your uncles for a drink. He's just as cut up about Jamie as we are. I think it's probably done him some good to stay over and talk to his brothers.'

'Oh.' Rosie looked relieved.

Meg guessed what her mother was feeling. She had already spoken to her about visiting Jamie and Joan's answer had been frank: 'Try to keep Rosie off the subject as much as you can, sweetheart, because we can't let her see Jamie at the moment. I'd rather you waited a bit as well, really.'

'Just tell me about him, please, Mum.'

'Well, for a start he has no hair. His head and more than half his face are covered in bandages. What would frighten her most is all the tubes and machines. When he's a bit better . . . when he comes round . . . we'll take her then.' That's what she had said, but Meg knew that even as her mother spoke she was fighting tears and praying that it would soon be the truth.

It was with a sigh of relief that Joan had closed the front door behind them. Now she had washed and dressed and was undecided whether to go straight to the hospital or wait until the morning rounds had taken place.

She had tried to concentrate on jobs to be done – rooms

to be tidied, washing put to soak, vegetables prepared for dinner that night, all the little things that still had to be coped with despite the trouble that had come so unexpectedly into their lives.

The ringing of the front doorbell startled her. She opened the door to find John Chapman on her doorstep. 'Good morning,' he said. 'I just wanted to offer my services in any way that might be of help.'

'Oh.' Joan was taken aback. This was so unexpected. 'That's very kind of you.'

'I know you don't drive so if you need a lift to the hospital at any time you've only to ask. I am a writer, I work from home so am freely available. Or perhaps you'd like me to keep an eye on the girls at the weekend. It would be no bother, you know. They get on well with Linsey and Mary.'

Joan stepped back. 'Would you like to come in for a minute?' It was the least she could offer since he was so kind.

'I owe you an apology,' she said, once they were seated at the kitchen table. 'You were kind enough to buy me a meal yesterday and I repaid you by falling asleep.'

He threw back his head and laughed. 'I felt guilty leaving you. You didn't look at all comfortable but it seemed such a pity to wake you. You needed the rest, you were exhausted, and I couldn't stay. I had to get back to get my girls' tea. Not that they couldn't have fended for themselves but I'd told them I wouldn't be long.'

'I did feel better for that sleep, and Matt was there when I woke up.'

Without asking, Joan set out two cups, cream and sugar, and lit the gas beneath the coffee-pot. Then she said, 'You cope very well on your own with your daughters. My two are full of praise for you. I'm just afraid that they take advantage, you running them about as you do.'

'Never think that,' he said sounding stern, but he was smiling as he said it. 'It's a pleasure, really it is. I'd do anything for my two and your two are good company, all of them being around the same age.'

'Must have been very difficult at first, coping on your own,' Joan remarked.

'In one way you could say that, but then again it was a great relief when my wife finally made the break. Everyone seemed to know what was going on except me. Even at the beginning you couldn't have said we had a good marriage.' He paused, as if deep in thought. 'Though out of it came Linsey and Mary, and for those two I shall always be grateful to my ex-wife. They fill my life.'

Joan remembered what Rosie had said on the day he had picked them up for tennis: that his daughters wished he'd find another ladyfriend. Joan felt sorry for him: he was an attractive man, kind-hearted and thoughtful. 'Now your girls are almost off your hands maybe you will meet someone else,' she ventured sympathetically.

'No, I don't think so. I get stuck into my work so I'm happy enough, and as long as my girls are too, that's all I ask.'

Joan poured coffee for them both. He took his black with no sugar. Joan helped herself to cream and sugar.

'Are you going to the hospital this morning?' he asked.

'Not yet. I'm going to see my parents and my nan. Then I expect my dad will go with me to see Jamie.'

'Oh, I didn't realize your folk lived nearby but, come to think of it, I have seen them here on several occasions, and Meg and Rosie often speak of them.'

'They're only at Merton Park. I can get a bus from the main road.'

John Chapman drained his cup, stood up and said, 'No need for that. My car is outside. If you're ready I'll willingly take you.'

Joan hesitated. She had been hoping that Matt would have rung by now. Of course she could phone him at the office but ten to one she would only get the girl who worked there. As it was Monday morning Matt and Stan would be out touring the sites, setting the men on for the week. The offer of a lift was pleasing: she didn't feel like standing about waiting for a bus and she could always ring Matt when she got to her mum's. 'I'll be five or ten minutes, if you're sure you don't mind.'

'Of course I don't. I'll wash the cups while you're getting yourself ready.'

Joan was touched, and didn't know what more to say than, 'Thank you.'

Not a word passed between them until the car was caught in traffic at South Wimbledon.

'You turn right here, then take the second left,' Joan directed him.

Within minutes they were outside the house. John switched off the engine, got out of the car, came round to her side and held open the door. 'Now, don't forget, if you need me just ring. I wrote my number down and left it on your hall table, though I'm pretty sure that either of your girls could have given it to you.' He grinned. 'They ring my two often enough.'

As soon as she was safely on the pavement he waved and drove away.

She had thanked him again, but it didn't feel enough.

She was pondering: was John Chapman a thoroughly nice man, a real gentleman? Or was he just a little bit smarmy?

Don't be so unkind, she chided herself. It's probably that I'm used to Matt. A rough diamond if ever there was one. But smarmy? No. Never. You couldn't use that word to describe Matt.

Chapter Nineteen

HER DAD OPENED the front door. Both Daphne and Hester were out. Bill Harvey held out his arms, and Joan rushed into them. 'Am I glad to see you,' Bill said, and he kissed the top of her head. Once he had her settled in an armchair beside the fire he bent down and took a good look at his daughter. He was appalled: the dark circles under her eyes looked terrible. 'Have you phoned the hospital this morning?' he asked.

'Yes, about seven o'clock.'

'And?'

Suddenly she couldn't find the words. Bill watched as she tried to hold back the tears. 'They said there was no change but that Jamie had had a comfortable night.'

'Has Matt gone to work?'

'I don't know. He didn't come home last night.' She had spoken without thinking.

Bill straightened up and patted her shoulder.

Joan sensed that her father was angry with Matt. 'What

with all that has happened already since Christmas, I don't think Matt can face much more,' she said quietly, not daring to voice what was really going through her mind.

'Oh? And what about you? Are your shoulders so much broader than his?'

'Please, Dad, you mustn't judge Matt. He really cares about Jamie, honestly he does. He just doesn't know how to handle it all.'

'And you do? You can carry all the burden on your own? Doesn't it make you angry that he's not here with you?'

Joan sighed. 'He never left me all Saturday night, and all day yesterday he stayed at the hospital. I think he felt he just had to get a break. If there was anything he could do . . . He feels so . . . helpless, I suppose.'

'I'll come to the hospital with you this morning. We'll leave a note for your mum to tell her where we've gone.'

The first person they saw when they got out of the car was Matt. He was standing outside the main entrance. He came running as soon as he spotted them. 'I was trying to make up my mind what to do. I went in to work this morning just to set things straight in the office, then I phoned home and got no answer so I came on here. I've been to the ward. Sister said there had been no change since last night and that the doctor would talk to us as soon as the ward rounds were finished.' He took Joan's arm and squeezed it, then turned to Bill. 'Bloody bad business all round, ain't it?'

Joan sighed. He had said nothing about not having come home last night and yet, in a way, she felt sorry for him.

Those were Bill's sentiments too: Matt looked spruce enough, well turned-out, clean-shaven, his short thick dark hair was neat and tidy yet somehow his spirit had been broken.

Later, the three stood in a group and listened to what the surgeon had to say: 'There has been no sign of an improvement in your son and we need to operate again.' Joan would have liked to put so many questions to this stocky, broad-shouldered man, who held her son's life in his hands. Instead she listened quietly as he talked to Matt and her father, and a few minutes later Matt was signing the necessary papers. 'We can see Jamie now for a little while. They won't be operating until later on today,' Matt told them, doing his best to smile.

Her father and Matt looked awkward as they sat side by side beside the bed opposite Joan.

She was leaning across the bed, holding Jamie's hand and talking softly to him. Now and again she stroked his arm. It seemed a long, long while, and it was something of a relief when a nurse quietly told them they must leave as it was time to prepare James for surgery.

The surgeon had said that he did not know how long the operation would take, which in itself was frightening. What were they looking for? Would they be able to repair the damage inside his head? All three were trying hard not to think of what might happen in the operating theatre.

They came outside into the damp, miserable April day and stood like three lost souls. 'I suggest we all go home to your mother,' Bill said quietly. 'She'll be only too glad to see you both, and she'll want to feed you. Besides, it will relieve your nan's mind if she hears first hand from you that Jamie's holding his own.'

Joan looked up sharply. 'Are you suggesting that we lie to her?'

'No, of course not,' Bill assured her. 'Jamie *is* holding his own so far, and we've got to hang on to that.'

'Good idea,' Matt said. 'I'll leave my car here if you'll run us back later on, Bill. But while you're getting yours out I'll pop back inside, let the ward sister know where we'll be if they need to telephone us.'

It was a long afternoon. After a tearful welcome from Daphne and Hester they had struggled to eat a late lunch but had little to say to each other. Hester started to reminisce once or twice about Jamie and the girls when they were small, but Joan couldn't bring herself to join in. Most of the time she sat quietly, lost in thought, wondering how she was going to answer Beryl Piviteaux's letter.

Matt was watching the clock, half hoping that the telephone would ring but dreading the thought that it might be bad news. At half past five he got to his feet. By then he and Joan looked as if they couldn't take much more. 'Come on, Joan,' he said. 'We'd best get back to the hospital. D'you mind running us there, Bill?'

'Course not. I'll just get my keys.'

First Daphne and then Hester held Joan long and hard. 'We'll be praying,' her mother said, as they stood on the doorstep. 'You'll ring straight away if there's any news?'

Joan nodded, tempted to say, 'Don't get your hopes up too high.'

When they arrived at the intensive care unit the sister said, 'James hasn't been brought back up yet,' so once again they sat in the waiting room.

It began to get dark outside and it started to rain again, spitting and splashing against the uncurtained windows, making them both feel grateful at least that they were inside in the dry.

The same stocky doctor came in to them at a quarter to seven.

'How did it go?' Matt leapt to his feet and stared down into the eyes of the shorter man.

The doctor smiled. 'We're all very hopeful. It went better than we expected.'

Matt was getting tired of that word hopeful. 'Please, would you mind explaining that in plain words,' he said.

'During the night we were worried about James. There was too much pressure in his skull from when his head hit the ground. We have succeeded in relieving most of that and now we feel there's every reason to believe that your son will make a full recovery.'

Joan wanted to stand up and thank him, but her legs wouldn't support her. She just sat there, saying silently over and over again, thank you, God.

The doctor was still talking to Matt. Most of their conversation went over Joan's head until she heard him say, 'It's a question of waiting now to see how he does and, of course, how long he remains in the coma.'

'You mean, he still won't come round and talk to us?' Matt was dismayed.

'Mr Pearson, the kind of injury your son sustained requires patience. Only time will give us all the answers we need.'

Matt sighed heavily and the surgeon turned to look down at Joan. 'Your son really is holding his own, Mrs Pearson,' he said gently. 'He's not out of danger yet but he's come though this second operation really well and that is an encouraging sign. For the next twenty-four hours we're going to keep him on strong medication. I suggest you both go home and get some rest. I promise we'll call you if there is any news.'

He shook hands with them and left. Matt and Joan looked

as if they had had the stuffing knocked out of them. 'If only there was something we could do,' Matt said miserably.

Joan raised her head and asked the question that had been niggling at the back of her mind since seven o'clock that morning. 'Matt, why didn't you come home last night?'

'I had too much t' drink so I stayed at my mother's,' he answered calmly.

'No, you didn't,' she said, without raising her voice. 'I telephoned Amy as soon as I got out of bed this morning because I was worried about you.'

'Does it matter?' he queried gruffly. 'I had a few too many. I was with Stan.'

'Yes, I know you went drinking with your brother, but he left you just after eleven o'clock.'

'What is this?' Matt's face had turned a deep red and there was an expression in his eyes that she hadn't seen for ages. Sheer rage was what she was looking at. 'Did you ring round all of the family just t' check on me?'

'No,' Joan answered. 'While I was talking to your mum, Stan walked in and he hedged, just said he'd get you to ring me as soon as you walked into the office. But you didn't ring, did you? I couldn't help wondering who you did spend the night with.'

Half of her wanted to push it further and ask, 'What about all the other Saturday nights you've spent away from home? Were you at your mother's, as you always said you were?' But now was not the time. All she said was, 'Maybe you'd like to tell me about it sometime,' in little more than a whisper. Matt looked away and didn't answer.

Slowly she got to her feet. 'Shall we go home? The girls will be worried.'

Chapter Twenty

JOAN WAS LISTENING to Matt tell Meg and Rosie what had taken place at the hospital that day. Their brother, he explained, had suffered a severe head injury. The first operation had not quite done the trick so today the surgeons had performed a second. 'Now all we have to do is wait for Jamie to come round, and by the time he's recovered from two lots of surgery he's going to be fine.'

The girls had prepared a meal and Matt opened a bottle of port, telling them that one glass would make them all sleep better. Somehow they passed the time until Meg and Rosie said they were going up to bed.

Joan went to the foot of the stairs with her girls, kissing them both in turn and saying, 'Goodnight, my darlings, try to get a good night's sleep. God bless you both.'

Rosie hesitated on the third stair. 'Mum,' her voice trembled, 'is it true that our Jamie's going to be all right? An' if it is, can I come with you to see him tomorrow?'

Meg looked her mother straight in the eye, and her face

showed that she, too, would like an answer to that same question.

'Well, my pet, the surgeon did say we all had to show a great deal of patience. Jamie is still in a coma but they're now sure it's only a matter of time and then . . .' Then what? She didn't know herself so how could she tell her girls? 'I will promise you one thing. The moment they say it's all right for Jamie to have visitors you two will be the first.'

Rosie looked doubtful and Meg put her arm around her sister and said, 'Come into my bed for a little while. Bring a book and we'll keep the light on and read together.'

Back in the sitting room Matt had his legs stretched out and was reading the paper.

'You shouldn't have told the girls that,' she said, more loudly than she had meant to. There were so many questions she wanted to ask him and now that the girls had gone to bed she could begin.

'Told them what?' he asked angrily. He knew that he was going to have to face up to the fact that Joan had caught him on the hop.

'You told them that Jamie was going to be fine. We don't know that for sure.'

'Oh, for Christ's sake! Now you're splitting hairs. That surgeon said our son has a good chance of making a full recovery. What more do you want? A bloody guarantee? Our girls are going through hell. They love Jamie t' bits. What was I supposed t' tell them, eh? Go on, answer me. What d'yer want me t' tell them? If it 'elps them through this it can't be bad, and if the worst comes t' the worst, well, we'll all 'ave t' face that, if an' when it 'appens.'

He was shaking with temper, and Joan couldn't stop herself saying, 'Feeling guilty, are you?'

'And what's that supposed t' mean?' he yelled. He hated the way this conversation was going, but he knew he was cornered.

'I was merely asking about last night. So far you still haven't said where you spent it.'

'It's got bugger all t' do with you.' He hadn't meant to say that, but there was no turning away now.

'Oh, Matt, I think it's got everything to do with me. Many a Saturday you take yourself off and I've never questioned where you go or who you're with, but this time you deliberately lied to me.'

'I've asked you t' come often enough but you just don't like drinking in pubs.' Matt was seeking any excuse he could think of.

'This wasn't a Saturday night it was Sunday, and the pubs close at ten o'clock. You said you were at your mother's, and by chance I found out you weren't, so is it too difficult to tell me who you spent the night with?' Joan was finding it hard to control her own temper.

'All right. OK. So you found out. You sure you want t' know the ins an' outs?'

Joan had thought she knew what his answer was going to be, but this outright admission knocked her for six. She had been hoping he would deny everything, come up with some plausible excuse. She hadn't wanted it to be true. But now he'd told her it was. It had to be faced.

'How long, Matt?'

He didn't answer her.

'Tell me, please. Has it been a regular thing? Who is she? Do we know each other?'

'I'm not going into all the ruddy details with you, Joan, so just leave it, will you?'

'No. I need a few answers. I think you owe me that much. Is it just a fling or has it been going on for a long time? Maybe all these years since we moved away from the East End.'

Matt sat down and stared at her. 'I should have put a stop to it ages ago,' he said, sounding confused.

'Is it serious, then?' Joan didn't want to know but felt compelled to ask.

For a long time he didn't answer. 'No, it isn't. Not on my part it isn't, but how can I make you believe that?'

'What d'you mean, "ages ago"? So it has been a long-term thing? And I'm asking you again, who is she and do I know her?'

'It began when we first moved here. I missed me mates and I missed the pub life. Then I put a stop to it. It only started up again when Clive Richardson appeared on our doorstep.'

'If it's a she, how can you say it was because you missed your mates?'

'Well, she used to get in the pubs I used with me mates. She was always on her own. Her 'usband was killed on the docks. I felt sorry for her. She was left with four kids.'

'I can't take this in,' Joan said slowly. 'First you say you took up with her again when you found out that Jamie was not your true son. Some way to get yerself over that shock, I must say. Then you're telling me she's a woman with four kids, so how come she could afford to go drinking on Saturday nights in the same pubs that you and your brothers used? What kind of a woman is she?'

'She's not a bad woman. She copes as best she can. She's not as intelligent as you but she always speaks highly of you.'

'God Almighty, so it is someone I know!'

'Yes.' For the first time Matt looked sheepish. 'Doris Shepherd, our next-door neighbour when we lived in Bull Yard. She got put into one of those high-rise flats and . . . I don't know . . . I guess I've always felt sorry for her. She needed a bit of comfort . . . someone t' talk to more than anything else. I did stop seeing her ages ago, more than three years, but then, well, I was almost out of my mind thinking we was going to lose Jamie.'

'Stop it. Just stop it, please.' Joan felt that if he said another word she'd kill him. She was asking herself why had she been so stupid. Out every weekend with his brothers! Those oh-so-important darts matches that meant he had to stay the night away from home.

Matt was watching her carefully. He ran his hand through his thick hair. 'In a way I'm glad it's all out in the open.'

For the life of her Joan couldn't understand why it had happened. Maybe if the other woman had been some London high-flyer, someone well groomed and sophisticated, even someone who was really beautiful, but Doris Shepherd! She had had four kids even when they lived next door to her. They must be all grown-up by now. She couldn't take it all in. Too much had happened.

'I'll knock it off. I swear t' God I will. Look,' he held out his hands, 'I don't expect you t' understand and certainly not forgive me. But listen t' me. Please, Joan, give me a chance. Let's concentrate on helping our girls to cope and praying that Jamie will come through with flying colours. Then perhaps you'll believe me when I say I will deal with this.'

Joan remained silent.

'I can't figure myself out,' Matt said, breaking the silence and making Joan jump.

'I'd made the break all that time ago, and you weren't hurt cos you were none the wiser. Then this bloody affair with the American family cropped up and I went to pieces. It was the daftest thing I've ever done in my life. Joan, can you believe me, please? I know I sound pathetic but I am sorry. I really regret going back to her.'

Tears were glistening in Joan's eyes as she and Matt looked at each other across the room.

'You deserve better than me,' he said, so quietly that Joan burst into tears. 'Can I make you a cup of tea?' He didn't know what else to say.

Through her tears Joan was smiling. To her knowledge Matt had never made a cup of tea in his life. 'Yes, please,' she murmured.

Twenty minutes later they were seated at the kitchen table and Joan was sipping quite a decent cup of tea.

'Joan . . . I do love you. I know it will take time for . . . I'm sorry,' he said softly, and made no move to stop her when she got to her feet.

'I'm whacked,' she told him. 'I have to go to bed.' Then she picked up her cup of tea and went out of the room.

Upstairs she closed the bedroom door and turned the key in the lock, then sat on the edge of her bed and finished her tea.

This year was a third of the way through. It would be May soon, springtime. New life, new beginnings. Could life throw anything else at her? She had had to face the truth that her dearly beloved son was not hers at all. Then that same lad had almost got himself killed and was by no means out of the woods. To top it all she had learnt that her husband had been having an affair, for a very long time, with a woman who had four children. All in all that didn't say much for her, did it? As she climbed into bed she was praying that 1965 wouldn't hold any more unpleasant surprises.

It was some time later that she heard Matt's unsteady footsteps as he came up the stairs. She listened as he turned the door-handle. Then came a terrific thud as he kicked at the door, then a string of swear words. He had been drinking. Since she had come up to bed he must have hit the bottle hard. Even when he moved from the landing the noise didn't stop. Downstairs he was banging about like a madman. She hoped against hope that the girls would have the sense to stay in their room; certainly their father must have woken them up. Only someone stone deaf could have slept through the racket he was making.

Joan knew what was biting him: she hadn't acted in the way he had wanted and expected her to. She hadn't crawled, hadn't said she understood or that she would forgive and forget, hadn't fallen into his arms or pleaded with him to go on loving her. In other words he had come off worst and because of that *he* felt hard done by and had let his temper get the better of him. What had been his main excuse? The fact that so much had happened, especially dealing with the solicitors over who were Jamie's rightful parents.

He couldn't take any more? What about *me*? He was always drumming into her that women were the weaker sex. Finally the noise lessened, the house was quiet, and Joan, exhausted, fell into a deep sleep.

Chapter Twenty-One

JOAN LOOKED DOWN at her son. He looked better, or was it her imagination? He still hadn't opened his eyes or said a word. Now and again he seemed restless, as if he was struggling to come out of the coma, and the nurses kept telling her that that was a good sign.

She leant back in her chair and stretched her arms above her head. She was trying to decide whether to go to the cafeteria for a hot drink, or whether to go home and make dinner for the girls.

The clock on the wall of this single room showed it was just coming up to two o'clock. It was Thursday, she reminded herself. Tomorrow would be the start of another weekend, and she shuddered to think what might happen.

She hadn't seen Matt since that awful Monday night. She had come downstairs on the Tuesday morning to find the living room a shambles and Matt gone. How could he do this, with Jamie still so ill? Every day she had gone through the motions of seeing the girls off to work then spending as much time as she could at the hospital. Now it was as if she didn't have the energy to get to her feet.

A nurse came out from behind her glass partition and said quietly, 'The front office have just rung through. Your mother-in-law is in Reception and would like to talk to you.'

'Oh.' Joan was flummoxed. Amy? Here? She'd made the journey? 'Sorry,' she stammered, trying to smile. 'I was just making up my mind to have a break, thank you.'

My God, look at the change in her, Amy thought, as she watched Joan come down the corridor. 'How's Jamie?' she asked. 'And you? How are you? I just had t' come.'

Joan felt Amy's arms wrap round her and she sighed. 'I don't know what you're doing here but, Amy, I was never more pleased to see anyone in my whole life. Jamie seems a bit better but actually there's no change. He doesn't even open his eyes.'

The two were feeling awkward now. Joan patted Amy's shoulder and broke free. 'We can't talk here, not with all this hustle an' bustle going on. I was about to go and have something to drink so shall we save all the questions till we're sitting down?'

'Those words are sheer magic,' Amy declared. 'One, me feet are killing me, and two, I could murder a cup of tea.'

Joan linked her arm through her mother-in-law's and felt Amy pull her close and squeeze her tight. It felt safe and comfortable as they walked along slowly together. When there was a sticky bun and a cup of tea in front of them it was Amy who opened the conversation. 'You must 'ave a 'undred an' one questions you want t' ask me. First off, I expect you wanna know 'ave I seen Matt. Well, the answer is no, I 'aven't. But I 'ave kept tabs on him an' he's been with our Stan for the past three days. He knows what I'll 'ave t' say t' him an' he's steering well clear of me.'

Joan shook her head. 'Did you know about Doris Shepherd?'

'Well, when you first moved away I suspected it, but I buried me 'ead in the sand, so t' speak. It wasn't none of my business. Stan dropped 'ints from time t' time. Always said his brother was a bloody fool. Besides, what could I 'ave done? Matt's a grown man. Honest t' God, though, I'd no idea it 'ad started up again.'

'Matt told me it was only since Clive Richardson came on the scene and we've had all this trouble with blood tests and the knowledge that Jamie wasn't our true son.'

'Yeah, Stan said he was using that as an excuse.' Amy sighed. 'Don't make my son much of a man, does it? But I never knew. Not this time. And that's the gospel truth. I'd 'ave torn him off a strip or two, leaving you at a time like this and for what? A woman older than 'imself with four grown-up children. I never even 'ad a suspicion, not until Stan came t' me this morning an' said Matt had been on a binge for three days now and he didn't know what t' do about it. How come you suddenly found out what was going on?'

'It was when I phoned you last Monday morning and asked to speak to Matt. You said he wasn't there, then Stan arrived and sounded so guilty, doing his best to cover Matt's tracks. I knew Matt hadn't been with him either.'

'Oh, Joan, what a mess.' Amy gulped some tea, then went on, 'I don't want the two of you t' split up. These last four months must 'ave been a ruddy nightmare for yer an' I'd give me right arm t' be able to do something t' help. I keep asking meself, what is there that anyone can do?' Her words ended on a sob.

'I know, Amy, I know.' Joan was sorry to see her so upset but she was glad too that she was with her.

Amy took a handkerchief from her big handbag and blew her nose. 'I'll admit that first off I thought you were a bit uppity for our Matt. Then I could see what a good mother you were, and there came a time when you let yerself go an' I began t' think Matt was dragging you down. Then yer bucked up, wanted to get a job an' make something of yerself and . . . well, I wasn't much 'elp, was I? Didn't want yer to move away from the East End either, didn't think it was right at all. But time 'as proved me wrong. Admitted as much at Meg an' Jamie's party, in front of everybody, didn't I?'

Joan was feeling calmer now, and smiled hesitantly. 'Yes, you did, Amy. At least I always knew where I stood with you.'

Amy shook herself. 'Now tell me the truth. How is Jamie?'

'About the same, as I said. Eat your bun, then we'll go back together and you can see for yourself.'

The staff nurse met them at the doorway. Joan introduced her mother-in-law, and the nurse said, 'I'll fetch another chair.' When Joan and Amy were seated side by side she told them, 'The doctors looked in while you were away, and they seemed satisfied with Jamie's progress.'

Joan wanted to ask, 'What progress?' but said only, 'Thank you.'

Poor Amy was crying quietly, upset to see her dear Jamie's face under all the bandages.

'His colour is ever so much better this last couple of days,' Joan whispered, 'and he's resting ever so much more peacefully.' She took Jamie's hand as she always did, and began talking to him softly. 'Your gran's here. She's come on her own. You ought to feel honoured, young man. Gran never leaves the East End unless 'tis for a very good reason. I haven't asked her yet but I'm hoping I can persuade her to come home with me and stay a few days. Then she'll be able to visit you again tomorrow.'

Suddenly there was a movement. The sheet that covered Jamie had lifted a little. Joan wondered if she had imagined it. She glanced at Amy, and from the look on her face knew she had seen it too. They turned their gaze back to Jamie, and he gave a shuddering sigh. Joan got up quickly and went towards the glass partition. The nurse met her halfway.

'He moved, well, not so much moved as sighed then settled down again.' Joan's voice was little more than a whisper.

'Would you mind waiting outside? I'll have to call Sister. She'll check his blood pressure and . . .' The nurse never finished the sentence. Joan and Amy were outside in the corridor and the door to the room where Jamie lay was firmly shut.

Amy looked angry. 'Why did she push us out like that?'

'Amy,' Joan said firmly, 'try to be patient. I've had to do a lot of waiting around. The sister will let us back in as soon as they've checked Jamie.'

Two doctors came, and it was some time before Joan and Amy were told they could return to his side. 'Your son is slowly coming out of the coma,' one doctor said, with a slow smile. Three nurses were standing at the end of the bed, whispering and watching.

'Thank you, thank you,' Joan muttered to no one in particular. Jamie's eyes were still closed but his breathing seemed different. She didn't know. She felt sure of only one thing and that was that there had been a real danger that Jamie would leave them. He had been so close to death but he had returned to her. Now he looked so peaceful. It was only a matter of time and, please, God, he would open his eyes and say, 'Hallo, Mum.'

She felt more peaceful than she had since the moment the policeman had called at the house to tell them that Jamie had had an accident. They had been given back their son. There was no mistake about it, and she would never, as long as she lived, stop thanking God for the reprieve.

Amy was crying unashamedly but they were different tears from those she had shed when she had first set eyes on Jamie's still figure lying in that bed.

As Joan and her mother-in-law left the hospital to go home, they were both struck by the power of prayer. Neither could put it into words but they would freely admit, sometime in the future, that there hadn't been a day go by since Jamie had crashed his motorbike that they hadn't prayed.

Joan was so grateful she felt light and happy. The misery and the anger she felt about Matt and his affair with Doris Shepherd didn't matter any more. She'd find the strength to deal with that somehow. It was impossible to explain, or to describe, but it was as if she'd been given an inner strength. Right now she was looking forward to telling Meg and Rosie that, any day now, they could visit their brother.

Chapter Twenty-Two

OVER THE WEEKEND, Joan felt as though her life had taken a turn for the better. Amy was still with them, much to the delight of Meg and Rosie, both of whom had now seen Jamie. And Joan no longer felt as if disaster loomed every time the telephone rang.

This morning, Sunday, she'd had a bath, washed and set her hair and had taken time to decide what to wear. She and Amy were going to the hospital after an early lunch, and then her father had offered to run Amy home. Despite all her protests Bill Harvey had been adamant. He wasn't going to allow Amy to travel back to the East End by train and then bus.

Yesterday Joan had taken Amy shopping, bought her a blouse, a pair of stockings, some knickers and a comfortable pair of shoes, because her mother-in-law hadn't come prepared to stay a few days. It was an outing they had both enjoyed and they had avoided all mention of Matt. Joan was aware that the girls had asked questions of their grandma but she didn't know what had transpired and she hadn't asked. It was sufficient for her to see that the girls had accepted some explanation of why their father was not at home. She herself had talked to them about Jamie and how his recovery would be a long-drawn-out business. Both girls had hugged her before she set off with their gran for the hospital.

The small room in which Jamie lay no longer seemed depressing: the screens around his bed had been removed and bright sunshine streamed in through the window. Both Joan and Amy looked and felt so much happier. True, Jamie had not come fully out of the coma yet but they were no longer terrified that he might die. And just seeing the sunshine made everyone feel so much better.

They hadn't been there long when Matt arrived. Told by the sister in charge that his son had turned the corner, he stood at the foot of the bed and let the tears trickle down his cheeks.

Amy knew it was a shock for him to find her there and her presence wasn't making it any easier for him to talk to Joan. She made a quick decision. 'Why don't the pair of you go for a walk? I'll sit with Jamie. There's a few things I'd like to tell him an' it's better done without either of you being here, whether he can hear me or not.'

Silently Joan thanked her for her tact, and said, 'All right, we'll have a cup of tea, then you can get yourself one when we come back.'

They left the room. Matt was feeling awkward. Joan was angry with him, he could see that from her face, and she had every right to be.

The cafeteria was packed. Sunday was a popular day for visitors at any hospital, and this one was no different. There were no empty seats, and children were running around chattering loudly.

'Shall we skip the tea and walk round the grounds?' Joan suggested.

Matt agreed, and soon they had found a bench on which to sit. It really was a glorious day: spring flowers were in bloom and the grass looked so green. Matt leant forward, his hands clasped between his knees. Without looking at Joan he said, 'Don't suppose there's much use in me saying sorry, is there?'

'Depends on what you're saying sorry for,' Joan replied sharply. 'If it's because you got found out, then don't bother.'

Matt straightened up. He looked grim. 'You shouldn't 'ave 'ad t' deal with this on top of everything else,' he muttered.

'You're damn right I shouldn't. But my husband had to find comfort away from home because too many worries were being thrown at him and he couldn't cope.'

'I deserved that,' Matt said bleakly.

'Would you like t' know what's really eating me?' Joan didn't wait for him to reply. 'The worst thing for me is that I was so blind. I would have sworn on our children's lives that we had a good marriage. Talk about deluding myself!' She shook her head. 'Been a proper fool, haven't I? You and Doris Shepherd must have laughed your heads off. Every weekend I stayed at home while you went off with her, an' I swallowed every story you told me. Special darts matches. Work to be seen to. Anything and everything I believed. Oh, I know it was my fault in the beginning that I wouldn't go on pub crawls with you but why couldn't you have stayed home sometimes and come on picnics with me an' the girls or taken them swimming or anywhere else they wanted to

go? You love them so much, you'd do anything for them –
that's what you're always saying, isn't it? Just goes to show
how cheap your talk is.'

Joan's voice had risen. Other people were walking in the
grounds and several heads had turned in their direction.

'I never thought of you as a fool, Joan,' Matt protested,
his voice low.

'Easy to say that now,' she said. 'I bet Doris Shepherd
did. She's been having the time of her life at my expense.'

Matt looked nervous. 'Are you going to tell me now what
you want to do about it?'

'Isn't that up to you and your ladyfriend?' Joan was trying
to be flippant. 'You probably can't wait to go back and live
in the East End. I bet you'll love it, living in a high-rise flat.
Might have a problem parking your car, though. Be quite
a change for you, won't it? By the way, are you coming to
the house today to fetch your clothes?'

'Are you throwing me out?' He sounded surprised that
she would dare even to suggest such a thing.

She smiled. It was a bitter smile. 'You really are amazing! You know that, Matt? You take the biscuit.'

'I never had any intention of leaving you,' he said stubbornly. 'You and the kids are my whole life.'

'Oh, I see. You want to have your cake and eat it too. You
don't want your image damaged, you still want to be seen
as a good father, head of a happy household. Doris is just
a bit on the side, is she? I wonder if she looks at it like that.
Perhaps I'll pay her a visit. Then she'll be able to tell me
her side of the story.'

By the look on Matt's face he was on the point of bursting a blood vessel. He ran a finger round the inside of his
shirt collar and took a deep breath. 'There's no need to start

being nasty. I've said I'm sorry and I mean it. It wouldn't 'ave 'appened if we 'adn't 'ad to go through all that flipping palaver over Jamie.'

'That's a fine excuse. Tailor-made for you. But if you think that's going to get you off the hook you've another think coming. Tell me about the first time. What's your excuse for starting the affair in the first place?'

Matt made no answer.

Joan pressed him. 'Come on, give me a reason. We'd moved to a lovely house, a nice area, and the children were all doing well. I thought I was the luckiest woman alive. Never dreamt you were going back to the East End to sleep with another woman.'

'It wasn't like that,' he hissed. 'Doris was lonely. She'd come into the pub where me an' me brothers were 'aving a drink, always on her own. It started, I suppose, cos I bought her a drink.'

'Oh.' Joan's voice was pitched high again. 'Her services to you in bed was her way of repayment, was it? Where the hell were all her kids when this was going on?'

Matt clenched his fists. 'I never thought you could be so nasty.'

'And I never thought that every weekend you were two-timing me,' she retorted.

Matt's anger was getting the better of him. 'Why you're 'aving to rake over old coals I can't fathom out. It 'ad been over between me an' Doris for years until I got knocked back with the news that my son belonged to a family in America.'

'So, I'm to understand that the pressure of finding out that we'd been bringing up the wrong boy for twenty years is what upset you. Drove you into sleeping with another woman. Or should I say drove you *back* to sleeping with her. Well, let me tell you here and now, Matt. That knowledge didn't do me much good either. What if I'd started an affair? I could have asked the milkman in, given him a coffee or something and asked him to comfort me.'

'Now you're being bloody ridiculous,' he snapped.

'Oh, I see. What's sauce for the gander doesn't apply to the goose?' Angry tears stung her eyes and she felt as though she might explode, but by now they both knew they were not going to solve anything sitting arguing in the grounds of Kingston Hospital, where their son still lay in the intensive care unit.

'Come on, Joan. Shall we call a truce for today? Let's go back and let my mother go for a cup of tea.' He was trying his best to keep his temper under control.

It was hard for him, she was well aware of that, and his suggestion was reasonable, but Joan was still too angry and she was about to tell him to get lost when he spoke again. 'Besides, Jamie might open his eyes soon. You wouldn't want to miss that, would you?'

She looked up at him and her heart ached. He was still so good-looking, his big brown eyes looked so sad and when he was . . . his normal self, she still loved him to bits. Right this moment if Doris Shepherd had appeared she would have killed her stone dead. I would share most things with someone less well-off than I am, but share my husband? *Never.*

'So, what you're saying is, we shelve . . . this rotten business and not talk about it till later?'

'If you think you can manage that, well, yes, please,' he mumbled, knowing he was asking a lot.

They got to their feet and walked back down the path,

which had such pretty flower borders. Joan wanted to ask Matt a hundred and one questions, the first of which was whether he was going to stay at home tonight. But she couldn't bring herself to do this. She didn't want to argue with him any more. There must be plenty more that hadn't been brought out into the open, such as Doris Shepherd's feelings in all this. More than likely she wanted to hang on to Matt. After all, she was on her own and it would seem that Matt had been showing her a good time. And what about Matt? He'd said he was sorry but he hadn't said he was going to put a stop to it, had he? Would she still want him if he did?

That was a difficult question to answer. When Jamie came round, and it might be any time now, thank God, he shouldn't be burdened with the fact that his mother and father were living separate lives. Dear Jesus, the lad still had to sort out in his head what he wanted to do about the Piviteaux family as well as struggle to become fit and well again.

Why, Matt? Why? I need you, Meg and Rosie need you, and most of all Jamie needs you. And what do you do? Go to pieces and go off with another woman. Comfort you, did she? Did sleeping with her feel good? She clenched her fists and held them close to her sides. Thank God there were people about or she might have done something she'd be sorry for. And knowing Matt and his temper, she might have come off worst.

They had reached the entrance. Matt held open the door for her, and as she passed him, she paused and stared into his eyes. She thought he looked angry, sad, even confused. She felt all of those things and more. Her husband had betrayed her and she had a right to be furious; she had been for days now, even though so far she had managed to keep

herself under control. At this moment she was almost longing for him to reach out and take her into his arms. Why?
After the way he had treated her? Because she was frightened,
lonely, and tired of trying to cope with so many troubles.

When they got home Joan was surprised that Matt offered
to lay the table. The girls were out but they had left a note
saying they'd be back by six thirty, and as it was almost that
now she set about making a huge salad and putting a
saucepan of new potatoes on to boil. Obviously Matt was
taking it for granted that he would eat with them.

The front door opened with a bang. The girls had seen
their father's car in the drive. Both Meg and Rosie threw
themselves at him and he lavished hugs and kisses on them.
Just watching them tore at Joan's heart. How could he go
off and leave them? They might be classed as grown-up but
they were still their babies. Mine *and* Matt's.

It was a proper family meal, Amy at one end of the table,
Matt at the other. It was Matt who carved the piece of
gammon Joan had boiled earlier on in the day before going
to see Jamie.

'Will you be here in the morning, Dad?' Rosie piped up.
No one else in the room would have dared asked that
question.

He looked lovingly at his younger daughter, gave her one
of his wonderful smiles and said, 'I will see you some time
tomorrow but, right now, when we've had our fruit and ice-
cream, I'm going to drive yer gran home. It's been a long
day for all of us.'

Joan protested, 'But my dad's coming over at eight o'clock.
He's going to take Amy home. We arranged it yesterday.'

'Yeah, I know,' Matt said sheepishly. 'Mum told me. While

we were at the hospital I phoned Bill, let him know that I was here an' that I'd take me mum home.'

'Oh . . . I see,' Joan stammered. He'd found a good excuse to go back to the East End again tonight then.

'I really do need to pick up some papers an' see a bloke in the City first thing tomorrow morning. I've let things slide a bit this past week.' Matt kept his eyes on his plate as he made that statement.

And whose bloody fault is that? Joan was tempted to cry out, but instead she said, 'Amy's got a few parcels upstairs, if you'd like to fetch them down for her.'

It was a sad little group who stood in the doorway and watched as Matt drove away with his mother beside him in the passenger seat.

'You and Dad are really mad at each other, aren't you?' It was Rosie again who popped that question.

Joan stared at her two girls, still so alike in looks, flawless skin and red-gold hair that set them apart in any crowd. In temperament, though, there was a vast difference between them. Meg was wise, tactful and understanding, while Rosie jumped in feet first, thinking only after the words had been said. God give me strength, Joan prayed. This younger daughter of mine dashes in where angels would fear to tread. 'Not really,' she lied. She couldn't face telling her girls the complete truth. 'Your father has a heavy workload on at the moment.'

Meg caught hold of Rosie's hand and said, 'Let's make Mum a nice cup of tea. We'll leave the washing-up till later. You go and put your feet up, Mum, and switch the telly on. We'll bring the tea in as soon as it's ready.'

For once Joan did as she was told and sighed with relief as she sank down into one of the big armchairs.

Rosie had always been the inquisitive one but this was the first time, as far as she could remember, that she had ever lied to her. For the time being, she told herself, it had been the right thing to do. She had no idea what future there was for her and Matt, so how could she tell the girls? Take one day at a time, she told herself. That's all you can do.

Chapter Twenty-Three

JOAN WAS IN a raging temper. It was bad enough what Matt was doing to her but he had lied to the girls, to Rosie in particular, and that was unforgivable. Four days had gone by since he had taken his mother home and promised he would be back the next day. Not only had he not put in an appearance, he hadn't even had the guts to pick up the telephone.

She had continued to spend a good deal of her time at the hospital while the girls were at work, but she missed Matt. She missed having him to talk to, missed his arms around her, and at night their double bed seemed so big and empty with no one for her to cuddle up to. At times she let her imagination run away with her. She couldn't help it. In her mind's eye she would see Matt being tender and loving to Doris Shepherd, see them in bed together, and it was more than she could bear. You shouldn't punish yourself like this, she told herself repeatedly, to no avail. In the corridors of the hospital, in the cafeteria, everywhere she looked, it seemed that there were couples. Old and young alike, everyone had someone except her. Some were celebrating good news, maybe the birth of a baby, others were consoling each other. Who did she have to turn to?

As if in answer to her own question the front doorbell rang. She was in two minds as to whether to answer it or not, then got up and walked down the hall. When she opened the door, John Chapman was leaning against the porch looking immaculate, his fawn trousers creased like a knife's edge, white shirt unbuttoned at the neck and a Prince of Wales checked jacket. His feet shod in slip-on casual shoes of the softest beige leather. Cautiously he held out a bunch of spring flowers, which Joan took at the same time stepping aside and saying 'You'd better come in.'

Hardly a word passed between them until Joan set two cups of black coffee on to the table and turned to take a jug of cream out of the fridge.

'Rosie spent last evening at my place,' John said. 'She came in with Mary, saying that Linsey had gone to the pictures with Meg and Brian Clarke and another lad.'

'Oh, she didn't tell me where she'd been.'

'Tell me if I'm butting in where I'm not wanted but she seemed upset. Said her father wasn't living at home any more.'

Joan was about to protest when the thought came to her that Rosie had spoken the truth. What answer could she make? None, she decided.

'This has been a very bad time for you, hasn't it?'

Joan gazed at him. 'Do you know more than you're letting on?'

John Chapman sighed. 'Kids talk among themselves and I did hear the bare bones about Jamie and the possible mix-up of the babies when he was born. Then came his accident. It can't have been easy for either you or Matt.'

Joan studied his face for a full minute. Was she right to trust him? 'Oh, there was certainly a mix-up at the time I gave birth to Jamie. It has been proved beyond doubt. I keep telling myself it had nothing to do with Jamie being knocked off his motorbike but at times I'm not so sure. He could have had his mind on other things when he came round that bend.'

'And Matt? Hit him for six. Can't blame him for that.'

'After twenty-one years of being married to him I can blame him for a whole host of things.' Joan was on the verge of tears. She hadn't meant to unburden herself to this charming man but, oh, God, she needed to talk to someone. Somehow she didn't feel she could tell her family how things were between her and Matt.

'Have a good cry if it helps,' John said. 'I know something of what you're going through.' He reached across the table and she smiled as his fingers touched hers just for a moment. 'Would you let me take you out for lunch?'

Joan looked bewildered.

'Sorry,' John said. 'Shouldn't have blurted it out like that. I know you go to the hospital every afternoon, Rosie told me your routine. I just thought a light lunch somewhere quiet might do you good. That's if you can put up with my company for that long.'

Joan kept her eyes down and didn't answer.

'Go on, get yourself ready,' he said, sounding as if he wouldn't take no for an answer. 'I know a restaurant where they have a wonderful garden and we can eat outside. It's a gorgeous day.'

*   *   *

He was right. The sun was warm, the sky was blue and the raised patio on which they were having lunch looked out over well-kept lawns and flowering shrubs. She could hear the peaceful sound of trickling water from two nearby fountains. And for the moment she was feeling better. Without thinking, she touched his face, saying, 'You really are very thoughtful.'

He put down his knife and fork and gave her a look she had never seen on Matt's face. It made her realize suddenly what a limited life she had been leading.

His hand was on her hair, which was not as unruly as it had been when she was young. Still a deep copper colour, she wore it high and smooth in the front and twirled into a neat French pleat at the back. 'You're beautiful. You could pass for a Greek goddess,' he teased.

Joan blushed. 'Now I know you're mad. Whoever heard of a goddess with red hair?'

He raised her hand to his lips and kissed her fingers, laughing. She felt the years roll away and she was young again. Of course she didn't believe a word he was saying but, by Jove, it had done her wounded pride a power of good.

It was just as well that a waiter appeared to remove their plates and John ordered coffee for them both. She shook her head thoughtfully. Things had been getting out of hand. But it had been nice to be told that she was beautiful and, yes, desirable. He might not have said that but his eyes had told her so quite plainly.

'I'll drive you straight to the hospital,' he offered, when they had drunk their second cup of coffee. It was an offer for which Joan was immensely grateful, yet part of her longed to linger in the peaceful garden where the birds were singing, the air was fragrant and she had no need to make decisions.

Her common sense rose to the surface. This was a dream world. The real world lay beyond this garden and she had no option but to go and face it.

Outside the hospital John Chapman opened the car door and helped her out. He kissed her cheek. 'You know where I am if you need me,' he said, holding her hand longer than was necessary. 'I'll see you tomorrow,' he added huskily.

Joan was wondering what he meant by that. She didn't trust herself to speak, nor did she wait to see him drive away. She merely nodded and made her way into the everyday life of a busy hospital.

'Mrs Pearson, James has regained consciousness.'

Joan stared at the staff nurse in disbelief. 'Oh, my God! And I wasn't here. I should have been.'

'It's all right, Mrs Pearson, really it is. He's sleeping so peacefully now.'

Joan smiled up at her and murmured her thanks. Then she took her seat beside her son's bed. She sat quietly for a time, then told him how pleased his sisters had been to see him and of all the celebrations they were planning for when he came home. She told him that the weather was glorious, and of how pretty all the flower-beds were looking, when suddenly Jamie opened his eyes, and moved his head slowly towards his mother. When his lips parted slightly and he half smiled she couldn't see it because she was blinded by tears.

The nurse, who had watched the whole time, handed Joan a paper tissue. 'Wipe your eyes,' she ordered. 'This is no time for crying. You've been through so much, a truly devoted mother.'

Jamie did not move again that afternoon, but nothing

could take away the joy Joan felt as she sat quietly watching him, holding his hand. Her heart was light as she kissed him goodbye and said, 'I'll be here again tomorrow morning.'

She called in to tell her parents and her nan the wonderful news, and as soon as she reached home she picked up the telephone and rang her mother-in-law. 'He smiled at me, he really did! He hears me, Amy! Now I know he does,' she told her, still sounding so excited.

Poor Amy was sobbing at the other end of the line, so thankful to hear the good news yet half afraid to let her hopes get too high.

'Amy, I really should phone Matt. He would want to know, don't you think?'

'Aw, pet, yer know he would, but if yer asking me where he is an' 'ow can yer contact him I honestly ain't got a clue.'

'Amy, please, surely he's been in to see you.'

'I swear on all I 'old dear 'e ain't never set a foot in this 'ouse since 'e dropped me off at the door when 'e brought me 'ome from your place. Stan ain't mentioned 'im an' I ain't asked. Best thing I can suggest is that you ring our Stan.'

Joan moaned softly, which broke Amy's heart. That bloody son of mine, she said to herself, needs someone t' tell 'im a few 'ome truths an', by God, I'll let me tongue rip the minute I set eyes on 'im.

Aloud she said, 'I'll do the rounds of the pubs. Someone must know where 'e's 'anging out. And if I find 'im I'll make sure 'e rings you. That's a promise.'

With that Joan had to be satisfied.

For the rest of the week she went into the hospital twice a day. Every day Jamie stirred a little more, but he never spoke. However, there were signs that he understood what was being said to him. He would move his head, open his eyes, squeeze her hand and even moan occasionally.

John Chapman called at the house with offers of a lift or was outside the hospital waiting to take her home in the early evening.

There was still no sign of Matt.

The weekend came again, and the girls were out with their friends when Joan opened the front door to see John striding up the drive. 'You look fantastic.' He stared at her in open admiration. She was wearing a sleeveless cream linen dress, with a jade green cardigan around her shoulders. Jade green went so well with her dark green eyes. With her hair piled up on top and high-heeled court shoes she looked a lot taller than she was. 'You must be feeling better,' he said. 'May I offer you a lift?'

'Why, thank you, kind sir.' Joan laughed as she got into his car, and he headed towards Kingston Hospital.

On arrival he didn't drive off but got out of the car and walked her slowly to the entrance. 'Will you have a meal with me later?' he asked softly. 'It has to be better than going home to an empty house. I'll be here waiting at about six.'

Suddenly she felt shy, and she was taken aback as he lowered his head and gently laid his lips on hers. They stood together, staring into each other's eyes, until he straightened up and murmured, 'I'll be here when you come out.'

Joan opened the door to the side ward and the colour rose in her cheeks. Matt was sitting beside the bed and Jamie's hand was between both of his. She glanced at Jamie and saw his head move. He was turning it slowly towards her, and she was thrilled by how quickly he had known she had come into the room. Joan caught her breath: her son was doing his best to lift his head from the pillow.

She covered the distance between them in three strides. Matt let go of Jamie's hand and got to his feet. Side by side they stood while Jamie smiled a real smile that took in both of them. Joan put down her handbag and drew nearer to him. 'Jamie . . . you look so much better. We're both here . . . your dad and me. It's OK, you're back with us . . . you are, aren't you?' She was speaking very softly as she stroked his hand. Then it happened. Jamie squeezed her hand and held out his other hand to his father, which Matt took and held tightly. Neither of them moved for several seconds. Then Joan looked at Matt and each saw that the other was crying.

They spent the next two hours talking quietly about Meg and Rosie. Matt asked if Brian Clarke was still seeing Meg. 'Very much so,' Joan told him, adding, 'I think you will soon have the expense of a wedding, the way things are going there.'

'Where 'ave all the years gone?' Matt murmured, half to himself. 'Doesn't seem possible that all our kids are grown-up.'

'No, it doesn't,' Joan agreed.

Jamie had slipped back into sleep, and Matt leant over the bed to kiss his son's forehead. Then he looked long and hard at his wife. 'As miracles go I'd say we've been granted one,' he said.

At that moment Joan would have given a lot for him to hold her close. She was thinking of all the years they had had together, blessed with three children, and how lucky they had been. Only right now they did not have each other. There was such a distance between them she didn't even know where he was living, let alone who with.

Matt looked at his watch. 'I have to be going. If you need to get in touch, ring Stan. He'll get a message to me.'

Joan looked at him in amazement. 'I think we need to talk right now.'

'No, sorry, Joan,' he muttered, having the grace to look guilty.

'What? You haven't seen the girls. You broke a promise to Rosie and now you turn up out of the blue and say it doesn't suit you to stay. You're pushing your luck a bit too far, Matt.'

Before she had finished, Matt was at the door. 'I'll be in touch, give my love t' the girls.'

If Joan had been at home she would have grabbed the nearest heavy object and thrown it at his head. Instead, she had no option but to watch as the door closed behind him and she was left with an unbelievable heavy silence and a great number of unanswered questions. The next few hours were some of the worst she had ever sat through. She felt so utterly alone. As the time drew near for her to leave she comforted herself that John Chapman would be waiting outside for her. Life has been treating me very unfairly, she was saying to herself. Surely I'm entitled to a break now and again. But was she just trying to get her own back on Matt? 'I don't know what to do or what to feel,' she muttered, as she bent over the bed and kissed her son goodbye.

John was as good as his word. He jumped out of his car as soon as he saw her, settled her into the passenger seat and headed for Epsom. 'I've reserved a table for two at the Chequers. We'll have time for a drink before dinner,' he told her quietly.

It was the most lovely hotel she had ever been in, and she felt special and spoilt as she headed for the ladies' powder room. She washed her hands, repaired her makeup and ran a comb through the front of her hair, then pushed the pins into the back pleat more securely. As she approached John stood up. He had chosen a table set in a bay window that looked out over the famous racecourse and drinks were waiting, a sherry for her and a lager for himself.

The head waiter brought them each a huge menu from which John chose smoked salmon for both of them as a starter. For the main course he ordered roast rib of beef, and Joan decided on breast of chicken in white wine. When a waiter came to tell them their table was ready in the dining room Joan had another surprise: a band was playing and the tables were set around the edge of a small dance-floor. Much later she gasped at the sight of the sweet trolley.

It was a marvellous dinner, an enchanting place, and John's attentive company, with a few glasses of wine, went a long way to smoothing her ruffled feathers caused by the fact that Matt had walked away from her without offering so much as the vaguest excuse. After coffee they danced, and Joan was only too aware of how close his body was to hers. She had tried to tell him she hadn't danced in years but he was in no mood to take no for an answer. It didn't matter in the least. He was a terrific dancer and she only had to go where he led.

They left the hotel at ten o'clock, Joan smiling like a Cheshire cat. 'This evening has done wonders for me,' she said. 'I just don't have the words to thank you.'

'We'll do it again soon.' He grinned.

John's footsteps were light as he walked her to her front door. Joan reached up to give him a thank-you peck on the cheek but that wasn't what he had in mind. He took the key from her and unlocked the door. 'May I come in?' he asked.

Joan stepped back and looked up to see that two bedrooms were showing lights. 'Better not. The girls are home, and as soon as they hear me come in they'll be flying down the stairs.'

It was as if he hadn't heard her. He stepped inside. The hall was in darkness. 'I'd better put the light on,' she muttered, but got no further. He had pulled her to him. They just stood there, in the dark, kissing, he touching her body as if he had waited all his life for this. Joan's mind was in a whirl. This shouldn't be happening, but didn't she want it too? Oh, yes. Very much so!

She wanted him to prove to her that she was desirable. She was human, she had needs and desires, and hadn't Matt betrayed her? Not just now but, as she had recently found out, many times over the years? The knowledge had hurt because she'd thought that they had such a good marriage.

John was caressing her with his lips, allowing his hands to roam over her whole body until she was almost moaning with pleasure.

'Mum, is that you?' Meg's voice floated down the stairs as a door was flung open and light streamed out.

'I love you,' John whispered, his voice throbbing, as Joan stepped away, tugging frantically to straighten her dress.

She found the light switch, snapped it on and gazed up at her elder daughter, who was looking over the banister rail. 'It's all right, Meg. Mr Chapman is with me, he took me for a meal. I'll be up to see you and Rosie in just a minute.'

'I do love you,' John whispered, as he kissed the top of her head and made for the door. 'I'll see you tomorrow.'

The door closed behind him with a click and Joan let out all her breath in a long gasp as she leant against the wall.

I must be mad, she was telling herself. Supposing the girls had caught her and John? What kind of explanation would she have been able to give them? That she was merely getting her own back on their father for what he had done to her? Of course not. That wouldn't have been the truth. Not the whole truth, anyway. Suddenly she couldn't stop smiling. It had been a fantastic feeling. Raw passion. Something that hadn't stirred in her for a long time. Oh, she and Matt still made love, but it hadn't aroused her like John Chapman had tonight for many a long day. She had felt wanted, special, the one and only lady in his life.

She kicked off her shoes and made for the stairs, then stopped. She had better stop trying to analyze her feelings where John Chapman was concerned or she may find herself getting in beyond her depth.

Chapter Twenty-Four

IT WAS BARELY ten o'clock when Joan opened the door to John. 'I think we have some unfinished business,' he whispered, as he took her in his arms. 'I love you so much, I haven't slept a wink all night.'

They stood together swaying as they kissed and touched each other. 'You're incredible,' he told her, as he undid the buttons of her blouse, murmuring 'Oh, Joan,' as he caressed her. Then they slowly climbed the stairs and she led him into her bedroom.

Her clothes fell away and she watched as he undressed. Then he lifted her gently on to the bed, and began to move his lips over her breasts. Their coming together was powerful, an explosion of need, until they lay spent in each other's arms, stunned by the force of what had happened.

'If the girls hadn't been at home when we got back last night I wouldn't have had to spend a sleepless night. Joan, you are great, and, oh, how I needed you,' he whispered.

She laughed with pleasure. 'It's amazing, isn't it?' she

pondered. 'We've been neighbours for years and never really known each other and now . . .'

'We're lovers.' He finished the sentence for her. 'We've found each other and from now on we can fill a need whenever the mood takes us.'

Joan was shaken by what he had said so casually. A moment ago they had been like passionate young lovers, barely able to tear themselves apart but now a warning bell rang in her head. He began telling her of places he would take her to, but Joan was only half listening. Later he said, 'This is a waste of time! I can't stand having you in my arms and not making love to you.'

Joan wriggled free and sat up. 'John, I don't know whether Matt and I will get divorced or not.'

'What the hell's that got to do with us being together?' he asked. 'Lie down again, my darling, and let me prove to you once more how much I love you.'

She swung her legs over the side of the bed. 'John, you are the most romantic man I've ever known, and your kindness to me has been a Godsend, but I think that what you and I want are two different things. I'm going down to make some coffee. The bathroom is the second door on the left. There are clean towels in there.'

Downstairs she washed and dressed. Her mind was working overtime and she couldn't believe how naïve she had been, acting like a rich man's mistress one minute and then, when the penny dropped that she was being used, she had reverted to being a housewife, telling him that there were clean towels in the bathroom. How would she ever look him in the face again?

She didn't wait long to find out.

He breezed into the kitchen, beaming. 'Too much for you,

was it? Wore you out, did I? It can only get better, I promise you. Next time we'll take it steady.'

'John, sit down.' Joan placed a cup of coffee on the table. 'I've only got ginger biscuits,' she added, matter-of-factly.

He roared with laughter. 'Well, I suppose there's always a first. Is that all I merit? A ginger biscuit? Come on, Joan, I can understand that you're feeling guilty but you shouldn't be. You're being silly . . . I love you.'

The amazing thing was he probably did, at this point in time, but it would never be a lasting love.

Joan sat down and sipped her coffee. She couldn't get her thoughts into any kind of order but she knew, without a doubt, that she was right. She had been feeling lonely, betrayed, unwanted, even, and John Chapman was a slick, charming man.

'You were just as hungry for me as I was for you,' he said, doing his best to tease her into a better frame of mind. 'As things stand, I'd say we're both free and there is nothing to stop us from indulging ourselves whenever the fancy takes us. Is there?' he asked hopefully.

Joan took a deep breath, then leant close to him and, almost in a whisper, said, 'To you I'm just a roll in the hay.'

He smiled wickedly at her. 'Is there anything wrong with that?'

'Not to your way of thinking obviously,' she said, but then she had to laugh. After all, it was she who had read his intentions wrongly. Like some starry-eyed school-kid, she had thought of him as a knight in shining armour coming to her aid when she most needed it.

He smiled. 'I was really hurt when my wife went off with another man and I vowed then I'd never let a woman get that close to me. I live for my two girls, and I love them very much. I'd never think of marrying again, but that doesn't alter the fact that I have my needs and when I meet someone who feels the same way, well . . .'

Joan couldn't argue with that. He had never promised her anything different.

John had been watching the different emotions flit across her face and felt sorry for her. Things could have been so great between them, given half a chance, but he could see that was never going to be. Joan Pearson was what he would term a good woman.

'I'd say it's game, set and match,' he said, and smiled. Then he looked serious. 'If it's any consolation to you, Joan, if I were thinking of taking a second wife I'd hope and pray that it would be someone as good and kind as you.'

'You don't have to say things like that, you did nothing to mislead me. It was my own fault.'

'Well, stop feeling so guilty. Shall I tell you what I think?' Joan made no reply, so he went on, 'You and Matt have gone through a terrible time just lately, but it will get better. I promise you it will. I can't see you two getting divorced. I hope you won't for the sake of your three children. I hope you manage to work things out.' He saw that her eyes were brimming with tears and it was all he could do to stop himself taking her into his arms. Instead he said, 'I have to go soon but before I do could you bring yourself to give me another cup of coffee and this time I would like a little cream or even milk, I can't stand black coffee.'

She looked straight at him. He smiled, looking mischievous and she found herself laughing at him. 'I think I can manage that.'

Just then the telephone rang.

Joan lifted the receiver but before she had the chance to

say anything she heard Matt's voice. 'I'm coming down to the hospital this afternoon. Shall I come to the house first and we go together?'

'Matt.' Joan hesitated. 'All right. What time will you be here?'

'Is two o'clock all right with you?'

'Yes, I'll be ready.' She heard a click and the line went dead.

'There you are,' John exclaimed. 'I'm so glad your boy's out of the woods and that now his father is beginning to see sense. It's time I faded into the background. Will you do one thing for me, Joan?'

'If I can.' She felt awkward.

'Don't go around feeling you've got to wear sackcloth and ashes. Don't ever let the girls get an inkling of what has been between us. They're great friends with my two and I wouldn't want that to change. We haven't become an item, much as I would have liked it,' he said ruefully. 'You've let me know that once was enough, so let's leave it at that.'

'I'll do my best,' Joan said thoughtfully.

'You'll do as I asked,' John corrected her gently. 'Confession might be good for you, but it would hurt a good many others and they'd end up hating us both. That's not what you want, is it?'

She swallowed hard, before saying, 'No, it isn't. I'll do as you say.'

At the door John bent his head and kissed her cheek.

She watched as he strode off down the drive. She was sure that his last words had been sincere and she knew she would miss him. She thought about the times they had spent together. He had been good to her. She hadn't read the situation right but neither had he for he hadn't truly got to know her – but, then, perhaps she didn't really know herself. But since John Chapman had come into her life, some deep change had taken place within her.

She leant against the wall, closed her eyes, and remembered almost every moment she had shared with him. His kisses. How he'd . . . She shuddered, feeling shame and remorse and now, above all else, guilt. How could she have allowed it to happen just because Matt had treated her so badly? Two wrongs never made a right She began to cry – bitter, reproachful tears. What had possessed her? What if the girls were to find out? That must never happen.

Never!

Chapter Twenty-Five

I WONDER WHY we're all so nervous, Joan thought, as she looked at Matt's twitching lips. Meg and Rosie were sitting in the living room. Both girls had taken great pains over their appearance for today they were going to the hospital as a family to fetch Jamie home.

'Do calm down,' Matt said. 'I promise you everything will be all right.'

How she wished she could believe him. A new relationship, different from any that had gone before, now existed between herself and Matt. He had asked, no, pleaded to be allowed to come home.

She had taken days to come to a decision. It had been as if she was carrying a heavy secret, and she had wished she had someone to talk to, to tell them about John Chapman. Friends were out of the question, and her mum and dad, even nan, wouldn't understand. So often she had come near to telephoning John. Yet she resisted the temptation. Life was already too complicated.

Did she want Matt back in her life? She hated him for the way he had deceived her with Doris Shepherd, but the answer was yes. She had had visions of living without him, and she hadn't liked the prospect. The feeling of loss would always be there. And he had been a good provider and a damn good father. The girls loved him so, and Jamie too. How could they bring Jamie home to a divided house? Hadn't he enough to cope with without them adding coals to the fire?

Over the past weeks they had all gone through a traumatic experience and now the end was in sight. They had so much to be grateful for.

Jamie was coming home. Although it would take time for him to be one hundred per cent fit again, they could thank God that he had not suffered any permanent brain damage.

There was still the matter of the Piviteaux family to be faced. What the outcome of that would eventually be only time would tell. Jamie would have to decide for himself. A small consolation had to be that they lived in America. Had they been in England contact would have been inevitable, and God knew what the result would have been.

Meanwhile, she had written twice to Beryl Piviteaux, the first time telling her that Jamie had been in an accident. However, in her second letter Beryl had sounded so kind and thoughtful that Joan was quite sure that, were they to meet, they would instantly become friends. But, Beryl's son Peter had been quite the opposite. A note from him, included in the letter, had been coldly polite. He had said in no uncertain terms that he was an American citizen and had no wish for ties in England.

Deep in her heart Joan couldn't blame him. And she reckoned that Jamie's views would run along the same lines as

Peter's. Given the choice she would have liked to wipe the slate clean, as though those blood tests had never taken place.

As for herself, she couldn't be a normal person or she would be longing to visit that family, to clasp in her arms the son to whom she had given birth to. On the other hand, could she ever have wiped away all the years she had nurtured Jamie? Put into her arms when only hours old, all the love, yes and heart-breaks, derived from various experiences only a mother would know about.

The short letter she had written to Peter had been one of the hardest tasks she had ever had to tackle. She hoped that she had been kind and considerate, and certainly felt that she had paved the way, should he ever change his mind. It must be awful for that poor lad. It wasn't fair on any of them and she shook her head in disbelief. A simple ordinary mistake made in the throes of a terrible air-raid over London and now, even after all these years, the repercussions were affecting so many lives.

'I'll get the car out,' Matt said briskly. 'They said we could pick him up as soon as the doctors had finished their rounds.' He picked up his keys and strode towards the door.

'Matt,' Joan's voice held a plea, 'we have so much to talk over with Jamie. I'm scared. What if he decides he wants to go to America? What'll we do then?'

Matt came back to where she stood and, very gently, put his arm round her shoulders. 'We decided to take one day at a time. "What if" never solved anything. All we can do is wait an' see. Come on, now, there's a good girl. You've been so brave all along and now we're all going to fetch our Jamie home.'

★   ★   ★

Jamie had been home for four days and the atmosphere was tense to say the least. His friends had dropped in, some making the journey from the university as soon as they heard that he had been discharged from hospital. Trouble was, he tired so easily. Though Joan felt that that was not at the root of what was troubling him.

So far not a word had been said about the blood tests. Both Daphne and Hester had to be persuaded to stop trying to spoil him. Meg and Rosie were reluctant to go to work – they wanted to be near their brother. It was as if they were half afraid that he might just go to America and they would never see him again. Jamie seemed more at ease with his father and his grandfather than he did with his womenfolk. With Matt the talk was of rugby and football, and Matt promised to get tickets for any match Jamie wanted to see as soon as he felt fit enough to face the crowds. Bill Harvey walked as if a great weight had been lifted from his shoulders. His beloved grandson was home, and at the first opportunity the pair of them were going fishing.

Joan woke with a start and struggled to sit up. Glancing at the bedside clock she saw it was a quarter to four. Matt hadn't stirred: he lay beside her, dead to the world. Things were so much better between them: they had talked for hours, and he had told her of how he had rented a bed-sitting room and literally drunk himself stupid in the days when he had disappeared. It had been a Salvation Army officer who had straightened him out. 'By the time he had finished with me I realized that the most important thing in this world was my wife and my family,' he had told her, with such frankness that Joan had cried as she listened to him say those words. 'I never thought for one moment you'd 'ave me back,' he had added later.

Now she was wide awake and she had to make sure nothing had happened to Jamie. Standing by his bed she looked down at his dear face, seeing it in the dim light that came from the landing. Her love for him was so great it made her whole body ache. How could anyone believe that they could take him away from her? No mother in her right mind would give up her son to a family that had never set eyes on him from the day he was born. She turned on tiptoe, about to go back to bed.

'Mum, I'm not asleep, stay with me, please.'

She drew his bedroom chair nearer, sat down and took his hand.

'I don't want to go to America and I don't want that family to come here.'

'Ssh, Jamie. Nobody's going to make you do anything you don't want to.'

'But before I went into hospital you said I'd have to meet them sometime.'

Joan considered. 'I think that what I said was that naturally they would want to meet you some time in the future. But you are an adult. There is no question of anyone forcing you to do something you don't want to do.'

'Dad said I'll never have to meet them. Granddad says the same.'

Joan had to stifle a little laugh. Both Matt and her dad were finding it hard to accept. Her two men were like small boys: neither would admit that it was true, and that worried her a great deal: there was no getting away from the facts and sooner or later they would have to admit it.

'You don't want to meet this family, do you, Mum?'

It took her a minute or two to compose an answer to that. 'No, I don't,' she told him sadly, 'but I can feel for that mother. Her situation is no different from mine. If she and I were to meet then I'm sure we could become good friends. But if she wanted to take you away from me then I would end up wishing her in hell.'

'What about the other boy? Peter Piviteaux. Dad said he's Polish.'

'That's not exactly true. His great-grandparents were Polish, but he says he's one hundred per cent an American boy and wants nothing to do with being English.'

'*He* told you that?'

'Well, that's the gist of a letter he wrote me.'

'Well, that's that, then,' Jamie said. 'He's happy where he is, and I certainly don't want to be uprooted. You've never known any son other than me, and that woman has had that lad all his life, so why, in God's name, did they start this investigation in the first place?'

'How many times have your father and I asked ourselves that very same question?' Joan said ruefully.

Jamie raised himself up on his elbows and looked gravely at his mother. 'Mum, do you and Dad still think of me as your son?'

The question broke her heart. 'Oh, Jamie! Do you really have to ask?'

'I know how Dad feels. He has never admitted that any of this was true right from the beginning, but . . . well, it must be harder for you and that worries me.'

She was surprised how well Jamie had summed up the situation.

'This lad who wrote to you, he really is the lad you gave birth to, isn't he?'

'Oh, don't, Jamie, please. You aren't doing me any good and you're torturing yourself.'

'Well, aren't you curious about what he looks like? Don't you feel the need to go and meet him?'

She sighed heavily. 'In a sense, yes, I do. I wonder about all of those things but have you looked at it from his mother's point of view?'

'You are his mother.'

She heard the break in his voice and felt she had to sort this out here and now, at least to a certain degree. 'If you feel so strongly about that, Jamie, then you have to admit that Beryl Piviteaux is your mother.'

The look he gave her tore at her heart, and the lump in her throat threatened to choke her. It was a while before she felt calm enough to speak again. 'Jamie, you can't have it both ways. Have you thought that Beryl might be just as frightened as I am that she'll lose the lad she has thought of all these years as her son?'

He made no answer.

'From the letters she has written to me I know she regards Peter as her son, just as much as I do you. Nevertheless each of us gave birth to a son that another woman has reared. I like to think that when Mr and Mrs Piviteaux were made aware of the mix-up one of their first reactions was to make sure that you had gone to a safe and happy home. I know if I had been told first that would have been my main concern.'

Still Jamie made no reply.

'Try to see it from Beryl's point of view. The fact that she feels the need to see you has nothing to do with her loving Peter, and were I to agree to see him at some time in the future it wouldn't alter my feelings for you, not by the tiniest scrap. I just can't put into words what you mean to me, Jamie. You'll just have to be content when I tell you I wouldn't swop you for all the tea in China. You *are* my son and I love you dearly. I just don't know how to put it more clearly than that.'

Jamie looked at her, his eyes brimming. 'Thanks for telling me, Mum.'

'Right, now you try to go back to sleep. We'll talk again in the morning. In fact, I'm going to get your father and granddad to have a word with you. If they can't convince you, well, we'll see.'

Back in bed Joan lay awake. During the past few weeks her mind had been centred on getting Jamie well enough to come home. Practically all thoughts of the Piviteaux family had been pushed to the back of her mind. Now there would be a lot more soul-searching before she came up with answers that would be fair to all concerned. Right now she felt too tired to think straight.

Chapter Twenty-Six

DAY BY DAY Jamie got stronger. In the middle of the third week since his homecoming Joan watched as he and her father set off on a fishing trip.

'I've made some coffee,' Matt said, as she came back into the kitchen. 'You're going to feel lost today, aren't you? Can't 'ave you left in the 'ouse all on your own. How d'you feel about coming up to town with me? You could spend some time with my mum, or I can drop you off in Haydons Road. I bet your mum and Hetty would be more than pleased to see you.'

'I think I'd like to go to my mum's,' Joan said. 'It won't take me long to get ready.'

'Sit down and drink your coffee first. I'm in no great hurry. Stan an' I are going after a new contract but we 'aven't got t' see the bloke till this afternoon.'

They sat in silence for a while until Joan murmured, 'I hope my dad manages to talk some sense into our Jamie.'

Matt put his cup down. 'Aw, Joan, you're not starting all

that again, are you? I've asked you time an' time again, for God's sake leave the boy alone.'

'That's the trouble. He's not a boy, he's a grown man,' Joan muttered.

'All the more reason to let him make his own decisions in his own good time,' Matt answered sharply.

Joan gave a deep sigh. 'You don't help, you know that, don't you? He's had a letter from Beryl, which he hasn't even let me read.'

'Quite right too. It's got nothing t' do with you.'

'How the hell can you say that? It's tearing me apart. Of course that family want to meet Jamie, they have a right to. Especially Beryl. They've suggested that if we don't want to visit them they will come to England but so far I haven't answered that letter cos I just don't know what to say.'

Matt got to his feet, his eyes blazing. 'Is there no end t' this bloody nightmare? How many times d'you want telling? Jamie wants nothing whatsoever t' do with them. He's our son and he lives 'ere with us an' as far as I'm concerned that's the end of the matter.'

'Oh, Matt, please. You don't help when you tell him things like that. You deny the facts and on top of that you won't let Jamie face reality.'

He brushed past her. 'You'll be telling me next that you can't wait to see that Peter, an' a fat lot of good that would do. Well, I'm not wasting any more time arguing with you about something that can so easily be settled. I've told you, let Clive Richardson write to Mrs Piviteaux and tell them to get lost. Now, if you're coming with me let's see you smile. Come on, you can go over it a dozen times with yer mum, if yer like, an' I dare say yer nan will want to throw her two-pennyworth in – that'll cheer you up – but just leave me out of it. I've said all I've got t' say.'

Joan was in two minds as to whether or not she should continue to argue with him. She decided not to today, but she was thoughtful as she made her way upstairs to get ready. When alone she freely admitted to herself that she would dearly love to meet the son to whom she had given birth. It did hurt, in a funny sort of way, that Peter had said in his letter that he wanted no contact with her. Oh, he hadn't been rude, but neither had he gone out of his way to spare her feelings. However, she still felt that at some point in the future it would be nice to meet him face to face. In no way did that alter the fact that she loved Jamie with all her heart. But what woman wouldn't be curious, if she found herself in this awful situation?

There were times when her heart ached for both Jamie and Peter. After more than twenty years to be told that the family that had loved and cherished you for the whole of your life was in no way related to you! It was enough to send any young man off the tracks. Each day that went by it became more apparent that both lads would prefer to forget that the truth had ever come to light. And who could blame them for that?

She could feel for Beryl, of course she could. But again there were times when she could cheerfully strangle her. All right, it wasn't her fault that a blood test had proved Peter was not her son and God alone knew how she must have felt when faced with that. But there were two ways of looking at this. One, she and her husband could have kept the information to themselves and not run the risk of losing Peter, whom they so obviously loved, or two, delve deeply and cause distress that, in the end, might turn to bitterness.

If the tables had been turned what would she and Matt have done? She had considered that question several times and, as always, she could not decide what her answer would have been.

Heaving a great sigh, she put the finishing touches to her makeup, picked up her handbag and made her way downstairs. Thank God she was going to spend the day with her mum and her nan. They would not be able to come up with a magic answer to all these problems but at least they would listen, rather than dismissing the matter out of hand as Matt did.

Matt stopped the car at the corner of the road in Merton Park. 'I'll be back about six, take you out for a meal, if you like. Just the two of us.'

In some ways life was improving. Only rarely did Matt suggest that the two of them had a meal out, but he was making more of an effort now. 'That would be a nice change,' she answered quickly, hoping he hadn't been able to read her thoughts.

'Remember to phone the girls and let them know we'll be eating out. Jamie won't mind staying on for the evening with his granddad an' we can pick him up later.'

'Yes, all right, I'll see to it.'

Matt leant across and kissed her cheek. 'See you t'night, then.'

Joan stood on the pavement, and within seconds the car was out of sight. She was thinking how grateful she was that Doris Shepherd was in the past. If it weren't for this American family business, life would be sweet. Matt was so much more considerate: he didn't take her half as much for granted as he used to. Thoughts of John Chapman came to her. He had helped her over a trying period and, though she now knew him to be an unreliable gadabout, she could smile as she remembered how charming he had been. And what a marvellous dancer! But all that was a dream world. Everyday life wasn't like that.

She looked about her as she walked down the road to the house she still regarded as her home. The corner shop was no longer there: three new houses had been built where it had once stood. In fact, nothing looked quite the same and she felt a bit sad until she reached her parents' front door, its paintwork bright as ever. It was such a comfort to take the key, with which she had never parted, from her handbag and open the door.

The smell of baking came from the kitchen. The door to the front room was open and the midsummer sunshine flickered on the wallpaper. There was no fire in the grate today but a huge bowl of ferns and dried flowers stood in the hearth. Photographs stood on the piano and on the mantelshelf. Taking pride of place was one of herself and Matt, and another of them both with the three children.

Feelings of love and security rose in Joan as she turned to see her mother standing waiting, arms outstretched. 'I heard the door open an' I guessed it was you. How are you, love? Yer dad said he thought it was more than likely you'd come over for the day so I started baking early. I've got the kettle on an' your nan will be in any moment now. I'd bet my last shilling she's seen you arrive.'

Joan was laughing. 'Give me time to get in the house, Mum. You go on as if someone has wound you up.'

'Good God, do I really?'

'I'm only teasing. I'm so darned glad to be here I don't care if you go on at me non-stop all day.'

'It's only me.' Hester's voice echoed down the hall.

'Told you so.' Daphne grinned.

'Oh, Nan, you look perky as ever,' Joan said.

'Come on, you two. I've got t' see to me oven,' Daphne urged, as she edged past.

Later as they sat around the kitchen table eating hot buttered scones, Joan said, 'I feel tons better already. What would I do if I didn't have you two to turn to?'

It was then, as she looked at these two dear faces, that the dam burst. She had merely meant to outline the reasons why she was still worried about Jamie and to listen to any advice they cared to offer her. But instead she found herself pouring it all out to them as she had poured out her troubles as a little girl, in the days when her nan and her mother were still full of beans and spent a lot of their time gadding about in dance halls. They listened to the torrent of words in silence, their green eyes attentive and concerned. 'Don't you see, Mum? With Matt and Dad refusing to face the facts and, more to the point, encouraging Jamie to do the same, it's like bashing my head against a brick wall. I haven't got a chance in hell of getting Jamie to answer Beryl's letter. And as for getting him to agree to meeting her, not a ghost of a chance!'

'But why didn't you tell us all this before now?' Daphne asked quietly. 'Did you think we wouldn't understand, or at least find a way to try to help?'

'Well, Mum, *you* might have tried to influence Jamie but . . . well, Nan, you're a bit like Matt and me dad. You've done your best to close your eyes and ears right from the beginning.'

'Just because I didn't much like the sound of those people in America doesn't mean I don't want to get things sorted out.' Hester sounded offended.

'No, I know you mean well, Nan, but you said quite frankly that you found the story of a mix-up at birth unbelievable, and you told Jamie that even if they did find out because of a blood test that the two babies had been given to the wrong parents they should have left it at that. That's what good parents would have done, you said, not taken the matter this far.'

'That,' said Hetty calmly, 'is still my opinion. Jamie is a serious young man, but he is also bright, decent, loving, and when it comes to the crunch he'll do what he feels to be right, no matter what you, I or anyone else has to say.'

'Clive Richardson has spoken to Beryl and her husband Joe several times, and he thinks they come across as nice, kind people,' Joan told her.

'Does he, indeed?'

'Yes. He was quite sure that they wanted what was best for everyone.'

Daphne chipped in, 'Well, the best for us on this side of the ocean is to forget we ever heard of them.'

'Oh, Mum! Not you too! Talking like that isn't going to help,' Joan rebuked her mother. Then turning to her nan, she said, 'If I were to be given three wishes, all of them would run along the same lines. I'd give the world to turn the clock back. And I keep asking myself, Why the hell didn't they just keep quiet about the blood test? But on the other hand I have to keep telling myself that Mr and Mrs Piviteaux started this investigation for all the right reasons. They appear to be quite prosperous, own a long-standing family business and somehow I do believe their main concern was to find out if their true son was healthy and well-cared-for. I can understand that. Can't you?'

'Yes, of course I can.' Hester was quick to establish that.

'But they could have achieved that by being much more discreet. Instead, what have they done? Churned up a right old hornet's nest and, from what I can make out, left two troubled young lads on the way.' Suddenly she felt she had been too outspoken and that now was the time to become the peacemaker. She added, 'Perhaps we ought to pray for a miracle. You know, something along the lines that the two lads meet and become the best of friends.'

'Oh, Nan,' Joan cried in despair, 'don't you think I've done my fair share of praying these last few weeks? Anyway, happy-ever-after only happens in fairy stories and this is real life.'

'No, it doesn't. Not always,' Hester replied. 'Happy endings happen every day somewhere in the world. If there's one thing I've learnt during my lifetime it is that if you have enough faith you can, as they say, move mountains. I prayed that Jamie, my great-grandson, would get well and come out of that hospital without the accident having affected his brain, and my prayers were answered.'

'Oh, Nan, we all said that prayer over and over again.'

'So, like I said, all our prayers were answered.'

'So now you're telling me that maybe an angel of the Lord could come down from heaven to sort out this horrible mess not only to our complete satisfaction but to give joy and peace of mind to the Piviteaux family as well.'

Hester sat up straight. 'And why not? Stranger things have been known to happen. There's no need for you to be flippant. As your granddad used to say, the Lord works in mysterious ways his wonders to perform. I shall pray for guidance – and for everyone concerned, come to that.' Then, getting to her feet, she added, 'About time we cleared this table and sorted out what we're going to do with the rest of the day. It isn't very often we get you to ourselves, Joan, so while I wash these cups you think about what you'd like to do.'

Daphne managed to get Joan on her own and, smiling broadly, told her, 'When your nan says she'll pray that the outcome of all this will see everyone happy, what she really means is she wants our Jamie to be just that for as long as he lives and that the Piviteaux family will remain where they are and get on with their own lives.'

Joan put out a hand to her mother. 'I don't care if it's an angel or the Lord Himself who's going to intervene. I just hope somebody comes up with an answer soon. All I really want, Mum, is for our lives to be normal again.'

Hester had overheard this last remark as she carried a tray out into the scullery, and thought, So do I. But I've got a feeling it's going to get worse before it gets better.

Chapter Twenty-Seven

DURING THE LOVELY summer months they all seemed to have reached an uneasy truce. As he had long been doing anyway, Matt refused to utter one word on the matter of the Piviteaux family. Jamie had gone from strength to strength: his skin was tanned, he looked fit and healthy and, more to the point, he was fun to be with. The only fly in the ointment was that he agreed with his father and grand-father that it was quite in order to ignore the American couple who were insisting that he was their rightful son. Joan's problem became harder.

Beryl had telephoned her, twice, which she had kept to herself.

Weeks went by. In spite of all her nan's promises, neither an angel nor the Lord Himself put in an appearance to help find an answer to satisfy everyone.

With the days now drawing in, the main topic of conver-sation in the Pearson household was that Jamie would be twenty-one in November, and all three females felt that if they kept on at Matt long and hard enough he would give in to their way of thinking.

'All right, all right,' he protested one evening, as they sat around the dinner table. Then to Joan, he said, 'I told you last year that they'd both want another do. Our children think I'm made of money.'

Joan had to raise her voice to be heard because Meg, Rosie and Jamie were rolling about in fits of laughter. 'Meg was quite content with her eighteenth,' she assured him, 'but we all feel Jamie's birthday this year is extra special an' not only because he's to be twenty-one.'

Matt glanced across at his wife. He knew what she was saying: first that they were lucky to have Jamie as he had been so ill, and second, that they had weathered the storm of his parentage. It had been a mutual decision that he would remain at home for the rest of the year, and would start work in the City from the first week in January. He hadn't lost out though. The university had recognised that his work had shown that he would have gained a degree had he not missed so much time because of his head injury and they had conferred a degree on him, a fact that had delighted Jamie and made the whole family really proud of him.

'I give in,' Matt muttered, doing his best not to laugh. 'What with your parents, not to mention Hetty and the way she's been going on, an' my old lady, you'd think there'd never been a lad reach the ripe old age of twenty-one before.' Seeing the wide grin on Jamie's face, Matt added, 'Think yerself lucky, my lad. It were 1944 when I 'ad my twenty-first an' not a soul offered t' do a damn thing about it.'

'You were in the Army an' there was a war on,' Joan protested.

'Exactly. That's the point I'm trying t' make.'

'Oh, come on, Dad,' Meg objected. 'You haven't done so badly since. Can we have Jamie's do at the same place? The Crown at Morden?'

'That would be smashing, Dad,' Rosie said. 'And while you're about it, you could book it for me too cos I'll be eighteen soon.'

'The Lord save us! I'll 'ave to see about robbing a bank,' their father said, turning away so that his children wouldn't see he was grinning.

'Tell us the old, old story,' Jamie sang, and as Joan got to her feet and began to clear the table she felt as though her heart was bursting. It had been such a happy meal. The children could wrap Matt round their little fingers. It was as if each and every member of this family realized that they had come close to losing so much. Matt could have lost all of them if he'd stayed away any longer, and the girls could have lost their brother if the tide had gone the wrong way.

And as to her own behaviour, she couldn't believe how gullible she had been where John Chapman was concerned. She had believed everything he told her and had wallowed in the attention he lavished on her because at that time she had felt the need to be wanted.

Having found out about Matt and Doris Shepherd she had been hurt much more than she had been willing to admit and taking up with John Chapman had been her way of getting back at Matt. But now she would readily agree, two wrongs don't make a right. In the end it was love, even with all the trials and tribulations over the years, the love they all felt for one another had held them together and helped them to weather the storm. For that she would be eternally grateful.

★　　★　　★

It was Monday afternoon, a nice windy day, and Joan had got two lines of washing dry. She was humming to herself as she stood in the kitchen doing the ironing.

When the telephone rang she put down the iron on its stand and went into the hall to answer it. She picked up the receiver and heard a female voice say, 'Joan?'

'Yes, who's speaking?' she asked, though the voice was familiar.

'Oh, sorry, it's me, Beryl. Beryl Piviteaux. I hope I'm not disturbing you.'

Joan's heart missed a beat. Not again! Why did she keep ringing? Joan knew the answer to that one. The poor woman was hoping that, just once, Jamie might answer the phone or at least someone might persuade him to talk to her.

'No, you're not disturbing me, Beryl. I'm the only one in the house at the moment.'

'Oh, I was hoping . . .'

'Yes, I guessed as much. Believe me, Beryl, I have tried to get Jamie to ring you, really I have. I don't know what else I can do.' Then, feeling that she shouldn't be bearing the brunt of all this, let alone made to feel so guilty all the time, she added, 'Surely it's no surprise to you the way he's behaving? After all, Peter's treating me no differently. He wrote quite openly that he wanted nothing to do with me or Matt – or Britain, come to that.'

There was an awkward silence. Then, her voice breaking, Beryl said, 'I have written twice to James. It bothers me that he won't admit who I am, or that Joe is his real father. It doesn't seem to count so much with you. It's as if you put it to one side . . . as if you don't care.'

'That's not fair,' Joan shouted. 'I have to deal with my husband and my parents who flatly refuse even to consider that Jamie doesn't belong to this family. I console myself that he has been mine from the moment he was born, and still is. I thought it would be the same for you. But it isn't, is it? You seem to want to lay claim to both of them.'

'Please, Joan, don't let us quarrel. The reason for this call is to tell you we're coming to England.'

'What? Really?' Oh my God!

'Yes, really, we're all coming.'

'Who exactly?'

'My husband, myself, our two girls and Peter.'

'Peter? Has he agreed? Does he want to come?'

'He hasn't been given a choice. He's coming. His father and I agree he has to meet you.'

Joan didn't know what to say. The boy to whom she had given birth was coming here. Suddenly she was afraid. Was she pleased that at last she would meet him? If she was offered a hundred pounds she wouldn't be able to answer that question. And Beryl must be feeling the same way, because faced with the family being here, in England, Jamie would have no option. He would have to meet his real mother.

When Joan remained silent, Beryl spoke abruptly. 'How it will all turn out I dread to think, but at least we will see their reaction face to face. We'll arrive about the sixth or seventh of November, staying at an hotel in Chingford.'

'Chingford?' Joan was having a job to take it all in.

'Yes. My mother moved out of London some years ago. She has a small flat in a block near Epping Forest. She found this hotel for us, the Ridgeway. It's only ten miles from London, about twenty minutes on the train, so she tells us. It should be convenient all round.'

Joan couldn't think of a word to say.

'Joan, are you still there?'

'Yes,' she muttered.

'I'll write you our full itinerary. I won't telephone any more as it's not always easy to get a connection and it is rather expensive, nor will I write to Jamie again. At least I've given you time to prepare him for this. So, we'll see what happens when we meet. 'Bye, Joan.'

The telephone clicked. Slowly Joan replaced her receiver.

She stood stock still. What now? How on earth was she going to tell her family that they had to come to Chingford or London or wherever to meet the family that had invaded their lives to such an extent that she didn't know what to do for the best. Matt, her parents and Jamie wouldn't want anything to do with the American family. They'd refuse outright even to consider meeting them. That was a dead certainty. What could she do about Jamie? Would it make any difference whatever she said? She had pleaded enough in the past to no avail. She could try to assure him, once again, how much he really meant to her and Matt. Ask him to give it a go. Be reasonable. That was a laugh for starters. From the day that Clive Richardson had come into their lives all reason had flown out of the window.

What about Meg and Rosie? How would they react? They probably wouldn't mind, they might think this visit was a great lark, even look forward to meeting the other family. As long as it didn't jeopardize their relationship with their beloved Jamie.

Her legs felt heavy and her heart was aching as she walked back to the kitchen. Why on earth did Beryl have to keep digging away at a problem that was far better left to sort itself out? She took a lot of understanding, did Beryl Piviteaux. She had said that she wanted to keep Peter as her son. She had brought him up all these years and the bond was too strong to break now. 'That is exactly the way I feel about Jamie,' Joan said aloud.

So what was the problem?

Was it just curiosity? Aching to find out how her real son had fared in these past twenty-odd years? Did she not realize that a meeting might go terribly wrong? Even if they did all meet face to face, eventually. Who's to say how it would turn out? Would it help matters if the boys hated each other? A sudden thought struck Joan, and the horror of it caused her to catch her breath so hard that she had to grab hold of the back of a chair to stop herself from falling. On the second of November both Peter Piviteaux and their own Jamie would be twenty-one years old! How could they have a celebration birthday party for Jamie knowing full well that within a few days they were going to force him to meet with the family that were claiming him as their own.

'Mum, are you all right?'

Joan shook her head, took a deep breath and waited a second for the colour to come back into her cheeks. Such had been the shock of her realization that she hadn't heard Jamie come in.

'Yes, son, sorry about that, it was only I felt a little dizzy.'

Jamie went to the sink and fetched a glass of cold water. 'Here,' he held the glass to her lips and she could see the concern in his eyes. 'Drink this slowly and then you can tell me what upset you cos by the look of you something has.'

Joan made a decision. He would be the first one she would tell. After all, it would affect him the most.

'Please Jamie, I want you to be patient and listen carefully to what I have to tell you.'

He sighed heavily. He knew that what was coming had

to be about the Piviteaux family. 'All right, Mum. I promise I won't say a word until you finish. What's happened now?'

Joan began with the ringing of the telephone and continued until she had related the whole of Beryl's conversation.

Jamie had been very tolerant, listening, taking in every word and not showing her how annoyed he was that once again that family had upset his mother. There was a brief silence, then, without raising his voice he began to repeat what were to him the bare facts of the whole matter.

'Mother, as I've repeatedly told you, I believe that the facts my blood tests turned up are true. Tests such as they were don't lie. But they haven't altered my feelings as to who I am and where I want to be. Not in the slightest. If the American family were hoping for a different reaction then I'm sorry. A mistake was made all those years ago and although that fact has now come to light in my book it's too later for it to be put right. That is my firm opinion.'

He paused and took a deep breath.

'I'm grown up, old enough to make my own decisions. They cannot come into my life just because they want me to know that my ancestors were Polish and are now one hundred per cent all-Americans. I am not interested.' He went to where his mother was sitting, bent down and took one of her hands between both of his.

'If you want the whole truth, Mum, I think fate, if that's what you want to call it, dealt me a great hand. I am James Pearson, have been since the day I was born, and as far as I'm concerned nobody is going to convince me otherwise. My parents are Mathew and Joan Pearson and I've two great sisters, grandparents and even a great-grandmother. My whole family love me and I dearly love each and every one of them.'

What could she say to that? What could she do about it?

She got to her feet, too choked with emotion to speak as her son hugged her close.

Later as they sat opposite each other drinking a cup of coffee Joan asked herself another question: What did she want to do about it?

Nothing, if she were truthful. Jamie's words had meant everything to her. In every sense that mattered he was her son.

Chapter Twenty-Eight

SEPTEMBER AND OCTOBER had given them an Indian summer, but now it was different. The first few days of November had been bitterly cold, and winter was about to settle in good and proper.

Joan didn't like that prospect any more than she did the proposed visit of the Piviteaux family. From the moment she had taken that phone call from Beryl, she hadn't had a moment's peace. Trying to convince her family that it would be in the best interests of them all to meet the Americans and get it over and done with had been the hardest task she had ever had to tackle.

Meg, Rosie, her parents, even Hester and Amy had come round to her way of thinking, but Matt and Jamie were still dead against it, and for the first time Jamie and his grandfather were at loggerheads. It had been a unanimous decision to postpone Jamie's twenty-first birthday party.

Beryl's mother had telephoned and introduced herself as Eileen Fowler. She had been kind and chatty, so Joan had no qualms about meeting her. Between them they had reached an agreement that the best way for everyone to meet for the first time would be in normal circumstances rather than in a hotel. Joan had invited them all to lunch on their first Sunday in England. She sighed and shook her head at the thought of it.

Christ knows how I let myself in for that, she thought. Would the whole day end up in ructions? Common sense told her she had had no choice. It was a bloody awful necessity that she had to get through. She would have to pull herself together and get on with making this family feel welcome.

She heard Matt and Jamie come downstairs and went into the hall. 'Where are you two off to?'

'Out,' Matt answered, surly.

'We're going for a walk,' Jamie told her.

His voice and the way he was standing, with his chin thrust out and hands in his pockets, infuriated her and Joan felt she couldn't take much more. 'I think the pair of you are acting very badly. The least you could do would be to sit down and talk to me properly. We've only a couple of days to go before they arrive and I'm getting no help from either of you.'

Matt flushed. Clearly he was angry. 'You invited them here, you deal with it.'

'That's the way I feel,' Jamie put in. 'How many more times must I tell you? I don't want an American woman fawning all over me telling me she's my mother.'

Joan felt it was time she stood up for herself. She was fed up to her back teeth with carrying the can all the time. 'Your mother was English, born and bred in the East End of London,' she flung at him.

'Really?' he said sarcastically. 'I thought you were born in Wimbledon, and if you insist on me meeting her on Sunday that is exactly what I shall tell her.'

Matt was frowning. He had never heard Jamie speak to his mother like that. He put his hand on his son's arm. 'Take your coat off, son, and come into the living room.' Turning to Joan he managed a smile. 'Go put the kettle on, love. Make us some tea and we'll 'ave a talk.'

There was a good fire burning in the grate, and the room was comfortable and cheerful. It was a whole lot better than arguing out in the hall. They were each drinking their tea. Jamie had retreated into silence: not a hostile silence but a melancholy one. Joan felt she had to start the conversation or they'd sit here all day. She took a deep breath, then said, 'Jamie, and you, Matt, I do wish you'd see things from my point of view. I could certainly do with a bit of help from somebody.'

'Oh, come off it,' Matt exclaimed crossly. 'You've got your mum and dad an' my mum all agreeing with you, what more d'you want?'

Joan sighed. 'They're not in this house. It's me who has to deal with all the animosity and it's not fair. This mix-up, or whatever you want to call it, was not of my making yet I seem to be getting the blame from all sides. Have either of you ever stopped to think about how I feel about it all?' She paused, and both Matt and Jamie had the grace to look guilty. 'I know it hasn't been easy for you, Jamie. Believe me, if I could wipe it all away I would. But, for once, just listen to me. This family has travelled all the way from America, and if I hadn't agreed that they could come here they wouldn't have just gone away. You'd better believe that because it's the truth. Would you rather that they followed you? Talked to you in the street? Besides, they've had the same trouble with their son. He doesn't want to know me. Has that ever struck you? I feel obliged to meet him, even if it is the one and only time. I honestly believe the best way to satisfy everyone is to let them visit us quietly here in our own home. That way, please, God, it will be over and done with.'

Joan felt such pity tug at her heartstrings as she watched Jamie look at his father. My God, he really is frightened, she thought. What on earth could she say or do that would absolutely reassure this loving, kind young man that he really did belong with them? How could he possibly, even for a minute, think she would allow another lad to come into her life and destroy all the ties that had taken years to grow between a mother and her son?

'Mum, I'm sorry, it's just that . . .' Tears weren't far away.

Matt took charge. 'All right, gal. I'll go along with 'aving them 'ere on Sunday, if that's what will make it easier for you.'

Joan sighed again, but this time it was a sigh of heartfelt thanks.

Now everyone was pulling their weight. Of course it was to be no ordinary Sunday lunch. Beryl and Joe Piviteaux were bringing Beryl's mother so that made six of them. Bill and Daphne would be bringing Hester so that was three more. And no one in their right mind would think of leaving out Grandma Pearson. Amy would never let them forget it if they did! So with us five I make that fifteen, Joan mused, as she made yet another list. Luckily, there were folding wooden doors between the living room and the front room, and although the dining table wasn't anywhere near big enough for fifteen a smaller one could be tucked on to the end. A sheet would have to serve as an undercloth with two fancy ones on top. Bill had promised to lend some chairs.

What to give them to eat? Did Americans like our kind of food?

'Give them good old roast beef,' Matt had said, 'and if it's not t' their liking they can always leave it.'

Joan had ordered the meat from her regular butcher, and when he had assumed that it was for a celebration dinner for Jamie's twenty-first she hadn't put him right. What he didn't know he couldn't gossip about to all his other customers. Hester had offered to make two apple pies on the Saturday so that they would only need warming through. Daphne had suggested that not everybody would fancy pastry after a big meal so her contribution was to be two bowls of sherry trifle, and with a good assortment of cheeses to follow that ought to fit the bill. Meg and Rosie were to do the vegetables on the Saturday, so all that remained now for Joan to worry over was whether or not to offer a starter and if so what? She was still pondering on this when the telephone rang.

She had hardly lifted the receiver when Amy's voice boomed down the line. 'It's only me, love. I just wanted to know if there's anything I can bring with me for the week-end an' don't forget to sort a few jobs out for me. Can't do with sitting about on me backside for hours on end.'

'Oh, Amy,' Joan laughed, 'I'm so glad you're going to be here. I'm dreading long silences when nobody knows what to say or where to look.'

'Don't let it bovver yer, love. I'll 'ave a thing or two t' say if they upset our Jamie.'

'Don't be rotten,' Joan scolded. 'Perhaps you can help me

out, though, because I can't think what to give them to start the meal off. I did consider soup but that seems a bit ordinary. Any suggestions?'

'Well, before Matt picks me up on Saturday morning I could nip down Petticoat Lane. There's always the herring sellers. Come to that, if you don't want roll-mops, 'ow about smoked mackerel, or a couple of crabs?'

'All a bit messy,' Joan said.

'Could always bring three or four pints of winkles, give 'em all a pin an' let them 'elp themselves.'

Joan had to hold the phone away from her ear because Amy's bawdy laughter was deafening. Even so she herself was giggling helplessly. She doubted very much if the Americans had even heard of winkles let alone eaten them. And the very idea of asking her guests to sit there with a pin, picking the tiny worm-like pieces of fish out of each shell, well, only Matt's mum would even think of such a thing.

'Amy, you've given me an idea. If you would bring a couple of nice dressed crabs and some fair-size prawns, I'll make seafood salads.'

'Okay, love. Yer wouldn't like some cockles and whelks just to add a bit of taste, would yer?'

'No, I wouldn't, an' just you remember t' be on your best behaviour over the weekend. You will, won't you?' Joan begged.

'Course I will. If that Beryl an' 'er mother were born and lived in the East End then I'm 'ome an' dry for someone t' talk to, ain't I?'

As she put the phone down Joan thought, The Americans are going to love you.

⋆ ⋆ ⋆

Everyone was attempting to keep busy, except Matt, who was reading the Sunday paper. 'For Christ's sake sit down an' get a grip on yerself,' he said, as Joan went over once more to gaze out of the window.

'I'm all right,' she answered, twiddling with a bowl of flowers. When he tut-tutted she dropped her hands to her side. 'Oh, how I wish today was all over. My mum and yours wouldn't let me near the kitchen and my nan has dusted and polished everything in sight. I don't know what to do with myself. God, why did Meg and Rosie have to go out? If they're not back when the Piviteauxs arrive I'll kill them. And Jamie wouldn't open his door when I called to him.'

She was working herself up into such a state that Matt was about to pour her a stiff drink when the two girls burst in. 'Dad, you'd better come. We think they've arrived. A car has drawn up on the opposite side of the road with hire-car plates.'

From that moment on Joan could not have said what happened or in what order. Suddenly there was a semi-circle of tanned-looking people standing in her hallway. Two girls in the front, both dark-haired and blue-eyed, were introducing themselves to Meg and Rosie as Karen and Betsy. Beryl Piviteaux was a short, good-looking woman, who in her early years must have been a natural blonde. Now the colour was fading and she could only be described as plump, though the suit she wore was well cut and fashionable. Now, looking at her smiling, good-natured face, Joan came to the conclusion that she was a happy lady.

The two mothers stood staring at each other, both near to tears. Suddenly they both spoke.

'Where is Peter?'

'Where is James?'

Joan turned round to Jamie, who stood against the far wall. In a low voice she said, 'Come and meet everyone, Jamie.'

Beryl was doing the same thing, almost dragging her tall son from where he stood behind his father. 'This is Peter,' she said.

Then both women had their arms around each other.

It was Matt who said, 'Come on, come on, give these folk a chance to get inside the house. They must be dying for a drink.'

Beryl and Joan broke apart, each fumbling for handkerchieves.

Hester, Daphne and Amy saved the day. They were taking hats and coats, ushering everyone into the living room down the end nearest to where the grate was filled with crackling logs. Bill Harvey was making small-talk and asking everyone what they'd like to drink. Beryl's mother was of the same age and type as Amy, and there was no hanging back between the two of them from the word go.

By the time Joan had wiped her eyes and got her breath back Joe Piviteaux and Matt had a glass in their hand and were acting as if they were old buddies. Now she could take a good long look at Peter, the lad to whom she had given birth.

He stood well over six feet tall, far taller than Joe Piviteaux, had big dark brown eyes like Matt's and his dark hair held the reddish tints of Joan's family. Their eyes met, then the lad's fell away. He looked so uncomfortable and clearly he had nothing to say to her.

She glanced at Jamie. He looked even worse.

Beryl was doing her best to engage him in conversation, and Joan felt sorry for her. And she had noticed that Jamie had taken his clear blue eyes and dark hair from Joe Piviteaux. In fact, he bore a distinct likeness to his natural father.

'I hope you're all hungry,' Joan said, making an effort to lighten the atmosphere.

'You must have gone to a whole lot of trouble,' Beryl answered, glancing at the long dinner table. Her face was very pale and Joan placed a hand on her elbow and led her to a chair. Matt offered a glass and urged Beryl to drink. 'It's port with just a dash of brandy to settle you down. Just sip it slowly.'

Jamie couldn't take his eyes off his mother. His insides were raging. His mum and this other woman were getting on like a house on fire. Doesn't my mother remember why this family is here? Anyway today, if nothing else, was all his mother's fault. Why had she had to ask them here? She could have stopped them if she'd tried hard enough. Their Peter was downright rude. He was standing with his back to everyone just staring out of the window. It had been a shock to see him. He was so tall, just like Matt, and there was no question that he had the colouring of the Harvey family. He'd seen his granddad's reaction as he'd compared faces, and when he looked at Nan he knew that she, too, had accepted the resemblance. He didn't like Peter. The quicker they get him and his family out of our house the better I'll like it, he cried silently. Besides, just look at Mr Piviteaux! Such dark hair even on the back of his hands and when he spoke there was no mistaking he was an American.

Then Beryl was on her feet again and crossing the room to where he was standing. She put out a hand and, automatically, he took a step backwards. Surely to God she wasn't going to kiss him – or, even worse, put her arms round him and start to cry. His heart was thumping against his ribs and he was thinking that he'd give anything in the world to be able to get out of the front door and start running.

'I'm sorry, James,' was all she said, awkwardly, and this time she made no attempt to touch him. She was making him feel even more uncomfortable, if that were possible. She merely stared at him, with such a sorrowful expression that as she turned and walked away he found to his surprise that he felt sorry for her.

Amy had come into the room to clear space on the sideboard for the vegetables but seeing her beloved Jamie looking so sad and forlorn she went to him. Resisting the urge to wrap him in her arms and hold him close – that would never do, not today, they might both just end up in a flood of tears – she whispered, 'Head up, Jamie! Get through this meal and we'll soon 'ave everything back to normal.'

'Oh, Gran, I wish you meant that,' he said, keeping his voice low.

'Course I bloody mean it. Every word. Come on, lad, show them what a man you are, a Pearson and proud of it.'

Joe Piviteaux was looking at him, though trying not to. He felt his gran pat his back, so he straightened up, did his best to smile and, seeing that Matt was dispensing more drinks, he made a beeline for him and asked, 'Can I give you a hand, Dad?'

'Will you all please sit at the table.' To Joan's surprise, Hester had given the command. She was certainly rising to the occasion!

Matt went to the head where his mother had placed a large dish that held the big joint of roast beef.

'Please, do sit down,' Joan urged, because no one had moved. 'Sit anywhere you like.'

The Piviteaux family arranged themselves down one side of the table and the Pearsons, in the main, sat facing them. Joan's head was spinning as she watched everyone toy with the first course, over which she had taken such trouble. Matt endeavoured to make jokes as he carved the beef, and it was a relief when Amy and Daphne got to their feet and passed round the plates, telling everyone to help themselves to vegetables.

Having this lot here was a terrible mistake, Joan thought. Jamie and Matt had been right. But I meant well. She was crying inside. When Peter bothered to raise his head he just glared at her, as if she had done him a terrible wrong. She knew he was having a hard job to curb his tongue. But if he did let loose, what would he say? Come to that, what would Jamie say to his real mother? It was worse than a funeral party.

Amy did her best to break the awful silence. 'You two lads 'ave come of age now. Did you 'ave a party for your twenty-first, Peter?'

He looked across at her, his eyes asking, What the hell has it got to do with you? He merely shook his head.

'We're having the neighbours and Peter's friends round when we get home,' Beryl answered for him.

They were laying their knives and forks down on their plates. No one could say a hearty meal had been eaten by all! The apple pies and trifles were brought in and Matt carried the cheese from the sideboard.

Joan got to her feet. 'Where are you going, dear?' her mother asked, the concern showing on her face.

She had to gulp back the tears. 'To make the coffee.'

Jamie watched her leave the room and there was hatred in his heart for the strangers who were sitting around the table. Why, oh, why had things been allowed to go this far? If only that American doctor had kept his damned mouth shut. If only they had accepted the truth but kept it to themselves. That's what Joe and Beryl should have done if they truly loved Peter. Instead look at the trouble they had caused. Every single person in this room was all twisted up and nobody had a clue how to sort it all out. There wasn't going to be a happy ending, and there was no use pretending there was.

The women seemed to be getting on better than the men. The older ones were in the kitchen doing the washing-up and talking away nineteen to the dozen. Joan and Beryl were clearing the table and folding cloths. The four girls had taken themselves upstairs because Meg had suggested they might like to freshen up and at the same time take a look at their bedrooms. If the truth be told, both Meg and Rosie loved listening to eighteen-year-old Karen and fifteen-year-old Betsy, and they wanted to know a whole lot more about life in America.

As Joan had watched them all climb the stairs she had wished so hard that the two lads had also formed such a quick and easy friendship. In the circumstances, though, that was an impossible wish. Amy came in, carrying a loaded tray of clean cutlery. She was smiling broadly.

'What's cheered you up?' Joan had to ask, even though she dreaded hearing the answer.

'It's all right, love, nobody ain't killed anyone.' Then, throwing her head back and roaring with laughter, she added, 'At least, not yet they ain't.'

Joan looked at Beryl and they, too, started to laugh.

'Oh, Amy, now I know I'm home. Listening to you I

hadn't realized how much I missed the East End. You're a gem, you really are,' Beryl said spontaneously.

'Glad yer think so, love.' Amy grinned. 'But you'd better 'ave a good look round while you're 'ere cos there ain't much of the old London left standing. Yer mum 'as been telling me 'ow glad she is she moved out t' Chingford. She's invited me to go an' see 'er place, an' I told her if she wants to breathe in the smoke again there's only me left in the 'ouse an' she'd be more than welcome to stay with me.'

Good Lord! Joan stared at her mother-in-law in amazement. There was no side to her. How did she do it? Most people would describe Amy as being rough and ready and yet she got on well with everyone and everybody loved her.

'Where have the men got to?' Joan asked.

Amy's grin widened. 'They've taken themselves down the garden, would you believe it?'

'But it's freezing cold,' Joan protested.

'Well, they obviously thought the atmosphere in 'ere wasn't exactly warm.'

'From the kitchen could yer see what they were doing?'

'Yeah. Matt and yer dad took Mr Piviteaux into the shed. The two boys were down beyond yer big apple tree. They 'adn't come to blows the last time I looked.'

By four o'clock it was getting dark as they all stood in the front garden saying goodbye. All the women hugged each other, the men shook hands and the four girls kissed. Only Peter and Jamie had nothing to say.

'Let's get their reaction tomorrow, after they've slept on it,' Joe Piviteaux said wisely. 'We've a while to go before we return to the States. We'll ring you – maybe we could meet up in London. Would you show us some of the sights? In particular I want to show my kids the place where I met

their mother and the district where we did our courting.'
He guffawed and Beryl blushed. 'But for today, well, we're
mighty grateful, even if we haven't expressed ourselves very
well.'

Matt assured him they had been more than welcome and
both he and Joan made noncommittal noises as regards
meeting again.

Once the car had turned the corner they all trooped back
indoors.

'I'll see about getting us some tea,' Daphne said, 'since
nobody ate much dinner.'

'I don't want any, Gran. I'm going to my room.'

Jamie had spoken quietly and Joan's heart ached for him.
She'd take a bet that it wouldn't be much different for Beryl.
She doubted that Peter would have much to say on the
journey back to their hotel.

They had somehow got through the first meeting, but
had anything been achieved? Somehow she felt more under-
mined than before. And as for both Jamie and Peter, their
minds must be in a terrible whirl. She would pray hard
tonight. But exactly what would she pray for? Guidance for
them all?

Chapter Twenty-Nine

JAMIE FELT HE had tossed and turned long enough. At two o'clock that morning he had gone downstairs, drunk a glass of milk and munched his way through a pile of cheese and biscuits. Even after that he still hadn't been able to sleep. He switched on his bedside light and saw it was a quarter to five. His mind was made up. Argue and turn it over as much as you like, when you boiled it all down it was himself and Peter Piviteaux who were most affected by this strange turn of events. But it had gone on too long. True, both his mother and Peter's had been shaken to the very core. How about the fathers? Matt took refuge in bad temper, making out that he disbelieved the whole damn caboodle from start to finish. That fact had Jamie loving him even more. At least he hadn't wrung his hands in despair and whined. Outright, with no hesitation, he had maintained that Jamie was his son and that was an end of the matter. Out in the garden yesterday Jamie had heard him say to Joe Piviteaux that he was his one and only son born on 2 November 1944 and he didn't care if folk wanted to talk to him till they were blue in the face it wouldn't alter his opinion one iota. Jamie had felt so proud. If Peter hadn't been watching him he'd have gone and thrown his arms around his dad and more than likely bawled like a baby.

It was just after that that Peter had said grudgingly, 'My dad feels the same way, I know he does.'

If that were true then it was only the women who were pursuing the matter. And he knew his mother hadn't been the instigator. That left only Beryl Piviteaux! When he had said to Peter that Beryl was to blame for the current situation they had practically come to blows. Then, reluctantly, Peter had added, 'You don't know the half of it. You don't have Polish relations and scores of ancestors clamouring away at you about their forefathers. None of you has the slightest idea what my mother has had to put up with. They just keep on to her. And at me.'

At that Jamie almost found himself feeling sorry for Peter.

Now, an awful thought came into his head. Were Peter's grandparents letting him think that if he was not of their blood they wanted nothing more to do with him? Straight on top of that came another thought. If those grandparents were such sticklers for their own bloodline, were they setting out to claim Jamie? If that was their aim, they were going to be disappointed.

It was about time he did something about all this, he decided, and climbed out of bed. He washed and brushed his teeth, then dressed. He folded some trousers, two shirts, underwear, socks and a few handkerchiefs, then added a washing pouch and put them all into the bag he used for his rugby kit. Money. He took ten pounds out of his drawer, then remembered his birthday money. God bless his aunts and uncles.

The house was still, but it wouldn't be long before his father was up and about. By the telephone in the hall he found his mother's address book. He turned the pages quickly and found the address and phone number of the Ridgeway hotel where the Piviteauxs were staying. He propped up the short note he had written, then pulled on his winter coat, wound a long scarf around his neck, opened the front door and closed it quietly behind him. He set off at a trot towards Morden station.

The warmth and the familiar smell of the Underground was comforting. Even at this early hour the train was fairly full and he looked around at the workers setting off on a Monday morning to begin the week. Come the new year, he would be joining them. The City held out good prospects for him and he had been looking forward to the opportunity that had been offered him. But, thank God, there were still a few weeks left before he had to think about it and hopefully by then he would have sorted out the mess that had been dumped on his family.

He came out into the hustle and bustle of Stockwell station, walked a few yards and turned left into South Lambeth Road. There he waited for a bus and when it came he climbed the stairs which gave him a jolly good view of the River Thames as the bus drove over Vauxhall Bridge. This reminded him of his days of sight-seeing with his mates on trips which had mostly ended up with them all paying a visit to his Gran Pearson. God, she could be a funny lady! But she had a heart of gold and there was never a person he had met that would dispute that fact.

The bus pulled into Victoria station. Suddenly he was very hungry. Except for the cheese and biscuits he'd eaten at two o'clock that morning he had hadn't a proper meal since Saturday. He wasn't going to waste his money on the posh cafeteria. His dad had taught him better than that. He made his way to the transport café behind the station.

Having put away a huge breakfast he decided it was time to make that telephone call. Less than an hour later the two young men were boarding a fast train bound for the West Country.

'I always did have a passion for travelling light,' Peter said, as he stowed his bag on the luggage rack.

'Did you leave a note for your parents?' Jamie asked

'Yes, I did. It wasn't the smartest thing I've ever done, running out on them like that, but what you said made sense.'

'I'm feeling guilty,' Jamie admitted, 'but I do believe it's up to us to have a few days away and decide what we think should happen.'

For the first time since he had heard the name James Pearson, Peter realized they were in the same boat, and it made sense for the two of them to be allies, not enemies. It was unthinkable to both young men that their lives should be turned upside down because of a mistake that had taken place over twenty years ago.

As the train pulled out of London they settled back in the corner seats of the carriage and their eyes met. Each could almost read the other's thoughts. Until now there had been little comfort in the situation and as time went on and nothing was resolved it was tearing their mothers apart. Would they be able to come up with an answer? They'd have to wait and see.

Jamie spoke first. 'I've no idea how we're going to carry on for the next few days, but whatever conclusion we come to, it won't be a victory for one of us and defeat for the other. How can it be?'

'I know what you're saying. But us clearing out of the way for the time being was a brilliant idea and at least it will give us a chance to . . . I don't know, certainly not find an answer to which everyone will agree.' Peter heaved a desperate sigh.

Jamie shook his head. 'Not a chance in hell of us doing that! Nothing short of a miracle would work now. But just because neither of us liked the sound of belonging to another family doesn't mean we don't care. I'd give the world to be able to ease the heartache both our mothers have been suffering.'

'The trouble with each of us is that we're pretty settled in the life that has been allotted to us and . . .' For the first time since they had met, Peter smiled '. . . well, James, we might even become buddies. You never know, do you? Just before we left the States my dad was telling us how he and Mom managed to grab a few days' honeymoon in Corn Wall.' He pronounced it as two separate words. His smile broadened. 'Wonder what made you think of us going to the West Country? Anyway, here we are, on our way there. We might even enjoy ourselves,' he said. That's if we don't end up coming to blows, he added to himself.

Meanwhile both mothers had found the notes and had arranged to meet. 'I can't believe it,' Beryl said, in the tea lounge of the Grosvenor Hotel at Victoria station that afternoon.

'No, but I was quite relieved when you rang and said Peter had gone off with Jamie. All Jamie's note told us was that he was going to telephone Peter.'

'I know what you mean,' Beryl said. 'While I sat here on my own waiting for you, I've been making mental notes of every single thing I wanted to tell you. And I imagined that it was going to be terribly difficult, and found myself searching for the right words and the best way to say them. But then you came through the door looking just as worried as I felt. My mind went blank. Now I've come to the conclusion that we both want exactly the same thing where our boys are concerned.'

'Oh, Beryl,' Joan cried, 'I've been so afraid of hurting or upsetting you that I've held back from telling you what was really in my heart.'

'Well, maybe the boys going off like this will prove to be a Godsend. Let's hope they come back friends. What did Matt have to say?'

'Much the same as your Joe did, I guess,' Joan replied.

'Yeah, well, I'm more than happy to shut my ears to that. Leave Peter and Jamie to get on with it. Now, I'm going to order coffee for myself and I guess it will be tea for you.'

Two days later Peter and Jamie, dressed in suitable winter clothing and heavy shoes, were sitting on a rock eating sandwiches. In all directions the moors looked bleak, but there were small shaggy ponies who were tame enough to nuzzle their hands and chew the crusts of bread they held out to them. They had spent their first night in an hotel in Truro, but on the advice of a hall porter had taken a bus out to Redruth, a tiny fishing village nestled at the foot of breathtaking hills. They had taken two single bedrooms in the village pub, with the offer of a hearty breakfast, a packed lunch and an evening dinner all inclusive for seven nights at twelve pounds each.

'We should at least send a postcard to our folks,' Peter muttered, as he crunched into an apple.

'No, I don't agree,' Jamie answered quickly. 'The post-mark would give away our whereabouts and we'd have the whole place swarming with relatives before we'd be able to turn round.' They laughed.

They were having a great time. The days were good, if bitterly cold, with whippy, freezing winds and an angry grey sea. Their evenings, perhaps, were the best of all. News of their presence had spread through the village, and the pub's evening trade was so good as a result that the landlord and his missus were thinking of asking the lads to stay on a bit longer.

With the curtains drawn and a fire blazing, the small bar was packed. The boys, who had had a hard job to get used to the thick Cornish accent, were not surprised to learn that Cornwall had once had its own language. But if they liked to listen to the locals, Peter's Americanisms and Jamie's London accent held the villagers spellbound.

The boys were told of how Redruth had been an important centre because of its tin and copper mines, but when the talk turned to the military activity that had gone on in the surrounding countryside during the latter years of the war they sat up straight and began to take notice.

''Tis true, lad.' The landlord came out from behind the bar. 'Quite a few Americans were here. Very inconspicuous at first, they were, but as time went on our narrow cobbled streets rang with the tramping of Army boots. Barbed-wire barriers were everywhere, certainly along the coastline. And many a night there was a jeep parked outside here.'

His missus wasn't going to be outdone. 'I could tell ee a tale or two,' she said to Peter. 'Further over the headland it's rugged country an' that's where they put the Nissen huts that became an American base.' She would have liked to tell him about the dance she went to up there. It had been a night she'd never forget. But one look at her husband's face and she decided against it.

'I was in the Home Guard,' one white-haired old gentleman quavered.

'Home Guard? Sorry, would you explain, please, sir?' Peter asked.

'Well, some of us had to defend our shores. At first, when we were formed in 1940, I suppose we were a laughing-stock. No weapons, only pitchforks and suchlike, but we drilled till we were dead on our feet, and as time went on we were well equipped. We'd have put up a good show if Hitler had sent his troops to invade us.'

'I'm sure you would have, sir,' Peter answered politely, even though he was having great trouble in taking in the fact that men had been doing their best to defend the shores of England with little more than garden tools in 1940.

He was so glad that Jamie had made that telephone call suggesting that they take off together. The funny thing was, though, that they hadn't even begun to discuss the situation. They'd spoken of everything under the sun but that. It was as if they were two old mates who had met up and decided to have a break in different surroundings. And of all the places to find himself! Redruth in Corn Wall!

It was so small, quaint, like nothing he could have imagined. He found himself wishing that he could invite James to visit America. How he'd gasp if they had a vacation up in the log cabin that the family used for holidays. Boy, he'd have to agree that was some beautiful country.

Here the narrow streets of the town were empty and quiet, except when a fishing-boat put into the harbour to land its catch. He could hardly believe that he was sitting here, in this pub that was a warren of stone-flagged passages, ceilings so low that he already had one lovely bruise on his forehead to show for it, and being made to feel so welcome, almost as if he and Jamie were long-lost sons.

He fell to wondering what these good down-to-earth folk would have to say if he and Jamie were to tell them their story. Hey, you guys, he's really the American, Peter Piviteaux, although he believes he's a Limey. And I'm the English one who should be going by the name of James Pearson. My father was an American soldier who came to these parts early in 1944 to spend a few days of wedded bliss, but quite recently we've learnt that man is really Jamie's father. Not mine! Surely they'd never be able to grasp those facts. He and Jamie were having a hard enough job as it was!

One of the women customers stooped to pile more logs on to the fire from the basket that lay in the hearth. 'Here, let me do that for you, ma'am.' Peter was on his feet in an instant.

Straightening up the woman looked at him, thinking what lovely manners he had. Then she turned her gaze to Jamie, a real English gentleman. She felt she'd love to dig deep into their friendship. There had to be more to these two than met the eye – God above, it was November and not the time of year to come sightseeing.

She thanked Peter, and asked, 'Haven't you got any tales to tell *us*? We'd love to know what's brought two big lads like you to our part of the country in the dead of winter.'

At this the boys stifled their laughter and did their best to dodge the question.

Much later when they were saying goodnight they came to the conclusion that the locals' way of life was different from anything either of them had experienced. The men seemed so elderly and so small, and there was hardly one among them whose hair had not turned grey. Take the governor of the pub: he wore an old jersey, and of an evening he'd take off his shoes and put on carpet slippers. You'd never believe he was the owner of the place. As for the other men, their hands were rough and horny – they might lead their lives at a slow pace but they worked hard.

Next morning, washed and dressed before eight o'clock, Jamie glanced out of the window and was surprised to see that Peter was already outside, standing by the big stone wall that surrounded the public house staring out to sea. He hastened down to join him.

'I was trying to decide what we should do today.' Peter gave him a cheery welcome. 'Although it's hardly light yet, I just know the sun is going to come out. I've been standing here imagining what a difference that will make to this place.'

They both gazed out to sea. Today it glowed with different colours. Over the rocks and seaweed that lay near to shore the water was dark. Far out, where a fleet of small fishing-boats were battling their way across the waves it became almost green. There was hardly any wind yet the sea was never still, swelling and dipping, constantly rolling.

Both boys were deep in thought until Jamie spoke: 'I think today we had better see if we can come up with some answers, don't you, Peter?'

'Yeah. Okay.' Then, as if thinking aloud, he said, 'My life was carefully planned. I had everything. Yes, and I took it all for granted. Now I wonder after all these years why a bolt out of the blue has been directed at my family. It has caused my mother such anxiety that I felt I could cheerfully kill the doctor who had laid the true facts bare. And to top that, she had my grandparents to contend with and they've convinced her somehow that she's an utter failure. It doesn't seem to count that she has two lovely daughters besides me.'

Jamie felt closer to him at that moment than ever before. 'I know what you're saying. I, too, wanted to lash out at someone when the proven facts were laid out for me. I blamed your parents for not keeping it to themselves. Then on my way home from university I had an accident. Got knocked off my motorbike. They tell me I hovered between life and death for some time. I do know that during those long days and nights my mother was never far away. I sensed her presence. She and my family willed me to live. All that time, the question of whether Joan and Matt Pearson were my true parents was irrelevant. So the answer, whatever it is, is no longer of any real importance.'

For one long moment they stared at each other. Then simultaneously they held out a hand, and grasped each other's.

'Something weird going on out there. Come an' look, me dear,' the landlord urged his life. She saw the two big lads holding each other in what she later described to her customers as a great big bear hug.

She would have been even more amazed had she heard the American and the Londoner swear to regard each other as a brother for as long as they should live.

'I'm ravenous,' Peter declared. 'Shall we go in for breakfast?'

'Yes, and I don't know about you but I feel as if a huge weight has been lifted off my shoulders.'

'Do you think we should make tracks for London?' Peter asked.

The very thought of it filled Jamie with dismay. 'What difference is a few more days going to make? Let's make the most of it, have a real holiday.'

Peter felt filled with the same need to stay on here in Redruth because there were so many more places for them to see and he was already making a mental list.

The time went all too quickly. They spent a few queasy hours out with the local fishermen, with an added thrill of seeing a shoal of mackerel being hauled aboard while the seagulls filled the sky with their screams. They tramped for miles finding yet more villages with maze-like narrow lanes. They found it pleasant to be alone. All the hurt and anger had been wiped away. They hoped that the same could be said for both sets of parents. Soon they would have to go back and face the music. But still, for a little while longer, they had each other's company.

One day they found a gift shop, filled with the sort of rubbish that tourists rushed to buy. Its windows were dusty and the door was closed.

'You boys looking to buy a present for your womenfolk?'

They turned to stare at a stout man in a leather apron. 'There be a factory down there.' He pointed with a gnarled finger. 'No rubbish, mind, handmade woollen garments finished off neatly on machines. Take a look. Won't cost yer nothing.' They were speechless but managed to nod their thanks.

They set their feet in the direction he had pointed. God, the way was steep, the road so narrow that there was no space for a pavement and the small whitewashed houses had steep granite steps up to their old oak front doors. Surely the man was wrong. No factory could exist in such a place. Where were the tall chimneys, Jamie wondered as he thought about the East End of London where his gran lived.

In a crooked corner they found it: a beautiful double-fronted cottage. A huge wooden board that had been painted bright blue was fixed to the stout wall: 'Shetland Wool Cottage Industry'.

As they stood there the door was opened by a little woman with rosy cheeks. 'I'm Mrs Benbridge. Come in.'

The boys looked at each other. Obviously she was a lady of few words.

Five young women sat working at a bench and when the ten eyes were turned on them the boys felt embarrassed.

Mrs Benbridge pushed back the mob cap she wore and scratched her head. 'For your mothers? Jumper or cardigan?' She pointed to a glass display cabinet.

The boys shifted their feet. The garments looked very nice, and it wouldn't be a bad idea to buy presents for Beryl and Joan, but what about size – and colour?

Peter was the first to recover and, using all his charm, he said, 'May we see one of each please, ma'am, and may we rely on your good judgement to advise us on size?' The approving sigh that rose from the girls as they stared at their American visitor was loud, and Mrs Benbridge quickly stared her condemnation.

Several items were brought forth and laid on top of the cabinet. They were indeed of the finest wool and skilfully hand-embroidered. Jamie whispered, 'Shall I buy one for Beryl and you buy one for Joan?'

'What a good idea.'

Mrs Benbridge snorted in disapproval. 'These cardigans are more suitable for your mothers. I'm sure they are sophisticated ladies.'

Peter couldn't bring himself to answer. This woman thought they were referring to their girlfriends. Good job she wasn't aware of the full story or she'd probably have forty fits.

Jamie came to the rescue. 'Joan and Beryl *are* our mothers,' he told her. 'I would like a blue cardigan, please, for Beryl. She's quite short and a little on the plump side.'

Before the poor woman could regain her composure, Peter said, 'And mine will be for Joan, who is tallish and has the most lovely red hair, so I think perhaps the green would suit her best.'

Still without a word Mrs Benbridge sorted through her stock and finally laid out two very fine cardigans in what appeared to be the right sizes. 'They be one pound ten shillings and sixpence each, and sixpence extra if you'd like them packed in a gift box.'

Both boys murmured, 'Yes, please.'

As they left the shop, each with a neatly packed box under one arm, they turned in the doorway and winked at the row of girls, who had stopped working and were craning their necks, following their every move, wishing to God that it was time for them to go home so that they could rush out and at least speak to these two gorgeous-looking young men, the likes of which they didn't often get to see in Cornwall.

Bags slung over their shoulders, the lads stood still and looked back. Half of Redruth must have gathered this morning to bid them farewell.

'Us'll never forget ye,' was what they had been told over and over again.

'And as long as we live we're never going to forget our time here in Redruth,' Peter said, as they went towards the bus stop.

'Nor the good it has done us,' Jamie answered.

Chapter Thirty

IT WASN'T A good day to be arriving in London. The spell of good weather had broken. The railway station was heavy with smoke and it was bitterly cold, the roads treacherous with ice. Having spent the last seven days entirely in each other's company, now came the time for parting. The comradeship Peter and Jamie had experienced over the past seven days could not have been imagined when they had first met.

'So,' Peter grinned, 'I guess we'll be meeting up again in the next few days.'

'Sure to be,' Jamie agreed. 'The whole family will want to compare notes. Oh, by the way . . .' He pulled his bag from his shoulder and took out the cardigan he had bought for Beryl.

Peter did the same. 'I've put a short message on the gift tag for Joan.'

'Me, too, for Beryl. Wonder what they'll make of us buying them a gift?'

'Floods of tears is my guess.'

'Yeah, but I bet you anything you like they'll wear them when we meet, just so they can compare with each other.'

'That's a safe bet, Jamie boy. Probably see you tomorrow, till then take care.'

'You too, Peter.' It wasn't enough. They had become too close.

Then Peter's long arms came round Jamie's lean frame and they hugged before going their separate ways.

Joan was looking out of the bay window when she saw Jamie coming up the drive. He hadn't noticed her. She rose to her feet. He looked well, very fit. She walked out into the hall and opened the front door.

She listened to the frosty grass scrunching under the soles of his shoes, and then he saw her. His face broke into a wide grin. She flew down the steps and he rushed towards her. His hand was in the air giving her a thumbs-up and he was laughing. Thank God for that! Jamie was home.

When they were settled with a cup of tea in front of them, Joan asked, 'Are you all right?'

'Did you think I wouldn't be?'

'No. But it was a bit of a long shot, you two going off like that. We didn't know for sure, until Joe phoned your father, that Peter had agreed to go with you. And we were worried sick. We had no idea where you were.'

'We got a train to Cornwall. We thought it best not to tell you our whereabouts. I'm sorry, Mum.'

'I'm sorry, too, son, we all are. None of us handled that first meeting very well.'

'I felt I had to get away and was pretty sure Peter felt the same way. Very fortunate we did what we did, the way things have turned out.'

'You sure about that? How does Peter feel?'

'Well, he's sent you a present. I'll fetch it and I suggest you read the message on the gift tag.'

When Joan had the wrapping paper off and the box open she exclaimed in delight, 'Oh, this is a really lovely cardigan! I've never seen one like it before.'

'Mum, you still haven't read what Peter has written on the card.'

Jamie watched in silence as his mother read the message and wasn't at all surprised when he saw tears spring to her eyes. It was some minutes before she was able to speak and when she did it sounded like a moan. 'Oh . . . isn't that lovely.'

The card said, 'To Joan, I hope we get to know each other a whole lot better in the future. With love, Peter.'

The words were very much the same as he had written for Beryl. He was about to mention this to his mother when she coloured and asked, 'What about Beryl? I wouldn't offend her for the world.'

'It's all right, Mum, really it is,' he reassured her. 'I bought one for her. Hers is blue and I wrote her a card too.'

'Oh, Jamie, bless you, bless you both. You must have wise heads on your shoulders, the pair of you. Us adults could have gone on wrangling for days and getting nowhere. You two lads take yourselves off to the West Country and it seems to me you've managed to become the best of friends. I hope it lasts.'

Jamie looked into his mother's eyes. 'Mum, that's one thing I can promise you. No matter what, Peter and I have agreed to be friends.'

He still had nagging feelings as to what *might* have happened but now they were pushed to the back of his mind. Between Peter and himself they had laid to rest a lot of the anguish. But the very shock of it all would never be forgotten. All those weeks when the possibility had hovered over him that the parents he had known all his life might now want to reject him. The very thought of him not having Joan for his mother had made him physically sick. And as for Matt! A giant of a man that everyone thought twice about crossing. He remembered his early days at school when he'd been bullied and he'd asked his father to meet him at the school gates one afternoon. He had deliberately hung back and come through the playground with the older boys that were troubling him. Seeing Matt, he had said real loudly, 'Come and meet my dad.' One look at the great hulk of Matt Pearson and those boys had never bothered him again. In fact they had gone out of their way to be his friend. And the beauty of it was that Matt had grasped the situation at a glance, although Jamie hadn't uttered one word of complaint. 'Well done, son,' his father had said to him, laughing, well aware his presence at the school gate had been put to good use. Praise from his father had been music to his young ears. All those years he had kissed Joan goodnight and hugged Matt. Of course they were his parents. Hadn't Matt carried him high on his shoulders when the crowds at a football match had been overwhelming?

These past seven days had been an eye-opener. The talking that had gone on between Peter and himself had not been for anyone else's ears. They had confided things to each other that they had barely been able to admit to themselves. With the calm that had followed had come acceptance. It was a strange tale that could so easily have ended up being a tragedy for two families. Not that it was perfect even now: that was asking for the impossible. But Peter and himself had come to the conclusion that they were the main characters in this drama, and if they could behave in a reasonable way perhaps they could prevent much of the heartache, or at least ease it a little. They had both grasped that in this life there were so many forms of love. Which made it a dangerous commodity for mere humans to cope with.

How long they had sat there Joan couldn't tell. She had watched the different expressions flit across Jamie's face and didn't need telling that her son had grown up a lot in the week he had been away from home. He certainly wasn't the angry tormented young man that had walked out of the house so early one morning. She hoped with all her heart that Beryl was having the same thoughts about Peter. Maybe there was hope for all of them yet.

Chapter Thirty-One

A TRUCE HAD been called between both families. Maybe it was more than just a truce. Time would tell.

During the evening of the day their sons had returned from Cornwall Joan had spent nearly an hour talking to Beryl on the phone. Neither of them had an inkling of what had taken place during those seven days, yet each knew that the outcome was good.

As Joan was about to replace the receiver Beryl mentioned the cardigans.

'What did you think when you were given yours?' she asked Joan.

'Overjoyed is the only word that comes to mind. It was such a surprise.'

'That's exactly how I felt. I want to wear it and yet I don't. I almost feel like having it put in a glass case to keep it safe for ever and ever.'

Joan laughed. 'That's not a bad idea. Imagine if we're lucky enough in the future to have grandchildren and we try to tell them the whole story. We could produce our gifts as evidence.'

'Dear Jesus,' Beryl said softly, 'I hadn't given a thought to grandchildren. As time goes on this mix-up is going to become quite a family legend, isn't it? Still, I suppose we just have to say, sufficient unto the day.'

At that moment Joan could easily have lost her temper. Pity you didn't think of that and keep the facts to yourself when you first got the results of that blood test, is what she had to stop herself from saying. No one could turn the clock back. At least everyone was on better terms than when the Piviteauxs had first arrived in England. That was something to be grateful for.

Long afterwards, when it was all over, Joan would remember the hectic remaining days that the Piviteaux family spent in England.

They had done the whole London scene on their own, but Daphne and Bill invited them for an evening meal. Considering how badly the Sunday lunch had turned out, Joan thought it was brave of her parents to make another attempt. She need not have worried. The Piviteauxs seemed different, relaxed. Indeed, they kept the conversation going non-stop.

Joe sounded like a tour guide as he described their visit to St Paul's Cathedral, starting with the fact that it was at the top of Ludgate Hill, in the heart of the city. It was only as Joan listened to how the monks had 365 stairs to climb in order to reach the dome, a fact that she had been well aware of since her school days, that she suddenly realized that this family were really interested in English history. Then Karen and Betsy were telling of their visit to the Tower of London. There was the most beautiful chapel in there, the likes of which they had never seen, they declared, and yet the place had been used as a prison. A fact that they found hard to believe.

Jamie, smiling broadly, told them that in the first place it had been used as a palace but was still most famous as a prison. And when Betsy raved about the crown jewels, again it was Jamie who told her that the Towers that housed the jewels were built much later. From there, they had gone on to Tower Gate on Tower Hill and Betsy had everyone in fits of laughter as she shuddered whilst telling of the poor souls that had been hung there. They still had to see Buckingham Palace, the Changing of the Guard and Windsor Castle, and when Beryl asked Joan to go to Windsor with them, she agreed happily.

My feet are killing me, Joan was muttering to herself and was as pleased as punch when she heard Peter urging his father to let up a bit and take them all for some refreshments.

'OK, son, we'll take a break,' Joe answered, taking his wife's arm and heading for the nearest café.

Take a break! God help us, Joan was thinking as she gratefully sipped a steaming cup of coffee. The flag above Windsor Castle was flying at half mast, signifying that the Royal Family were not in residence. That meant that the State Apartments, round tower, stables, Saint George's Chapel and the Albert Memorial Chapel were all open to the public. And Joe had made sure that they had done the lot!

Their last day had arrived. Their flight was booked for six p.m., which meant they didn't have to be at Heathrow airport until four thirty.

Matt had booked a luncheon for the Piviteauxs and the Pearsons. He had also invited Beryl's mother. They would all meet up at the Goring Hotel at twelve thirty, and two cars had been ordered for two thirty to take everyone to the airport.

Matt was indeed a wise man. His choice of the Goring had been a good one. Everything about the building, the staff and the décor reflected the best of the British way of life. As Matt had become more prosperous in his business dealings, he had taken Joan there for a meal, and once they had stayed the night there after the theatre. Everything about the hotel had impressed Joan, and now it was having the same effect on Joe and Beryl.

'Old-world splendour,' Joe had stated, as Matt ordered drinks from an immaculate waiter.

'Will you have them in the main lounge or on the enclosed terrace, sir?' the waiter asked.

'Oh, the terrace, I think,' Matt told him: the elegant windows of the terrace overlooked the beautiful garden.

'Wow,' Joe exclaimed loudly, 'this place is something else.'

And so it was. It was only a few minutes from Victoria station yet it was like going back in time; stepping out of a cab one could leave behind the hustle and the bustle of London town. Dressed in the distinctive uniform of a great family hotel, a porter would open the taxi door and welcome you to the Goring Hotel. And from that moment it was personal attention down to the finest detail.

As they were a party of eleven, they were served in a private dining room It was a spacious room yet cosy. The meal was excellent, the service discreet and professional. When it was time for them to leave Joe Piviteaux was beside himself, shaking hands with everyone in the entrance hall and saying, 'We sure as hell ain't got anything like this in the States. Fantastic! Not like an hotel, more like a family house that belongs to an important aristocrat. And to have been made so welcome!' These Americans certainly hadn't the reserve for which the British were so well known. One young man, attired in morning dress, thanked Joe for his compliments.

'Don't know how you Brits do it,' Joe had answered.

'Sir, when your name is above the door you try that much harder,' the young man said, smiling.

'Your family own this hotel?' Joe spluttered.

'My great-grandfather opened it in 1910 as the first hotel in the world to have a private bathroom and central heating in every bedroom.' What could Joe say to that? Except to make a firm promise to return.

The drivers had already warned them that out at the airport there was a 'right pea-souper'. And they weren't wrong. The cars had crawled the last few miles because the fog was so dense. However, it wouldn't have mattered if they had arrived late, because the flight was delayed. Nevertheless it wasn't long after they had checked in their baggage before the passengers were being called into a departure lounge. Since this was beyond Passport Control, folk seeing off their friends and relatives were not allowed to enter.

The final moment had arrived. Both families formed a line to say goodbye. Everyone was hugging someone, and the girls were clinging to each other, promising not to lose touch.

Peter stood in front of Joan. She bit her lip as she watched him struggle with his emotions, willing him to put his arms around her. Come on, please, just this once, she begged him silently. Don't go without touching me. Suddenly he moved, and once he had taken that final step that brought him so close to her she held out her arms and he came into them. She was really holding him in her arms! In that moment, the touching of mother and son, she felt many things. She couldn't have explained the feeling, but she simply knew that a bond *did* exist between them and that from that moment some kind of seal had been set on their future relationship.

Beryl had been taking her leave of Jamie. Joan hadn't seen what had taken place between them, but as they looked at each other, she knew.

Both mothers understood that they would have to tread warily, but they also knew that their new bond was permanent.

Matt and Joe were clasping hands, Joan and Beryl were crying, Beryl's mother was cuddling her granddaughters. Only Peter and Jamie seemed quiet.

'Wipe your eyes, you two,' Joe ordered Beryl and Joan. 'We have to go.'

'We could go up to the observation area and watch your plane take off if it weren't for this damn fog,' Matt said.

'Never mind. When you all come to the States we'll show you what sunshine is. We'll go up to the cabin, do a bit of fishing, or even down to Florida.'

Meg and Rosie pricked up their ears. The Pearsons go to America? It was something to think about.

Then, gently and without haste, Beryl kissed Joan and whispered, 'So far, so good.'

BOOK THREE

ASHTEAD, SURREY, 1980

Chapter Thirty-Two

MATT DROVE HIS new Ford Granada slowly along the empty country lane. It was the beginning of May, a spring day with bright sunshine and clear blue skies. The trees were heavy with blossom while the hedges were green with fresh leaves. Away in the distance he could see a lone farmhouse and flocks of sheep. Over the past few weeks he had travelled this road daily and had often stopped the car to watch the lambs nestling up to their mothers' thick fleece.

Hopefully it was the promise of things to come. Sunshine always made everyone feel better.

Well wrapped up in the passenger seat, Joan was thinking how wonderful it was to be away from the hospital and all its smells of disinfectant. She thought that she had never seen the countryside look so beautiful

Matt turned his head and smiled at her. Ahead stood the wooden fence that fronted their long ranch-style bungalow, which Matt had had built for her four years ago. She leant forward, gazing at the clumps of spring flowers, remembering when the girls had planted bulbs beneath the trees and in scattered clumps over the lawn. She felt so happy. The white gates were open. Matt drove through them and drew the car to a stop at the front of the house. He opened his door, got out and came round to the passenger side. 'Come on, my love, we're 'ome.' He held out a hand to assist her and watched as she winced with pain. She had been so ill he'd thought they were going to lose her, but she had refused to go into a convalescent home, for which he was glad. She would be far better off at home. He would see that she had everything she needed. And when she was well enough he was going to take her on an extended holiday, maybe a cruise. That was if he could persuade her to be away from the children for any length of time. Children? They were all grown-up and some even had children of their own.

'Shall I carry you in?' he asked.

'I'll be fine,' she said softly. 'Oh, Matt, it feels so good to be home.'

'Well, at least take my arm. Everything's ready for you, loads of pillows on the settee. Mrs Simmonds has been a Godsend while you've been away. I'd be the first t' admit I never wanted t' 'ave a char-lady in the 'ouse, knowing all our business an' gossiping to 'alf the village, but she's turned out trumps.'

The first door in the wide hall was open and a well-banked-up fire burned in the grate. Joan went into the sitting room and sat down. Matt propped pillows behind her head and carefully lifted her legs up from the floor. She let her shoulders sink back and sighed with relief. She was home.

As soon as she felt a bit stronger she was going to walk

this bungalow from one end to the other. She had never got over feeling how lucky she was to have such a wonderful home. When Matt had first shown her the plans she had cried, 'God, I'll need a bike to get from one end of the hall to the other!' Now she loved every inch of it. The three bedrooms, the dining room, this lovely sitting room, and it had an office too for Matt, which kept him happy and out from under her feet.

The kitchen was something else. It had taken her weeks to get the hang of using the Aga, but now she wouldn't be without it. There were two bathrooms and many was the time she'd lain soaking in deep, sweet-scented water, thinking of how she'd had to wash all three of her children in a tin bath in front of the fire when they'd lived in Bull Yard.

It truly was a grand bungalow and lying here she could see beyond the windows to her garden, showing off all its springtime beauty.

'I'm just going to the car to fetch your case in,' Matt said, bending over her and planting a soft kiss on her forehead. 'Then you can tell me what you'd like to eat.'

'Oh, Matt, there's only one thing I'm longing for.'

'Well, tell me what it is an' if it's possible I'll see that yer get it.'

'A decent cup of tea.'

'You're something else, you are, Joan. You know that, don't you?' he laughed. 'I'll have a pot beside you just as quick as I can get the kettle to boil.'

While he was gone she took a good look around the room. There were several get-well cards on the sideboard as well as the host she had received while she had been in hospital. She hadn't realized they had so many friends.

Everything was fine. Mrs Simmonds was indeed a treasure. Left to Matt her house plants would surely have shrivelled up for want of a drop of water, but all their leaves were shiny and green. Nothing had changed. This was a beautiful room.

Matt came back carrying a loaded tray, which he set down on a side table. He should have looked awkward, a big man like him, handling bone china, but he didn't. So much had happened over the years and her husband was a different man from the one he had been in the early stages of their marriage.

Life had been good to them in so many ways. And yet, some regrets? Of course there were. Whoever said that life was going to be easy?

He placed another table near her so that she could easily reach her tea. Then he sliced a Victoria sponge, sandwiched together with thick cream and early strawberries. Placing a small wedge on a plate he ordered, 'I've been told to see you eat that. Mrs Simmonds came early this morning just to make it for you. Her way of saying welcome home, I guess.'

Joan did as she was told, savouring the lightness of the sponge and the sweet taste of early English strawberries. She drained her cup and smiled as she held it out for Matt to refill. By God, the hot tea tasted good. How come it didn't bear any resemblance to what was handed out from the hospital trolley? Matt's expression was serious as he took it from her. He was so relieved to have her home again. They'd had their share of rough times and right now all he wanted was to look after her and see some colour come back into her cheeks.

Joan was thinking what she would have liked to do now

was walk through the whole of this bungalow. Open every door, inspect each bedroom, because she knew some of the children had stayed here during the three weeks she had been away. She would know by their perfume which girl it was that had occupied which room. She wanted to touch her furniture, to see the curtains she had so carefully chosen. To make sure that everything was still as she had left it. She knew it was a daft idea but she had come so near to never coming home she needed reassurance that nothing had changed.

Matt piled logs on to the fire and the dry kindling flared and crackled, sending flames high up into the chimney.

Joan felt blissfully warm and cosy. She really was home. If only she didn't feel so tired. She knew why it was. Only too well. The doctor had said it was imperative that she had an hysterectomy, then all would be well. It hadn't been that simple. Not for her it hadn't. She was fifty-five years old and after the operation she had haemorrhaged. She had suffered such a blood loss that she had had transfusions and was kept in hospital much longer than she had expected. Now she felt weary. But it was a different kind of weariness to what she had felt as she lay in that long ward.

In hospital she had never had a peaceful night's sleep. So much was always going on even during the night: admissions, trolleys being wheeled along the corridors. Then there was that poor soul in the next bed who was always crying. During the time she'd been there Joan had come to realize the woman had never had a visitor and she had felt so sorry for her. Now she looked across to where Matt was sitting and as he smiled at her she felt his love flow across the room. She had so much to be grateful for. The last fifteen years had turned out so well. It was unbelievable, really. It was as if she had two families. And she knew Beryl Piviteaux would say the same.

Now they each had one son in America and another in England. Over the years it had given both families experiences that otherwise they would never have known.

'Joan,' Matt said, as he came to her side, 'I'm just going to switch on the electric blanket and then I'm going to see that you get undressed and into bed.'

'Oh, Matt, I'm so comfortable here.'

'Never mind that. You know what they said before you left the hospital: at least another week in bed before you start putting your feet to the ground.'

'All right. I do feel as if I need a good sleep, but what am I going to do lying there for another seven days?'

'You've got several new books the girls brought you. You can't have read them all.'

'No, I haven't read even one. A look at the daily paper was about all I managed. There was never enough peace and quiet in the hospital for me to settle down to a good read.'

'Well, now's your chance,' Matt told her, sounding masterful.

A sudden thought came to Joan. Yes, she felt she could easily sleep the rest of today away, and probably all of the night as well. But tomorrow she'd ask Matt to bring her six special books into the bedroom for her; they'd keep her happy and contented. They weren't scrapbooks, more a record of what her three children had achieved and how their lives had become entwined with the three Piviteaux children's. They regarded Peter, Karen and Betsy as their extended family, and as far as it had been possible she'd kept a kind of diary on all three of them as well as her own three. Now she and Matt saw more of Karen than Beryl and Joe did.

I shall go through each one slowly and carefully, she promised herself.

She was beginning to feel stronger and certainly much more optimistic.

Chapter Thirty-Three

JOAN WAS GOOD at sitting in silence while others liked to keep up a lively source of conversation. She didn't dislike her own company and she was actually looking forward to a few hours on her own today.

Matt was worried because Mrs Simmonds was taking her granddaughter to the dentist and wouldn't be coming to work, and he had had a phone call from Stan saying that he was needed at a meeting.

'Matt,' Joan pleaded, 'just get yourself ready and go. I'll be fine, honestly I will.'

'Well, if you're sure. I 'ave rather left Stan t' carry the can these last few weeks but I'll be 'ome no later than four o'clock.'

'Stop fussing,' was what Joan felt like screaming at him, as he checked that she had plenty to drink near her bedside.

'I've made you a salmon sandwich and I've cut all the crusts off and there's plenty of fruit if you fancy it. Are you sure you can get along to the kitchen all right on your own?'

'Matt, I go to the bathroom, don't I? I'll be fine.'

He put his arms around her shoulders and kissed her, reminding her of how it had been when they had both been young and so much in love. In spite of all their setbacks, it wasn't so very different today. They just took life at a slower pace. She watched as he shrugged himself into his jacket. At fifty-seven he was still a sight for sore eyes, his movements quick, his hair still dark, though showing grey around the sides, and the big brown eyes that flashed with the same smile that had captivated her when they had first met. By any standards Matt was a fine-looking man.

She had been home now for three days and he hadn't allowed her to lift a finger. To tell the truth she had slept most of the time.

The minute she heard his car drive away she threw back the bedclothes and put her feet into her slippers. Then, with her dressing-gown wrapped around her, she headed for the third bedroom, which overlooked the front garden. From the inside shelf of an oak tallboy she took down two parcels, one labelled 'The Pearsons' and the other 'The Piviteauxs'. She smoothed her hand over the cover of the second and replaced it on the shelf. I'll get to you lot later. Then, tucking the other set of books under her arm, she made her way back to bed.

Minutes later with her pillows arranged behind her back and a bedjacket tucked round her shoulders, she opened the first volume. It bore the title 'James Pearson'. She turned to the first page. The date was January 1965 and it was a record of the first visit to their house in Morden of Clive Richardson, followed by a catalogue of the events that had swiftly followed in those troubled times. She skimmed through these pages. She didn't want to dwell on that dark

period of their lives. It was the happier days she was after.
Then she came to a page headed 'Our Holiday'. She smiled.
That was when they had returned the Piviteauxs' visit.

It had taken two years after Joe, Beryl and their family
had returned home for Matt to agree that they should go
to America. But at last they had managed it. That had been
some holiday. So much had been packed into such a few
weeks.

Beryl and she had become the closest of friends, because
of the love they both had for their children. And both she
and Matt felt a great affection for Joe too. He was such a
considerate man, and he'd been a tower of strength to Beryl
through all the sorting out of Peter and Jamie.

The seeds that had been sown during those three happy
weeks had been nurtured and had grown. Almost on their
first day in the States, Karen had introduced Jamie to
Pamela, her best friend. Within two years the pair were
married. Joan felt lucky that they had decided to live in
England. They had a beautiful house in Chelsea, not far
from Albert Bridge. Their firstborn was a son, named
Matthew, much to Matt's delight. Eighteen months later
their daughter Beryl had arrived. That had sent the phone
lines crazy across the Atlantic.

When Hester, Jamie's great-grandmother had died, everyone had been devastated and none more so than Grandma
Pearson. The funeral had taken place the same week as Amy
had received notice that her house was due for demolition.
The council welfare officer had suggested that she go to live
in a council-run home. Amy had had other ideas. And loudly
and firmly let everyone know her objections.

Joan laid down the book, took a long drink of her lemon-
barley water and smiled to herself. She remembered it as if

it were yesterday. Matt had taken it for granted that his mother would make her home with them, and Joan would gladly have gone along with that arrangement.

Amy's response had been to the point. 'If you think that I'm comin' 'ere to be buried alive in Surrey you've got another think coming. Where would I do me shopping? Ain't a decent market for miles. No. I was born in London an' in London I'm gonna die. Whether the council like it or not. But it won't be with a load of white-'aired old folk that spend two-thirds of the day dozin' an' if they do wake up long enough to feed their faces they dribble 'alf of it down their clothes. I know cos I've been to visit a few of me friends what 'ave got shoved into them places.'

Joan chuckled. Amy hadn't altered even now. At the ripe age of eighty-nine she wouldn't let anyone consider her old. Tears came to her eyes as she read of the kind way in which Jamie and Pamela had acted. The solution? A granny-annexe had been built on to their house, and to this day Amy reigned there like the Queen Mum. As she said, she only had to get on a bus and cross the bridge and she was near enough into her part of London.

Joan chuckled. When she and Matt had first been married she'd had the occasional set-to with her mother-in-law, but over the years a great affection had developed between her and this large jolly warm-hearted woman. A woman who had taught her that love could still exist despite the traumas that life threw at you. She loved it when Amy honoured them with her presence for a few days. Her larger-than-life figure filled the house, her bellowing laughter, her spoiling of the little ones, her witticisms which made them all laugh.

Funny when you came to think about it: Jamie had always been Amy's favourite. Not that she didn't love Meg and

Rosie, but Jamie had been to university and was now holding down a successful job in the City. You might have thought he would have outgrown his gran but nothing was further from the truth. He was very proud of her. And not only of Amy, Joan thought. He had never abandoned any of the family he had grown up with. He was wont to say that he had just spread some of his family across the Atlantic which was great when it come to holiday time. As for sharing his love, Jamie had proved that he had more than most to give.

Remarkable really that such a catastrophe had brought so many people together. At least every other weekend Pamela and he would bring Mathew and little Beryl to see her and Matt. At this thought Joan looked out of her bedroom window. The sun was shining, and it wouldn't be long now before it was warm enough for them all to have barbecues in the garden.

Soon after she and Matt had moved here, Matt had built a brick fireplace for the barbecue in a sheltered spot at the far side of their garden. He had come home from America determined that they would have one built in their 'backyard', as Joe Piviteaux would say. For the past three years it had been put to good use, with everyone sitting outside to eat, the adults at one table and the children at another, the sound of laughter filling the garden. When it got dark, Matt always lit candles in tall narrow glasses to prevent them being blown out by the breeze.

She hadn't made any entries in these books for some time now, but soon she would take up her pen again. She had only to sit back and listen when the children were talking and she would hear how their lives were proceeding.

Joan sometimes thought that of all her children Meg needed her most. She certainly led a much more ordinary life than her brother or sister, yet it seemed fraught with complications.

She opened the book on her eldest daughter and was surprised to see a photograph taken at Meg's wedding lying between the pages. She hadn't remembered placing it there. Such a carefree, happy couple they looked, Meg and Brian.

Meg had married her faithful Brian Clarke and had two children, John and Josie. They still lived within a short distance of the Pearsons' old house in Morden. She and Brian had a good lifestyle. He was now a partner in the same firm of chartered accountants that he had started out with, Macdonald and Partners.

It was the children who caused the trouble – though when they stayed here neither Matt nor she had had any complaints – or maybe just one: both children wanted to sit in front of the television set all day. Josie was a sweet girl, but she sucked the end of her pigtail, which annoyed Matt no end, and you couldn't get her to open a book, let alone read one. John wasn't much better: he hated school and all forms of sport. Perhaps the fault didn't lie with the children.

Brian had been lucky with their house. Situated at the top of Wimbledon Hill it had been a vicarage in the past. It was the most lovely old house with a large garden, and Brian employed a gardener-handyman, Harry Evans. As Joan read what she had written she chuckled again. What Matt had said had seemed funny at the time, but sad to say it had turned out to be true.

'That bloody man Evans is so slow I doubt he could catch a cold, and as for 'im producing vegetables, well! If he does get sprouts to grow he'll be too lazy t' pick 'em. Probably believes if he leaves them in the ground long enough they'll grow into cabbages. I was there once when he was supposed to feed the dogs. Know what the lazy bugger did? Put the bowls down and a tin of meat in each, but never opened the tins!'

Of course, the last bit hadn't been true, though it had caused a lot of laughter, because everyone knew Evans.

Joan sighed. Brian and Meg's life read like a depressing saga. Their children were always suffering from some ailment and Meg continually rang home for help. Matt called her 'The Drama Queen'.

It wasn't until the next afternoon that Joan got round to opening the book that told the story of her successful younger daughter's life.

The previous day Matt had been as good as his word, arriving home by three thirty to find Joan propped up in bed, fast asleep, with her book on Meg lying open across her chest. He hadn't disturbed her, merely removed the book and gone to the kitchen to prepare a light dinner for them.

While he stood peeling a few potatoes his mind was centred on Joan. What a woman! What a mother! She kept in close touch with all three of their children, didn't interfere, mind you, but was there if and when any of them needed her. And not only their brood: she'd taken on Peter, Karen and Betsy too. Not that he minded that in the least. His views on the Piviteaux family had changed since he'd spent so much time with them. He himself had come from a big family and the fact that they had all scattered sometimes worried him. The only ones who seemed to care about their mum these days were himself and dear old Stan.

It was different with his children: they were always

coming home for the weekend, and if they weren't they never failed to pick up a phone and chat to their mother. They had all rallied round while she was ill: a fact for which he was eternally grateful. Add to that the American side of it and how close they had all become and it was pretty unbelievable!

Why, some folk would never understand it if you were to sit down and tell the story till you were blue in the face. And though there weren't many folk to whom he would make this admission, he had felt, over the last fifteen years, as though he had two sons. Which, of course, he did.

That reminded him. He'd had a telephone call from Karen while he'd been at the office this afternoon and she'd be coming home next weekend. He would tell Joan when she woke up. Home to Karen Piviteaux was here in Ashtead, or at least while she was working in England. Her own parents heartily approved of this. Bit of a mix-up all round when you thought about it – his Rosie lived in the States now. Matt tossed a peeled potato into the saucepan. No wonder Joan kept books on them all. It was the only way she could keep tabs on them. He had let Joan get out of bed and come out into the lounge to eat their meal. She'd had a wash and brushed her hair and the atmosphere as they sat in front of the fire was relaxing. When Matt had brought in ice-cream and a pot of coffee, Joan had felt a bit guilty because he was waiting on her so much. Later, seated on the settee, nestling back against his broad chest, his arms encircling her, Joan had felt that she was indeed a lucky lady.

Today there was no need to light a fire: the morning was bright with warm sunshine. Unable to resist Joan's pleading that she'd had more than enough of being in bed, Matt had settled her in an armchair from where she had a good view of the garden.

He placed a stout stick beside her chair and said, 'I'm going to be working out there for a while so if you need anything just tap on the glass an' I'll come in. Do you want me to fetch you your books?'

'You're a darling,' she told him.

'Anything for a quiet life,' he retorted. 'Anyway, better make the most of it because we'll probably end up with a house full in a week's time. At least on the Sunday, they'll all be wanting to check up on you. Make sure I'm not ill treating you.'

'Get on with you,' she smiled. 'I'm glad Karen is coming. Do you know if Meg and Brian are?'

'Most probably, more than likely they'll bring some of Evans' wonderful garden produce.' Matt couldn't resist that sarcastic gibe.

Joan gave a little laugh; it was difficult getting Matt to agree that Brian and Meg did their best. All she could do was try and make a joke of it, so she answered sweetly, 'And if they do I'm sure they will be the best we've ever tasted.'

'Hmm, some bloody 'opes you've got.'

Joan squared her shoulders, her voice shaking with laughter. 'Well, you'll be the one that has to cook them.'

Matt had reached the door, then hesitated, turned round, and said, 'That's where you're wrong, my old darling. With a 'ouse full of women and kids I'm going to shut myself in the bedroom with you. But if you insist on getting up and pretending you're well enough to be the hostess then I'll be off down the pub.' He closed the door firmly. Only to open it again and say, 'Use the stick to bang on the window when you feel like a cuppa.'

What a real family man Matt had become. He could be gruff, but the girls could still wind him round their little fingers. These days she did worry about Meg and Brian. Meg didn't help herself. Which made it nigh on impossible for anyone else to offer her help. Funny thing was that she belonged to the Women's Guild and several other clubs, where it seemed she was well able to cope with organizing events and meetings, yet she was scarcely able to control her own two children. Just thinking about Meg was fairly draining and it was with a heavy sigh that she laid down that book and picked up the book about Rosie.

How could two sisters turn out so different? If she had been asked to foretell the future when both her girls were small she would have laid a penny against a pound that Meg would be the more successful of the two. And how wrong she would have been! On leaving school it had been Meg that had landed a job in a solicitor's office while Rosie had been content to be a mere clerk in the offices of the Water Board.

She began to read. Rosie had been nineteen, coming up twenty, when Matt had taken them all to America to stay with the Piviteauxs for three weeks. Against Joan's better judgement, and despite all her protests that Rosie was far too young, Matt had given his permission for Rosie to stay on with the family for another month. From that time on Rosie had been fascinated by the American way of life. If it had been only that, perhaps she would have settled down in the country in which she had been born and, like the rest of the family, been content to go to the States on holiday. However, at the end of her stay when they'd met her at Heathrow airport she had been full of the fact that if the Piviteauxs were allowed to sponsor her and she were to be granted a work permit she had a job waiting for her in New York.

New York!

As Joan read on, and relived those months, she remembered how sad she had felt that her younger child not only wanted to leave home but go and live on the other side of the Atlantic Ocean. How could she or Matt have stopped her? They couldn't.

Rosie had always been a story-teller. Even at school she got high marks for all of her essays, and to be offered a job in a publishing company was the icing on the cake for her.

Joan turned to the pages that told of her own visit to New York just five years ago. She had travelled alone, which would have been unheard of before the war. Matt had insisted she go. He was up to his eyes in contracts and couldn't possibly accompany her.

Joan hugged herself as she recalled those two weeks. The main reason Rosie had so badly wanted her to be there was for the launch of a book she had written to be published by the firm she worked for. The party was held in New York, and Joan wouldn't have missed it for the world. To see her daughter being made so much fuss of and listening to compliments coming from all directions had to be seen to be believed. Today Rosie was a successful author with half a dozen best-sellers to her name.

Betsy Piviteaux was an editor with the same firm, and the girls shared a flat in a building so tall that terror had gripped Joan's heart: whatever would they do if the lift was out of order?

'Mum, it's an elevator, not a lift, and the Americans always have a back-up service,' had been Rosie's reply.

She was so proud of her baby. No matter how old she

was she had been Joan's last-born and therefore would always be her baby. It seemed such a long time since Rosie had been home; seven years, in fact, though she and Matt had been over to stay. And while she had been in hospital the nurses had wheeled the phone-trolley beside her bed so that she could take a call from Rosie. Twice that had happened, and each week a huge bouquet of flowers had been delivered to the ward with a card bearing such loving words from her.

She mustn't complain. She had a wonderful family.

To be honest though, she did worry about Rosie – not in the same way that she worried over Meg – there was no need. The truth was it was more wishful thinking on her part, rather than a cause for concern. It was just that there was never any mention of men in Rosie's life. Everyday workmates, oh, yes! While she had been staying with Rosie she'd been introduced to several handsome young American men. Quite a few of them had seemed to be very much at home in the girls' apartment. When she mentioned it to Matt he always laughed and told her not to be so daft.

Joan hadn't asked questions because what she didn't know supposedly wouldn't hurt her, but she belonged to a generation that attached great importance to marriage. Marriage was the beginning and the end for a well-brought-up young lady. It was all very well for Rosie to have a career, even such a successful one that she'd carved out for herself, but what about the dreams Joan had had of her getting married, looking beautiful in a flowing white dress, walking up the aisle on her father's arm? Didn't Rosie want to have children? It might not matter to her now – she was thirty-two – but her body wouldn't stay young for ever.

It was some time later that Matt opened the sitting-room

door. Joan woke with a start as he laid a hand over hers. 'It's ten to seven. You've been asleep for three hours. I know because I've checked on you three times. Dinner is all ready but I can keep it hot if you'd like to freshen up first.'

Joan stretched her arms. 'Oh, Matt, I'm sorry.'

'Nothing to be sorry for,' he told her. 'Sleep is the best medicine you could have.'

Suddenly she smiled and said, 'Would you like to know something? For the first time in ages I'm hungry.'

'Good. Shall I bring our meal in here or shall we eat in the kitchen?'

'Give me a few minutes in the bathroom and then I'll come out into the kitchen.'

Matt laid his cheek on the top of her head, and they shared a quiet moment, each grateful that they still had each other.

Then she struggled to get out of the chair, moaning, 'If only I didn't feel so weak.'

Matt laughed. 'You always did want to walk before you could run. Will it help if I tell you how much I love you?'

'Yes,' she told him. 'You know it does. It helps a great deal.'

Chapter Thirty-Four

JOAN WAS READING the book on Peter Piviteaux, and promising herself that she would do exactly as Matt had told her and keep her legs up. He had been right: the rest she had had over the past few days had worked wonders. She felt so much better. Peter. It was still a wonder to her that she could feel such deep love for the son to whom she had given birth yet not brought up. It was the same for Beryl where Jamie was concerned and that point alone had both mothers thanking the Lord for the way things had eventually turned out. She had often wondered just what had been the incentive that had made each of them fight so fiercely for the right to keep their sons. They both had two girls and knew full well of the intimacy that existed in a mother's relationship with her daughter. Didn't the well-known saying state that a daughter is a daughter for all of her life but a son is a son until he takes a wife?

And yet isn't there that very special affinity that sparks a mother's fierce love and loyalty to a son? She only knew that of all the many happenings in her life Jamie, from the moment he had been put into her arms, had to be looked upon as the best. And now she regarded Peter as a terrific bonus.

Peter still lived with his family in America, but was no stranger to her and Matt. At the moment he was in Sweden. She knew because he had telephoned her the minute he had been told she was home from hospital. Today the world seemed so small with all the children getting on planes and going places in the way that she and Matt used to catch buses.

The Piviteauxs' company had expanded. She and Matt had been told that it had started out as a dry-cleaning business. Now it offered hotel-, office- and furniture-cleaning on a huge scale. With several members of the family involved, they had won many contracts and employed more than a hundred people. Peter had been chosen to oversee the purchase of new equipment, which would come from several different countries. It was a feather in his cap to be responsible for such expensive items.

'Let me see,' Joan murmured, turning the pages slowly. When she came to the record of his first marriage she sighed. Things hadn't gone all that smoothly for Peter. He had been on holiday with some of his mates, hunting and fishing, staying at the family lodge, when he'd met Abigail. He had found her extremely attractive. The long and short of it was, she'd turned up pregnant three months later claiming that Peter was the father. She wanted him to take her home, face her parents and marry her.

'Home is where?' Beryl had questioned.

'Down south.' And that was about all the information Abigail had offered.

It had not been an easy time for Joe or Beryl. They had shown their disapproval, only to get up next morning to find that the two had gone. They had suggested that Abigail stay with them and get to know them before the pair applied for a marriage licence.

Joan sniffed back tears at the memory of Beryl on the phone asking her advice. Joe had talked long and hard to Matt. 'The greatest gift a parent can give his son is independence,' Joe said, 'and, God knows, I've done my best to give him that.'

Matt had told her afterwards that he could hear the sobs in Joe's voice when he was telling him that Peter had thrown it all away for some little trollop. Beryl had blamed herself. Perhaps they should have been a little less ambitious for him, or even more tolerant of Abigail. But it was all too late. Peter had left with her, and they hadn't an address or a real inkling of where she lived.

Joan searched for and found the two letters she had folded between the pages. They gave an end to this story. One was from Beryl, showing relief, if nothing else, and one from Peter telling her he realized what an idiot he had been. Joan smiled as she read. It hadn't been hard to see things from his point of view. Hadn't they all been young once? Hadn't they all done things they later regretted?

As he was over twenty-one he had had no trouble in obtaining a marriage licence, but the honeymoon period had lasted all of three weeks. The next five months Peter described as unbearable, but he had stayed for the sake of the unborn baby. When the little girl had been born, he said, he had been rooted to the spot. Not that she wasn't the prettiest thing, with huge eyes and thick tight curls, but her skin was coffee-coloured. She was not his daughter.

Poor Peter. He had tried to do right by Abigail but she had made the mistake of thinking he was a simpleton, which of course he most certainly was not.

But thanks to his father he had weathered that storm. Joe had set the wheels in motion and had the marriage annulled. It had taken time for the hurt to heal. It didn't seem fair that so much deceit and trouble should have been heaped on one young man's shoulders.

But again God was Good, the right young lady had come along, and although she and Matt had not made it to the wedding in New York they had been pleasantly rewarded. Peter and his lovely bride, Louise, had come to London for their honeymoon, staying at the Goring Hotel. Twice she and Matt had had a meal with them. Louise was the kind of girl that every mother would want her son to marry, and both she and Matt had loved her from the moment they had met.

Karen's book came next: not that she needed to familiarize herself with what Karen was getting up to because hardly a week went by when she and Matt didn't have the pleasure of her company. Karen had chosen nursing as her career and now specialized in children's welfare. Where better to gain experience than at Great Ormond Street Hospital in London, the most famous of children's hospitals?

Beryl said she had breathed a sigh of relief when Matt had assured her there would always be a bedroom in their house for Karen whenever she had days off and wanted to get out of London. Eighteen months she had been over here now, and Joan would be sorry if and when Karen decided it was time to go home.

Karen was an absolute beauty, always full of energy, turning heads wherever she went. She had come to visit Joan in hospital, wearing black slacks and a white silk blouse with a scarf tucked in at the neck. She was a kind, caring person, like her mother. She talked about several boyfriends but had only ever brought one down to Ashtead for the weekend, a doctor at the hospital where she worked. His name was Alex, a rugged, handsome man in his late thirties. Matt said he looked more like a rugby player than a doctor.

Karen acted calmly and quietly when he was around, which made Joan think she might be serious about him. 'I hope so,' Beryl had said, when they were chatting on the phone. 'After all, she is thirty-four.'

But girls didn't get married so young, these days. In fact, many of them didn't bother to tie the knot at all. They just found themselves a young man, and before they had time to get to know each other they were openly living together.

These were hard times for mothers, especially when the world was their children's oyster and they could take a plane to any country in the world that took their fancy. Getting pregnant out of wedlock was no longer frowned upon. In my day, Joan was thinking, you would have been an absolute outcast, someone dirty and disgusting if you had a baby before you got married. Not today. They talked about having a love-child with their partner! Joan felt she was in an awkward situation and when she voiced her fears to Matt he laughed. Yes he had! Even going so far as to say she was jealous that the Pill hadn't been around when they'd been young. He'd laughed even more when she blushed and called him a cheeky bugger.

Anyway, Karen was coming down on Friday and Joan began to wonder whether she would be bringing Alex with her. Wait and see, she chided herself, and took up the last book, which was all about Betsy.

She couldn't think about Betsy Piviteaux without coupling her with Rosie. They both worked for the same publishing firm and they shared a flat. Or, as they were more apt to say, an apartment. She had shut her eyes to some of their goings-on when she had stayed with them for two weeks. They certainly lived a different life from anything she had known. There were times when she didn't know what to make of either of them. Their moods seemed to change with the weather. This last month they had been in high spirits. Apparently Rosie had been away from New York, on a tour to publicize her latest book and to sign copies. When she came back Betsy was going to tell her that she had everything planned out. It wasn't going to happen until December, six months away, but Betsy was full of it, right down to the last detail. Rosie, she and two male companions were going to spend Christmas in Switzerland. It sounded, from Betsy's account, an enviable way to spend the festive season. But – and it was a big but – by the time December came, would they still be friends with these *male companions*?

Joan laughed and shook her head, saying out loud, 'I don't suppose so.' What it was to be unrestricted! The life that young women could live nowadays was beyond her comprehension. Still, she would be daft to start worrying about what might never happen. As Matt was fond of telling her, 'That would be putting the cart before the horse.'

Chapter Thirty-Five

IT WAS FRIDAY morning and Joan knew something was going on but couldn't put her finger on what it was. Matt seemed always to be answering the telephone or making calls of his own.

This weekend was going to be marvellous, especially tomorrow. Matt was taking her to lunch at the Crown Hotel in Morden. It would be her first real outing since she had been discharged from the hospital. Karen had rung to ask if it would be all right for her to bring Alex home with her so, of course, Matt had said yes and extended the invitation to include them in the special Saturday lunch.

Shortly after three o'clock she watched from the window as Alex and Karen got out of the car. To her surprise they had brought Amy with them.

'You don't mind if I park meself on yer for a few days?' Amy asked, before she'd set foot inside the house.

Karen kissed Joan warmly, offering no explanation as to

why they had her mother-in-law with them. Alex shook her hand, saying how pleased he was that she had been discharged from the hospital, then warned her to take things easy for a while.

Though their evening meal had passed quietly enough Joan sensed that everyone was hiding something from her. She couldn't stand it any longer. As Karen got up and went to the sideboard to pour coffee, she turned to her mother-in-law. 'Amy, are you going to tell me what's going on? Cos I know something is.'

Amy grinned. 'Do you?'

Joan nodded. 'Yes, I can smell you're up to something a mile off.'

'Aye, well,' Amy said, 'you're a clever clogs. But, then, you always have been.'

Joan burst out laughing. 'And for your information I know when you're trying to soft-soap me.'

'Now, would I do a thing like that?'

'You're losing the battle, Amy.' Karen laughed, as she set the tray down on the table.

'Shall I be referee?' Alex asked.

'Oh, I don't think it will come to fisticuffs.' Karen smiled gently at the rugged, well-built man, whose bright blue eyes were telling her that he was happy to be here with her.

'Well,' he pursed his lips, 'I think I should take Matt down to the local for a pint and leave you ladies to sort yourselves out.'

'You've never 'ad a better idea.' Matt got up and came to stand behind Joan's chair. 'You don't mind, do you, dear? We won't be late but if you want to go to bed Karen will see you're all right.'

'Of course not, I'll be fine.' Joan reached up to pat his cheek.

With the two men out of the way, the three women sat over their coffee. It was Amy who broke the silence. 'I'm sorry I didn't get down t' see you while you were in 'ospital, Joan. Me legs were playing me up. But I'm downright pleased t' see yer looking so well. I'd never 'ave forgiven meself if anything 'ad 'appened to you.'

Joan patted her workworn hand. 'Well, nothing did happen to me, did it? As you can see I'm almost as fit as a flea, so you needn't worry. And I really am so pleased that you're here now.' Then quickly, as an afterthought, she added, 'But I still think there's more to this visit than either you or Karen is letting on.'

'You're letting your imagination run away with you,' Karen said, and sprang to her feet. 'I'm going to get your nightdress and dressing-gown and put them in the bath-room. It's time you were tucked up in bed.'

While Karen was out of the room Joan seized her chance. 'Amy, what do you think of Alex?' she asked.

'So far so good. He seems a fine man, not too young. What I did like, having listened t' them talking in the car, was that he doesn't sound t' me as if he's for the social lime-light. You know what I mean, London an' all the parties an' goings-on. No, I think he'll suit our Karen cos he's the steady type.'

'Oh, Amy, I'm glad you say that. I feel responsible for Karen, what with her own parents being so far away.'

'Bit like tit-for-tat, ain't it, gal? They keep an eye on our Rosie and you do the same for them with Karen.'

'Keep an eye on them is about all we can do,' Joan muttered, more to herself than to Amy. 'I used to think that by the time they were twenty-one you didn't have to worry about them any more. As it turned out, the real worries started at just about that time. And, these days, it seems to me that they do exactly as they please.'

'My, my.' Amy chuckled. 'Feeling old, are we? Our brood ain't youngsters any more and if that makes you feel yer age, what d'yer think it does t' me?'

'Time for bed. Big day tomorrow,' Karen announced, coming back into the room.

Joan latched on to that. She was even more sure now that something was afoot. Ah, well, better do as she was told and take herself off to bed.

'How does she look to you?' Karen asked Amy, once they were alone.

'Bit thinner, but better than I'd expected, thank God.'

'I just hope tomorrow isn't going to prove too much for her. Do you think we've done the right thing?'

'Aw, pet, course I do. She'll be that 'appy, she'll be over the moon. You wait and see. It will be just the tonic she's needing.'

'I hope to God you're right,' Karen said, beneath her breath, and even to herself it sounded like a prayer.

As it was Saturday lunchtime, the bars of the Crown were busy. Matt had a firm hold on Joan's elbow as he guided her through the customers. Suddenly a voice from behind her was saying, 'I'm so glad to see you again, Mrs Pearson.'

Joan turned her head and smiled. The man who had spoken was the manager, and just seeing him brought back memories of the happy family parties they had held here. 'I'm glad to see you too, Mr Curtis. It's been a while since I was here.' She studied his face: he hadn't aged, with his curly iron-grey hair and tanned complexion. She wondered why he was welcoming her personally. His eyes were bright and twinkling as he turned to Matt and said, 'Everything is ready outside. Shall I lead the way?' His voice was remarkably soothing and he had an old-world charm about him as he offered his arm to Amy.

Two young men held open the double swing doors for them. At the far end of the lawn a marquee had been erected.

'Went up a treat,' Mr Curtis murmured to Matt. 'Always best to be on the safe side in case it rains, though the forecast is good.'

Joan stood still. It was a glorious day with the sun high in the sky, the green grass stretched in front of her to where a brightly coloured marquee had been erected. It was a sight to behold, plastic windows in each side and the opening appeared to be a huge front door. Now she knew her instinct had not been wrong.

She looked at Karen, who merely smiled. Amy's head was turned away.

Joan was feeling bewildered, even a little apprehensive as to what might be going to happen next. Nothing in this world could have prepared her for what did happen. Her younger daughter was coming towards her.

Joan stared in amazement. She tried to go forward but her legs wouldn't move quickly enough. Arms outstretched, Rosie reached her.

'How did you get here?' her mother asked, her voice little more than a croak.

'I swam the Atlantic,' Rosie said, and threw her arms around her mother. 'I love you, Mum,' she whispered.

'My God,' Joan gasped, 'I've missed you so much.'

'Me too, Mummy, and I worried so much while you were in hospital.'

Rosie calling her Mummy after all this time! It tore at Joan's heart. Tears were pouring down her cheeks and Rosie said, 'Oh, please, don't cry, Mum.'

'I'm not crying because I'm upset,' Joan spluttered, 'I'm crying because I'm so happy to see you. Have you got a handkerchief?'

Matt came to her side, holding out his own big white one. 'I've a feeling you're gonna need this even more when you see everyone else that's here to wish you well.' He took her arm, making sure she was close to his side. 'Come on, my darling,' he whispered, 'I just know you're gonna 'ave a happy day. You've nothing to cry about. Nothing at all. Just remember I love you very much and so does everyone else that's here.'

Now she really cried.

Matt stepped aside, letting Rosie lead her mother forward into the centre of the marquee.

Joan was dumbfounded. 'Just look at you all,' she said.

It took ages for everyone to hug her, to tell her how glad they were that she had got over her operation, Jamie and Pamela, Meg and Brian, Matt's brother Stan and his wife Hazel were here. And all her grandchildren were outside in the sunshine enjoying themselves.

Betsy Piviteaux popped out from behind a chair. 'You didn't think I was going to let Rosie swim all that way on her own, did you?'

Then her mum was holding her close, telling her how afraid she'd been that they were going to lose her.

'Not today, Daphne,' Bill Harvey reproached his wife. 'No more tears. This is going to be a good day.' With that he bent his big frame to take his daughter into his arms. 'Love you, Joan. We all do.'

'Love you too, Dad.'

There was a moment's confusion as everybody moved back to the sides of the marquee. Then, once more, Joan just could not believe what she was seeing. Beryl was the first to move, covering the space between them in no time. Joan held her arms out wide, feeling enormous pleasure that her dear friend was here today. And then came Joe: 'Hi, how you doing?' There was no holding back, his strong arms lifted her until her feet were no longer on the ground. 'We couldn't let you guys have a party without us being here, now, could we?'

Beryl's mother kissed her on both cheeks.

The last to appear were Peter and a very pregnant Louise. The hug that Peter gave her seemed to go on for ever. A head came over her shoulder and she twisted round to kiss Louise.

To say the very least it was a lively lunch, and as Joan settled back in an armchair Amy came over to her and said, 'Well, Joan, love, 'ow d'yer feel now?'

'I just don't believe that so many people were that concerned for me that they came all this way to wish me well.'

Amy gave a deep laugh. 'They're all so grateful.'

'What d'you mean, grateful?'

'Well, let's face it, gal. They could 'ave all been gatherin' 'ere dressed in black. Much better t' be 'ere drinkin' yer 'ealth.'

'Oh, Amy! Only you could think of something like that!'

Amy thought it best to keep the rest of her thoughts to herself. Nevertheless she still thought she wasn't far wrong.

Most of the adults had gone off to help amuse the children, and even Meg had offered to organize a game. She seemed so much happier today, Joan thought. Let's hope it lasts, especially for Brian's sake.

She turned her gaze to where Matt was standing just outside the opening of the marquee. Joe Piviteaux was beside him, and the two men seemed to be deep in conversation.

Joan had been so relieved when those two had become friends. The last few years had changed Matt so much. When the truth had come to light about Peter and Jamie he had been rebellious, angry, determined not to face the facts. Now she could see that he and Joe were watching their sons with pride on their faces. Despite the heartache and against the odds they had all survived, and everything had fallen into place.

Now Matt was making his way towards her. 'What are you doing sitting here all on your own?' he asked.

Joan looked up at him standing over her, his eyes twinkling. He took her hands and pulled her to her feet. 'Later on our grandchildren are going to sing a song for us. There are some deckchairs out there if you feel up to it.'

'Yes,' she said softly, 'that will be lovely. But while we're on our own, Matt, I want to say thank you for today. And for so much more. No man could have done more for their wife than you have.'

'Just so long as you're happy. We've come a long way, ain't we? Mine an' Stan's business 'as turned out even better than we 'oped and that pleases me cos I'm able to give you an' the kids so much more. All I want you t' do is get a bit stronger and then I'm taking you off on a long holiday. Will that make you 'appy?'

'I am happy, Matt.'

'Then that's all that matters.'

She sighed. 'Things have turned out so much better than we could ever have imagined, haven't they?'

'You can say that again. We 'ad our rough passages, by God we did, but we weathered them. Right now, though, I think we'd better go outside. Everyone will be worried as to where you are.'

'Oh, do we have to?' Joan asked playfully. 'Can't we just stay here, the two of us?'

'No, we can't. We've family and friends t' see to.' Suddenly he grinned wickedly. 'You could go so far as t' say we've got double trouble cos we've got two families to contend with.'

'I heard that, Matt Pearson, and what goes for you two goes for the two of us!' Joe Piviteaux was smiling broadly as he and Beryl came to stand beside them. Then, with a theatrical flourish, he produced a bottle of champagne from behind his back.

It took a while for Joe to release the cork, but then he was pouring the foaming wine into four glasses. 'Here's to us two sets of parents,' he declared, raising his glass. 'Good health, and may we always be friends.'

'I'll willingly drink to that,' Matt said, 'but I'll add a bit. To Anglo-American relationships.'

All four were laughing as they drank, but when Beryl and Joan looked into each other's eyes they couldn't help but see the glint of tears. Then Beryl said, 'I'll make the next toast.' She raised her glass and, with her eyes fixed on Joan, she said, 'Here's to our two sons.'

The air was so charged with emotion that it was a relief when they heard, 'Oh, so this is where you're all hiding.'

Both women blinked away their tears and smiled as Jamie and Peter came striding towards them. Then, in unison, they said, 'We're just coming, son.'

Chapter Thirty-Six

'THEY DO A pretty good job at the Crown,' Matt said, the next morning, as he stretched out in an armchair. 'And it all went off very well, even if I do say it myself! There's usually someone who gets upset at a family do but this time everyone was remarkably well behaved. All getting older and wiser, I suppose.'

'Trust my husband to take all the credit.' Joan grinned

Joe and Beryl both laughed. It was good to see Joan looking so relaxed, and it was true, Matt had given everyone a great day. They were sitting close together on the settee which was drawn up close to the fire.

Joe and Beryl were staying for a few days with Matt and Joan. Rosie and Betsy had stayed the night with Meg and Brian, and Stan and Hazel with Daphne and Bill. Peter and Louise had gone off with Jamie and Pamela, while Karen and her new friend Alex, with Amy and Beryl's mother, had come home with Joan and Matt. Tomorrow most of the Piviteauxs would be flying back to New York, but today it was open house here in Ashtead.

Joan was thinking that yesterday had been a most wonderful day, and today, with all the family around her in her own home, was the icing on the cake.

'Who'd have thought it, eh? All of us under one roof.' Beryl's voice was soft.

Joan laughed. 'Took time but we got there in the end. I wish my nan was still here to see us all together.'

Amy and Beryl's mother came into the room carrying plates of food. 'Shall we lay the table or just set up a buffet for everyone to help themselves?' Amy asked.

Joan and Beryl grinned. 'Why ask us? You're in charge.'

'Then a buffet it will be. Much less washing-up.' Amy had always been jolly but since having her own flat at Jamie and Pamela's house she had blossomed even more. She loved living there, still so close to the East End and with company on hand if and when she needed it.

'Joan, your mum and dad are here. I've just seen their car pull into the drive,' Karen called from the hall.

Daphne burst into the room, followed by Bill who said to Joan, 'Your mother's thrilled she hasn't got to cook Sunday dinner. And as I haven't had to do all the vegetables here's my contribution.' He held out a cardboard box containing three bottles of white wine and three bottles of red.

'Thanks, Bill.' Matt relieved him of the carton. 'You're a man after me own heart.'

Stan and Hazel followed close behind. 'All right, are you, Joan? Yesterday didn't tire you out too much?'

'No, love, I'm fine.' Joan got up and kissed her sister-in-law. 'I expect there's tea on the go in the kitchen but if you want to join me and Beryl ask Matt to give you a glass.'

'What you two drinking, then?'

They raised their glasses, and Beryl said, 'Try some. It's Bucks Fizz.'

By now a host of women were setting out enough platters of food to feed an army. The doorbell rang and, seconds later, it appeared as if everyone had arrived at the same time. The whole room was in an uproar.

John and Josie, Meg and Brian's two children, with young Matt and his sister Beryl, Jamie and Pamela's two, were all claiming the right to kiss their grandma first.

Meg bent over her mother's shoulder. 'Are you all right, Mum?'

'Never better.' Joan smiled at her elder daughter. Meg looked happier than she had for ages. She was a bit too thin, but her skin was good and she still had a gorgeous head of hair with the reddish tints inherited from the Harveys.

Joan transferred her gaze to Brian as he lowered his head to kiss her hello. This son-in-law of hers was a good man, a bit of a stick-in-the-mud but steady. Just lately she'd had the feeling that he and Meg had weathered their storms, and that much between them had changed for the better. She hoped she was right. Nobody had an easy ride through life.

Pamela bent over Joan and said gently, 'It was a lovely gathering yesterday, and we're all so pleased to see you on the mend.'

Joan touched her daughter-in-law's cheek. If she'd searched the earth she couldn't have found a more loving wife for her beloved Jamie.

Now Louise crouched in front of her and took her hand. They say pregnant women take on a special bloom and it was certainly true where Louise was concerned. She looked so nice in her navy blue maternity dress which had a wide white lace collar.

'Stand up,' Joan urged her. 'You shouldn't be crouched down like that.'

Louise did as she was told but grinned as she said, 'I'm having a baby, I'm not ill.' Her voice was full of happiness as she hugged Joan.

Beryl and Joan looked at each other and raised their eyebrows, what with the children and the adults it was beginning to be confusing. 'Best we stay where we are and let the youngsters get on with it today,' Beryl suggested.

Suddenly Rosie and Betsy clapped their hands and when order was restored they said in unison, 'Grub's up. Come and help yourselves.'

The two mothers looked at each other. Both of their daughters looked stunning. It was easy to see why they set the pulses of their menfriends racing. They were the modern young woman personified, in their tailor-made suits, sheer nylons and high-heeled plain court shoes.

The glance that went between Joan and Beryl was one of understanding and amazement. Everyone in this room loved everyone else. The old were adored by the young. These two women, who at one time might have hated each other, were firm friends. Today it was as if two completely different families had been moulded into one, each member had accepted the inevitable, all happy in their own ways, and glad to be here. The story of their coming together would go down in family history. Their children would tell their own offspring, and so it would live on. No one could have foreseen that what had happened on 2 November 1944 would have brought such heartache and then such joy.

Joan felt Beryl's hand take hers and they looked into each

other's eyes. The rift that might have ruined their lives had been healed. They were confident women with loving families of their own and yet they shared a part of each other's. They reached for their drinks, then raised their glasses in a very personal toast, just for the two of them.

The silent toast was 'To our two sons.'

A.

DATE DUE

OCT 1 1 2005	MAR 1 7 2012
OCT 17 2005	APR 23 2012
NOV 1 1 2005	
MAR 2 4 2006	
AUG 1 5 2006	JUL 0 5 2012
AUG 0 2 2009	JUN 0 4 2013
AUG 2 3 2009	AUG 2 4 2013
MAR 0 6 2010	SEP 1 6 2013
NOV 2 3 2010	
FEB 2 2 2011	
MAY 1 7 2011	
JUN 0 8 2011	
JUL 0 4 2011	